BOOK THREE

OATH BOUND

ЯuniK Press

ISBN: 979-8-9883406-3-8

BOUND BY

A WEB OF WYRD

TRILOGY

RENATE ROWLAND

Runik Press

Author's Note

Dear reader,

Thank you for choosing to stick with my characters in this Web of Wyrd, and welcome to the final title in my trilogy. I want to remind you again that this book is intended only for an audience of 18+.

Now, without further ado, get ready for the conclusion to my characters' quest for love, honor, and destiny.

Renate

This Story Contains:

Explicit sexual scenes

Graphic language

Self-harm

Psychological abuse

Torture & violence

PTSD

Pregnancy loss

Mentions of murder & death

Sexual assault (non-descriptive)

Playlist

Disguise – Motionless In White

Skin – Beartooth

Nightmare (The Devil) – Fame on Fire

Psycho In My Head – Skillet

HOUSE ON SAND – Nothing More

Welcome to the Chaos (feat. Spencer Charnas) – Fame on Fire

Parasite – Set It Off

Numb – Sleep Theory

Battling My Demons – Jeris Johnson

Bleed Me Dry – Memphis May Fire

For What It's Worth – Silent Theory

Look The Other Way – Beartooth

Emptiness in You – Silent Theory

Straight to Hell – Falling In Reverse

Misery – Memphis May Fire

Loser – Falling In Reverse

Made Me This Way – Silent Theory

Prequel – Falling In Reverse

Watch Me Burn – Silent Theory

Room 138 – Asking Alexandria

Fragile Minds – Silent Theory

Vultures – Asking Alexandria

The Fight Within – Memphis May Fire

Hurricane – I Prevail

Fallout – Sleep Theory

Paralyzed – Memphis May Fire

Drowning – Atreyu

Another Way – Sleep Theory

Superhero – Falling In Reverse

Necessary Evil – Memphis May Fire

Safe And Sound – Point North

Into The Fire – Asking Alexandria

Bad Guy – Falling In Reverse

Six Feet Under – Silent Theory

Watch Me Burn – Atreyu

Like A Stone (Reimagined) – Atreyu

Heroes – Zayde Wolf

Get up (feat. Dan Murphy) – All Good Things

Rise – State of Mine

Immortal – Atreyu

Forevermore – Atreyu

Pronunciation Guide

Ægishjálmr – Aeyishyaulmr

Æsir – Ayesr (Ásgarðr faction of Gods)

Álfar – Owl-ver (Elf folk)

Angrboða – Angre-botha

Ásgarðr – Ows-garth

Askja – Ahskia

Bifrǫst – Be-fruhst

Dúlla – Doo-la

Dynja – Dun-ya

Fenrisúlfr – Fenris-oolf (Fenrir)

Fólkvangr – Folk-vahnkr

Freyja – Frei-yah

Frigg – Frick

Hǫðr – Huhrth (Haðarson: Son of Hǫðr)

Hrafni – Rabne

Huginn – Hooy-in

Hvergelmir – Kvergelmir

Iðunn – Eathun

Jǫrmungandr – Yuhrmun-gahnd

Kjan – Ki-an

Kjartan – Kiahrtan

Kría – Kri-a

Kristján – Kristiaun

Miðgarðr – Mith-gahrth

Miðgarðsormr – Mithgahr-thorm (Midgard Serpent)

Mjǫllnir – Miuhtll-nir

Muninn – Moo-nin

Narfi – Nahrvee

Níðhǫggr – Nith-hock

Níflheimr – Neevle-heym

Óðinn – Oh-thin

Raf - Raff

Ragnarǫk – Rahg-nah-ruhk

Seiðr – Seyth

Sigyn – Siggen

Skaði – Skahthee

Skuld – Skoolt

Sleipnir – Slehpnir

Strákur - Straukur

Styrr – Stir

Týr — Teehr

Urðr – Oorth

Valhǫll – Vahl-huhtll

Váli – Vow-lee

Valkyrja (singular) – Vahl-kyria

Valkyrjur (plural) – Vahl-kyryr

Vanr – Vahn (Vanaheimr faction of Gods)

Verðandi – Vehr-thahndi

Völva – Vahlva

Web of Wyrd – Web of Veert

Yggdrasill – Eekdrasil

Þórr – Thohr

Thórunn (Þórunn) – Thohrun

Months:

Heyannir – Heya-nir (Hay Work – July time frame. The name refers to the farm work that had to be done that month)

Jól – Yohl (Yule - The pagan celebration of the winter solstice; lasts 2 months)

Ýlir – Eelir (1st month of Yule, begins in late November)

Mörsugr – Muhrsur (2nd month of Yule; begins in late December)

Miðvetr – Mith-vetr (Midwinter; late January; end of Yule)

The Old Icelandic calendar has 6 months of summer and 6 months of winter. Find the list of months in the annotations at the back of the book.

Runes:

ᛒ : Bjarkan (Berkano) – bierkaan

ᛇ : Eihwaz – eye-whas

ᛉ : Algiz – ahl-ghiss

ᚹ : Kaun – cown

ᛏ : Ár – owhr

ᚱ : Reið – rhight

ᛏ : Týr – teehr

ᚨ : Áss – us

ᚾ : Nauðr – neuyth

ᛟ : Othal

Þ : Thurs

ᚢ : Ur

ᛋ : Sol

"BRAVELY AND GLADLY A MAN SHALL GO
TIL THE DAY OF HIS DEATH IS COME."

HÁVAMÁL: 15

ÓÐAL

(Homeland)

It represents:

- Homecoming
- Family strength or group prosperity
- Legacy and spiritual heritage
- Experience
- Fundamental values
- Inheritance
- Greater peace
- Heaven on Earth

It predicts:

- Aid in spiritual and physical journeys
- Source of safety
- Increase and abundance

PROLOGUE

THE RAVEN

He cocked his head at an angle, watching the mortal vessel with the woman who had ruined everything.

How can an insignificant thing like her cause the downfall of a God?

His beady black eyes twitched in contempt. The son of Hǫðr couldn't possibly be content with this truce. A divine spirit trapped in the body of a mortal?

Blasphemous! It was beneath him.

The Gods had ignored the boy until he had broken from his destiny. If he could get their attention, then the Raven could do the same. His own existence had gone unacknowledged for long enough.

He ruffled his feathers, a nervous twitch like cracking his knuckles.

The Raven, too, was a misfit. A reject. A social and racial outsider because he defied authority and conventional tradition. Like the Godling, he had been cast out and shunned since the day he was born. He had been forced to wither in the shadow of his heritage, and by losing his home, he had lost his identity.

He had tried to make amends. Tried to fit in. But wherever he went, he was met with the same persecution. Prejudice had followed him to the ends of the worlds, so he had turned the tables. He had embraced the role they had cast him in.

His croak echoed through the silence with another ruffle of his wings. What made the two of them so special? This Kjan had been given a second chance, as had the Haðarson. Why had they been accepted, where he had been passed over again and again?

Unlike him, they both had blood on their hands. They were murderers, monsters by their own actions, unlike his brothers, yet the God's chose to pardon them while disowning him.

And now, due to this woman, *they* had an alliance. An alliance that should have been *his*. The Haðarson was only freed from his prison because of him. The Godling owed him after what he lost. After the sacrifice *he* made.

. Was the life that had been taken from him worth less than that of this man? *This mortal?*

Talons clutching the branch, his vision refocused on the one who called himself Kjan. For his self-sacrifice, the Gods had welcomed him into the fold. They granted him a place among the noble warriors, which he had declined to return to *her*, this meddlesome woman!

But the Raven would use that to his advantage. They didn't know what he knew.

The Gods would take notice of him now. Violence was the only language they understood. The only means they acknowledged. He would get his vengeance. He would balance the scales. Where the Godling had failed, the Raven would not.

His talons bit deeper into the branch underneath him as his ire grew, the wood creaking in defeat. He never caught them apart—the vessel and his female. Never one without the other close by. They were inseparable, practically joined at the hips.

It wouldn't last, though. It was the calm before the storm. Love and acceptance were always conditional. Give them a reason, doubt, no matter how small, and your so-called family will turn against you.

Impatiently, he had been watching them from afar for days, first at the high-rise and now back here at the cabin. But his plan was already in motion, all the little gears turning, the seeds of distrust sown. All he had to do now was wait and observe. They would tear each other apart with their constant doubt and jealousy. In the end, they would be just like him.

Alone.

Renate Rowland

CHAPTER

I

KJAN

October—

Kjan tied the rubber tourniquet around his upper arm a second time. He didn't bother wiping down his skin before he pinched the butterfly and inserted the large 17-gauge needle into the median cubital vein on the inside of his left elbow again. He probably should have switched sides, but he didn't want to do this left-handed. He could. He just didn't want to.

The veins down his forearm bulged, and he placed a small strip of tape over the tube to hold it in place. The needle stuck out about an inch below the previous insertion.

Squeezing the little stress ball, he relaxed back onto the pillow. With his right arm folded behind his head, he watched the mechanical tray beside him agitate the bag to mix his blood with anticoagulants. The one-pint bag held about an ounce and a half for each of them. Minus Eve.

He always filled two.

Kjan endured the hassle because it was better than the alternative. He wouldn't let them draw directly from his vein. Not even that first time. He had used the offering bowl at the temple then, but he healed so fast that he had to repeat the process multiple times, and that got old quickly. This was more tolerable in the end.

The timer on his phone went off, making him jerk from the start.

Straightening on the bed, he released the tourniquet first, then pulled the needle. A few drops splattered onto his arm, and he wiped them with a patch of gauze he lifted from the nightstand before lowering his sleeve. His motions were hardly more than automated. Like the little machine churning his blood.

Kjan switched it off and cleaned up his supplies. Both bags in hand, he made his way downstairs. With the heavy thumps of his boots on the wood, he wasn't surprised that the group's chatter in the great room fell quiet as he approached. Not in an awkward silence kind of way, just quiet as though he had interrupted their conversation.

My *house, but whatever.*

He handed one of the bags to Kristján when laughter erupted from the door across the room that led to the sublevel. Eve and the rest of them were goofing off in the gym.

He followed the sound of their voices down the steps. The garage with the Harley was to the left, the gym to his right.

Rounding the corner, he slowed his stride. He could hear Caleb's grunts of exertion as he finished what was hopefully his last rep. Any more, and he was likely to pull something.

Kjan lingered out of sight in the corridor for a moment, listening to Eve and them bond.

Why does that make me feel guilty?

Erik's baritone voice gave some words of encouragement to Caleb, and then the bar clanked loudly onto the rack's supports.

"That was only eight," Claire chimed in. "You came up one short."

"That's bullshit!" the boy cried in return. "She bench presses more than me."

Kjan chuckled, knowing he was referring to Eve. Pushing off the wall, he caught his Dove's smug grin.

Claire nudged her side. "Way to go, girl. You really are the Black Widow to your Winter Soldier."

Right, because she kicks ass and I have a split personality.

Caleb grimaced. Rolling his left shoulder backward, he remained seated on the bench. Erik stood behind him as a spotter.

"Hey Kjan, what's your one-rep max?" Erik asked. He wasn't as broad or tall as Kristján, but the amount of time he had slaved in the gym hadn't been in vain.

"More than we have here," Kjan answered, sauntering into the room.

Caleb rose to his feet, still muttering under his breath. He scowled at Eve, who held her chin high, hands on her hips, to challenge him.

Tail tucked between his legs, he walked off, ruffling the shaggy mess on top of his head.

Kjan slapped the other blood bag to his chest as he passed by on his way out the door. "Don't forget to share," he told him.

"I'll try, but I can't guarantee it. You're too delicious." Caleb winked, then his grin disappeared around the corner.

"Tell me about it," Eve drawled in agreement. "I know *I* can't get enough."

She could have whatever was left of him, but he better not mention that he had passed out briefly before the second draw finished.

Kjan pulled her up close by her hands, linking them behind his back, and she raised onto her toes to meet his kiss halfway, every move second nature.

"He's not very happy that you bested him, huh?" Caleb's frustration was tangible. *Losing to a girl…*

She pinched her brows. "Not in the slightest."

"I would pay to see you take him on in an arm wrestling match," Erik said, hooking Claire in an embrace.

"My odds are on you, Dove. I remember you giving Dynja a run for her money, and she is twice your size."

Her sharp eyes focused on him. "Thanks to you. You're the one who taught me everything I know."

Not quite. There were things she was better at than him. But he wouldn't admit that in company, so instead he said, "Sounds like my work here is done."

"That's right. The student has become the master," Eve exclaimed smugly, draping his arm over her shoulder.

EVE

Behind her, Kjan slumped onto the sofa. Pulling her into his lap, he wrapped his long limbs around her. The warmth of his body spread straight through the marrow of her bones, making her melt into his embrace.

"Hmmm," she purred, reaching up to clasp his scruffy cheek. The ¼-inch growth of his beard was harsh against her skin as he nuzzled her neck, but she loved every bit of the burn. "I missed your touch already."

How long did it take this time? An hour?

"Same."

His heavy arms enclosed her waist tightly like a seatbelt, and a smile tugged on her lips. One of his hands always found its way under her shirt.

Skin on skin—that was all he needed to recharge.

Well, that and sleep.

He no longer needed blood himself, thanks to his divine passenger, but feeding all of them took a brutal toll on him. Good thing he didn't have to do it again for another couple of weeks.

All but Eve still occasionally fed on willing humans, taking a few drops here and there. Their saliva had healing properties as well as a numbing effect on the wound, and the control they had over how much they took was always on point. Kjan's blood was a supplementary source. It didn't just sustain them for longer periods of time. It also made them stronger and more resilient to sunlight.

Eve rubbed her hand along his leg where it pressed against the outside of her thigh as she sat cross-legged in front of him, and he dropped his chin on her shoulder.

She could tell he was dozing off when his head leaned heavily against her own.

His thumb slowed in stroking her belly. The others talked among themselves, but Eve wasn't tracking the conversation. She always focused on him.

"Earth to Eve," somebody said.

She jerked to attention at the sound of her name. "I'm sorry. What was the question?"

"What food do you miss the most?" Parker repeated. "I already picked pizza. Caleb took hamburgers. Doughnuts for Emma. Fries over here"—he jerked his thumb toward Dynja—"Kristján's and Kría's, I'm not even gonna repeat. *Gross*, by the way. Bacon. Mom's corned beef brisket. Hotdogs. And spring rolls," he finished, pointing at Askja, Nessa, Erik, and Claire individually while reciting the rest. "What was your poison?"

"Hm, I don't know. Tacos, I guess." She lifted her unoccupied shoulder in a half-shrug to not disturb Kjan. "I don't really miss anything."

"I wonder what he used to eat," Caleb uttered. "Seal maybe?"

Eve felt Kjan's chest bounce with a low rumble against her back as he chuckled. "Fish or lamb, mostly," he mumbled without lifting his eyelids. "But seal is delicious. Has a gamey, iron-rich taste to it. Kind of like organ meat. Shark is good, too."

"Shark! *That* I can get on board with," Parker shouted from his spot on the floor, pointing at Kjan. "But ram testicles? Seriously? You guys are fucking disgusting."

He chucked one of the small cushions he'd been using at Kría, who sat in Kristján's lap on the sofa chair across from him. Caleb and Emma were snuggled up on the floor together while the rest of them took the big couch, leaving the loveseat to Kjan and Eve.

Lucas had made himself scarce per usual, showing up late and checking out first. Nevertheless, Eve loved it when they all came together like this. Everybody got along. Everybody was happy. It felt like family. Maybe even better.

Their living arrangements hadn't changed much over the last three months. They were spread out into four places over Portland now: Askja and Nessa in Greenhills; Kría stayed with Kristján in Portland Heights; Dynja, Erik, and Claire in the Pearl district; and lastly, the loft downtown, where Emma, Caleb, Lucas, and Parker lived.

Kjan and Eve usually stayed at the cabin, and everybody was always welcome, but they'd kept their little hideaway in the city's Waterfront district for whenever they didn't want to be disturbed. It remained their sanctuary. Their refuge.

Eve gently nudged his head with her own. "How about we get you to bed?"

Kjan raised his weary eyes to hers, and they didn't hold their usual sparkle. "Yes, ma'am," he replied with only a half-cocked smile.

Eve tugged on his limp arm, and he rose to his feet.

"Happy Birthday, Eve," Erik hollered after them.

"And thanks again for not making us dress up in Halloween costumes," she heard Parker add.

"You know you would've loved that French maid outfit I got you."

Caleb's heckle was followed by a rustle and the *thud* of another pillow being flung across the room. But it must have missed him and hit Emma instead because an unamused 'Watch it!' burst from her mouth.

"Your aim sucks, dude," he said, sending the pillow through the air again.

Eve hoped they wouldn't destroy the house completely.

"Hey, who do we have to talk to to get a pool table around here?" Caleb called after her and Kjan before they made it to the stairs. "I'm just sayin'. That could be fun if we all start hanging around here more often."

"I see what I can do," Kjan grumbled over his shoulder, his hooded stare on her as she dragged him upstairs and out of sight.

Dim wall sconces illuminated their way through the dark wooden hall. Down the corridor, Eve stepped backward into the bedroom, her scrutinizing eyes studying his demeanor on a deeper level.

"You look exhausted," she noted.

"I'll be fine."

Kjan shut the door behind him, then his hands were on her jeans, grabbing onto the waistband. He gave a sharp pull to jerk her toward him, nearly knocking the wind out of her as she hit his chest.

Eve scowled up at him, searching for the truth behind those tired, green irises. "You always say that."

"Because I will be," he drawled, his busy hands working the front of her pants with efficiency. "As soon as I get to touch you. The more, the better."

He didn't give her a chance to argue back—or take a breath—before his mouth cut her off. His fingers brushed across her lower belly and then slipped to the back, squeezing her ass as he groaned into her.

Kjan walked her backward toward the edge of the bed. Eve knew he was deflecting, but she felt the heat welling between her thighs, making it impossible to keep her mind straight. Underneath his thin, dark red Henley, her hands skimmed up his chiseled pecs and then around his neck with a will of their own.

When his lips roamed across her throat to her earlobe, she had to force her thoughts to stay on track. "Can I ask you something?" she cued as her legs met the side of the mattress.

His only reply was an impatient grunt, muffled against her skin.

For weeks now, she'd been mulling over that night at the temple, replaying it over and over in her head. After possessing Kjan's body, his Sire had taken over the minds of the coven and controlled them to the point where they'd been forced to obey his every command blindly.

Pitting friend against friend, brother against sister, Kjartan had bent them all to his will and intended to do the same to Eve by combining their powers with his in the lunar ritual.

If it hadn't been for her sacrifice and the breaking of his unintentional blood oath, he would've succeeded, too.

Kjan had felt no remorse for his Sire's acolytes. He'd wanted to leave them behind to die for betraying Eve, but she'd made the plea on their behalf because, for a brief moment, they'd welcomed her into their midst and given her a sense of family.

Kjan's powerful blood had saved them from turning on each other after the loss of their alpha had left them violent and crazed. He'd given them back their rational, conscious awareness.

"Do you regret it?" she asked. "Giving them your vein, I mean. You only did it because I asked you to—"

"Eve, stop."

"—and I'm afraid that you're going to resent me for it one day," she rambled on.

He straightened and slapped a palm over her lips, his eyes stern. "Stop! I love you. More than anything. You're not making me do anything. Understand? So quit beating yourself up about it. They need my blood, and I need you."

Without another delay, his hands dropped and grasped the backside of her thighs, plummeting her onto her back.

Eve yelped.

He yanked off her jeans next. She scrambled on the mattress to put some distance between them, but she couldn't match his speed, and he pulled her back by her ankles, wrenching her legs apart.

"Dammit, woman. Gimme!" he growled.

His eyes burned with a hunger that sent a jolt through her body, igniting the same ravenous craving in her. His grip firmly on her hips, he dipped his head between her thighs, licking and nipping higher along the sensitive inside.

The stubble of his beard was rough, as were his fangs whenever he chose to remind her.

Eve's hands came down to graze through his hair, nails scraping at his nape while she rolled into him. His deep, gravely moan drove tremors through her.

Whimpers poured from her lips under his inescapable attention. Higher and higher she climbed on his command.

With the unrelenting heat of his tongue stoking the flames, she chased the spark in her core until it exploded like wildfire. The force of the inferno consumed her. Writhing against him, toes curled, she cried out.

Kjan kept her going. He flicked and sucked, his fingers digging harshly into her skin, squeezing her curves while she rode out the wave.

He emerged with a dark, self-satisfied grin on his face, teeth tugging on his bottom lip. Bracing his weight on his hands, he kneeled between her legs, spreading them wide as he hovered over her to admire his handiwork.

Her pulse still racing, Eve twisted the front of his shirt around her fingers and pulled him down to her. But he only lowered himself to his elbows, keeping his hips at a distance.

He chuckled at her disapproving frown. "Not satisfied?"

"Never," she snorted, already going for his fly.

Kjan grabbed her hands and pinned them above her head, fingers entwined. "You're insatiable, Dove," he rasped with an enticing lilt.

His expression had changed, however. Trapping her under his massive body, he closed his eyes and dropped his forehead to hers.

His warm breath against her cheek fell steady, unlike her own, and Eve realized he was cutting himself off. He wouldn't take it any further tonight; not with the gang in earshot.

Kjan sat back on his heels, pulling his shirt over his back, and when he finally lowered his full weight down on her, his head was level with her stomach.

He dropped his cheek on the back of his hand while his other arm hooked around her.

Seeing how tired he was, Eve relented and gladly settled for this. She ran her fingers through his hair, stroking the back of his neck until he fell asleep, snoring softly.

He wore his hair shorter now. Gone were his soft, long locks and the Mohawk. The sides had grown back, but he kept them short so the raven tattoos above his temples were still visible beneath the blackish-brown. The top was barely more than two inches. He'd also shaved the goatee and grown his facial hair back evenly, full beard, and stache.

Her fingertips lingered on the raven as she brushed along the side of his head. He was trying so hard to erase it all and start over. His scent was dulled and muddled, much like his eyes had been earlier. There was no vibrance.

Eve had no doubt that he was holding back on how much it was wearing on him. It was obvious and not entirely surprising either. Sustaining twelve vampires had knocked his sire out cold, and Kjartan was an immortal who technically didn't need sleep to function.

Kjan had never desired to lead a coven. She'd forced this on him, and while watching the effects unfold, guilt was eating her up inside.

Her greatest fear was that he would one day regret his decision to stay here with her instead of joining his family in Fólkvangr. After all, he'd made that choice without anticipating inheriting a coven with it.

CHAPTER

2

EVE

She woke with a chill despite the fur comforter draped over her. Fall in the mountains was no joke. The sun was just starting to set, drastically lowering the temperature outside the cabin as well as inside.

Kjan's body served as a much better blanket to keep her warm these days, even if it felt like a ton of bricks on her chest.

Eve turned her head toward the window. Music blared from the shed at the far end of the driveway, letting her know that he was already in his forge. She couldn't remember the last time they'd woken up together.

He was having trouble sleeping again.

Another shiver ran over her as she pictured him working by the fire. Without him, the bedroom seemed like an icebox in comparison.

Bracing the cold wind, Eve followed the long driveway around the front of the cabin where the previous owner had built his forge. The little building flanked the main house on the left, standing across from the entrance of the underground garage and sharing the cul-de-sac. The dead end turned into a stone footpath that led to the patio in the back.

The new barn doors, which Kjan and Kristján had recently installed stood wide open, and Eve could see him moving about inside. He was shirtless, naturally, not wanting to ruin his wardrobe with the sparks. His skin was much more resilient than the delicate fabrics.

Appreciatively, she took in the view of his muscled shoulders, rendering a perfect V-shape that tapered down and disappeared into his jeans in a sexy curve at the small of his back.

And then there were the tattoos on his upper body—a lot of them—all Norse-based and traditionally hand-poked, unlike the newer ink on his head. Two full sleeves covered his arms up to the shoulders: the Midgard Serpent Jǫrmungandr on his left; the wolf Fenrir on his right, flowing into the Helm of Awe on his right pec.

The animals' forms were intermingled with bands of Elder Futhark runes. Eve refrained from asking what they spelled out. He had always been emotionally closed-off when it came to his heritage.

From his upper back down to the center of his spine, the branches of the World Tree Yggdrasill fanned out into a V. Its roots formed the shape of Mjǫllnir, Þórr's mighty hammer.

Kjan also had a second set of Óðinn's ravens on his torso: Huginn stretched across his right shoulder blade and traps;

Muninn ran down the front at his collarbone, framing the middle and bottom of his left pec.

He was a true masterpiece. The huge muscles in his upper body flexed with each movement, the light of the flames bringing them to life when he pulled the metal from the fire.

His chest glistened from the heat as he swung the hammer. Kjan was every bit the savage Viking that slumbered in his DNA, and with his jeans low on his hips, her gaze trailed the perfect curve of his back. Eve could watch him. All. Damn. Day.

His lips moved vaguely along with the lyrics of the music, but it was so subtle she couldn't make out the words. The growls in the song didn't help since she wasn't familiar with a lot of Slipknot.

His eyes shot up before she made it through the doors. He took off his gloves, tossed them onto the workbench, and turned down the music. "I'm sorry. Did I wake you?"

Eve trailed her fingers up his bare chest, ogling the ridges and the deep valley in between his pecs, which were level with her eyes. He stood almost a foot taller than her. "No. I woke up because I missed you."

His skin was so hot when he kissed her; steam practically rose under her touch. All she wanted to do was crawl back into bed with him.

She clasped her hands behind his neck, and Kjan flashed a weary smile. He still looked tired.

"I miss waking up with you. How long have you been out here?"

His eyes flicked to the side for a split second. "Maybe an hour."

"You haven't been sleeping well," she noted.

Before she'd moved to Seattle with him a year and a half ago, he'd survived on four hours of sleep a day. But things had changed since their relationship had grown deeper and he'd restored the torn part of his soul. The nightmares were gone, and so were the secrets he'd been keeping from her.

Or were they?

"Do you want to talk about it?"

"There is nothing to talk about." He unlinked her arms and dropped them by her side.

"You never talk about the *elephant* in the room." She was, of course, referring to the seven months of torture he'd suffered trapped in his own body while his Sire had been in control.

Kjartan had forced him to surrender by threatening Eve. Kjan's spirit should have died in the process, but somehow he'd managed to hold on, fully aware of everything that was happening yet powerless to stop it.

His expression hardened. "And why the hell would I want to talk about it?" his voice snapped.

The violent shift in him startled her. Then he sighed, and the rigid lines on his face softened. "Don't push it, Eve. Please."

KJAN

Fuck. That look on her face hurt like hell. It tore him open.

He turned his attention back to the blade on the table, pushing stuff around, pretending to clean up, eyes on anything *but* her.

Talk about it? Like it was so easy to acknowledge that he had let an immortal being use him? Violate him? He rather preferred to block it out.

Too bad he couldn't. He couldn't even rely on sex as a means of disassociating.

He had woken up painfully stiff with the voice in his head, lusting for Eve, but Kjan wouldn't give *Him* the satisfaction. He had come down to the forge to distract himself. *Two and a half* hours ago, actually.

He hated that the lies were beginning to creep into his words, creating a rift between them, but he didn't want to worry her more. It would only compound the issue.

Goddamn, he had wanted her too. Wanted her *still*. Her pheromones had given him an instant hard-on, and then her ice-cold fingers on his neck had sent a shockwave through him. His skin was on fire. He wanted her hands all over his body. Wanted to warm her with his own.

The way those gray knit leg warmers with the faux lacing pattern and the little black bows stopped just short under her oversized sweater teased him with two inches of unrestricted view of her mid-thigh, leaving whatever else she did—or did not—wear under it up to his imagination. He briefly considered putting his hands to better use and taking her right here.

'Don't you dare!'

"Shut up," Kjan bit back, pinching the bridge of his nose. He hoped Eve hadn't caught the remark.

She shuffled her feet in his periphery. Of course, she was barefoot again.

Why is she always barefoot? What was her obsession with wanting to feel the ground beneath her feet?

Not like she could catch a cold, but she had to walk across the freezing concrete of the driveway to get here, for crying out loud. The woman was a true rebel to the core and occasionally utterly unreasonable. Sometimes he wondered if she was doing it just to piss him off.

"What about the trip?" she asked timidly, fidgeting with the clunky heirloom on her thumb.

The clenching sensation around his chest tightened even more. He had known the question was coming; she had been talking about it for days. "You still want to go with them?"

She cocked her head to the side. "I want to go with *you.*"

"I'm not going." He braced himself on the table with a long exhale and then shook his head slowly. "I can't."

She threw her hands up. "What's the big deal? You went back last year."

Physically, yes. His Sire had taken his body back to Iceland, but Kjan had receded too far into his mind at that point. "That… that wasn't me. I shut down for most of it."

He had hated the entire experience. Every single minute. And then Eve had shown up at the club, making it a million times worse. He had felt the pull too, just like his Sire, and it had yanked him out of his semiconsciousness. It had been one of the worst moments of his life. The panicked choking sensation her presence had spurred—

"But it's Christmas," she begged. "Plus, it's like an anniversary for them."

Right. How could he forget? His Sire had shared his *gift* with his minions after claiming Kjan's body during the first blood moon of the lunar tetrad last winter, turning the street kids from Portland first and then moving on to the rest of the crew in Iceland.

Kjan kept his head down, the muscles in his shoulders flexing. "Are you trying to convince me to go or giving me more reasons to stay? You know my stance on the topic, Eve."

Thórunn had died in the summer, at the end of Heyannir. He had endured the pain of her and their daughter's loss for three more cycles. Once Ýlir, the first month of Jól, had rolled around, he hadn't been able to take it anymore. He had become desperate. The Winter Solstice and New Year's were still a sore spot for him. They reminded him of his mortal death and his rebirth as something else. Where they considered it a celebratory occasion, he did not.

"I'm not going to keep you from joining them, but I'm staying here." She could very well make her own decisions. He had no right to control her.

Eve didn't reply. The forge was quiet, and when he turned around, she was gone.

Guilt burned in the back of his throat. His hands gripped the edge of the table with force and hurled the whole thing into the air. The new blade, tools, and everything else on it went flying, scattering on the floor as it landed; top down, legs up.

With panting breath, Kjan dropped to his knees, and once the ringing and clatter of the metals against the wood floor died, there was only the rapid drumming of his heart left.

Well, that and the voice in his head.

'Feel better?'

"Much," he sneered.

'Who is the one with the bad temper now?'

Kjan clasped his head, heels of his palms driving into his temples, as he repeated the words, "Shut up. Shut up! SHUT UP!"

KJARTAN

He obliged. After all, what was the point of taunting him further? They were in this together. Literally. Two minds in one body, he was stuck with Kjan in control, but that did not mean he was entirely cut off. His constriction was only limited to his host's physical movement. He could feel everything Kjan felt. His anger. His frustration. But also *her*.

Through his vessel, he could feel Eve—the warmth of her skin, the taste of her lips. Kjan hated that fact. He hated that he had to share her. His *son* would restrain himself just to deny him.

Kjartan remembered the time when their roles had been reversed: him in command, Kjan the passenger. Eve had been his. Physically, anyway. Her heart had never belonged to him.

Kjan had chastised him for his violent behavior then. Now he was the one with the raging tantrums.

True, they had things in common, like their value of loyalty and their love for the same woman, but they were not the same person. Kjartan's thoughts often spun in a different direction. Especially when it came to Eve.

He had never forced himself on her. Never meant to hurt her. She was fragile compared to him. Delicate, precious, like a porcelain doll. What he had done at the end still haunted him months later. The fear of losing her had driven him mad. He had refused to accept being abandoned again. He needed her.

Needed them *both*.

Kjartan was the outcast, the one nobody wanted, and he had lived every day of his life with that painful knowledge. Locked away in a cave, cursed, and eventually abandoned by his mother, he had spent over 1600 years searching for a place where he belonged. A home. A family.

He had not found it. Not even after siring a coven. That was as close as he had come to having a family of his own. To know kinship. But his jealousy and obsessiveness had destroyed everything.

Kjan was a better leader, and Kjartan was grateful for that. The vampires were all he had. His own kind wanted nothing to do with him. The Gods had made that very clear when they cast him aside for no other reason than being born.

There was nobody like him. He had no friends. No one to confide in. Kjan was the only one who could even hear him, and that was why he would grant him peace. For tonight.

Until he got bored again.

CHAPTER

3

KJAN

He sought her out in the backyard after he took a cold shower. Eve sat huddled under a plush blanket on the wicker daybed, brooding over her laptop.

She still worked in different entry-level advertising jobs. Insisted on it, even though his passive income granted them a very comfortable cushion in their bank accounts.

He watched her through the glass that lined the entire wall of the living room. Her face held a somber expression illuminated by the bright light of the screen.

She seemed so small in the giant pod that was nearly as big as their bed upstairs. Huge cushions surrounded her on all sides, engulfing her in a fluffy pile. One of her bare feet stuck out from under the blanket, and he rolled his eyes.

The vision of her brought a smile to his face. She was luminous. A radiant pearl inside of an oyster, seamless in his regard. Like any other ocean bead, she had started out as a mere irritation before growing into the most exquisite treasure, priceless and irreplaceable.

She was so beautiful, she took his breath away.

Her warm chestnut-colored hair lay brushed over one shoulder as she looked down, offering an unobstructed view of her profile. He knew every detail of her: her deep blue eyes, her flawless skin that was smooth as silk, and those sweet strawberry lips he couldn't resist. Her intoxicating scent of wildflowers and bilberries was the icing on top.

That primal longing raged through him again, and his hand reached for the door to slide it open before he made the conscious decision to do so. He was the moth to her flame.

The cool air on his bare chest didn't bring much relief. The bouquet of her fragrance hit him with force the second he stepped outside.

He didn't miss the skittish look in her eyes as they shot up to him and then quickly back to her laptop while sucking that naked foot back into the warmth.

For the millionth time, he wished he could read her mind.

Kjan slipped into the pod behind her, pressing a kiss on her shoulder. She was still wearing the fuzzy, oversized sweater that hung off-kilter on her delicate frame, and his stare immediately dropped to the deep plunge, following the long chain of her necklace down her chest to where the pendant rested between her breasts. Goosebumps prickled across her taut skin.

A bolt of need shot through him. His breath stalled, and he had to pry his eyes away to keep the desire in check.

"You're cold. Let me light the fire," he offered, his body primed to jump into motion.

"No, it's fine. I'm almost finished anyway."

He watched the arrow on the screen dart to the floppy disc icon in the top left corner as she saved her work. Then she powered the laptop down and set it aside, giving him her undivided attention.

Her brilliant sapphires stared up at him. There was no grudge, no bitterness, in them. He hated to bring it up again.

Weaving his fingers through her hair, his thumb traced her jawline, and the words coiled in his throat, choking him. "I understand why you want to go. You fit in with them. I don't."

She flinched at his admission, looking genuinely surprised. "What are you talking about?"

How can she not sense it? "They accept me, but I'm not one of them, Eve. Lucas doesn't respect me. Askja hates me."

"She doesn't hate you. And Lucas doesn't respect authority; that's nothing personal. He didn't respect Kjartan either. Feared him more likely."

Kjan's fingers tensed. He hated it when she called *him* by that name. The way it rolled off her tongue struck something painful in him, twisting his stomach in knots.

His Sire had never been bestowed a name of his own by his mother since his entire existence had been a secret. He had instead assumed Kjan's original given name.

The immortal had also embraced the persona of a former alias whose reputation had come with consequences. Running a black market business under the identity of Donovan Morgan had attracted the attention of old enemies from Las Vegas, where he used to own a nightclub while dealing in various illegal activities over the span of thirty years.

Kjan withdrew his hand, turning his eyes toward the trees to hide his discomfort. "You should go."

With his gaze on the distance, he sensed her confusion rising, like dense smoke engulfing her aura. Sifting through the fog of her emotions, he tried to recover her scent in the cloudy haze. He knew she was right there next to him, but somehow she felt worlds away. His heart fluttered in a panic.

Out of nowhere, her hands clasped his face, yanking him back. "Where are you?"

"I'm right here," he stammered, his eyes refocusing on her concerned expression.

Her stare narrowed. "Liar. I know I'm losing you."

He dimly shook his head, unable to form the words to deny it.

"Prove it."

Her lips crashed against his, demanding validation with an authority no other held over him. And she was right. *He* was the one pulling away. Not her.

A hand snaked into his hair to give a sharp tug at his roots. Raw carnal instinct replaced his sanity at her fierceness. His body responded without delay, wrenching her into him and spreading her naked thighs around his waist.

His lips parted with a hoarse groan. A strip of lace was the only thing covering her.

"Why must you torture me so, woman?"

Eve gave a soft chuckle, and her tongue flicked out to slide against his.

His blood heated. Meeting the uninhibited inferno between her legs, his hunger for her raged, but instead of nudging Eve onto her back, he encouraged her confidence. Kjan directed his aching palms underneath her sweater to find skin as she straddled his lap and let her take the lead.

Pressing her down on his swelling cock, he submitted to his own needs. Heat seared up his spine and spread with the friction between their bodies.

Kjan's touch skipped lower. He gripped her ass, grinding the hard ridge of his shaft into her.

"Dove," he moaned, unable to contain his response to the building wetness that seeped through his fly.

With her arms locked around his neck, Eve rolled her hips into him. Her nails grazed up his nape, fingers tugging on the longer ends of his hair.

Sparks of pleasure darted over his skin. Kjan jerked underneath her, throbbing against the blazing heat between her thighs as more needy groans erupted in the back of his throat to urge her on.

"That's more like it," Eve acknowledged, her heady rasp pulling away from his lips and traveling down his jaw. "Now I believe you."

Her words robbed him of breath. He loved the sound of her voice like that. So rough. So raw with need. And when her arms unlinked from his neck to nudge him backward, he complied without thought.

Kjan lowered them both down, his right hand drifting up her body in the shift. Despite the soft texture, her sweater felt harsh compared to her skin.

His lungs expanded. He drew in her sweet scent, letting his fingers fan through her silken locks until his palm settled at her nape.

"Don't leave me again," she murmured, her tone contracting an edge of warning.

Eve repositioned her small figure on top of him. Already straining desperately against the unforgiving resistance of his jeans, Kjan sucked in a sharp breath as her hand skimmed down between them, playfully teasing lower.

His grasp on the back of her head tightened even before her descended canines scraped along the front of his throat. Her fingers fumbled with his fly. She released the zipper to spring his erection, then her gentle hand closed around him.

Hissing through his teeth, he rocked into her touch as everything else fell away. Only him and his mate remained, with one primal need. A single joined force.

Eve stroked the whole length of him in a steady pace while dragging her fangs lower. She nipped at him, drawing blood, becoming more determined each time as his back arched and the sweet sting of pain shot up his spine.

The link between them screamed at him to follow through. Making her come wasn't enough. He needed to be inside her. Needed to bury his cock in her and feel her body tremble against his.

Kjan couldn't stop what she set in motion. The tidal wave began to build with irreversible force, and he knew he couldn't keep doing this. The urge to satisfy the bond's call rose to a critical degree. Every time he denied himself to be with her, he craved her more.

More scrapes flared in rhythm with her palm. More lazy swipes of her tongue charting the trail of blood down his chest before she pressed a warm kiss to the scar above his heart.

The velvety touch of her lips moved along his abs. Inch by slow inch, she descended. The anticipation was pure torture.

Weaving his fingers through the tangles, he gathered up her hair and swept it out of his view. Her eyes stayed on his.

Then her mouth came down on him.

Pleasure riddled him as her lips formed a slick, hot seal, sliding lower and retreating. With each bobbing motion, she pulled him deeper, stretching until she took him in fully.

Eve swallowed to adjust, and the back of her throat narrowed with a moan that sent ripples from the sensitive head all the way down his shaft, spreading through his thighs.

His fist clenched at the base of her skull. He watched the rise and fall of her mouth pick up the rhythm while she worked him to climax. The sharp sensation surged, cranking him into overdrive, and it didn't take much to push him over the edge. His entire body drew tight. The muscles in his neck strained from gritting his teeth.

He held her stare until he couldn't take it anymore. Letting himself go, he relinquished to her liquid fire enveloping him. His hips bucked off the bed in a violent arch, and his head flung back. The euphoric force sliced through him like a knife, crisp and clean.

Kjan felt the immortal's presence in his head even if he didn't speak—sensed his gratification now that he had given in. But this wasn't over. He wouldn't let his little dove go hungry.

He lifted his head, and his sight landed back on Eve. There was a wicked twinkle in her eyes as she swirled her tongue at the tip of his still-aching shaft in her palm. The muscles in his thighs gave another spasm.

Freeing the growl in his chest, he seized both of her wrists, then flung her around, crushing her body underneath his.

Her pheromones filled the air vividly. They came to life in his lungs. He could taste her arousal on his tongue, smooth with a subtle burn like Bourbon down his throat.

Everyone would get what they wanted—what they needed—tonight.

CHAPTER

4

EVE

November—

Eve set her foot down on the last available step of the ladder and reached for the hand Kjan was holding out to her. The final three rungs were gone.

"I don't like this," he said, pulling her up onto the roof of the abandoned building.

He'd been sure the brittle iron would collapse beneath them before they ever made it up. Or that the entire fire escape would come loose from the brick of the factory's side wall.

"I thought you loved running."

"Yeah! On the ground, not jumping between buildings." Holding on to the iron rail, he leaned back over the edge and gave Nessa a lift.

The ground he was referring to currently ran approximately 100 feet below them. They hadn't gone out on the trails since the first frost; the landslides and steep terrain of Mount Hood were too treacherous to pick up speed.

But this was about more than just having fun. It was about bonding. Kjan was becoming seemingly more restless as the weeks went by, and Eve stayed hopeful that she could sway him in time for Christmas. She wanted to help him integrate. She'd been wanting to do parkour for months, and since he wouldn't let her go alone with the guys, this was a win-win.

Did he suspect her ulterior motive?

Kjan didn't hide how much he hated the idea. Eve had gotten over her initial apprehension about the height, but she did feel safer with him around. Lucas was so far ahead now that she couldn't even see him anymore. He always took the lead and gave no regard for the safety of the rest. That was why the duty to make sure no one got left behind or hurt fell to Kjan.

As usual.

He remained in the back, even though he was arguably more proficient than anyone else—in anything. Nessa and Eve were the least experienced in the group and therefore nowhere near Lucas' speed. Bayley was the only one who could keep up with him. Parker and Claire formed the middle, along with Dynja and Erik, who had quickly advanced in their skills.

"What's taking you guys so long?" the Icelander hollered over from the adjacent building. "You're supposed to stay in motion to keep your speed up."

The gap to the next one was only about eight feet or so. Eve had managed similar challenges.

Kjan went first, clearing the distance with the ease of jumping a puddle.

After landing softly on the other side, he stayed close to the edge in case one of them came up short or slipped—not that it had ever happened; Nessa was as tall and athletic as everyone else. How Bayley, Lucas' girlfriend, managed to keep up with him was a mystery. The skill level she contained in her tiny stature made her a freak of nature.

Eve took aim at the gap and got her legs into gear. Putting all her weight on her right foot, she pushed off just before the dead drop.

As she went airborne, she caught sight of Kjan's proud grin. Despite his complaints about the process, she knew he was pleased with the progression of her skills. When she landed on both feet right next to him, he didn't even flinch. His hands hung lax, making no motion to step in.

His full confidence and the silent praise in his eyes sent an arousing flare through her. She shot him a wink before stepping aside to give Nessa room.

The succeeding line of rooftops was grouped tighter on this street, which was why they had chosen it. Without stopping, they cleared building after building and managed to catch up to the lead party.

Eve recognized Bayley's pleading voice first, then Parker spoke over her, "Dude, that's over 20 feet."

Lucas gave his friend's worries little consideration. He was standing with only his heels on the edge as he gauged the distance. "What's the world record for the long jump?"

"29 feet, four inches," Kjan weighed in. "That's on track. Don't be stupid. You're not going to make it up here; you won't get enough speed. It'll be closer to a broad jump. 15 feet is ambitious. 20? Impossible!"

Parker shifted nervously. He was now flanking Kjan. "I agree, man. I don't feel like scraping you off the concrete on the bottom. That's a long ass drop."

Lucas' back muscles tensed in the silence that followed. He didn't have to turn over his shoulder to know that everyone was siding with Kjan's assessment.

"I can make it," he insisted nevertheless. "I can clear 15 feet without a running start."

Kjan rolled his neck, and the annoyance in his demeanor grew. "That'll still leave you a few feet short," he snapped.

"So I do a cat leap."

"What if you miss the ledge? You're gambling with inches."

Nessa's elbow nudged into her side. "Did this just turn into a measuring contest?" she heckled under her breath.

Eve didn't laugh. Her nerves were strung taut. She kept her eyes on Kjan. He'd taken a step closer to the edge in an effort to gain control of the situation. "Don't do it," he warned again, trying to talk sense into Lucas.

"Scared? Wouldn't that be a surprise if I could do something that Wonder Boy here can't—"

"Aaaahh!"

Everyone jumped in alarm. Nessa's poignant shriek tore through the tension as she swatted frantically at the rat that had dropped down on her shoulder from the rain gutter above. It tangled in the dense locks of her hair.

She gave it a good whack and knocked it to the ground by Dynja's feet where it scurried off into the shadows.

Her chest heaved with panicked breaths. "Where'd the wee shite go?" she asked in between gasps. Her face was paler than usual, her green eyes huge.

Eve pinched her lips between her teeth, trying not to laugh when Kjan's attention snapped around. His body moved so fast, she felt the whiplash from watching.

Fingers of his right hand gripping the neck of Lucas' sweatshirt, he ripped him backward, slamming him onto the rooftop's gravel.

And speaking of whiplash. There was the crisp sound of a snap coming from his spinal cord. Eve remembered being at the mercy of that very same force once.

"I totally had it," Lucas barked, shoving him off. His arms and legs thrashed furiously.

For a moment, Eve expected things to escalate into a full-on brawl, but Kjan was calm as he let go and straightened. "You don't know that."

"It wasn't your fucking call to make," Lucas gnashed, kicking to his feet.

His heated stare flicked to Bayley and then back to Kjan. He was beyond pissed. The expression on his face was one of raw hatred, making the air around him ripple. It lifted the hairs on Eve's neck and arms even though they were covered. She had only ever felt this around Kjartan.

On a sharp exhale, his glare landed on Eve. She saw his nostril flare before Kjan stepped in between, cutting into the intense connection like a shield. The visual was gone, but she could hear him take off.

Eve felt a rush of pity. No one made a motion to follow him. In her periphery, Erik shot Claire a knowing look. Bayley picked nervously at her fingernails, eyes downcast. To her left, Dynja stood beside Parker, her arms folded over her chest.

Kjan's shoulders sagged before he spun around and instructed everyone to go home. His tone carried a heavy note of remorse. He knew that his interference had emasculated Lucas in front of his girlfriend while he himself came off as the hero to his own. She knew that hadn't been his intention.

Parker nudged his chin toward Dynja, and then everyone dispersed, leaving the two of them alone on the roof.

Why did Lucas continue to push his luck? Did he feel the need to prove something? At what cost? He had tried to use the distraction of the rat to his advantage, and it had almost worked.

Unfortunately for him, Kjan had a sixth sense. Eve had noticed his muscles contract a split second before Nessa's scream.

CHAPTER

5

KJAN

ecember—

His stare was fixed on the dance floor, watching Eve and Emma with the guy who couldn't catch a hint. She had already told him off once, yet *Mr. oblivious-to-his-quickly-approaching-expiration-date* kept eye-fucking her. Kjan was fully aware of how captivating she looked in that outfit, hands up by her head, swaying her body to the rhythm.

He tried not to let his mind dwell on her trip next week—crammed those harrowing thoughts way deep down.

"Why aren't you out there with her?"

He nailed Caleb with a hostile look from the corner of his eye for suggesting it. "I don't dance."

"Yeah, me neither." The kid slouched back against the bar, hiking his elbows up on the ledge.

Kjan kept his hands in his pockets, fingers clenched around his keys like he was trying to strangle them. He forced the stuffy air of the club into his lungs and back out, jaw as rigid as his grip on the sharp metal in his hand.

It wasn't helping.

He noticed Eve's demeanor shift, her awareness triggered by a sixth sense. She leaned toward Emma, speaking directly into her ear over the music, and the girl's head bobbed in acknowledgment.

The muscles in his back relaxed when she pivoted and made her way up to the bar in the black stilettos, which made her toned legs appear twice as long.

His fingers unfurled in response to touching her. The smooth, red silk slid across her skin like water, shifting with the seductive swing of her hips. She wore nothing underneath—and he meant absolutely zilch. No bra. No panties. *Just her sweet peach, ripe for the taking.*

The parasite beneath his skin stirred, and Kjan swallowed the growl rising in his tight throat.

"You okay, man?" The concern in Caleb's tone registered.

"Fine," he replied in a grating voice. He was far from, but what was the kid going to do? Kjan was beyond finding any form of escape from his personal hell.

Eve quirked an eyebrow in her approach. The tips of her lavish breasts perked, beckoning him to suck them between his teeth.

"You want to leave, don't you?"

Fuck yes. "No," he lied. He didn't want to spoil her fun. He tugged her closer by her hands and planted a chaste kiss on her lips while imagining her spread across his lap.

"I can see the wheels in your head turning. You don't look particularly amused."

He lifted one of her hands over her head to give her a spin, then pulled her backside flush against his chest.

Slinging his arms around her narrow waist, he dropped his chin on her shoulder, mouth pressed to her ear. "I'm perfectly content just watching you. Though, I would opt for the more exclusive kind of entertainment." *With her legs wrapped around my neck or sprawled out on the hood of the Charger, her back arched, perfect tits begging for attention.*

"I'd be happy to give you a lap dance in a private room," she offered.

Fuuuuck.

He smothered his curse with the gravely sound of his exhale at the crook of her neck. Her response was exactly the reason he wasn't drinking tonight. Or in public places with her in general.

Kjan had to keep his mind sharp. Whiskey would obscure his firm conviction about not making a public display of his *affection* for her. All it took was a few minutes of lowered inhibition, and she was already making it so easy for him. Under the influence of alcohol, he wouldn't turn down a lap dance with a happy ending.

Alas, her on top wouldn't work. He needed to dominate her body. Needed to feel in complete control. Even if he wasn't. "I know you can handle yourself, but if that guy touches you again, I'll turn him into a PEZ dispenser."

"I'm fully aware of your animosity," she snickered. "I could feel it rippling off you from 20 feet away."

She thought he was joking. After watching the horny prick get all up in her business, Kjan was so fucking tempted to make her cry out his name in a state of perfect ecstasy and show everyone who exactly she belonged to—

WITH! *Dammit*. Who she belonged *with*. Eve was not his property. She was not an object to be taken or owned. She gave herself to him, and he was damn fortunate that she did.

"You put too much faith in my self-control, Dove," he said, forcing his tone casual. He was seething, and Eve knew it.

"You know I'm not doing this on purpose to make you jealous, right? I'm not some immature 17-year-old who seeks attention."

"Yeah, I know. But that doesn't mean I tolerate his proximity." His jealousy meter was at 200%—max for each consciousness occupying his awareness.

Touching her through the thin texture of her dress didn't impart enough relief. The sensitive pads of his fingertips ached to feel her skin. That would at least lower the critical level down to the standard 100%.

"Why are you wearing that dress anyway? It's not really you," he noted. Eve was confident, but she never flaunted herself in public.

"Emma talked me into it."

"Since when do you let anyone talk you into doing things you're not comfortable with?"

The comment came off like a reproach, and he immediately regretted it.

"I don't know." Her shoulder gave a weak shrug; her voice was low. "It sounded like a good idea at the time."

Had he given her the impression that she needed to make an effort for him? "You are perfect the way you are, Dove," he assured her.

Eve preferred casual clothes like himself: jeans and sneakers. She rarely wore dresses, and that was fine with him.

He loved her curves in the snug denim. He would have her naked beside him soon enough.

"Just be yourself. That's who I want."

"I'm hungry," Caleb mumbled next to him, his eyes canvassing the crowd.

Kjan's followed the path. They brushed over Emma. Her black hair was matted down by sweat, and she was still going strong on the dance floor by herself, but not exactly alone.

Caleb didn't seem to share his obsessiveness. The notoriously vocal girl worked as a dancer at another club in town. It was the one where Claire served drinks at the bar and Lucas was a bouncer. The kid had procured a job for Kristján at the same establishment while Kjan handled the necessary paperwork.

Under his Sire's charge, they had all agreed to move to the States permanently. But now they had their freedom, and with that, the option of going back home.

Caleb's head made a sharp 90-degree turn when a young blonde took the stool next to him, her natural bouquet strong enough to overpower the boy's own obnoxiously sweet scent.

"Not her," Kjan snapped at him in his periphery. "Anyone but her."

"Why? She smells fucking delicious. And Em won't mind."

"Here's a free tip for you: don't feed on a pregnant woman. No matter how early the stage, trust me, her hormones will fuck with your own. The effect is similar to taking Ecstasy. You won't know what hit you and are more likely to lose control."

HCG was a powerful aphrodisiac—better than any artificial stimulant he had dabbled in. Plus, the kid wouldn't want to raise his oxytocin level and unintentionally mark her. He didn't have the experience that came with practice. In their hypersensitive systems, the slightest shift in hormones could have catastrophic repercussions. Their bodies were even more regulated by the wretched chemicals than a human's.

Kjan caught Eve staring at him blankly over her shoulder. "What?"

"Nothing." She gave a subtle shake of her head, directing her field of vision back toward the dance floor.

Was she surprised that he could tell? He had skipped over the scientific details and dumbed his answer down to the basic minimum for the kid. It was one of her pet peeves when he sounded like he had a degree in this shit.

Or was it his experience with drugs that ruffled her?

Caleb cocked his head, his boyish features twisted in a skeptic grimace. "How do you know she's pregnant?"

"That intensely sweet trace underneath her natural scent. It's hard to describe. Kinda like… cantaloupe."

"Huh. Good to know. Thanks for the heads-up," he said with a wink, jabbing his forefinger toward Kjan.

Eve remained awfully quiet after that. Her arms were crossed over his at her waist. The index finger on her right hand rubbed back and forth along the shape of the ring on her thumb.

She knew it was a nervous tell, but she couldn't help doing it whenever she was deep in thought. Maybe she was trying to come up with the number of pregnant women he had killed.

"The exact amount you're looking for is zero," he assured her before she could make a wild assumption.

Her big, stunning eyes refocused on him, and a few rapid blinks washed away the glassy haze. "Amount of what?"

"I have never killed a pregnant woman, Eve." He had left them all very much alive—safe and sound—in their own beds, and with no desire to mark them or even return for seconds. He had only been chasing the rush of dopamine that came with each new conquest. Once he had enjoyed them, their appeal quickly dwindled, and he had lost interest.

"I wasn't accusing you of doing so."

"You were giving me that look."

"What look?"

"The one I can't read." When her mind disassociated and her aura practically vanished into thin air right in front of him. It propelled him into instant panic mode.

Eve knew about his fucked-up past. He couldn't change any of it. Or sugarcoat it for her. But he needed her to know that there were lines he had never crossed. She was the only one who had ever overwritten his self-control. The entire attack was a blur to the point where he couldn't recall the taste of her pure, human blood.

But the frenzy that had compelled him to kill her had not been chemistry, not been hormones running amok. It had been fate. He was sure of it.

"You're reading too much into it," she said, dismissing him again.

Or maybe it wasn't the number of pregnant women that gnawed on her mind. Maybe it was the number of women as a whole. And not just the ones comprising his death toll.

He couldn't sugarcoat that either. He could only assure her that, in 953 years, there had never been one like her.

Kjan uncurled his arms and spun her around to face him. When his lips feathered across hers, everything else disappeared. The lights shut down. The music faded into a far-off hum. There was no more crowd. Not even a Caleb.

He pulled Eve's lithe curves into him, his hand cradling her head while his thumb caressed the flawless contour of her cheek.

With a lengthy moan, she tipped her head back further, and Kjan unfurled completely. He didn't need booze. He didn't need cigars. All he needed were her pheromones on full blast, and he was done for.

His mouth went to her throat—to the pulsing vein beneath her skin—and his fangs answered the call. He wanted to bite her. Wanted her in total submission. He was falling, and he needed her to catch him.

Legs entwined, her body melted into his, their two shapes becoming one. But she held out on voicing her pleasure as openly as he craved it. He needed to hear her wailing and whimpering without restraint… needed to feel her fingernails in his back.

Sex in public meant none of that. It also meant tolerating his passenger's ride-along in the front seat.

But he would never make it back to the refuge of Mount Hood.

Kjan's hand shackled around Eve's wrist. "Take care, Caleb," he hollered over his shoulder, dragging her along behind him.

He welcomed the harsh bite of the November air into his feverish skin, but Eve hadn't brought a coat and the Charger wasn't parked in the main lot. It was tucked away, facing into the alley around the corner. A very dark, very secluded corner.

Kjan pulled her further down, strategically positioning them at the front end, so the vehicle blocked their view of the street.

"What's gotten into you?" Eve asked, flustered and short of breath when he nudged her onto the hood with obvious intention.

"Distract me." His hands gripped her thighs, splitting them around his hips. "It's either this or I will go back inside and tear that guy limb from limb for touching you. You have no idea how many ways I came up with to skin him alive."

Kjan's mouth closed over hers in an attempt to shush her thoughts as much as his own, which continued their drilling assault.

Trailing kisses over her cheek and down her neck, he sank into her fragrant nest. More heat flooded him. She let her head fall back, granting him free rein as he pressed her into the car.

When his coarse facial hair scraped at her throat and collarbone, he felt her go weak, her body growing wet and needy for him.

Eve's hands dropped from his chest to undo his fly without a verbal cue from him. Mouth hot at her throat, he licked across her pulse point, savoring the rapid beat against his tongue as she reached down between them.

Her fingers closed around him in a moan, and she stalled, treasuring his ardent arousal for her. Kjan felt himself swell even more at her appreciation.

Moving up his shaft, she gathered his pre-cum with a swipe of her palm. Her grip became slick, and he rocked his hips toward her, meeting her halfway while she worked his entire length up and down.

Eve stroked him at a deliberate yet restrained pace, granting him only a taste of her heat with each of his thrusts. The slickness made him shiver. Her touch didn't bring the needed relief. He ached for her soft, molten core.

Kjan straightened his head, hovering over her. His tongue flicked her top lip. "Don't make me beg," he whispered.

Then his mouth came down on hers, kissing her softly and slowly as he entered her body on that first lazy thrust.

Her arms wound around his neck. Lifting her leg by the back of her knee, he opened her more and sank deeper.

The scent of her arousal hit the back of his throat like a flower in full bloom. He retreated, then slid back in, unhurried and gentle, again and again as he pinned her down on the hood.

Little whimpers fused with her breath. Eve was about to come.

"Bite me," he told her, easing up on her lips. "I need to feel your teeth when you come."

Watching her face, Kjan caught a flash of white. Then she plunged her fangs into his traps, right above his clavicle.

Eve claimed him with her bite and her body. He was aware of every pulse, her contractions working him to his own release. The force of it built in his thighs and stomach. Shudders raking through the muscles, he spilled himself into her on a final thrust.

With his left palm heavy on the hood, he felt the metal give under his weight. It irked him that he was forced to keep her quiet, but he didn't want to draw attention to them.

Three was already a crowd.

CHAPTER
6

KJAN

he's an adult. She can make her own decisions. She'll be fine, he told himself. *It's only one week.*

'Don't let her go.'

Almost two months had gone by in a flash without Kjan being able to emotionally prepare himself. He stood in the door, watching Eve pack and ignoring the parasite itching under his skin.

Kristján's Suburban had just rumbled up the driveway, the low throttle of the engine forcing his heart to sink deeper into the pit of his stomach. He wasn't taking her to the airport himself. Wouldn't be able to let her go if he did.

Anxiously, he went downstairs to let the Icelandic giant in. He was technically no longer his enforcer, but he was still the only one Kjan trusted with her safety. At the human age of 38, he was the most responsible one.

"Hey." He nodded at the tall blond as he removed his shades and stepped inside.

Kristján flashed a subtle grin, sporting a five-o'clock shadow. The morning sun flooded through the front door behind him, but at 6'7"—and a build like a brick shithouse—he blocked out most of it.

"She'll be down in a minute," Kjan said, swinging the door shut.

Kristján trotted after him into the living room. His subtle leather and sandalwood scent mixed with traces of his mate's: vanilla and elderberry. There was also a distinct nuance from that pack of smokes he still carried as a keepsake in his pocket. "No worries. We got plenty of time."

The flight left around two in the afternoon, and they would land in Reykjavík before 10 p.m. Daytime was a non-issue for any of them now.

They came to a stop at the bottom of the staircase, one on either side. "Thanks again for giving her a lift."

Kristján propped his arm on top of the newel post. "Sure thing. The others won't be ready for a while anyway. You should see how much Kría is packing. You would think she was staying for a month." He laughed, shaking his head. "Hey, did you finish the new sword yet?"

"No. It fractured. I have to start over." Not even a lie. It had been one of the victims of his latest outburst.

Kristján seemed disappointed. "That's too bad. I was really excited to see it."

"I'll have plenty of time to work on it." Kjan shoved his hands in his pockets and leaned back against the wooden post behind him, his chest tight.

"Don't worry. I won't take my eyes off her," Kristján said in his thick accent, as if reading his mind. "She is perfectly safe."

"I know," Kjan responded without looking at him.

Eve came skipping down the stairs in her fur boots, coat in hand, backpack slung over her shoulder. The sight made him nauseous. His stance stiffened.

"That's all you're bringing?" Kristján scoffed in surprise. "Kría could fit that entire backpack in her purse."

"It's only a few days," she replied.

"Whatever. I'm sure the girls will want to take you shopping. You're going to need a better coat."

"He's right. You'll be cold," Kjan agreed, tugging on the front of her sweater.

Actually, the temperatures weren't any lower than Portland in December. He just couldn't get the image of her twirling barefoot in the snow out of his head, light, white flakes settling on her nose as she stared up at the sky.

Eve's features didn't soften, and a faint prickle of resentment brushed him. Kristján immediately picked up on the tension too. "I'll wait outside."

Kjan vaguely heard the giant excuse himself to give them a few minutes alone.

He sighed, cradling her face in his hands. He couldn't resist drawing her into him. "I'll make it up to you, I swear."

"You don't have to." She jostled her head dismissively. "It's fine."

"I don't want you leaving angry."

"I'm not angry."

"No, you're disappointed, and we both know, that's worse," he argued, keeping his voice gentle. "Eve, I love you. I'm trying to move on, not move backward. I don't want to relive my past. I can't go back there."

He pressed his face to her cheek, lips trembling against her warm skin. "I'm too afraid of what I'll find."

Her fingers twisted the front of his shirt. "What could you possibly find that would change things between us?"

Kjan didn't really know the exact answer to that. If he had made different choices then, he wouldn't be here now. Wouldn't be who he was. Wouldn't have Eve.

But he had always felt guilty, as if he could have somehow prevented Thórunn's fate. It was absurd, of course. She died in childbirth; there was nothing he could have done, and they had both wanted children. Yet the nagging feeling persisted. He had no desire to return to that forsaken island. It was a curse to him, like it had been to his father.

"You're being unreasonable."

"You're right. I am," he admitted.

Nudging her chin up, he kissed her deeply, his lips moving against hers with a sense of desperation. He drew out the goodbye—needed it to last him all week. She was the air in his lungs, and he would have to hold his breath until she returned to him.

When he pulled away, he clasped her hands on his chest and squeezed them affectionately, searching her eyes again for any unresolved grudge. "I'll miss you," he said, feeling the need to reassure her.

"I'll miss you too."

Lips in a tight line, her fingers flexed as she freed them, and a shiver of dread trickled down his spine.

"I'll be right here when you get back," he added before letting Eve slip through his grasp.

Kjan watched her walk out the door. She didn't look back.

'You fool.'

CHAPTER

7

EVE

Kristján had been right. Dynja and Kría insisted on taking her shopping as soon as possible. It was all they talked about the entire flight. Their excitement made Eve's ears ring.

Unfortunately, since their plane landed in Reykjavík late Monday night with the shops already closed and people preparing for the Winter Solstice, the wild spending spree had to wait until Tuesday afternoon. Nessa and Askja both declined, but Emma accompanied them, making it a fun girl's day out nonetheless.

Eve didn't really get the point. Her parka was more than adequate for the weather. Unlike her more elaborate solo tour back in March, they would be sticking to a crawl down the city's main street. She wasn't exactly planning on going for a hike out in the cold.

She'd once been to Nebraska on a family trip with her grandparents. -15F with the wind chill—now *that* was cold. Iceland wasn't much worse than Portland in the winter.

While Kría and Emma browsed the racks for her, Eve ambled through the store, her ears perked to catch little conversation pieces of the other shoppers. She identified a few words here and there, like a disgruntled man scolding his wife for buying yet another scarf when she already owned a thousand.

Eve stifled a grin. She knew she got the number right, but surely he was exaggerating.

"Here!" Emma exclaimed, shoving a puffy gray parka at her.

Several more outfits hung draped over her arms, dwarfing the girl under the pile, but Eve refrained from asking how her friend was going to fit all that into her already bursting luggage.

When leaving the store, Eve gave the Doberman guarding the door a wide berth. Despite its gorgeous, sleek black and rust-colored coat, it was arguably the meanest one she'd ever seen. Lips curled back as she passed by, it growled at her for no reason. She felt the urge to assure the dog that she wasn't shoplifting.

Back out on the street, they turned down the rainbow path toward the church at the end that stood out among the cute, colorful two-story houses. The street was buzzing with people during the meager hours of daylight, and at a little after 3 p.m., the sun was already beginning to set.

Pausing to stare up, Eve focused on the large clock on the tower. The bells had chimed on the hour, but the time was not the same as on her phone.

"It's off," she pointed out to Kría.

"That happens a lot. The wind messes with the hands."

No surprise there. Hallgrímskirkja dominated the skyline. Its towering steeple sat at a height of 244 feet, if she remembered correctly. The winds up in the bell tower must be quite something. Eve had never gone up in the elevator.

"Have you been inside?" Kría asked.

"I have. It's definitely the most beautiful one I've ever seen. Inside and out." Eve's neck strained as her gaze followed the long way up. The design was utterly unique. The exterior with its steeple and wings was styled after the unusual volcanic basalt formations along Iceland's coastal cliffs.

"The view of the city from up there is amazing. We should go and catch the sunset. Trust me, you have never seen anything like it."

Go up? Eve gulped. Not that she didn't believe her friend's judgment, but the awe-inspiring height made her nauseous. She would've preferred to have Kjan by her side. He had never seen it either.

Unless…

"Do you know if Kjartan ever went up?"

Kría shrugged. "I'm not sure, but I don't think so."

Eve's heart felt heavy. This could've been something they experienced together, had he not chosen to stay behind.

He'd once told her about all the amazing European architecture he'd seen in his long life: churches, cathedrals, and palaces in various styles he'd visited on his own. Gothic being his favorite—all dark and broody, go figure.

She wasn't sure where an Evangelical Lutheran church fit into his interests, but for once she could've been by his side when his eyes beheld something new to him.

"I think I'd rather keep my feet on the firm ground for now," she said, then lowered her stare to the plaque above the heavy bronze doors.

"Can you read it?" Kría probed, gauging Eve's frown from the corner of her eye.

"I wish, but my vocabulary hasn't increased much." Kjan refused to teach her. *Anything to keep me from poking around his past.* "Will you read it for me?"

Her friend obliged, and Eve followed the carved words as she pronounced them. The sound of the language triggered an ache in her chest that she couldn't place. She had to blink rapidly to fight the tears from welling up.

"What does it mean?" She needed to know, even though she wasn't religious. It was about the language, not the hymn.

"It roughly goes, *Come into God's house. Keep well in mind, my pious soul, do not mock your Lord. With a pure body, bend your knee, flesh, and heart. Your promise and prayers be filled with love. You will have no honor in deceit.*" Kría cringed, embarrassed. "I'm sure you can find a better translation somewhere."

"That's alright." Eve chuckled. "I appreciate the effort." She knew there was a rhyme to the words in the Icelandic tongue that had gotten lost in the translation.

"How about you give the doors a try?" Kría suggested with a nod toward the bronze slabs. "That shouldn't be too hard."

Eve grinned. It wasn't. "Komið til mín—Come to me," she translated on her own. And that brought some of her pride back.

The cottage they were staying at was just a short drive from the city's center, but still somewhat isolated to give them privacy in the busy capital. It was also easily big enough to fit them all comfortably without making it too crowded.

Especially now that Caleb and Emma were dating, Claire was with Erik, Kristján with Kría, and Dynja was hooking up with whomever.

Everybody had their own little personal space.

On the first two nights, they had all hit the local bars and clubs together, with Erik giving them a private tour of his favorite hangouts.

The scene was much different than what they were used to in the States, and naturally, the kids from Portland were immediately hooked. The legal drinking age in Iceland was twenty, but since none of them were engaging in alcohol, even Caleb didn't need his fake ID.

Eve had enjoyed herself for a while but lost interest after a few hours; it brought back memories of her trip here last year. She vividly recalled the night she encountered Kjartan for the first time, his red eyes as they burned into her with a strange recognition, hovering on top of another woman in the cozy seating area while possessing Kjan's body.

Eve didn't want to relive that night. Didn't want to remember anything about the immortal. It only made her miss Kjan more. And while the shopping trip had compounded her feelings, it was on that first night out that she started to regret her decision to come here.

The second night had made it worse.

Eve was bitter. But she didn't want to be the one to cave and reach out first. There had been no communication between them. No messages. No calls. The two days of radio silence from him made her anxious. It hadn't really been a fight, and yet it still felt like one.

Watching the happy couples around her rubbed salt into her wounds. Music filled the living room. Dynja was dancing with Lucas, who appeared to be in a better mood now after his spat with Bayley. According to him, she hadn't been able to get time off from the clinic for the trip, but Eve wondered whether his girlfriend was avoiding the group intentionally.

Is there more to their little quarrel?

Mama Askja seemed more reserved than usual toward Eve as well. Almost as if she were avoiding her. It reminded her of Kjan's remark. The woman had always been kind to her before, but lately, she felt a distinct coldness wafting her way.

Eve crossed the living room, and Caleb seized her by the arm, interrupting her straight shot for Nessa. His usually messy brown hair was spiked on top tonight.

"What do you mean, you're not going?" He frowned down at her, dumbfounded.

"I don't feel like dancing," she replied with a retort.

He might have a few inches on her, but everyone still considered him the baby of the family. He had barely been 19 before becoming a vampire last year. Eve was almost two whole years older than him.

The golden sunbursts in the center of his irises flared. "You're kidding, right? You *have* to go."

"Uhm, I'm pretty sure I don't!" she countered derisively before pushing past him. Last she checked, she could damn well make her own decisions. She was here, wasn't she? No one put a leash on her.

Eve caught up with Nessa in the hall when Askja ran back upstairs. "What's with her lately? She seems kinda distant. Like her mind is somewhere else."

"Aye." The redhead's green eyes shimmied uneasily. "She misses… *him*, ye know?"

Eve shuddered. There was no need to say his name. The thought of him rolled like ice down her back.

Askja was the one who had found Kjartan in Iceland when he had still been cursed to live as a never-aging 12-year-old boy. She'd been his confidant and only friend for 14 years. Eve had seen the affection between them firsthand.

"Don't take this the wrong way," Nessa continued in a hushed tone. Sweeping an auburn curl behind her ear and leaning closer, the scent of her cucumber mint lotion amplified. "They had known each other for a very long time, and they were very close. She was like a mother to him. He wasn't as bad as ye make him out to be."

Riiight. He had only hunted down and killed all the vampires he'd ever sired, possessed Kjan's body, and tried to turn the coven into his personal slaves. *No big deal.*

Nessa sighed, her glance shooting around the room to make sure nobody was overhearing. "She wants to be happy for you two, but she's hurting. She's lost a child before… years ago. She doesn't like to talk about it."

Her eyes shot over Eve's shoulder, and she suddenly looked uncomfortable. Askja came hopping down the stairs, her straight, dark blonde ponytail bouncing behind her.

"Please don't mention to her that I told ye." She turned away and then followed her mate outside.

Askja lost a child? The female was in her mid-thirties, Nessa eight years younger, but still… Eve had never considered the possibility. She knew next to nothing of anyone's background. Claire had barely touched the subject of her and Parker fleeing from a grabby foster father. How much deeper did the coven's scars run?

"Come on, Eve," Caleb pestered again. "Everyone is going. Why would you want to stay here by yourself?"

He sure was relentless about changing her mind to join them. She rolled her eyes at him, annoyed. "I'll be perfectly fine. Go have fun."

Emma tugged on his arm. "Leave her be, Caleb. She doesn't want to go."

"Let's roll!" Parker yelled from the open doorway. They were the only ones left.

"Get out of here already. And stay safe." Eve specifically glared at Parker on that last part. She would never get the image of him nearly dying on the sofa out of her head.

"Yeah-yeah," he mumbled with his back turned.

Caleb still hesitated, hands twitching nervously by his side. "Maybe I should stay, too. I really don't like leaving you by yourself. What if—"

"Enough!" Eve stomped her foot in anger. "I don't need a goddamn babysitter. Nothing is going to happen, I'm not going anywhere, and I'm perfectly capable of entertaining myself for a few hours."

"You heard her," Emma hissed impatiently, setting her hands on her hips.

The tiny girl had a fire in her cold blue eyes. She would never let him off the hook if he stayed behind with her. Eve could see the conflict in his face, jaw ticking from tension. He had been loyal to Kjartan, and now he was loyal to Kjan. He was very aware of his responsibilities. He had learned them the hard way.

"Get. Out." Eve turned her back on the two, formally relieving him of his duty. He was about five seconds away from dealing with her wrath.

She was downright fuming as she lit the firepit outside. The anger rolling off her seemed to give fuel to the flames. She almost expected the freaking tank to ignite from a spark of her fingers.

Nah, she didn't have Kjan's powers. No one but him had that magic touch.

Grateful that the gas hadn't blown up in her face, Eve plopped onto a lounger on the deck. The back of the cottage was quiet and peaceful. A few small trees lined the property, and she could hear wildlife in the bushes scurrying about.

She wasn't exactly sure what kind of animals were native to the region, but that huge black bird looked out of place on the skinny branch. Its head twitched in her direction, and the fire of the pit reflected in its eyes, giving them an ominous amber glow.

A prickle went up her neck.

Eve watched it curiously as it inched its talons along the branch, rustling its feathers, and cocking its head at her in a nervous twitching motion.

It suddenly flinched in alarm, tearing off with an angry caw, and a split second later, the heavy glass door behind her slid open, scaring not just the hell out of the bird but also her. She nearly jumped out of her skin.

"For fuck's sake," she snapped before turning around. "I'm going to kill you myself if you don't leave—"

"How unfortunate. And here I came all this way just for you."

Her anger dropped when her eyes landed on Kjan in the doorway. Hands in his pockets, he leaned into his shoulder, grinning from ear to ear.

"You came," she muttered tearfully. "What changed your mind?"

He slid the door shut, then sat down on the lounger with her, clasping her hands in front of him. "Forgive me. I was a fool for thinking I could make it through a single day without you. I'll follow you to the end of the world, Dove."

He kissed her right palm reverently and pressed it to his cheek, closing his eyes with a steep sigh of relief that Eve could relate to. She felt like she hadn't seen him in weeks.

"But there is one more reason why I had to come back." He opened his eyes and appeared to study her face for a minute, his own expression somber, brooding. Or maybe it wasn't actually Eve's face that he was seeing.

He tenderly pulled her chin up to him, his beautiful emeralds darting over her features. Her throat tightened like a noose, and her mouth got suddenly dry. She knew who was on his mind… because she supposedly looked just like her.

"I feel like I'm competing with a dead woman," she blurted out.

His eyes narrowed into slits, his expression changing from thoughtful to utter bewilderment.

"Her ghost haunts me like a part of her is still here, and I have to find her to understand why you would choose me over her."

The corner of his mouth twitched, and he gave her a thin smile. "Dove, too much has changed—*I* have changed," he murmured. "I'm not the man she knew then. Far from it. She was the dominant personality in our relationship, not me."

Eve raised her eyebrows in disbelief. "You, submissive?"

Kjan chuckled. "I like where your head's at, but there's more to a relationship than sex. She made the important decisions, and I went along with them. Usually." He smirked, his thumb brushing along Eve's bottom lip.

"Let's just say I knew what she needed, and I was happy to oblige. Others were less agreeable with her strong mind. There were plenty of conflicts, but I always had her back. Unquestionably. She knew she could count on that. But you're right. I can never break the tether to this place and move on until I confront my fears. I have been pushing it off for a millennium. It's time I get this over with. I couldn't do this with anyone but you. It's you and I," he whispered against her lips. Then he drew her in, finally crushing his mouth to hers.

Eve inhaled deeply, his scent filling her lungs. He smelled so good. Tasted even better.

She climbed into his lap, her gums throbbing, fangs itching to sink into his skin. She clung to his chest as it rose and fell in short breaths matching her own.

With her heart rushing the blood through her veins faster and a pounding in her ears, she clutched his shirt in her fists. "I want you," she whimpered while grinding against him. Her body ached for his touch, but he kept his hands annoyingly decent.

"Not out here." He broke away from her lips on a gasp, roaming her throat. His tongue soft and his beard rough against her skin, he continued teasing her.

Eve moaned, sinking deeper. "Why not? We're alone. Are you afraid of the birds watching?"

Kjan chuckled again, nuzzling the crook of her neck, his breath searing hot at her jugular. "No. It's too cold for you."

"You're doing a fine job warming me up," she drawled.

He flinched abruptly and pulled away like he had a realization, his eyes set in a deep scowl. "Why are you alone?"

KJAN

"Why did they leave you by yourself, Dove?"

It had taken his brain a moment to catch up. Getting his hands on her was the only thing that mattered when he saw her. "I thought I made myself clear. Kristján or Caleb were supposed to stay with you at all times."

"Don't blame them. I sent them away."

His hands at her sides tensed possessively. "Now why would you do that, knowing how I feel about you being alone?"

"I don't need a babysitter, Kjan."

With her thighs spread wide across his lap, she leaned toward his ear. "I'm a big girl," she breathed provocatively. "I can take care of myself."

Her hips gave another slow grind against him, and a growl rippled through his chest. His palms skated lower to cradle her ass. "You're trying to distract me."

A dark hint of amusement laced her voice. "Is it working?"

His grip on her ass tightened, fingertips dimpling her flesh through the cotton. She could damn-well feel him harden beneath her. "Not yet," he lied. "Are you particularly attached to these leggings?"

"No. Why?"

Kjan's hands slid from her hips inward, gripping the fabric and splitting it at the seam. He slipped his fingers into the opening, pulling the skimpy thong aside and brushing his knuckles over her bare cleft.

Eve whimpered in his ear. Her body arched into him, her breasts jutting into his chest.

"So, they just left you?" he asked, teasing her clit with lazy strokes. "Without argument?"

Her breath began to judder. "No. I had to repeat myself three times."

"Three times?" He watched her face as she rocked herself against his hand. "How impudent of you. Do my rules mean so little? Perhaps I should remind you."

He increased the pressure of his strokes, flicking over the sensitive bundle of nerves until she let out a soft cry. Her body convulsed in pleasure.

"Yes!" she gasped, coming down. "You should definitely remind me." Her hands wandered down his chest to work the front of his pants. "To make sure they *really* sink in this time."

Eve's weight lifted, and he hardly caught the sound of the zipper going down over the rushing blood in his ears. Her hands working to free him choked his breath.

"I mean, as long as we have the place to ourselves… why not take advantage of it?"

His touch left her sides briefly to raise his hips enough for her to scoot his pants down and expose him fully. *Yes.* There was one upside to him finding her alone.

Her gentle grasp closed around his shaft. Hovering, Eve stroked the tip of his cock across her seam and then sank down, swallowing all of him in one long, slick glide.

Fuuucck me!

Kjan's mind scrambled. She was utterly magnificent, and he almost forgot what they had been arguing about.

Almost.

Grinding down hard, she forced him deep into the curve of her passage.

There! At the very front…

A long groan ruptured free. The sensation was just as pleasurable for him as it was for her, and Eve knew it. She knew how to work him into herself to get what she was after.

Her body bounced on top of him as she hit that spot over and over, her breaths coming in shallow huffs. Beads of sweat made her skin sparkle.

But that wasn't enough for him.

"Open your mouth for me, Dove," he urged, his fingertips tracing the seam of her lips.

Eyes on him, Eve complied, and Kjan eased two fingers past her fangs, sliding them over her tongue toward the back of her throat.

Closing her lips around his knuckles, Eve moaned.

"So eager," he mused, his cock straining against her walls as it swelled in response.

And *that* still wasn't enough.

His free hand rounded her waist to slip into her leggings from behind. The matching pair of fingers working her back entrance at the same time, he filled every part of her to the brim. And she was so into it. Eve's movements became more urgent—his *not*-so-innocent little dove.

Kjan fed on her arousal. Fed on her lust. Her sweet sounds. *That* was what he needed.

His mouth latched on to her throat, his tongue slicking across her pulse point, feeling the rapid beat while Eve sucked his fingers deeper. She gripped him with her body, and when she climaxed again, his skin prickled. He felt it everywhere.

With a restraint on his own depraved desire, Kjan loosened his embrace, retracting his hands and, at last, his cock from her heat.

Eve's brow furrowed. "You didn't finish."

"Don't worry." He clasped the back of her neck. "I have every intention to fill you thoroughly. Upstairs. *Now!*" he growled into her ear.

Her muscles tensed on top of him, ready to leap off, but he gave her hair a sharp pull to hold her in place for another second. "I'm giving you a ten-second head start, but you better be naked when I catch up."

The instant he released her, Eve launched herself off his lap to make a run for it. Kjan allotted her the promised advantage before he gave chase.

Catching up to her in her room upstairs, he swung the door shut behind him. She spun around to meet his eyes, and he nodded toward the bed. "All fours, Dove."

He watched her crawl up onto the mattress. Braced on her forearms and knees, she bared herself to him. Her pink seam swollen and glistening spurred the primal, possessive beast in him.

Kjan stripped his clothes too. He wanted to be bare for her the way she was for him. Wanted this to be raw—no layers between them.

Ears perked to the rapid drum of her pulse, he drew out his approach. He wanted her eager… ready… waiting. He knew the anticipation was killing her.

Coming up behind her, he granted her that first touch. He ran a splayed hand along her spine, tracing the steep curve with subtle pressure.

His painfully stiff cock jerked at her responsiveness. Eve's body adhered on reflex, bending to his authority and his guidance.

The small taste of her downstairs only made him that much harder now. The mattress dipped as he set his knees down on either side of her, pinning her thighs together and bringing himself flush with her.

Fingers clasping the back of her neck, he urged her head down while letting her feel his throbbing length.

Eve squirmed against him, aching to be filled again.

"Nu-uh, Dove. I'm in charge now. And this time, you'll be good and follow my directions."

Face buried in the pillow, she relinquished a stifled whimper of acknowledgment he knew all too well.

"Now," he prompted, easing up on her to reach in between their bodies. "Tell me again, how many times you told them to leave." He dragged the side of his hand through the wetness of her slit.

"Three times," she groaned as she spasmed from his touch.

"Fight it, Dove." He made another slow pass over her clit. And then a third.

"I know you're dying for me to make you come. I can feel you trembling. But not yet. I want you to come with my cock buried in your ass."

Eve's fists clenched the sheets, and she granted him a small whimper as her body shuddered. One more stroke over her clit would unravel her.

Grip on his shaft, he speared her core, nearly splitting her in half, but he knew she needed the external stimulation to come. And he wasn't ready to give her that. The more he edged her, the harder she was willing to take him.

When he pulled out and sank back in, it was at a slower pace. Eve's curse was muffled by the pillow, but not inaudible to his ears.

He rocked into her a third time, then pulled out all the way. Guiding his slick cock up her ass, he eased just the head into her.

Her whimpers turned desperate.

"Not yet, Dove. Fight it."

His own muscles burned from restraint. Eve ground herself back, slowly welcoming as much as he offered but never going over the edge.

"So good," he muttered under his breath.

Releasing the grip on her neck, he set his hands on her hips and watched her take him. Her tight rim stretched, swallowing another inch. And then another.

"Just a bit more."

When he pushed in to the hilt, she quivered from tension, and Kjan gave her a few lazy thrusts to make sure she was adjusted.

"So, so good," he repeated. "Now you're full and ready."

His fingers found her clit as he gave two quick, hard thrusts. By the third, she shattered.

"That's it. Let me feel you come."

Her body gripped him, her moans so sweet as her passage collared around him, clenching and unclenching his shaft with erratic pulses.

It took every ounce of self-control not to speed up yet. Keeping his thrusts going in a lazy rhythm, he lowered himself down on her.

Eve's knees buckled underneath him as he pinned her hips, pressing her into the mattress.

"Hard and fast?" His voice went up in question for her consent.

"Hard and fast," she echoed in the next beat.

A breath of relief left his lungs, because the fear that one day she would reject him remained ever present.

A burn flared at his canines.

"Bend for me, Dove," he said, his weight braced on one hand, the other one fisting her hair to force her head back.

Eve craned her neck, and her blue gaze lit him up when it landed on him—more than just a window into her soul, but a sliver of his own, ever inseparable, and more than that still.

My Mate.

My Chosen.

MINE.

The acknowledgment triggered a nerve, and his fangs descended fully.

"Remember, it's not punishment," he breathed against her lips.

"I know." Eyes full of trust locked onto him. The message in their depths was clear even without her uttering the words.

Then Kjan delivered.

Drawing back, he rammed his cock into her again, harder and faster with each thrust. He was so close to his own climax there was no slowing his momentum now. The building pressure rippled through his muscles.

Eve's quickening breaths and whimpers only spurred him on. He railed into her, deep and relentless, and this time, the friction was enough to get her off. Her walls squeezed him.

Her tight fit… the smooth glide on each full thrust…

Kjan was done fighting his release. A roar ruptured free when he burst inside her, trembling from the violence behind the act.

Beads of sweat rolled freely down the side of his face as he stilled, drawing her pleasure into himself like oxygen, filling his lungs with the sweet, flowery scent of her arousal.

The effect her body and the mate-bond had on him—the gift of her unconditional devotion—*that* was what he thrived on. Fleeting touches were merely crumbs. Not enough to feed him. Or heal him. He required more.

Kjan had locked himself in the study after Eve left with Kristján. But two days of solitary confinement in the dark with *him* had driven him mad. It had become his own personal hell. As a danger to himself, he couldn't even be trusted with the tools in the forge.

He had resorted to suppression with Bourbon and cigars instead, but that had hardly put a muzzle on the pesky leech. Audibly and physically, he proceeded to show his contempt for Kjan's cowardice.

His Sire had enjoyed bragging about the fact that he would have gone with her if the choice had been his. It was easy for the immortal to criticize others. He wasn't the one who had to face his traumatic past.

Or was he?

CHAPTER

8

KJAN

While the love for Thórunn was still alive in his heart, it was true: they were no longer compatible. He had been the submissive; parts of it still showed in his general concern for the people around him and his keen awareness of their needs. He had always found happiness in meeting those needs and being of service.

But with her death and the torture by his Sire, not to mention a thousand years on his own, Kjan had changed. He had become the dominant, making all the decisions on his own and dealing with the consequences and mistakes of his actions.

Eve was his match now. There was no question about it. Though she looked like Thórunn, was stubborn and fierce like her with a personality that lit a fire inside him, she was not the same.

No. Kjan grinned to himself. The two were very different in one significant manner. His *not*-so-innocent Dove had a particular way of cooling his engines, and after finding out they had left her alone at the cottage, he had been ready to rip someone's lungs out if she hadn't taken full responsibility for her actions.

Multiple times.

They had gone at it again in the shower, and then one more time after before he deemed her properly reminded.

But his anger had only decreased to a low simmer, not vanished entirely. Kristján was in charge, and he had promised to watch over her. Kjan shouldn't have trusted them. They couldn't possibly understand what she meant to him.

He had a hard time letting it go. Eve fell asleep before the others returned, and he sat in the living room, cracking his knuckles, waiting for whoever would show up first to collect the honor of his fist and the grand prize of a black eye. Beneath his skin, he was itching for a fight.

Fuck. Kjan dropped his head into his hands. This wasn't him—wasn't his approach to conflict. Yet it wasn't completely out of character, either. He had long ago changed his mindset and trained himself to react calmly in situations he couldn't control, but it was so much harder now. The tendency to explode had doubled.

Leaning forward on his thighs, he raked a hand through his hair, rubbing the top of his head in thought when the door flew open and Caleb strolled in.

Ding-ding, we have a winner, Kjan thought, but then the boy shrieked and took cover behind Kristján, cowering like a child under a tree for protection during a lightning storm.

"What the fuck? You gave me a heart attack," he gasped, clutching his chest overdramatically. "I told you, I felt something." He glared up at Kristján. "A disturbance in the force."

"Simmer down, Padawan," the blond giant laughed.

"I'm a fucking Jedi Master, and don't you forget it," Caleb wagged his finger at Kristján, who collapsed onto the couch, dragging Kría with him.

"Then take a seat," he shot back.

Emma snorted behind the kid's back as he passed her and dropped into the chair across from Kjan. "Why are you sitting in the dark like a damn vampire?"

"Appreciating the quiet," he replied bluntly, but even he couldn't keep a straight face anymore.

Knees spread wide, he slouched back in his seat, stifling a smile as he set his elbow on the armrest and propped his chin. The storm inside him had dissipated. The boy was safe after all.

Askja's reaction to his unexpected arrival didn't slip his notice. She gave him the hairy eyeball, per usual, and quickly disappeared upstairs with Nessa.

"Where's Eve?" Emma asked, sliding into Caleb's lap. She brushed her slick black hair over one shoulder like a satin curtain.

"Sleeping," he muttered in response.

Jet lag was a bitch. He should really be headed upstairs to join her. He had left her naked in the sheets.

"Did you wear her out already?" Kristján's head poked around Kría's dark blonde locks. "Seriously, you've been here five minutes."

Fuck yeah, I did.

Kjan's mouth twitched with a guilty tell behind his fingers, jaw cradled in between his thumb and pointer. He was nothing but efficient in making Eve squeal. Especially when they had the house to themselves.

Caleb shifted nervously between the cushions of his chair. "Look, man, if you're pissed that I left her, I'm sorry. I didn't want to, but she looked ready to kick my ass out personally. She is scary for a girl."

Emma nudged him with a glare, and the boy's eyes flitted sheepishly to her, and then back to Kjan. "I'd rather take it up with *you* than *her*."

"Good call," he acknowledged. "She took the blame, though. You're officially exonerated." If the boy had so much as touched a hair on her head, he would be dead meat now. "Where are the others?"

"Erik is giving Claire the 'private tour'." Caleb added air quotes to his insinuating grin. "Dynja, Lucas, and Parker are AWOL, but they're out together as far as I know."

Kjan swung his attention to Kristján. "Text them. Make sure they're being careful. We still don't know who was following them the last time they were here. They might pick up the trail."

He still remembered Kría's distress call earlier this year when she, Dynja, and Erik had stayed behind in Iceland while Kristján had relocated to Portland with the rest of the coven. Someone had been hunting them, and though his Sire had flown out to assess the situation, he hadn't been able to track the entity. Whoever it had been possessed magic powerful enough to cloak themselves completely, and the thought that even his Sire, a God, had no clue as to who it might have been was terrifying.

"That has crossed my mind too," Kristján replied. "I told them to keep their eyes open."

The man still acted with the duty of a lieutenant, always protecting those in his charge. Dynja, Kría, and Erik had been his friends for years before they were all turned, but he considered the entire coven his family. Kjan knew he would kill to keep them safe. He and Askja had been the backbone of the coven from the start.

"Looks like you're on top of things." Kjan rubbed his hands across his thighs and rose from his seat. "Eve and I are headed out tonight. We won't be back until morning, and you probably won't be able to reach us."

"Safe trip." Kristján nodded, and Kjan turned toward the stairs.

He heard Caleb exhale in relief before he reached the top. "Fuck me," the kid mumbled. "I thought he was going to rip my head off. I nearly pissed myself."

Kjan smirked. His reputation was starting to slip, but Eve would be proud.

"Seriously though, I think I have to take a leak. Get off, babe."

"How much water did you drink?"

"Obviously more than I can sweat out," the kid yapped back. "I like to stay hydrated. Just to make sure the plumbing still works, you know? Don't you miss it?"

"You're weird, man."

"Whatever."

Okay, maybe their company isn't so bad after all, Kjan admitted to himself. At least they were good for a laugh.

CHAPTER

9

EVE

K jan's arm slithered around her waist as his nose brushed the base of her neck.

When promising to fill her thoroughly, he hadn't exaggerated. *Three times* he'd finished on top of offering her his vein. Must've been all that pent-up frustration of missing her.

And she'd felt it too.

Eve backed her bare behind into him and scowled at the rough contact. "Why are you dressed?"

He chuckled darkly, his stubble tickling her skin. "Does that mean you're not sore?"

A flush warmed her face when remembering the sweet sting of his palm on her ass. "No," Eve drawled, inching back further. He *had* punished her afterwards, and she was tempted to break more of his rules if it resulted in a spanking. The experience had been exhilarating.

Kjan must've been thinking the same thing, because he purred like a very large, very content cat and tightened his hold on her.

Pulling her closer, he trailed kisses along her neck toward her ear. "As much as I would enjoy continuing where we left off this morning, it will have to wait." He yanked the covers off and Eve got hit with a cold blast.

"What! Why?" she shrieked, tugging on the blanket to regain the warmth he had just ripped from her.

He gave it another sharp pull, and it slipped through her hands. "We're going on a trip."

She watched him toss the comforter aside and wedge himself between her knees. His forearms dug into the mattress on either side of her head, trapping her underneath him.

"All of us?"

He leaned down and closed his eyes. "No. Just you and I." He brushed the tip of his nose along the bridge of hers.

"Where are we going?" Eve pressed with curiosity. He was really drawing out the suspense.

Kjan pulled away, his face hovering an inch above her. He pinched his lips between his teeth and exhaled sharply through his nose, taking a few seconds to answer. "To the cave."

"The cave? You mean, *the* cave?" Eve gasped in shock. "Kjan, I-I never expected you to go back there."

He tipped his head to the side, his jawline tense beneath the dark scruff. "I know. But I have to."

"Why?" she asked again.

His tone was curt when he lifted off. "Unfinished business."

Eve hadn't pressed the matter further. She'd gotten dressed—parka, beanie, gloves, hiking boots; everything he insisted on—and climbed into his rental truck.

They were on the road for over four hours, his grip around the steering wheel tense, matching the expression on his face when Kjan pulled into an empty parking lot and killed the engine.

"You're really sure you want to do this," she asked after he made no move to get out.

She could feel the subtle trembling of his hand as he laced his fingers with hers. His eyes were facing forward, but he didn't seem to be focusing on anything. He just held her hand. She had the sense that he needed the physical connection for assurance.

"I will do this once, and then I'll never come back here. This is it. No turning back."

He exhaled a purposeful breath and sprung the door on his side. "Let's get this over with."

Soaring mountains awaited them. They loomed in the darkness with snowy peaks, imposing on the desert plains of ash.

Eve pictured the eruption of the massive volcano, large amounts of ice melting all at once, causing devastating floods to crash down and wipe everything in their path.

Nevertheless, fire and ice *shared* dominion over this land, coexisting side by side in a natural rhythm. The interplay of volcanic activity and glacier ice provided fertile ground for moss and other vegetation to thrive.

It was extraordinary.

Kjan led her across the black wasteland of ash and sand, not slowing in his steps. The crashing sounds of falling water grew louder every minute they advanced on the towering glacier. Its continuous movement crackled like thunder.

Eve's gaze traced the dark lava columns rising up the sides of the cliffs, a stark contrast to the cascading white waterfall and lush green moss even in the dim moonlight. Broken pieces of basalt in a perfect hexagonal shape lay scattered at the base. As resilient and invincible as it seemed in its size, the rock moved with the land, just like the glaciers, in an endless cycle of destruction and rebirth.

The stunning feature wasn't their destination, however. His hand still firmly clasping hers, he dragged her along, the wind whipping around them.

Something wasn't right. He seemed… off.

They left the assigned trail and ascended on a rocky path that looked unused, his body pushing onward with one clear objective: a runaway train, in motion and unstoppable.

Eve briefly wondered how he knew where he was going. When the glaciers thawed in the summer, meltwater would carve fresh paths through the ice, forming new and unique caves. They changed constantly in shape, and he hadn't been here in a thousand years.

Sensing her worry, he squeezed her hand. "We're taking a different way in than the tourists," he said over his shoulder. "The opening is much smaller than the main entrance to the glacier, but it will get us where we need to go."

And then Eve saw it. *Small* was an understatement. She couldn't picture Kjan's broad shoulders fitting through it. "That's barely big enough for a child to squeeze through. This is how you got inside?"

"No."

Their eyes met for a split second as she remembered his Sire in the body of a 12-year-old.

"Oh, right." It was how *he* had gotten *out*.

"Here." Kjan handed her a headlamp and shrugged out of his parka, which was an unusual sight on its own, but Eve was surprised to see him wearing a sweater underneath instead of a T-shirt. It would still be a tight fit for him.

Lowering himself down, he kicked some of the loose rocks with his boots, and they tumbled down the black hole.

Eve's stomach did a nervous flip.

He wedged his body into the fissure. "The cavity is only a few feet and then opens into a narrow tunnel, but it's a bit of a drop."

"Great," Eve mumbled under her breath, strapping the light to her head.

"Don't worry, I'll catch you," he added quickly before he disappeared.

And just like that, Eve stood alone at the edge of the massive black glacier, wind howling and ice cracking in the distance. The landscape was striking and terrifying at the same time.

A sudden sadness struck her heart. How could someone abandon their child like this?

KJAN

'Please don't do this. I'm begging you. You have no reason to go back. Leave, while you still can.'

He didn't waver. "You wanted me to come here, now I'm taking it all the way. If I'm forced to confront my past, then so are you," he argued with the voice in his head in the dark tunnel. "We can't move on unless we do."

After Kjan had made his intentions clear, his Sire had become strangely quiet, probably hoping that he would change his mind.

But the silent treatment hadn't lasted. The tables had turned. He was afraid.

Kjan hated the idea of being back here too, yet the fear pulling under his skin was *not* his own. The 1800-year-old in his head was having a full-on meltdown worthy of a deathly terrified toddler. Once it became obvious that his host would not back down, he retaliated, protesting every step of the way.

Kjan had ignored him until now.

'You don't know what will happen. I can't go back to being trapped. What if you don't make it out? Is it really worth the risk for you?'

The Goddess Freyja herself had put a curse on the immortal child, condemning him to a life in darkness and imprisoning him inside the ancient volcano. "The spell was linked to *your* body, not mine. We will make it out. Have a little faith."

Eve slipped from the cleft in the stone and dropped into his arms a second later, the bright beam of her headlamp piercing his retinas, penetrating like a scream.

"You okay?"

"Yeah." Her coat had taken some damage, but it had protected her from the sharp rock.

His head ringing from the noiseless wail, he set her down safely. Beneath their feet, the rock was completely iced over, turning into an underground skating rink.

"Careful, the ground is slippery. You don't want to land on your butt," he mocked her affectionately, referring to the one and only time she had challenged him on the ice.

"Uh-huh, I remember. I swore to never go skating with you again."

"Watch your head, too." He pointed out the array of stalactites above them.

"Wow."

While gawking at the black ice walls, the beam attached to her head bounced spastically through the otherwise dark tunnel. She brushed her fingertips along the smooth surface that interlaced the jagged stone. "This is incredible."

"Volcanic ash gets trapped in the sheet, making it black," he explained. "Without the ash, the ice appears bright blue in daylight. One of the most beautiful things you'll ever see."

His eyes lingered on her face, adoring her own natural beauty as she gaped at the glacier. She rarely wore makeup, and her image was as pure and undiluted as the melting rivers running from the ice.

The merciless waters could destroy, but they were also essential for giving life. Kjan wondered if Eve knew the meaning of her name. She had saved him from himself that god-awful night in the woods and brought him back from the brink of death.

He reached toward her and seized the front of her coat, crushing the down insulation of her parka in his fists. "Thank you. For being here."

"You're the one who brought me," she answered with a sly grin. "I can't imagine how hard this is for you."

'Hard for YOU? I'm the one who doesn't have a choice. I don't even want to be here. What thanks do I get?'

Kjan clenched his teeth with a soft growl and drew Eve to him, silencing the jabbering noise in his head with her lips. It was the only way to shut him up, but the leech was still there with them.

Always.

CHAPTER

10

KJAN

She pressed her soft curves flush to his chest, and all tension left his body. When he drew back, her eyes were gleaming.

Kjan dragged in the rewarding scent of her arousal, then nudged his head over his left. "Come on. We're close."

Eve's hand was warm as it slipped back into his, and he tugged her further down the narrowing passage. He could hear the soft brush of her other hand, scraping along the glacier's wall for guidance.

"Close to what?"

"You'll see." He pressed along, his mood slightly elevated. The cave was calling to him. Like a beacon.

"You're humming," Eve abruptly remarked from behind him.

He snickered, bemused. "No, I'm not."

"I mean your skin. It's buzzing. Like an electric charge."

Kjan stilled. He felt it too now, a different tingling sensation spreading through his body. And his eyes. They were itchy and irritated.

What's happening to me?

His throat constricting painfully, he glanced back over his shoulder.

Eve gasped. "Oh my God, Kjan… your eyes… they're shimmering. They're reflecting the light like those of a cat, making them glow. They never did that before." She paused. "What do you see?"

He blinked rapidly, getting them to refocus on the crystal walls of the cave and the many hues of red, orange, and yellow interlaced with turquoise ice.

"Everything!" he exhaled in awe, unable to keep his gaze on anything.

The multicolored layers of lava covered by a thin layer of clear ice became iridescent. "Colors. So many colors. It's all brighter. More vibrant."

His vision had always been equal to that of an eagle, watching insects crawl on the sidewalk below from on top of a 10-story building, but his eyes had apparently upgraded. The cat-eye reflection Eve described sounded like tapetum lucidum, the mirror-like layer behind the retinas of nocturnal animals.

Owls had some of the best night vision, and sharks could see clearly in dark, murky waters. Kjan remembered reading something about frogs that could observe colors in near darkness because they had two different types of rods in their eyes. There was also a species of butterfly that had additional cones compared to humans that were stimulated by different rays of the light spectrum.

The once seemingly useless knowledge in his head came in handy more than he could ever have imagined.

With shock, Kjan realized what was happening. He squeezed Eve's hand.

"What is it?"

"I-I think my body is adapting... to the cave... to the darkness. It's evolving. Just as *his* did over the centuries trapped in here."

The magic manifested around him like a gentle caress. It made him fucking giddy. His quest would not be in vain. The answer was here.

Kjan tugged on her hand again, towing her the rest of the way until they reached the crystal-clear pool of glacier water. This was the antechamber. The *doorway* was submerged within the depths of the underground lake.

It was just like he remembered it. The same magical blue glow illuminated it from below without plausible cause. There was no source. It was just that! Magic.

955 years ago... almost to the day.

He had made his descent on the shortest day of the year and been held down here in the darkness for eleven nights—endured eleven nights of torture—before being released back into the world as a monster.

"How come no one's found this part of the glacier yet?"

"It's warded." He felt a buzz in the air. It was still here. Only not as strong. "Humans can only see or pass through the opening during Mörsugr, the second of the two Jól months. Our calendar was based on lunar cycles, not days of the now commonly used Gregorian. The Winter Solstice three nights ago signaled the beginning of Mörsugr and the middle of Jól. Miðvetr—Midwinter—in late January will mark the end. But the glacier is strictly off-limits during that time. That's how it remained undisturbed and shielded from humans."

"What about *you*— I mean *him*? Could he get inside anytime? He's a God."

"Currently stuck in the body of a human," Kjan pointed out. "He might have been able to see it, but pass through…"

He let his words drift, lingering on the emotions whirling inside him. Yes, he could feel the nearly paralyzing fear. "He was too scared to try."

"So he was biding his time here, *clubbing* and *partying*," she stressed with derision, "until the portal would open again next winter? That's why he left Kría, Dynja, and Erik behind?"

He gave her a weak shrug in response. He didn't want to elaborate on the graphic excursions his body had taken under the direction of another.

Kjan approached cautiously, drawn to the water. He could feel it. The curse. It was weakened.

He lowered himself to the edge, leaning into his reflection. A subtle vibration hovered over the surface, similar to the hum of his skin. His body began to shake as the immortal thrashed violently in his head.

Enduring the stabbing pain at his temples, he forced his trembling hand steady, then touched his palm to the liquid mirror.

The instant his skin made contact, the luminous blue glow of the water magnified, spreading out from his hand and creeping across the length of the pool to the outer edges. He felt a pull from his chest to his fingertips, like a magnet stretching toward its polar opposite.

The beating of his heart doubled. Could this all end here, now?

Kjan still hadn't decided if the real reason he had come was to trap his Sire. He had passed through the magical barrier twice before, once as a human and then again after his transformation, but things were a little different now. What if the leech was right?

There were three possible outcomes:

1. The spell could eject his divine spirit, imprisoning him within the cave to haunt it for all eternity like a ghost.

2. It could trap them both together. Forever.

Or 3. Nothing.

How desperate was he to be rid of his passenger?

Kjan swallowed with a heavy heart. He wanted to be free, but not like this. It was immoral. It wasn't fair.

"*I will not abandon you here*," he whispered in the old language. "*I swear it.*" They would leave this place together, he vowed.

Kjan had hardly spoken the words when the pool's illumination receded before his eyes. And so did the pulling sensation, as if the spell had accepted his decision.

A calm washed over him, and he turned to look back at Eve, who stood pale-faced in the opening of the antechamber.

"The entrance is down there."

Her eyes went wide. "What! You said it's underground. You never mentioned it's also *underwater*."

"I have to go." He yanked the sweater over his head. "I need to see it through his eyes."

"The hell you do. Are you nuts? It's freezing."

Kjan pulled the leather cord from his pocket, the matching set of iron bands dangling from it clanking together silently.

He made a shaking fist around the rings. He remembered forging them, twisting, and bending the hot metal. They were simple, but Thórunn had loved them. He recalled her smile and the way her eyes had lit up. He hadn't been able to part with them when he buried her in the cold ground. Hadn't been ready to let go. But he was ready now.

"I have to put them back," he said, looping them around his neck. "He never should have taken them. They belong here."

Eve gave him an understanding nod, her eyes full of concern nonetheless.

He swept the unruly strands of her hair behind her ear and tilted her chin high. "I'll make it back," he promised.

Holding her stare, he stepped back. His hands went to his fly, and he unzipped his jeans in front of her, watching the worry melt from her expression.

Eve sucked in her bottom lip, the tips of her brilliant white fangs making a quick appearance when punching down on the plump shape.

Her reaction stirred a swell in his chest. He fucking loved that blush on her cheeks.

"Look at you. Sweater *and* boxers," she teased. "I never thought I'd see the day."

Kjan smirked, dropping his pants to the ground. "Don't get used to it."

With a rough grasp, he crushed her against his chest, his hands engulfing her face and her palms warm on his skin as he kissed her forcefully.

"Wait for me." His breath feathered across her lips before pulling away.

Time to test that shark theory.

CHAPTER

II

KJARTAN

Kjan plunged into the frigid depths of the lake, the icy fluid piercing his skin and sending his muscles into a numbing shock. A tight fist around his throat and chest squeezed the air out of his lungs.

How the humans survived the dive had always baffled him. Though he had known that it wouldn't kill him, even Kjartan had considered it immensely painful.

The doorway had been the real impediment. He had touched it so many times, seeing only his reflection in the mirrored portal. And then the night had come when the spell had weakened, allowing him to shatter the mirror with his small fist and break through to the other side.

Receding from the light in the antechamber, the darkness in front of them swelled. Kjan forced himself deeper, his hands brushing along the irregularities of the rough rock until it became smooth and glass-like. He held his breath effortlessly, descending further still, the pressure on his body increasing with each foot. His heart was racing. They were close.

When the black arch appeared in view, fear rose in Kjartan again, and every instinct told him to turn back.

Alas, in command of their shared vessel, Kjan disregarded all concern and pushed on, adrenaline pumping through his veins. Retreat was not an option.

Kjartan saw no mirror. No reflective boundary. Only empty space beyond.

It seemed too easy.

Squeezing through the portal felt like passing through an invisible force field. The subtle drag turned into a propelling motion once he reached the halfway point, ejecting him on the opposite end.

Then it was gone.

The pressure on his body decreased rapidly as Kjan shot upward, drawing the crisp air back into his lungs the instant he broke the surface.

He emerged from the blackness of the water's depth. Without his eyes utilizing the light from Eve's lamp, his night vision adapted once again. The colors were muted, yet not invisible.

The grotto on the other side of the pool was smaller than the rest of the caverns that made up his tomb, but by far the most beautiful. Kjartan recalled the image in daylight vividly. The memories flooded back with an unstoppable force as aquamarine ice filled the little gaps in the stone, the cracks glittering like stars in the multicolored layers of different lava rock, not just on the ceiling but all around him. Filtered through the ice was the only way he had been able to tolerate the sun, his sole link to the outside world.

The singing of the glaciers was the only *voice* he would hear. He couldn't recount the infinite number of times he had gently tapped the stalagmites to produce the melodious, resonant ringing. In the dead silence of the cave, the harmonic sounds and music had been a comfort. Almost hypnotizing.

His mother, Iðunn, Goddess of Eternal Youth, had raised him on the God's Apples of Immortality in secret. He had aged normally until Freyja had cast her spell. Then the curse had locked him in the body of a 12-year-old and trapped him inside the cave.

Discarded and buried deep beneath like a forgotten relic, he had suffered alone, praying every day for his mother's return. For 1600 years, he had waited. He had been angry at times as the centuries passed, his rage and anguish shaking the rocks. As a child, he had not understood why the Gods had punished him.

Eventually, the reasons behind his imprisonment had become irrelevant. He had found a different purpose. By cursing others to a similar fate, he had lashed out and retaliated, so the Gods might take notice of him and end his unbearable existence. The immortal too had longed for death as salvation. Just like the mortal men who had come looking for him.

After all this time, he still wasn't over the pain and the loss he had suffered in here. Kjan was right, he had to face it to move on. Eve had once asked him if he resented the Gods for their conviction, but he had denied it. He had trusted their judgement and believed that there was in fact something wrong with him; that he was a monster and needed to be locked away. It must have been the reason why his mother had abandoned him in the end. Even she couldn't bear to look at him.

He had never met his father. Hǫðr, God of Darkness, had been executed for the murder of his twin brother before Kjartan was born. The twins hadn't returned to Ásgarðr until after the great war of Ragnarǫk.

The boy had waited, serving his sentence, but there had been no pardon for him. He had learned the truth upon his escape. He was nothing more than a mistake, banished from the minds of those responsible.

And yet, he still couldn't bring himself to hate them. He was just that broken.

Kjartan felt the warm tear on Kjan's cheek. *'Why would you do this? Why show me mercy?'*

"I understand. I can sympathize. You did nothing to justify this life sentence, and anyone else in your position might have acted the same. Including me," Kjan admitted. "I'm sorry."

'I don't deserve it. I have done horrible things. Things I can never atone for.'

"Do you feel remorse for what you did?"

Kjartan hesitated. *'I believed my actions were warranted. I see now that I went about them the wrong way. I'm sorry for what I did to you.'*

"If you repent, then you deserve redemption."

There was no spite in his voice, but Kjartan couldn't trust his host's intentions. The truce was difficult for him to handle. Kjan didn't hide how much he hated their current *arrangement.* Unfortunately, there were no other alternatives.

"Let's finish this and go home," Kjan urged, his wide shoulders brushing the jagged rock walls as he weaved around stalagmites of various sizes down the tunnels. Fiery magma that once flowed had been replaced by ice, creating a labyrinth, a lost world, that remained frozen in time.

Slippery steps led to the largest chamber, a vast cavity of massive ice sculptures and stalactites hanging from the ceiling like crystal chandeliers. They stirred a more recent memory within Kjan's mind as he recalled his friend Eleanor's lavish taste for Baroque décor and architecture.

The cave was eerily quiet, besides the pitter-pattering drip of water from the ceiling onto the ice floor. Among the wide range of delicate ice creations, red lava rocks had fallen to the ground and were being covered with more layers of ice, the glacier swallowing them up.

This was it. The main chamber of his crypt. The place where he had turned Kjan and the others.

There had been no need for him to lurk in the shadows; blindly his victims had stumbled around in the dark. He had followed them, sometimes for hours, drawing out the excitement and stalking them through the maze that only he knew by heart.

The attack had always come as a surprise for them. With his fingernails, filed to sharp points on the rough stone, he had cut their throats open and watched them bleed out. Then he had dragged them back here… to his torture chamber.

In his original form, he had no fangs. He was a God, not a vampire. But he had indeed been born differently. Sustained himself in other ways even before the curse had affected him. He could nourish himself on the emotional energy of others, first his mother, and then on the terror of the occasional human wandering too close.

"You think fear is powerful? You have never tasted true love. Pure, unconditional love," Kjan remarked.

But he had. He had fed on his mother's feelings for him. They had been honest. And pure. He became a soul-eater rather than a blood-sucker.

Initial curiosity had driven him to lap up the dark red liquid from his fingers, not the thirst for it. He could see visions of his victim's life in front of his eyes as though they were his own, little glimpses allowing him to live in their past and forget about his curse.

That was when he had seen her for the first time— Thórunn—plucking her image from Kjan's memory when he had spilled his blood… tasted it.

She had returned to him in his dreams. Every time the loneliness had driven him to the edge, she had pulled him back. She had been his salvation.

"You didn't even know her."

'I knew her through you.*'*

"What you felt were *my* feelings for her. You… you don't understand what love is," Kjan reproached him.

'How can you love them both? Still?'

"Eve understands."

'Does she?' He thought about what Eve had said to Kjan at the cottage.

"It's not the same. I loved Thórunn as a human, with all my heart, but it will never be more than that: the love of a mortal. Eve is different. She is… she is a part of me. That bond will never die."

'It did with Andromeda.'

Kjartan had struck a nerve. Kjan wavered in his response. "What I feel for Eve is stronger. It broke my commitment to Anne."

'The breaking of your devotion was clearly mutual.'

He paused before admitting to the miscalculation on his part, which had led to Kjan taking his best friend's life. *"She was only supposed to bring you to me. I swear, I didn't know she would try to kill you.'*

Askja's attempt at slipping him a dose of Kjartan's toxic blood through his supplier in Seattle had failed. And so had Nessa's at the gala. By going behind their backs, Andromeda had nearly ruined everything.

"Water under the bridge." Kjan's shoulder gave a jerk, eyes scanning the cave.

'How does the bonding mark work?' Kjartan had bitten Eve but never marked her. Never pledged himself to her the way Kjan did. *'I know it's more than just turning her with your blood. I have felt the pull toward the neophytes I sired, even an empathic connection, but it was unlike what you have with her.'*

Sire and fledgling shared a profound psychic link, but the bond to a mate ran so much deeper than he could have ever anticipated.

"It's not really a conscious decision," Kjan elaborated. "Some part of you will take over—a primal instinct I guess— and it will make that decision *for* you. You will commit to that person with everything you have. The vow will become a physical addiction… the need to be in her presence. Like a drug. Deficiency causes painful withdrawal symptoms, but it won't kill you. I lived through it after leaving Andromeda. If you can call it living," he added in a contemptuous note.

"But some part of you *has* to want it. *Has* to want to give yourself over to that person wholly and without reservation. When you accept the bond, their life becomes your life, their happiness, your happiness, their sorrow, your sorrow, and their death, your undoing."

Become dependent on another and give up their own selves? *'Why would anyone choose this?'*

"Like I said, you don't understand love," Kjan scoffed.

The emotional and physical connection of the bond made Kjartan curious. *'Perhaps that's why you failed to kill Andromeda the first time. She was still your mate. And perhaps it was for the same reason that she had to work through someone else to get to you. She couldn't kill you directly. In her heart, you were still her mate.'*

Was it physically impossible to kill the one you are committed to?

"Perhaps," Kjan's voice echoed absently.

He finally found what he was looking for. His father's beautiful 9th century Viking axe had been the only trophy the immortal had kept from all his victims. Passed down from one generation to the next, each owner leaving their own personal mark on it, it had at last ended up in the hands of Mýrkjartansson, the last of his line.

Since he had no heir, Kjartan—the human—had intended to be buried here with it, dying in battle with the weapon in his hand. But fate had intervened, diverting his path to Valhǫll, never to be reunited with his wife and daughter.

It felt lighter in Kjan's hands now. The single-handed axe had undoubtedly been lightning-fast and deadly in the mortal man's skilled grasp. The handle was original ash wood from a Viking longship known as *drakkar*, getting its name from the Norse term *dreki*, which referred to the dragon at the front of the boat.

Kjartan sensed the sentimental value the weapon held for his host. Exquisite carvings stretch down the length of the aged wood with bands of Futhark runes and the image of the God Týr on the knob. An 8-inch blade at the axe's head was secured with a wedge and pin technique.

Kjan's fingers flexed around the grip's leather wrap. The cross stitch was worn and weathered from the hands of his ancestors who had wielded it and from being forsaken in this ungodly place. He wouldn't leave it behind a second time.

When he returned to the grotto, Kjan swung the blade at the frozen ground, cleaving the ice and the lava rock underneath it. The fractures extended from the split like the web of a spider.

He removed the twin wedding bands from his neck and wedged them into the rift. Cutting his palm open with the axe, he mixed his blood with the loose ice and filled in the cracks. The steady drips from the ceiling would soon reseal the gap altogether. The pool was the only way in or out. No one would ever find them here.

Before Kjan dove back into the icy pit and through the doorway, Kjartan speculated again. Could he really trust the seemingly pure benevolence of his vessel's character?

Renate Rowland

CHAPTER

12

KJAN

He reached the surface, and sharp, painful breaths shot into his lungs. He barely had enough energy to hoist himself up. Rocks crashed into his shoulder as he collapsed onto the rough stone that was only slightly warmer than the frigid water.

Stretching out on his back to slow the rush of oxygen, he let the ground warm his body.

Eve shuffled about in his peripheral vision. The muscles in his neck were tight from the cold, but his head jerked up in shock.

"W-what are you doing?" he stammered as he shivered, watching her from the corner of his eye shake off her coat and yank on her sweater.

"Raising your temperature. Duh!"

"Please, stop," he rasped, brushing a hand through the top of his hair; water sprayed from the short ends. "You don't have to. Just give me a minute." His balls were already blue. They didn't need the extra attention.

Eve ignored him, shimmying out of her jeans next, and pressing her lithe, practically naked body up to him.

The searing heat of her skin ignited him like a flare. He instinctively wrapped his arms around her, pulling her on top so her body wouldn't touch the cold ground.

"Why are you so stubborn, Dove?"

"Me, stubborn?" She smirked while her feathery-light touch wandered down his chest. "You know I can warm you up a lot faster, right? Show me what other upgrades you got."

He blocked her hand before things got even more critical. If only his mind wasn't so goddamn crowded.

"Ignore it," he hissed through his teeth, deterring her from his raging hard-on. "We're not doing that here."

Entwining his fingers with hers, he pulled her left wrist to his lips and kissed the branding. The bindrune, a union of *Bjarkan—or Berkano—*and *Eihwaz*, was *his* symbol. His Sire might not have bound himself to Eve, but he had still claimed her in some way.

The brand made Kjan wonder. *Bjarkan* gave life, and *Eihwaz*, the rune of the immortal's lineage, symbolized death and rebirth, the cycle of all living things. He had carved it into Kjan's heart, twice, and then sealed the wound with his own blood. He had found new life in shedding his own body and transferring his essence into a willing host. What kind of impact did the mark have on Eve's skin?

His grandmother had preached ad nauseam about the ancient magic the old symbols channeled. Unlike the younger runic alphabet used for writing, the Elder Futhark had retained its significance in spellwork. He had purposely neglected to mention that to Eve. He wanted to keep it a personal concern.

Exasperated, Kjan let his head fall back against the hard rock underneath him. He sincerely hoped the decision to preserve the truce wouldn't come back to bite him in the ass.

EVE

Eve leaned her head against the window. They still had the long drive ahead of them to beat the sunrise, and after the chilly 40-minute walk back to the car, her eyelids were beginning to feel heavy.

The vehicle's deceleration and subtle shift jerked her awake.

"We need to get gas," Kjan said as he slowed to exit the highway that ran along the southern coast.

Nearing the closest town, he pulled into the gas station and got out.

Eve watched him disappear from view. She listened to the beeping of the machine, and the rushing of fuel from the pump to the tank. Her senses were on full alert, the drowsiness gone.

Eyes on the bare fields and mountains in the distance, she suddenly felt restless in her seat. Something was nagging at her. She needed to get out of the truck.

Right now.

Her mind went blank, but her legs were moving—fast. She was running toward something, her body responding to a call. The answers she sought were just beyond those rolling plains. She could feel it in her bones.

Eve sensed a presence… something familiar. She'd never been here before, yet somehow it felt like coming home. Images appeared in front of her eyes, pictures her brain couldn't process: sprinting through tall grass, the sun high in the sky, wildflowers in the fields, someone hot on her trail…

…and she wanted him to catch her. She felt the cold rush with the thrill of the chase.

When her foot met a divot in the ground, she tripped, but a strong arm captured her around the waist, snatching her up in mid-air before she went down.

He held her above the ground, laughing, while she squirmed.

Eve knew this wasn't real… this wasn't *her.*

Hands seized her upper arms, ripping her backward with force.

"NO! Let go! I need to see—" She twisted uselessly in his grip.

"What are you talking about?" Fear seeped through his words as he tried to shake her out of the dream. "There's nothing here."

Caught in a manic frenzy, her mind strained to grasp at the delusion before it slipped away.

Eve snapped out of it, her nails digging into Kjan's sweater where he stood facing her now. Her eyes refocused. Fresh snow covered his shoulders and the field they were in. Big flakes were still coming down in the dark of the night, adding to the inches that had already landed on the thick, white blanket.

She looked around, perplexed. "W-what? When did it start snowing?"

"I've been looking for you for half an hour," he replied frantically. "You took off… I couldn't find you anywhere."

"Couldn't find me?" How had he not sensed her presence? The sliver of his soul within her was like a beacon.

"Something was blocking me… I couldn't feel you… you just vanished."

Eve shivered in his embrace from the cold, but it was *his* heart that was bounding out of his chest from the scare. She could read the panic in his eyes. "What happened?"

Renate Rowland

CHAPTER

13

KJAN

A queasy feeling coiled in his gut. He was putting the nozzle back on the pump when he sensed her absence. The front passenger door stood wide open, and her parka was still on the seat as if someone or something had ripped her clear out of the car.

Warning sirens went off in his head. Following the empty feeling in his chest, his eyes searched the horizon while icy winds whipped across his face.

Kjan's heart dropped like a stone. He recognized the landscape—knew those plains like the back of his hand. How had he not realized where they were? The small town had changed, naturally, but the terrain was untouched by time. The river was to the west and the waterfall almost a straight shot south across the highway.

He was home.

Kjan spun around in a panic. Their truck was the only other vehicle at the gas station, and the roads were empty too, but even if they had been overcrowded with people, he should have been able to sense her.

He didn't.

He felt nothing. No draw to his mate, no spark from his soul, no pull from the blood in his veins toward its reflection in her. It was like she had never been with him in the first place.

He sent his feelers out again. Focusing harder, Kjan pictured her in his mind. Lifted her scent from his memory to strengthen the image.

But his efforts were useless. Instead of locking on to her presence, they rebounded every time he tried to reach for her. Something was shutting him out, keeping them separated.

'It's magic. There is someone else out here. It's the same force I sensed last time. It's too powerful for me to penetrate. I can't help you find her.'

Kjan's body was already in motion when he heard the worry in his Sire's tone.

On a hunch, he set off south, leaving the truck behind. He didn't know what in the world had compelled Eve to run off, but a familiar voice in his head told him where to go. For once, it was not the same voice he usually heard.

Following her direction, his boots beat across the open field as fast as his feet would carry him. He fought the rush of the memories as they crashed down on him—disregarded the images of blooming wildflowers in spring while his boots hit the frozen ground. Her long hair billowed behind her, and her laughter reached his ears, snapping his heart nearly in half. The vision was too real. Too painful.

They had been happy here. Countless times he had chased her through these plains… caught up with her before she reached the marsh by the river. It was so close to where he had laid her body to rest.

Thórunn was guiding him. He just knew it. But was she leading him toward Eve, or was her spirit the one keeping them apart? He had seen her after he died in the temple. Could her ghost really be haunting this place?

Dread grew heavier in him as snow began to fall, the sky still dark as night hours before sunrise. The storm picked up quickly, and flakes so dense he couldn't see his own hands in front of himself whirled around him.

'*Catch me,*' she pleaded again enticingly, her voice no more than a whisper.

Cold, hard fear snaked through his veins, nearly crushing his hope. The lack of footprints was unsettling. He prayed that he had picked the right direction. Eve was somewhere out here, blind in the snowstorm and unfamiliar with the landscape. Because of the waterfall, the layer of ice covering the river was always thin, even in December. It wouldn't hold her. He had to reach her before she made it to the water.

Still sprinting, his heart pounding beneath his ribcage, a second away from leaping out of his chest, Kjan stayed true to his heading. And then he felt her—a subtle echo to his beat dead ahead. Whatever magic was playing tricks on him was starting to fade.

Why is she out here? Of all the places…

Yards ahead, Eve wasn't slowing, but her blue sweater was rapidly gaining proportion against the dark gray backdrop of the scene as he cleared the distance between them.

With the boundary of the ice less than ten feet from her, he ripped her back from the edge.

"NO!" she cried out, flopping in his arms like a fish while trying to shake him loose. "Let go! I need to see." Her body steered toward the water, fully committed to walking right out on it.

Kjan whipped her around by her shoulders, his grip too harsh in his panic. "What are you talking about? There's nothing here."

That finally got her attention. Eve blinked owlishly. "W-what? When did it start snowing?"

"I've been looking for you for half an hour. You took off… I couldn't find you anywhere."

She frowned. "Couldn't find me?" She knew it was highly unlikely for him not to sense her.

He let out a huge sigh of relief and pulled her into his chest. "Something was blocking me. I couldn't feel you. You just vanished."

He wasn't sure how much detail about this crazy trip he should include. He didn't want to freak her out. "What happened?"

"I-I don't know. I saw something. I knew it wasn't real, but I just couldn't stop."

"It's okay, Dove." Tucking her head into his chest, he kissed the top of her hair and inhaled her scent.

Now that she was safely back in his arms, even the snow stopped falling. Kjan didn't want to tell her about his suspicions yet. He wasn't exactly sure what he had seen himself.

That was when he heard the hysterical, high-pitched laughter over the whistling of the wind.

"Come on." He nudged Eve in the direction he knew was north. "We need to get out of here."

Someone was going through a lot of trouble, and he did not enjoy feeling like the prey in this hunt.

HRAFNI

His fingertips twitched. Standing on the thin layer of ice, he watched them turn tail.

A sadistic smile danced across his face. He could not have planned it better himself. They were playing right into his hands, and they didn't even know it.

He sneered over his shoulder at the dark figure lurking in the distance. His attempt might have been foiled, but it was all coming together now.

"Let them feel safe for a bit."

He would catch up with them soon enough.

CHAPTER

14

EVE

hould I have told him about the vision I had in the plains? Eve was a voyeur glimpsing a private moment he'd shared with his wife a lifetime ago.

She had been so happy. Eve had felt her love for him, her heart full to the brim, threatening to burst. And she'd known that he felt the same. He was her home. In his arms, she was safe. In his heart, she was immortal.

Kjan was quiet as they drove the rest of the stretch. They made it back to the cottage shortly after the others had returned from their bar crawl. Most of them were gathered in the living room, and the house was buzzing with chatter as they gave detailed accounts of their night.

Eve glanced at Kjan, who shook his head in opposition, brows set in a deep frown, his mouth askew. Neither of them was interested in sharing their unusual adventure. The subtle nudge of his eyes toward the stairs was more along the lines of getting her naked and forgetting about the entire ordeal.

Her cheeks burned as he slid his fingers in between hers and tugged on her hand.

"You two really missed out," Dynja called from the couch, her 6-foot Amazon-body stretched across Parker's and Lucas' laps. Her accent wasn't as thick as Kristján's or Erik's, yet her r's rolled almost like Nessa's.

"Doubt it," Kjan shot back at her in an oddly hostile tone. Eve hadn't been tracking the jabbering until now, but his grip tensed on her hand as if he didn't like where this was going. He towed her across the room with clear purpose.

"Call me nostalgic, but it would have been a lot more fun with all of us there. That one is definitely my favorite. You know, the one with the big sofas."

Eve froze, her hand slipping from Kjan's. She noticed the expression on his face darken. He exchanged a nervous look with Kristján, and then it dawned on her too. She knew exactly where Dynja's story was headed. Knew the club she was referring to personally.

"I mean, I can get creative anywhere, but the one at the other place hurt my back. I like to be comfortable—"

"Dynja..." Kristján growled. Face set in a deep scowl, he made a chopping motion at his throat, trying to get her to shut up, but she didn't hear him over the sound of her own voice. She babbled on, clueless as usual.

"—Too bad I never found that ring I lost between the cushions. Small price to pay, I guess."

"*Dynja!*" the giant's voice boomed a second time.

"What?" She glared at him. Then understanding bloomed in her mind, and her jaw slackened.

All eyes turned to Eve as the details she had blocked out came back to her. Her gut twisted into a knot. The blonde woman under Kjartan at the club back in March had been Dynja, and Kristján was the giant she'd stumbled into. They'd all been there. They all knew. She was such an idiot. How had she not put the pieces together sooner?

"Oh man. Shoot! I'm… I'm so sorry, Eve," Dynja stammered. "I didn't mean to… I thought you knew."

Her blood boiled beneath her skin. Eve lifted her eyes to Kjan, but he didn't look at her, pinching the bridge of his nose to hide his shame.

Acid burned in her throat. Eve stormed up the stairs. Alone. She could accept that Kjartan had been with others while possessing Kjan, but knowing it was one of *them*, someone she actually knew…

Her shoulder blades bumped into the door, and she thought about all the other little things she'd missed right in front of her eyes. Kristján had sent her to *this* room specifically and practically assigned the rooms to the others. He'd moved around the place like he was well acquainted with it, and so had Kría, Erik, and Dynja. They'd been here before. Even Kjan had known which room was Eve's. This was not some random Airbnb. This was *their* cottage—Kjartan's house.

Eve's eyes fell on the bed. *His* bed. Had they been together here too?

But it didn't matter *where* or *how many times* it had happened. The fact remained that *she*, Dynja, her friend, had been with *him*. And although she acknowledged that it had been Kjartan, not Kjan, that was still a hard pill to swallow.

Eve paced around the little bedroom, hands balled into fists. She still hated him with every fiber of her body. Taking it out on the house wouldn't change anything. She had no one to be angry at. Couldn't blame anyone for the way she felt.

Damn. This house wasn't big enough to fit all her emotions. Blinking back tears, she refused to break down. Kjan dealt with the knowledge that she'd slept with the monster, and he never held it against her. And unlike him, she'd been a willing participant.

They'd been through too much together. This was just something she had to process and then move past. She could do that. She was not a hypocrite.

KJAN

The lights flickered. Kjan forced the rage bubble inflating in his chest back down. The only person he wanted to hurt for this wasn't physically in the room, and he couldn't take it out on the parasite without punishing himself.

His Sire squirmed under his skin at the personal attack.

The room fell eerily silent after Eve left. They were all on edge, awaiting his reaction.

Dynja shifted nervously, sitting upright now, wedged between the guys. "I really am sorry."

Kjan waved her off. It wasn't her fault. It was his. He should have cleared the air with Eve sooner. Should have never let it come to this.

He sat down at the bottom of the stairs and hung his head.

"Let's clear out." Kristján rose to his feet; Kría, Dynja, Parker, Caleb, and Emma followed suit. "Move it, kid," he barked, kicking Lucas' outstretched legs.

"Worst Christmas Eve ever," the boy muttered from his seat on the sofa.

"Give him a break. He's only half a person without his woman."

Kjan rolled his eyes. This day couldn't possibly get any worse, could it? Rubbing the sides of his head, he considered his options.

'I never meant for any of this.'

"Don't start," Kjan growled, applying pressure to his temples.

'I didn't remember her.'

"You knew I had a mate when you took me. I have not forgotten how you threatened her to force my surrender. Actions have consequences. You didn't care. You only cared about yourself. We were pawns in your game, easily sacrificed to guarantee your advantage."

'That's not true.'

"Bullshit! How many of your worshipers have you wasted? Besides the one that you fed to Andromeda?"

'They were martyrs.'

"Right," Kjan snorted. "As were the ones you sired before me… hunted and slaughtered for the greater good of a God." Forking his fingers through his hair, he raised his voice. "You were free. Why wasn't that enough?"

Then he burst off the steps. "Spare me your sob stories. You will get no more pity from me. I will honor our peace, but I am not your friend. Eve belongs with me."

'And every time you touch her,' his Sire taunted in his head, *'every time you are with her… I am there. Feel everything you feel.'*

"But I'm the one she will choose. Every. Time. *I'm* the one she loves. Not you."

Kjan knew he had hit a sore spot. A coldness flooded his body like he had been dumped back into the glacier water. Only this time, it spread from his core outward, originating inside his chest and stretching through his limbs, reaching his fingertips last.

The acidic taste of anguish caught in the back of his throat, burning slowly as it lingered. He felt it too. The same agony.

The prickling heat of his own rage faded as their emotions mixed.

Eve sat on the chair in the corner, knees pulled into her chest, when he entered the bedroom.

"I'm sorry." The words shot out of her mouth.

"What for?"

"For getting mad. It wasn't you. I'm not blaming you. Or Dynja. I know I have no right to be angry." Eve paused as her voice cracked. "I just can't help the way I feel. The thought of you with her… it hurts." She sniffed and wiped at the tears on her cheeks.

Kjan dropped to the floor in front of her and crossed his legs as if he could make himself appear smaller. "You have every right to be angry."

"No." Eve shook her head. "Nobody did anything wrong. You never had a choice. *I* did. I could have turned him down."

She squeezed her legs tighter, and he noticed her nails biting into the skin on her upper arms. She had changed into her sleep clothes: a black tank top and lime-green shorts.

Kjan's hands twitched in his lap. He had the urge to comfort her but was afraid she would flinch away from his touch. He couldn't handle that rejection right now. Not after the declaration he had made to his Sire about Eve choosing him. He hoped his words would be enough.

"You asked me to talk about it, and I refused, but you should have heard it from me. It was only a matter of time before someone brought it up."

His fingers twitched again, and he curled them toward his palms, keeping his gaze steady on her face. "It wasn't a secret that I tried to keep from you, I swear. I'm the one who didn't want to face it. Talking about it made it real, and I… I didn't want it to be real."

Eve stared down at him. Her eyes were so blue the tears in them shimmered like diamonds, and he cursed his newly enhanced vision. The look on her face was heartbreaking. He couldn't deny how much it pained him to remember all the ways his Sire had used him, but the last thing he wanted was her pity. He could barely accept the fact that he had been victimized. He was used to being on the dealing end.

Eve uncrossed her arms and slid out of the chair, right into his lap. No matter what kind of distrust the immortal tried to plant in his skull, Kjan would always hold his woman. Always welcome her touch. Their love was stronger than anything he could throw at them.

His Sire laughed softly. *'Are you sure about that?'*

Kjan kissed Eve's forehead, ignoring the distraction. He would not let him ruin this moment.

She curled into his embrace and put her head on his shoulder. "I want to go home."

CHAPTER

15

LUCAS

"**Y**ou there raht now, ain't you?" Her tone challenged him to deny it.

He couldn't. Not without lying.

Caleb, Emma, and he had taken Kjan's offer to fly them home on Christmas Eve, and even though Lucas had his issues with the guy, he'd been grateful for the opportunity to return sooner. For more than one reason.

"Ah knew you didn't come back for me. You came back to see *her*."

Yeah, he'd been lying to the others about why he was so moody lately. Lying about his fights with Bayley too. She was the only one who knew the truth.

"You want my commitment, but you're the one who can't let—"

The notification sound of a new text cut off her words. Lucas angled the phone by his ear to give the screen a glance, though he already knew it was from Caleb.

They were supposed to meet up, but he'd canceled at the last minute, pretending to hang out with Bayley instead when she was actually working a double shift tonight. One of the other nurses had called in sick, and she always picked up extra hours. The clinic downtown was small, but got plenty of traffic due to its location.

The lie about her being busy over Christmas hadn't been far-fetched, but the real reason why she'd declined was that she hated being forced to keep his secret. She'd caught him lurking on the roof a few weeks ago and been pestering him to come clean ever since. But he wasn't ready.

"You can't live two lahves, Luke," her voice stressed from the speaker. "You can't keep going back to her."

He could picture the contemptuous twist of her lips. Lucas paced the rough pavement a few steps, rubbing his palm across his buzzed scalp.

Why can't she just understand?

Bayley didn't like him hanging around the strip club, but it was the only way he got to see her. Even if it was only for the short walk from the car to the door. He only went on the nights he knew she'd be there. Never went inside; he wasn't a stalker. If he were, he'd taken her with him months ago.

Hell, he didn't even know her name. That bitch wouldn't tell him. Who knew what he'd do if he ever found himself alone with the girl?

Probably steal her away.

And that scared him. The fact that he'd even contemplated it. He wasn't like that—didn't want to be like that. But he could. He could just take her and run. She was *his* goddammit. She didn't belong with that guy. What if he hurt her?

Lucas would bring hell down on him, that much was sure. He'd make the guy suffer and regret ever laying a hand on her.

Through the phone, he caught the sound of Bayley swinging the clinic's door open. "Ah gotta go. My boss is gonna laht a fire under my behind if Ah'm late again."

Man, I love that southern bell drawl of hers.

He was about to give her his usual lame apology or, God forbid, say something worse but snapped his mouth shut and stopped himself from becoming any more of a simp.

Bayley wasn't the committing type; she looked out for herself. And who could blame her? She was over 200 years old and had even been married before being turned at 23. She'd been in more relationships than he could count on his fingers and toes.

He wasn't bitter. Love didn't last forever—he knew that from personal experience—and he'd tried to keep things casual between them too, yet he couldn't deny how hollow he felt without her. Dynja had only made that more evident.

Lucas found his voice, though the words came out with a note of desperation clinging to them, "Can I see you when you get off?"

"No," she replied short. "Ah think Ah'd rather sleep alone."

He heard the click and sighed as the line disconnected on her end. He felt his shoulders sag.

Dropping his ass on the raised ledge of the roof, he kicked his legs over the side and replied to Caleb's text. He used Bayley as an alibi more often than he cared to admit. He didn't like lying about his whereabouts, especially not to Caleb, but he didn't want anyone else to know.

He set the phone down beside him and kept his eyes on the entrance of the back lot where all the staff parked when the white '08 Accord he'd been waiting for pulled in. And then he saw her, with that big smile on her face and her dark waves around her cheeks.

Pain and warmth spread through his chest simultaneously.

She got out of the car, and for a second, her eyes went up to the roof where he was sitting as though she knew he was there. She was looking right at him, her curious stare meeting his, and he felt his lips curve to return her smile. She was so beautiful.

Lucas couldn't help but wonder whether he would've taken Kjartan's offer had he known about her sooner.

No, he probably would've chosen to remain human just for a chance to be near her.

He scrubbed his palms across his face and up his head for the millionth time, trying to think. He knew he had to let her go. He couldn't take care of her. And he couldn't lose Bayley over this. The fights were getting to him.

That damn migraine was flaring up again. *What the fuck?* He'd never had this shit before. And that scraping under his skin like claws? He felt like peeling it off altogether just to make it stop. It was worse than the bullet in his head.

At least one good thing had come from getting shot. Bayley!

Though her dainty presence had seemed completely out of place in the shady part of town, her eyes had been the first thing he'd noticed about her—irises the color of smooth chocolate silk full of concern for him.

And that little wrinkle in between her brows…

Yeah, her eyes had pulled him under. She'd found him just before he'd taken Kjartan's advice on removing the slug himself. By taking a dive off Fremont Bridge with a nylon rope around his neck.

No more head, no more agony, he'd figured.

He'd been okay with making death stick at that point. The drilling pain had been excruciating. Even the dagger through the heart during their initiation hadn't been *that* bad.

He'd had no idea that there was another stage of pain. The one he was in now. Bayley was the only one who could take it away. The way her touch soothed him was magic.

Damn. He was in too deep with her, he couldn't fuck that up. He had to see her after her shift and hope to God that she wouldn't turn him away.

What if she tells me to get lost for good? What the hell am I gonna do then?

Another explosion went off inside his skull at the thought, pummeling him with a heavy blow to his temples. He clutched the sides tighter and screamed inward. He couldn't take it—

"JUMP!" someone shouted.

Lucas flinched at the start, flinging himself sideways on the ledge and tucking his head underneath his arms.

His heart hammered against his sternum as hard as the migraine had been a second ago. The voice had come out of nowhere.

And once he lifted his head from its cover to look around, he confirmed that he was still very much alone up here. Everything was quiet.

Lucas straightened. His eyes shifted across the roof space. There was no movement.

He blew out a sharp breath, and his pulse smoothed out after a few more slow inhales. But he knew that voice. It was the same one that had told him to jump the other night when they'd been out here running. Right as everyone had been distracted by the rat in Nessa's hair and *Wonder Boy* Kjan had taken charge.

The command had really been inside his head then, too. There was no one on the roof with him.

Am I hallucinating now?

CHAPTER

16

EVE

She blinked out of the strangest dream, her skin itchy from the sensation of being buried alive. Eve double-checked her fingernails for dirt. It had felt so real. She could still smell the fresh earth in her hair.

After spending a few days at the condo downtown, she and Kjan only returned to the cabin last night. While Caleb, Emma, and Lucas had joined them on the last-minute charter flight back to Portland on Christmas Eve, the rest of the gang had stayed behind to finish off the week in Reykjavík. They wouldn't get in until tomorrow.

Even the hot shower couldn't shake the nightmare from her mind. Eve felt the need to scrub her skin nearly raw before giving up, and yet the tingling remained.

Kjan was in the forge. He'd made himself scarce since their return. While keeping busy at the penthouse, he'd seemed disconnected and absentminded. Eve knew he missed the work, needed the outlet, and it had been her idea to get back a day early, but as soon as they'd made it to the cabin, he'd withdrawn physically.

He was hiding out.

Things just weren't turning around for them. Every time she thought they were finally moving forward, they ended up taking two steps back.

Eve worked through the load her boss had pushed her way without complaint. She welcomed the distraction, since spending all night in bed with Kjan wasn't an option.

When she went down to the forge, she found him with his earbuds in, his lips moving along to the lyrics like he was arguing with himself. Steampunk goggles gave him a mad scientist vibe as he wielded the blowtorch. A *sexy* mad scientist, all sweaty and shirtless.

Yeah, I would totally let him experiment on me.

A smile grew on his face, and she knew she had been caught. With a sideways glance, he eyed her leaning against the frame. "Why do you always lurk by the door?"

"I like watching you. How did you even hear me?" Eve pushed off and strolled toward him, putting some extra sway into her steps.

He killed the torch. "I didn't," he replied nonchalantly. "I can feel you."

Kjan ripped the goggles off his head and ran his fingers through his wet hair, wiping them on the back of his jeans before picking up his phone to turn off the music.

"So there really is no sneaking up on you? Ever?"

He took out the earbuds and met her halfway. "Any particular reason why you would want to?"

"Nope. Just checking." She winked, linking her arms around his neck and pulling him down to her lips. Not that he was putting up a fight. With a firm hold around her waist, he lifted her toes off the ground.

Eve was a split second away from wrapping her legs around him when he dropped her back down and pulled away.

How disappointing.

She glanced at his phone on the workbench, wondering what he had been listening to.

"The Devil in I?" she asked, nodding toward the device over his shoulder.

He creased his brows. "What?"

"Slipknot," she clarified.

"Oh, right. I don't know." He shrugged with indifference. "I wasn't paying attention."

"Really? It looked like you were singing along." She had clearly seen his lips move.

"Was I? Hmm." His tense jaw ticked like he was grinding his thoughts.

Odd. He must have been really engrossed in his project. "What are you working on?"

Kjan towed her to the workbench and placed a solid piece of steel in her hand. "It's a karambit."

Eve looked down. The little, curved blade had small holes in the handle and a big ring at the end. *He made this?* "Wow, It's beautiful."

"It's simple, but effective," he stated humbly. "It's perfect for close combat. The basic purpose of the ergonomic handle and the ring is to ensure the safety of the user. You can't drop it in a fight, attacking or defending," he went on, explaining the unique shape. "I made it for you."

"For me? I don't know how to use that."

Kjan chuckled. "I'll teach you. You're fast. This will make you deadly. When you put your thumb or finger in the ring, you gain significant control over the knife, and no one can take it from you. It's a great backup weapon to have in your arsenal."

Eve put her pointer through the finger hole and held it in her open palm, getting a feel for the weight before she closed her fist around the grip. "It looks like a claw from Jurassic Park."

"The shape is based on a tiger's claw, actually. And it's not just a stabbing weapon. It can serve as a grappling tool as well."

Kjan guided her hand to his throat, the tip of the steel right up against his jugular. "It's mostly used to slash, not stab. The sharp blade can do severe damage to your opponent's arteries, tendons, and nerves," he said, dragging the point across his skin with a steady grasp on Eve's hand. "Due to its curve, it can dig deeper to hook, tear, and flay. Strike near the collarbone, ribs, and other body parts to go past the flesh, then hook the knife into the bones," he elaborated while vaguely demonstrating on himself.

"It will immobilize anyone, and in the hands of an adept user, the bones don't just break,"—he yanked her fist toward the center of his chest to mimic a punch—"they shatter if you put up enough force."

Eve felt a shudder down her neck as her knuckles made contact and the curved blade's tip punctured him. The idea of accidentally hurting him was unbearable.

She let go of the handle, dropping it into his hand.

"The bend in the steel is also very efficient at deflecting an attacker's jabs and kicks," he said, leaning back against the bench. "Maybe even more effective for self-defense than for fighting."

He put the karambit down and picked up another blade. "I've also made a few of these."

This time, he was holding a plain blade in the shape of a dagger out to her. It was only an inch at its widest point and completely straight with a double-edged head.

"The karambit is not meant for throwing, but this is. Give it a whirl." He pointed at the target on the wall behind her.

Eve glanced over her shoulder and then back at him, raising her eyebrows. "You sure?"

He shrugged as she took the knife. "What's the worst that could happen? It's pretty well balanced, and it's light, so you don't need a lot of force. It's not about power. It's about refining the motion. Keep it fluid."

She adjusted her grip on the handle, remembering how Kjartan had shot the paring knife through the kitchen at Lucas' head. He'd made it look so effortless.

Eve raised her arm toward the target and took aim, eyes glued to the circle he had drawn on the wall.

Is that Sharpie? Whatever. Focus!

She reached her arm back and released the knife on the forward swing—

The lethal blade came flying back at her faster than a boomerang. Kjan's hand snatched her out of its path just in time, and they scrambled for cover.

"You were saying?" Eve retorted.

Kjan laughed as he pulled her to her feet. "If you throw a knife from the handle, it will need one full rotation to land point-first. If you hold it by the blade, it will need to turn one and a half times. The more you bend your wrist down when you draw your hand back toward your ear, the more you increase the speed of the knife flipping in the air."

He moved her arm up to demonstrate. As he arched it backward, his fingertips brushed over her tattoo in a deliberately slow motion, inciting sparks with his touch before he reached the center of her palm.

Kjan stalled there, the gentle pads of his fingers conveying a much deeper desire she wasn't immune to.

Caught in the moment, their eyes met, and he flashed a crooked smile. Then he cleared his throat and continued. "That's necessary if there's not a lot of distance between you and your target. For long-range, keep your wrist unbent. It will keep the knife from turning too much."

"Small detail to skip, you think?"

"You did fine. You managed one and a half turns, but you held it by the handle. That's why it hit with the butt instead of the blade."

He picked up another one and placed it gently into her palm, tip toward her. His green eyes were so bright and clear. He was practically beaming, enjoying the opportunity to teach her a new skill.

"Pinch it carefully. Put your thumb on the front and your fingers on the other side. Pinky at the tip of the knife."

He guided each one of her fingers to its proper spot, one at a time, and then dragged his hand lazily along her forearm… right to her waist.

He closed in behind her, planting his hands on either side of her. "Left foot forward, but don't angle your hips when you shift your weight to follow through. And don't release the blade until your arm is straight out in front of you. Just let it slip through your fingers. Hold it firmly but delicately. And remember…" He gave her hair a quick pull, yanking her back just a little to force a sharp inhale from her. "*Finesse*. Not brute strength."

He spoke the last words softly as he leaned down right by her ear, letting his voice coat her like honey before he kissed her cheek.

Eve's body grew heavy, her knees weak. Her hormones raged with his front pressed against her backside. It really wasn't fair how he could so easily manipulate her, and he knew it too. Kjan lingered, his beard tickling when he smiled against her skin.

His remaining hand on her hip tightened its grip briefly, then he released her, ripping his warmth away and taking a step back to give her space.

She wouldn't have judged him for taking cover again. He healed fast, but he probably couldn't regrow an eye.

Eve stretched her arm toward the target a second time and took a deep breath. Then she drew it back and swung her arm straight out like he had shown her, letting the steel slip from her grasp.

The blade stuck.

She grimaced. "Well, that sucked slightly less."

Kjan pursed his lips. "You only missed it by two feet." The metal tip had struck the wooden wall well below the target's outer circle. "You'll get better," he added, cocking his head.

He retrieved the knives and put them back in her hand, along with four more from the workbench. "Again!"

Eve gave him an exasperated eye roll but took the knives as ordered.

Kjan didn't approve of her attitude. He grabbed her chin to tilt it up. Holding her gaze, his tone turned raspy and low. "Humor me, and I'll return the favor."

A blaze rushed her chest with his rough grasp and that unrelenting stare, causing the butterflies in her belly to flap their delicate wings a little bit faster even before his lips sank down on hers.

Then he straightened and gave her butt a light slap. "Show me what you got. And you better make it good."

'Good!' The way that word rolls off his tongue…

But Eve was getting ahead of herself. "Don't worry. I'll make it worth your while," she muttered under her breath.

Taking aim again, she darted the knives at the board across the forge, 1… 2… 3… 4… 5… aaaand 6.

Every single one of them hit the target, and the last one pierced it dead center.

"See!" Kjan praised, coming up behind her. "You're a natural. All it takes is the right motivation."

"I'll show you motivation." Eve swung around, hands raised, clasping his face as she crushed her mouth to his to affirm her need for him more directly.

Fueled by an insatiable ache to feel him, her breaths strained, her thumbs grazed through the scruff along his jawline, her body arching into him, hungry for his touch.

Only when it came, it wasn't in the way she'd hoped. Kjan's fingers wrapped around her wrists to peel her off.

"Slow your horses, Dove. Let me wash up first."

"I don't care," she groaned against his lips, palms falling to his chest, reluctant to pull away.

"But I do." He straightened and released her wrists, his eyes as stern as his tone. "I'll meet you upstairs."

Eve sighed. "Fine." But before caving, she let her hands wander slowly down the center of his chest, scraping her nails along the solid muscles of his abs and the happy trail that disappeared into his jeans.

Gripping the waistband, she gave it a harsh pull, joining them at the hips with her moving toward him—Kjan being the unmovable mountain with his own gravity pull.

Eve scowled, making her acute displeasure known while walking backward. "Don't take too long," she reminded him, one hand still attached to his. "I might fall asleep waiting."

Her arm stretched toward him as both of them treasured every second of the touch, and she didn't turn until the connection broke at their fingertips.

"I guess I'll just have to wake you up then."

"Deal," she shot back over her shoulder, sashaying out the door.

Over an hour later, Eve was stretched out on the bed, glaring at the door. She'd been kidding about falling asleep, but Kjan was taking his sweet time. It had been an eternity since he stomped up the stairs in his heavy motorcycle boots; they weren't exactly sneaky.

Why is he using the shower in the hall instead of the one off the master bedroom?

Eve momentarily contemplated pulling her laptop back out.

Finally, she heard him approach the room. Turning her back, she closed her eyes to feign sleep but kept the little lamp on the nightstand lit.

The door fell shut silently behind her, and two seconds later the bed dipped under his weight. Kjan laughed softly, the towel wrapped around his waist rubbing against her backside as he showered her with kisses.

"You're not fooling me," he said, rolling her onto her back.

"Took you long enough."

Eve twisted her fingers through his hair as she reached for him and pulled him to her mouth. "You smell so good," she purred.

Their breaths mingled with the feathering touch of his lips against hers. "Worth the wait?"

"You always smell good."

A warm, woodsy trace of cedar weaved through his matching aged Bourbon shampoo and body wash set, but it was the underlying fragrance of his natural scent that penetrated her senses, the rich dark chocolate and black cherry blend an embodiment of forbidden temptation.

Kjan nipped at her bottom lip, giving it a gentle tug. Legs entwined, one arm around her waist, his free hand slid higher on top of the slick, green satin nightie she'd changed into.

Through the thin texture, the brush of his fingertips sent subtle jolts of electricity across her skin, a skill he'd only revealed to her a few months ago. He was tapping into the power line of the house, drawing on the charge, then sending it back out through his touch.

His hand trailed higher up her side. Cupping the swell of her breast, his thumb swiveled over the nipple that was barely covered by the black lace trim. It hardened under his attention.

Eve gripped his shoulders tight, his muscles flexing beneath her skin. "You like?"

"I like," he drawled. "But you don't need to try so hard. I take you any way you come," he added with an extra husky rasp.

She chuckled. "Let me guess, no pun intended?"

"Oh, it's definitely intended." Rolling the pebbled tip of her flesh with his thumb, he sent another spark across.

Eve pressed into the warmth of his palm encouragingly, whimpering under the torture. She was aching for him.

Kjan hummed with glee. He teased her for a moment longer, then pulled her onto her side, bringing her body flush with his.

The annoying towel shifted between them but kept what she was after covered when she coiled her leg around him. Eve needed to feel his hard length against her core, skin on skin. She was bursting with need.

Rounding her ass with more of his wispy touch, Kjan caressed her thigh and inhaled sharply.

"Fuck… your skin is so smooth," he moaned against her mouth, the timbre in his voice even darker than before.

He kissed her again and again, needier each time his hips rocked into her. Eve felt her own patience dwindle.

His phone went off next to the bed.

A deep growl erupted from his throat, but Kjan ignored the call. It would take more than that to divert him.

With her lips parted, his tongue went on an exploratory cruise. He prodded past her teeth as he slid his hand under the silky fabric of her dress.

His fingertips brushed the ticklish area at her hip bone, and Eve wriggled against him while he teased small whimpers from her. Each flick of his tongue against hers carried the same electric tingle his touch gave off.

As his hand inched upward toward her ribs, he rewarded her with a more thorough stroking that forced needy groans from her into his mouth. His touch was everywhere at once, so intense, so full of longing.

Breaking from her lips, Kjan ventured along her jaw to the crook of her neck, a blazing trail chasing his path.

The lamp on the nightstand buzzed, and the light jittered in the view of her half-closed eyes when the sharp points of his fangs cut into her skin, deeper than usual with each nip.

Tension built in her spine. Kjan never took from her vein anymore. Avoided any major artery altogether; *she* fed on *his* blood, not the other way around.

It wasn't too long ago that she'd loved to feel his bite; when they'd shared the kind of raw passion that marred skin and left scars on bones, all those times they'd made a complete mess out of the sheets. Her blood or his, it hadn't mattered.

Now she dreaded it.

Every time his teeth scraped along her throat, her mind went back to the immortal. Eve felt her pulse spike, and her fingers tensed at his nape, remembering how Kjartan had torn into her jugular and nearly drained her. Twice. The memory was still so close to the surface, rushing back like it had been yesterday.

Would she ever be able to shake it? She didn't know how to tell Kjan without hurting him. He had his own PTSD to deal with.

His phone started ringing again. He cursed and peeled himself away from her to reach for it.

"It's Caleb," he said, checking the screen.

Eve groaned in response, dropping her head on the pillow.

"WHAT?" he barked into the phone.

She could immediately hear Caleb's voice screaming through the speaker. Kjan's face dropped, his eyes wide, darting rapidly as he followed the words on the other end.

"I'm on my way." He hung up and leaped off the bed into the closet.

"What's wrong?" she asked in alarm.

"It's Lucas." His clothes rustled while he got dressed. "He's planted himself on the railroad tracks and refuses to move."

"What! Because of Bayley?" The two of them were constantly on again/off again. Who could keep track?

Bayley wasn't like them. She was a different kind of vampire, not sired by a Norse God of Immortality and Darkness. At least not directly, as far as anyone knew. Eve's ex, Jordan, had been like Bayley. They couldn't tolerate sunlight and didn't heal as fast. Therefore, she didn't always fit in. And she was older, too. Turned in 1820, if Eve remembered correctly.

"What happened with Bayley?" he shouted back from the closet.

"I don't know yet."

But I'll definitely find out.

"Maybe it's his way of going on a bender," she suggested. "Since he can't drink his troubles away." None of them could. No one but Kjan.

"Then he should talk to someone."

"Like who?" Eve scoffed. "A shrink?"

Lucas was used to dealing with his problems alone and had always been closed off. She wondered whether he ever opened up to Caleb. The two of them were close—as close as Lucas would let anyone get. Besides the occasional hook-ups with Dynja.

Eve knew about those for a fact, but they didn't make a big deal out of it. There had been threesomes with Parker, too.

The rest of the coven usually avoided him. His dark eyes and buzzcut gave him a violent edge, but Eve wanted to believe there was more to him than this angry kid from the streets.

She shuffled off the bed to grab her clothes, but Kjan interjected when he returned from the closet. "Stay! I'll be right back."

"I want to help," she protested.

"There's nothing you can do, Dove."

He quickly pressed another kiss to her lips and charged out the door, cutting her off from whatever was going on between him and Lucas.

CHAPTER 17

KJAN

When he rolled up to the tracks a few miles from the loft, he could already hear the train approaching. It was due to haul past here any minute. Caleb and Emma were still there, trying to talk sense into the bastard.

"I owe you," the kid said, tugging on Lucas to make him move. "If I had been there… you know I would've gladly taken that bullet for you."

"You don't owe me shit, man. We're good. Now beat it," he snapped, shoving his friend off.

Kjan caught only the last bits of the argument, and he wasn't going to waste his breath. Caleb locked eyes with him for a split second before pulling Emma back.

His prey didn't see him coming. Kjan charged him from behind, locking him in a rear chokehold while the other two ran for cover.

Lucas squirmed, his body arched, but Kjan kept him in a vise, one arm bent at his throat, his other hand unrelenting at the back of his skull.

The train was rolling near, they could both see it through the trees around the bend.

"There's your light at the end of the tunnel, asshole. Is that what you're waiting for? All you need to do is ask, and I'll be happy to oblige. I would do us both a favor," he hissed.

He felt Lucas' heart racing at his jugular as he clawed at him, barely leaving marks on his skin. Kjan didn't flinch. He waited, his pulse unfazed.

3…

2…

1…

The kid collapsed.

Kjan yanked him away from the tracks and dragged him into the woods. He slammed his body hard against a tree, forearm across his collarbone, fist clenching his shirt.

The boy's scent triggered a memory. The air of hot iron and burning flesh winding through Kjan's nostrils fueled his rage. "I'm tired of your shit, Lucas," he went off. "You want to die? Do it on your own. Don't drag innocent people into this."

Lucas pushed him off, thrusting the heels of his palms into Kjan's chest with as much force as he could muster. "I didn't force Caleb and Emma to stay behind."

His dark blue eyes were cold, no shred of remorse in them when he turned to walk away.

Where the fuck does he think he's going? Kjan ripped him back, his knuckles colliding with the boy's jaw in a single motion.

Lucas toppled to the ground, spitting blood, and Kjan put one knee on his chest before he could get up again. "I'm talking about the humans on that train, you selfish prick. This is the only warning I'm giving you," he said, reaching into his boot. "I hope it sticks."

Before Lucas could blink, Kjan snatched up his right arm, pinned it next to his head, and rammed the point of the 8-inch throwing knife into the center of the boy's palm.

Through the soft, damp soil, he drove the steel to its midpoint, painfully slow, while the kid screamed and twisted underneath him.

"Pull a stupid move like that again, and the next one goes through your heart," his voice gnashed. Then he pushed to his feet and stomped off, leaving Lucas to pull the knife free on his own.

Maybe he would use the time to reflect on his reckless behavior.

Vampires were emotional creatures, acting on their impulses without considering the long-term consequences. It had taken Kjan centuries to reign himself in, and he had always shunned others for this exact reason. He had never felt the desire for a coven or the interest to lead one. He had made that clear from the beginning, and yet he was the one they called whenever there was a problem.

Lucas' rebellion was only part of the issue.

The kid didn't respect him and didn't bother hiding it. He made a point of letting Kjan know that he didn't belong every chance he could get, but he was right. Eve and he didn't belong with them. Kjan could never see them as anything but an extension of his Sire. The immortal had controlled them, turned them against her, and they had followed him unconditionally. Now they were only loyal to each other. Kjan couldn't trust them. It wasn't *his* blood in their veins.

'Your whining is pathetic.'

"We both know it's the truth."

The second he touched the Harley, sharp pain exploded between his shoulder blades like the stab of a knife. Prickling sparks triggered the nerve endings along his spine as if he had touched a live wire with his bare hand.

'You don't see what you have… how lucky you are. I would give anything to trade places with you.'

"I'm very aware of that," Kjan spat. He held on to the handle, absorbing the charge his Sire was drawing out of the motorcycle. "And if you still had a body to get back to, things would have gone a lot different in the—"

His head snapped around. He didn't see anybody. Didn't sense anybody. But it was definitely the same laugh rustling through the trees. That same high-pitched snickering, here, in Portland.

"You heard that too… I'm not hallucinating?"

'No. It's him. He's here,' his passenger confirmed. *'You best be ready once he chooses to reveal himself, because I can't tell who or what he is.'*

Eve was asleep upstairs when he returned, the sun just rising to the east. The soft and steady rhythm of her heartbeat spread through the house, setting it aglow with the warmth of her aura. To him, the cabin had a luster that reflected her light. Her presence made it home.

Kjan pulled the bike into the garage and kicked off his boots before creeping upstairs, so he wouldn't wake her.

He slid into bed, fully clothed. Eve voiced her displeasure with a soft snort when he curled his arm around her waist.

"Sleep!" he told her, nuzzling her hairline, his face pressed snugly against her cheek.

She was still wearing the deep green satin, and he was, again, painfully hard when feeling the delicate fabric shift over her smooth skin. It was almost better than having her naked.

His Sire had a point. Marking a mate was madness. No one really knew how it worked. It was rare for a vampire to pledge his or her entire sanity to another. Kjan had only known four with the same *affliction*, and each one of them had died shortly after their consort. He had made the lunatic vow of devotion to a single lover not once, but twice.

What if fate forced you to share your mate? Could it actually kill you, slowly, from the inside? Or would they eventually turn on each other out of jealousy?

Kjan had been arguing with the parasite earlier. Even with the water running ice-cold, his skin had felt like it was on fire, every muscle fiber in his body twitching to keep him at bay. Hence the long shower.

He never felt clean enough for her, either. Making love to her the way he wished to was too fucking intimate. He couldn't stand having his Sire lurk in the back of his mind.

Being rough was easier because the immortal hated it. He despised the way Kjan handled her while Eve loved it and craved it just as much as he did. But it wasn't everything. He needed the intimacy they had shared long before all this, before they had ever had sex. Things had been simpler then. No Gods. No monsters. Just he and his little dove.

Eve had changed so much since then. She was no longer the naïve girl. In the past two years, she had become a strong and confident woman. He couldn't deceive her. She knew what was going on with him, even if she didn't know the details. He could feel her worry. It ate him alive.

It was these thoughts that had trapped him in the shower. These thoughts that kept him up during the day. Like a drug addict, he had been kicking it up a notch every time lately and was getting dangerously close to hurting Eve.

Kjan ground his teeth. He wanted her to himself and be alone with her for one goddamn night. No voice in his head. No pulling under his skin. Just Eve and him.

He squeezed his eyes shut, trying to drown *him* out. Feeding off her pheromones had him walking on the edge. All it would take was a little push.

But a bigger threat was afoot. He could feel it. One that would shake their very existence to the core.

CHAPTER

18

KJAN

Eve ripped him from a dreamless sleep as her torso shot upright next to him, her breath panting and her eyes frantic while she oriented herself. When they found him, her breathing eased.

Kjan frowned. He was the one with the recurring nightmares, not her. "You okay?"

She shook her head briskly and then flung herself at him, sadness bursting from her. Puzzled, he wrapped his arms around her small frame.

"What is it, Dove? Talk to me." He held her tight, and she buried her face deeper in his chest.

Fanning his fingers through her hair, he rocked her gingerly, waiting for her to find her voice.

"I couldn't see anything. It was so dark… and cold. Just like last time."

"Last time? You had the same nightmare before?" What else was she keeping from him?

"Exactly the same."

"When?"

Eve straightened, her fingers playing with her ring for emotional support like a security blanket. "Last night."

"Why didn't you tell me?" He kept his tone light. He didn't want to come off as reproachful.

Looking up through her lashes, she tugged on the front of his shirt. "I didn't want to ruin the moment. Honestly, I didn't think much of it." Her brows furrowed. "But now it's kinda freaking me out."

"What did you feel?"

Kjan remembered his own nightmares about being trapped in a box like Anne at the bottom of the ocean. He hadn't been able to see either, but he had heard the crashing of the waves and felt her fear.

The tip of Eve's tongue made a quick appearance to wet her lips. "I was being held," she started, gazing off. "I could feel someone cradling me... trembling. I was shivering, and I couldn't stop.

"No." Her eyes shifted as she corrected the details. "I was cold, but I wasn't the one shaking. I think the person holding me was."

Kjan watched Eve's breath stall while she appeared to focus on the other person in her nightmare.

"Then I felt myself slipping into the dirt," she continued, blinking herself free. "Not dropped, but placed gently, like I was being laid down on a bed. The ground was so cold... *I* was so cold."

Her naked arms revealed a subtle twitch, as if the sensation persisted in her bones now, and Kjan could see the little hairs on her skin rise.

The emotion in her tone neared a sob. "Something small was placed in my arms. It made my heart ache. I-I remember crying. But not for myself. I was worried for someone else. I didn't want to leave…"

Her lips attracted a quiver, and her hand made a quick swipe beneath her eye. "Ugh, it was awful." She tucked back into the crook of his shoulder. "If I never have that dream again, it'll be too soon."

Kjan didn't blame her. It sounded dreadful, and it was too much like his own nightmare. The darkness, the cold; they had felt real to him, too.

But her recount also reminded him of something else. Something he would rather not dwell on.

One look at Eve snuggled up close to him in that skimpy piece of satin forced the chill crawling over him away, steam rising quickly in its stead. There was something about that dark shade of green that got him all riled up.

Finding himself distracted, his eyes roamed the black lace trim. Her breasts were already tight-tipped under the see-through material.

"Speaking of not wanting to ruin the moment." He dragged his finger lazily down the deep plunge, exposing one of her dark pink nipples.

Her skin flushed as he admired the view. He pinched it, watching it pebble under his touch.

Leaning down, he extended his tongue and licked at the peak, moistening it in little circles.

Eve's chest heaved with a sigh. He felt her fingers diving into his hair, and he shivered when her sweet, floral scent amplified. Her pheromones engulfed his senses. They called to him, and he complied like a dog summoned by its master.

Eve rolled her hips to meet him, moaning softly as he sucked her nipple between his lips.

The roar of a truck out front made them both cringe at the same time. "Tell me that's not Kristján's truck," she uttered, notably peeved.

Kjan let out a frustrated groan and dropped his forehead on her chest, clinging to the beating of her heart. If he didn't get inside her soon, he was going to burst.

"I'm sorry we have to postpone this again." He raised his head and straightened her top. "Next chance I get, you're mine," he rasped, pulling her mouth to his, hips pressing into her, nudging intently against the blazing heat between her thighs.

The doorbell chimed, and Kjan growled as he pulled away, forced to leave her perfectly unsatisfied.

"Wait!" The sheets behind him rustled when Eve sat up. "What happened with Lucas?"

Kjan kept on walking. "He's still alive." *For now.*

"Did he really try to kill himself?" The sincere concern in her tone for the kid left a bad taste in his mouth. Then again, her general compassion wasn't a surprise.

Swallowing his resentment, he opened the bedroom door and glanced back. "I pulled him off the tracks. I didn't ask for details. Maybe you'll get it out of him."

Then Kjan went downstairs to let the bunch of undesirables inside while Eve got herself dressed.

"Boy, sure hope we weren't interrupting anything important." Nessa winked and pushed past him, her auburn curls bouncing around her face.

Kjan rolled his eyes. "You wouldn't care if you did."

"Not true. Ye could've made us wait. I understand the essential things in life." She grinned wide at Askja, pulling her by the hand.

"I'll remember that for next time." He met Askja's warm, honey-colored eyes. A soft cloud of lavender surrounded her. "How was your trip?"

"Long."

Her smile seemed forced, and Kjan felt a heavy weight in his chest. It was strange to remember how close they had been once.

Well, not *he*, technically. At the human age of 22, she had become a substitute for a mother the perpetual boy had barely known. Even though the memories weren't his own, Kjan recalled every moment of the 14 years they had traveled together. In a way, she was to the immortal what Eleanor had been to him. A companion and a confidant.

Kristján's broad shoulders blocked the entryway. The blond giant's frame barely fit through a standard door.

His face was lit up with excitement like a child on Christmas morning. "Can I see it now?"

Kjan smirked and motioned with his head. "It's in the forge."

Shuffling awkwardly back against the wall, his former second-in-command surrendered his dominion over the doorway and made enough space for Kjan to slip past.

Eve affectionately referred to him as a big teddy bear, which was pretty accurate most times, but Kjan also knew the fiercely protective side of him that she had yet to meet.

"I looked into that Cooper-kid again like you asked me to," Kristján mentioned, circling back to a conversation they had had before their trip to Reykjavík. "He is still lying low. Mostly. At least nothing that affects us. And his bodyguard didn't suffer any brain damage after he got beaten to a pulp, either." He chuckled, shaking his head. "That was epic. No offense."

Because it hadn't actually been Kjan throwing the punches, and he probably wouldn't have approved of the rather extreme strategy either. "None taken."

He recalled it making quite the impression on Eve as well, only in a distinctly less enthusiastic kind of way. She had never seen him in a fight before.

"So, yeah, he should not be a problem anymore."

"What's his situation? Does he have family?" *Someone to mourn him?* Kjan knew next to nothing about his former business partner's offspring.

"Wife. No kids."

A wife? "Hmm."

Kjan mulled that one over. The old man had been known to smack women around, and although she wasn't his concern, for her sake, he hoped that the younger Cooper hadn't picked up the same habit.

He gave Kristján a skeptical look. "You really think he has given up the search for his father?"

Kjan had left a lot of things unfinished with Cooper. He prayed he wouldn't have to go back to Vegas to silence the kid after all.

"I think he has accepted that his father's dirty business caught up with him. And who knows, maybe that will encourage him to follow in his old man's footsteps. But I will keep tabs on him to make sure he doesn't become a problem in the long run. And so will Caleb. You have my word on that. No one's going to threaten her or us."

"Thank you."

"Sure thing."

Kristján followed him down the driveway, where Dynja hung back with Parker, lips locked. They were partially blocked from view between the vehicles, and Kjan did a quick double-take to verify what he was seeing. Her white-blonde hair spilled around his dark skin. Yep, sure as shit; it was them.

Dynja wasn't his Sire's first sexual experience. There had been many human women before her and even a few men back in Iceland. She had been the only vampire, however, besides Eve, other than the threesome with Parker when he had walked in on them together at the cabin.

'Wanna join in?' Her sly lilt scraped like a rusty nail through the back of his mind.

That was how he had ended up with Parker giving him head. Then Dynja had done the same for the guy while his Sire had watched before he had indeed joined in, taking Dynja from behind as she had finished Parker off.

Though Kjan had had his fair share of kink in 980-some years, he wasn't the least bit attracted to men. He had always considered Jeremy's attention flattering, but Eleanor's assistant had never crossed the line of professionalism. If he had, Kjan's response would have been a hard pass.

Yes, he had fed on men and women alike in the past. Yes, drawing them in was a lot easier when they were attracted to him. And yes, feeding straight from the vein carried a highly erotic charge, which enriched the blood's taste, therefore affecting him to a certain degree as well. *BUT* he had always left it at that.

His Sire, on the other hand, had been a lot more intrigued by the concept, eager to explore firsthand that which he had been denied in his former body. And it was his impeccable memory that made Kjan want to smash his head repeatedly into a brick wall to give himself a concussion. Amnesia sounded pretty fucking tempting.

"Here." He tossed Kristján the axe, and he caught it with both hands.

He had been itching in his pants to see the weapon ever since Kjan mentioned it. It was made from *crucible steel*. Due to its purity in conjunction with an insanely high carbon content, the strength of the Viking metal was legendary and usually reserved for swords—and even those had been rare, only produced for the occasional nobleman. Kjan had never heard of it being used for an axe besides this one.

Other than carbon, the second crucial requirement for the process was heat. Iron was melted with carbon to create the desired steel in a furnace, or so-called crucible, that had to be heated to 3,000 degrees to separate the impurities of the metals and create the high quality. Impurities caused weaknesses and rendered the blade prone to breaking from repeated strikes against shields, armor, and other swords.

Instead of restoring the original owner's modern furnace, Kjan had opted for an ancient clay and brick crucible in his forge in order to create the desired steel. It was the same type that had been used in the Middle East to first produce Damascus. It could take a skilled blacksmith over ten hours of labored pounding to shape the blade and several more days to polish it.

Too bad he had ruined the sword he had been working on. He would have to start over from scratch.

"Damn, that's beautiful," Kristján noted while giving it a few swings. His face showed surprise as it cut swiftly through the air. "And fast. Not as heavy as I expected."

Kjan snorted a laugh. "I thought the same thing."

"Family heirloom, I assume." The giant turned it back and forth in his hands, admiring the carvings.

"A few generations." Kjan stuffed his hands into his pockets and leaned back against his work table. "My mother gave it to my father when they were wed. The wood is in surprisingly good shape. I replaced the leather wrap and just need a couple of days to polish the blade."

"Nice." He brushed his thumb along the butt-end of the handle. "Is that Týr?"

"Yeah. Each owner added a carving of personal significance to the wood. Usually runic inscriptions. That one was mine," he stated modestly.

Kristján's expression revealed only genuine appreciation. The man was as honest as they came; there was not a deceitful bone in his body. Which was crucial if you needed to know whom to trust. "It's an incredible piece, Kjan."

"Thanks." The compliment made him uncomfortable. Other than Thórunn, no one had ever admired his work. "So, Dynja and Parker, huh? Is that still a thing?" he asked now that they were out of earshot.

"I don't know." Kristján gave him a half-shrug. "I'm pretty sure they're just fucking, but it's none of my concern. They're consenting adults."

"Well, good for them. The two are made for each other," Kjan muttered. Neither of them was looking for anything serious. Let them fuck to their hearts' content. At least someone got some action around here.

Kjan wasn't bitter. Not. At. All.

Kristján cleared his throat and set the axe down. "I'm sorry about her slip-up."

"Don't worry about it," Kjan dismissed him offhandedly. It wasn't his fault, and things were better this way. One less secret to worry about.

His brows dropped heavily, darkening his blue eyes. "So Eve didn't stay mad for too long?"

"Nah, she's fine." He was back in her good graces. Though he hadn't had a chance to express his gratitude and officially make it up to her.

"Hmm." Kristján's grim expression didn't alleviate. "Mind if I ask you something?"

Oh boy! His lungs halted mid-inflation. Did he like where this was going? "In regards to…?"

"Eve. What are you waiting for? I mean, what's keeping you from making an honest woman out of her already?"

Marry her? Kjan swallowed. Vampires had mates and consorts. They didn't get married. "What makes you think that's what she wants?"

"She's a female. It's what they all want."

Kjan didn't respond, his eyes downcast, the muscles in his jaw tense. Eve had never shown any inclination toward the subject, and honestly, it had never crossed his own mind. It wasn't going to happen now. Not like this.

"Look, again, I mean no offense." The giant threw up his palms. "It's none of my business. And who am I to give you advice any—"

Kjan ducked out of the way at the last second as the football came flying at the side of his head. It hit Kristján square in the jaw instead.

"Let's go, bitches. You owe me a rematch." Caleb stood in the center of the open barn doors, pointing his scrawny finger at them.

"Oh, I'm gonna kick that little shit's ass," the giant roared.

Kjan picked the ball off the ground and punched it into Kristján's chest. "Here is your chance, big guy."

CHAPTER

19

EVE

She took a spot on the sidelines with Emma, Claire, and her brother Parker. The *field* they played on was neither flat nor big, but it was the best they could do. The ridge had a sharp drop just a few yards beyond the trees across the clearing.

"You're sitting out?" Eve glanced in surprise as Nessa plopped into the grass next to her. "I thought you were itching for a rematch too."

"Nae. Kría is taking my spot on Kjan's team."

"Not Kristján's?" His mate chose to play against him? *This ought to be fun.*

"Watcha know? Maybe it's their new kind of foreplay." Nessa shrugged, then hollered toward the field. "Let's go, lads!"

Erik and Caleb joined Kjan's team. It was usually four-on-four and always him versus Kristján. Despite the evident size difference, they were an equal match. Kjan's speed and agility posed a distinct threat. Cradling the ball in the crook of his arm, he charged the giant, jerking left, then right, and then wheeling around him in a backspin at the last second to break past the block.

Caleb doubled over, huffing for air after being steam-rolled by Lucas. He was a decent runner, though his slimmer build couldn't match the other guys.

"Hurry the feck on, ye dope!" Nessa heckled.

The smell of kicked-up earth—like a freshly dug grave—brought her recent nightmare back to the surface. Stiffly, Eve turned to her. "What do you know about reincarnation? Do you believe it's real?"

Askja's mate narrowed her sharp green eyes. "What a weird thing to ask. I dunno. Maybe not necessarily reincarnation, but I do believe our ancestors live on in us. DNA carries knowledge, memories…" she droned on. "What exactly are ye getting at?"

She glanced at Kjan on the field, and then shuffled her butt two inches closer to Nessa. "I had this dream the other night. It kinda freaked me out. I told Kjan about it, but he shrugged it off."

"Well, what was it about?"

Eve sighed. "You're gonna think I'm crazy," she started to explain. Her hands were trembling again. "I was lying in a grave. I knew I was dead, but I still felt a physical connection to my body in the ground. I could feel what was happening to me while I was watching the scene. All I could think about was not wanting to leave him."

"Him who?" Nessa's forehead creased as her brows winged up.

Eve chewed her bottom lip. "I didn't tell him that part, but I'm pretty sure it was Kjan. He was cradling our baby, and I kneeled next to him… put my hand on his shoulder…"

She began to stammer, her eyes watering as she recalled the details. "I felt his sorrow. He was all alone. I wanted to comfort him so badly." Eve blinked back tears. "The thing is, it didn't feel like a dream. It felt like a memory. But that would be impossible, right? I mean, how could I remember something that never happened?"

"Well, maybe it *did* happen. Just not to *you*," her friend said. "Some people believe a soul can be reborn within the same bloodline."

"But I have no relation to the woman."

"Are ye sure? How far back can ye trace yer family tree?" she asked, emphasizing the *r*s in her Irish brogue.

"Not a thousand years. And definitely not back to the Vikings." Eve shook her head. "It's not that I could ask my uncle about it."

She hadn't seen Joe in nearly a year and a half, since before she'd moved to Portland. She'd cut ties with him and her old life to protect him, but she still felt guilty for leaving him without an explanation.

"Ye have an uncle?" Nessa met her with surprise. "Ye never mentioned him."

No one but Kjan knew. She wasn't even sure Kjartan had known; Kjan had locked away all memory of her in his head to deny his Sire access.

"Joe raised me after my parents died in a car crash. He's the only family I have… as far as I know." Her last set of grandparents had passed away years ago. Joe was her dad's sole sibling, and her mother had been an only child.

"I think anything is possible," Nessa prompted with an encouraging lilt. "It's important to know yer heritage. I have some Scottish in me myself. I was born in Ireland, but when my mum split from my dad, she took me back to Scotland with her. I didn' return to Ireland until way later. That always made me an outlander on both sides. You should ask Askja, though. She knows more about this stuff than me." She nodded at her girlfriend out on the field, standing next to Dynja on Kristján's side.

That would be a lot easier if it weren't for the current rift between her and Kjan.

Half-heartedly, Eve turned her eyes back on the game. Caleb passed the ball to Erik, but it dropped short and missed his reach by five feet as he dove for it. He landed stretched out in the dirt.

"You throw like a girl," Parker hazed Caleb from the sidelines. His head sported a fresh buzz along the temples, leaving the dense, curly hair of his fro with a little over an inch. The stubble along his jawline and his thin mustache were immaculately groomed.

Kristján's boisterous laugh hollered across the field. "Scream like one, too," he bellowed with his throaty Icelandic accent.

Then he high-fived Kjan, who snickered along with him. Eve felt a spark of joy seeing him interact with the guys. He really wasn't the outsider he thought he was.

Kría glared at the two of them with her hands at her hips. Her long braid flopped over her shoulder with dramatic motion. "Say that again."

"Present company excluded," Kristján quickly apologized, eying her sheepishly.

Nessa nudged Eve in the side. "Someone's not getting laid tonight," she whispered, and they both joined in with all the laughter.

"Screw you, Parker," Caleb yelled across the field. "Your aim isn't much better."

Erik got back to his feet and dusted himself off. He was the only one of the Icelanders whose hair wasn't one of fifty shades of blond. His spiked top and goatee were as dark as Kjan's. He was a lot shorter than Kristján and had a warm-hearted smile that Claire had taken an immediate shine to. The two of them had been inseparable since they met.

Well, almost. Nobody wanted to remember the night of the ritual at the temple. Mistakes were made; water under the bridge.

Still grinning, Kjan picked up the football and pointed toward the ridge behind the pines. "Yo, Caleb, go long."

"Oh, ha-ha, very funny." He slapped his palms on the seat of his jeans without considering the suggestion. Everyone knew about the dead drop past the tree line.

"Aye, the wee one is a hacker, not an athlete. He doesn't know his arse from his elbow."

But he isn't one to quit trying, Eve thought. Caleb always gave his best effort.

The teams broke from their huddle to set up the next play. The score was a draw. Kjan called for the hike from Kría, then launched the ball to Caleb on the outside, who made it approximately two yards before Dynja knocked the wind out of him and the ball out of his possession.

Ooh, that had to hurt. That girl was tough.

Caleb was still standing, though hunched over, hugging his stomach from the impact of her shoulder. He was heaving so hard, it looked like he was going to hack up a lung.

Erik, who was closest, dove for the fumbled ball bouncing down the center. Lucas, on Kristján's team, was supposed to cover him but vacated his position to plant himself in Kjan's path on the opposite side of the field instead.

After he'd sent the ball to Caleb, he'd made his way around the outside, where he usually had to break through the big man's block. Everyone was paired up with someone of appropriate mass: Kristján blocked Kjan, Askja matched Kría, Dynja got Caleb, and Lucas had Erik, or vice versa, depending on which team was on defense.

But since Lucas had left Erik unguarded, it was now up to Askja to stop him… or make it to the fumble first.

Neither was possible.

"Oh shit!" Emma cursed next to Nessa.

Erik scooped it up, and Askja narrowly dodged his elbow to her head as he sent the ball soaring back to Kría.

Luckily, Kristján's woman thought fast on her feet. She set off downfield, following the route Kjan was clearing for her.

Lucas charged him like a bullet train with an expression that looked more personal than sportsmanlike. Kjan didn't give a shit. He ran him through, aiming the full force of his good shoulder below Lucas' center of mass, and tossing him over his head.

Then it was on to Kristján. Kjan tackled him around the chest, throwing his entire weight at him to knock the giant off balance. They both hit the ground. Neither of the guys nor Askja were able to catch up with Kría as she ran for the end zone markers.

"What the hell, man?" Dynja shouted at Lucas. She wasn't happy about Askja nearly losing an eye because of his piss-poor call.

Or something along the lines of that. She mixed some Icelandic words with her English, and Eve had to guess the meaning from context. But the blonde Amazon wasn't wrong; he'd blown their defense.

The only response she got out of him was, "My bad."

That was when Kjan stepped up and got right in his face. Eve couldn't hear what he was saying, but she knew he was pissed; his lips were moving fast, his shoulders squared.

Lucas' words didn't travel either. He kept his voice low as Caleb joined, never shifting his eyes away from Kjan. But his mouth was definitely moving. And not in an apologetic way, judging by Kjan's reaction.

"You better check your attitude."

Lucas scoffed. "What's the big deal, so I changed things up…"

"Askja can't block him," Kjan barked. "Defenders are paired up for a reason. You should've played your fucking position."

Lucas' fingers twitched, his body slanting slightly forward.

"Whoa, dude, chill…"

"…Don't do anything stupid," Eve whispered, matching Caleb's lip movement to a T as he tried to keep things from escalating.

Too bad he hadn't been there on the roof the other night. *But then again…*

Lucas ignored his friend. He stared Kjan down as though expecting him to cave first, then took a step closer, bringing his chest level.

Caleb's eyes widened at the sheer audacity. No one challenged Kjan.

"Stand. Down," he warned. It came out like a growl, and Eve got goosebumps, though she was yards away.

"Is that an order?"

Nessa groaned. "Not this again."

Eve couldn't agree more.

"Enough!" Askja stepped in between the two hotheads, a hand to either's chest, but her eyes pinned on Lucas. "You both stop. No one got hurt. It's over."

A few more glares were exchanged, and Eve felt the tension in the crowd on the sidelines.

What a great start to the night.

CHAPTER
20

EVE

After the heat of the game had settled, everyone went back to the house. Kjan had converted the study into a billiard room to accommodate Caleb's request from the night of her birthday, and from the sounds of it, Erik was currently getting his butt kicked by Kjan.

Kristján's bellowing laughter made it all the way out to the patio, as did his friend's swearing. Eve had never heard Erik use such explicit language.

Emma stretched out on the lounger while Claire and she sat on the half-wall that surrounded the patio. Her floral perfume gave off spring vibes with her proximity. Parker's older twin was braiding blue highlights into Eve's long, brown waves. The cobalt shade matched the current color of the strands in her own dark hair.

Her hazel-green eyes cut to Eve. They weren't as luminous as Parker's *lady killers*, but their faces had the same exquisite bone structure, identical noses, and smiles. "You like it?"

"I love it." Eve fingered through the multitude of intricate braids. "Where did you learn to do this?"

"Askja taught me," she chirped with a twitch of her shoulder.

Her outgoing attitude and lightheartedness had made an instant connection with Eve the night they met. She'd been the last one standing in Kjartan's way during the ritual. Claire had defied him till the end, pleading for Eve because she'd saved Parker's life.

"I really do enjoy our"—Caleb walked up with Lucas, his hands raised—"*dinner parties*," he accentuated, adding air quotes. "They're rather unorthodox."

He dropped into one of the many wicker chairs around. His fingers drummed annoyingly on the armrests, waiting for the punchline to sink in.

"Because they're *pagan*," he blurted when nobody took the bait. "Get it?"

"*Heathen*, actually," Eve corrected.

"Too bad the menu is always the same, though. You know what it reminds me of? The Last Supper."

Everybody looked at him confused. Lucas dropped his head into his hands as though he were embarrassed to be associated with him.

Caleb always tried to lighten the mood with his jokes, but seriously, he was putting on the clown routine a little thick. Eve got the feeling he was overcompensating for failing to talk Lucas down after the game. He knew him best. Did he believe the threat of him doing something stupid wasn't over?

She took a deeper look at the young man in front of her. His hood was raised, setting his face in a shadow. A distinct hostility shot from his glare. His blue eyes were so dark they appeared black.

His mood was always difficult to place, but it usually matched his abrasive exterior. She couldn't tell what was different tonight. Everyone had been giving him a wide berth. The air around him tasted indistinctly bitter, the opposite of Caleb's sugary cotton candy nuance.

At least, there're no train tracks near here to stand on, Eve mused.

"Arggh"—Caleb let out a frustrated groan, dropping his head back—"you know what I mean… the whole 'this is my blood' and the goblin."

Goblin?

"I think you mean gob-*let*," Lucas barked. "It's called a *chalice*, dumbass. And we only did that once."

Caleb threw up his hands. "Whatever. Tomato. Potato."

Maybe he'd gotten hit in the head too hard earlier?

"Ah, perfect! Here comes our 'Lord and Savior' now."

All of them snapped around as Kjan appeared behind the glass, whiskey in hand. There was no way he hadn't heard the stupid joke, but he took no offense. Never did.

Though he seemed casual as always on the outside, Eve worried about him nonetheless. He had the habit of bottling things up until he couldn't handle anymore, and she'd started counting the days.

She remembered the way he used to laugh, scrunching his nose, eyes squeezed tightly shut. She missed the way it used to set off fireworks in her chest to see him happy. It had been brief, but Eve knew *that* Kjan was still somewhere in there.

He slid the door open and stepped outside.

On cue, Lucas jumped to his feet. He turned on his heel, taking the long route to the front door around the back through the driveway instead of brushing past him to get straight into the house.

Eve didn't want to believe his attitude toward Kjan was personal. He'd even challenged Kjartan's patience, which had already been thin. But she wondered whether there was more to the story of the train incident than Kjan had let on. The two of them couldn't even share the same space anymore.

"I got next game," Caleb shouted.

"Later." Kjan didn't take his eyes off Eve perched on the wall while he closed in on her.

"Come on, man. I bet a hundred bucks that I can beat you."

"You'd be the first. I don't want your money." He swung his leg over the narrow wall and wrapped his arms around her, hugging her snugly against his chest without spilling his drink.

"How would you know? You've never played me."

"Kid, I've been shooting pool in Vegas for a lot longer than you've been alive. You don't play in my league. Take it up with Erik."

He took a sip from his Glencairn, and Eve got a whiff of the fragrant aroma as it went by her nose. The vanilla and maple syrup nuances were the strongest next to the cocoa, but the overwhelming chocolate scent was probably his own.

It reminded her that although each one of the others carried a unique scent, even after eight months, none of them had triggered a specific affiliation. Kjan represented forbidden temptation, and Joe and the Snickerdoodles were her connection to home, but no one else's scent embodied a deep, personal relationship.

Eve leaned her head hazily back against his shoulder, reveling in the intimate comfort of his embrace, and he pressed his lips to her temple.

Why has this become so rare?

He'd taken her to a concert a few months ago. Just the two of them. And he'd hated it. Not the music, but being in a large crowd. She knew he missed their intimate moments too.

Letting out another huff, Caleb took the hint and went inside. Emma and Claire coasted after him.

Kjan pinched one of her skinny braids between his fingers and pulled it gently. "Blue?"

"It matches Claire's."

"So I see." He brushed her hair over her shoulder to the front.

"You don't like it," she assumed, a little disheartened. His comment at the club about not wanting her to be anyone other than herself still lingered in her bones.

Leaning down, he pressed another kiss to her neck, exhaling against her skin. "It's beautiful."

She caught his eyes wandering down her cleavage. The slim white gold necklace she was wearing had been his birthday gift for her. He had it specially made, just like the Viking cuff that covered the branding on her left wrist.

Eve took in his scent as he hugged her tighter. "You showered."

"I did." He laughed wickedly. His beard tickled along her skin, and his left hand slithered under her fuzzy sweater. He showed no intent to restrain himself.

Fireworks boomed in the distance, lighting up the sky. Sparkles of red and gold rained down as they crackled.

"Happy New Year." He toasted to himself and tipped the rest of the whiskey back, then set the glass aside.

Kjan didn't go for the fancy, expensive Bourbon, though he could easily afford it. Eve knew which one was his favorite. He'd shared it with her only once, by the means of a kiss, his lips even sweeter from the hints of fresh plums and cherries.

It wasn't necessarily dangerous to any of them, but due to their hypersensitivity, the effects of the alcohol hit them much harder. The craving for blood grew substantially, and low inhibitions for vampires could have a disastrous outcome.

But he was different.

And this wasn't just New Year's. It was also the day he'd emerged from the glacier as a vampire, his 're-birthday' making him 28 plus 955 years old.

Kjan's body could handle more because he was older and because they weren't created equally. He was the only one who received the immortal's blood raw and *unpolluted*. Each one of the others had been created through him as a proxy, and Eve had no Sire-bond to the God at all. She was bound to no one but Kjan.

Eve glared over her shoulder at him. "So unfair. Can you even feel it?"

"I can feel it," he assured her. "I can also feel *you*."

The pulsing effect of his low and sultry voice rippled all the way down to her bones. Her body went rigid. His hand skimmed from her stomach down between her legs, cradling her pubic bone in his palm.

Heat pooled between them. His appreciative moan in her ear sent a signal down to her thighs, making them twitch, and on a reflex, she arched back to rub herself against his touch, hips rolling on the rough stone surface.

With Kjan, there was no in-between. No gray-area. He was either ravenous or he would keep her at a distance, and Eve was never quite sure which it would be until he pounced. She didn't mind the savagery in him. It was the *dry spells* that had her worried.

Eyes closed, Eve felt his fingertip trace the delicate chain's contour from her collarbone down to the arrowhead pendant with the triangle emerald that dangled between her breasts.

"I need your sublime tits back in my mouth," he groaned into her ear.

Eve suppressed a laugh. "Aren't you frank?"

"Why beat around the bush? You already know what I want."

"We have company," she reminded him, her voice a pleading whimper.

Did she want him to stop? Or did she want him to keep going regardless?

Kjan wasn't into doing it in public places with her. Didn't like taking the chance of having someone watch them or catch a glimpse of her naked. Eve wasn't exactly quiet either. The other night in the alley had been a fluke. Like his mating bond with her had taken over his common judgment.

"We can go into the woods… get lost on the trail. There are no more tourists around. I'll even let you keep most of your clothes on."

Out in the open? His kinky proposition made her heart palpitate.

"You know I got skills. I can't get you drunk, but I can make you fly."

"Make me fly? I think *you're* drunk."

"Let me prove it," he said, suddenly sounding dead sober. He slid his fingers in between hers and pushed off the wall, pulling her to her feet.

Son of a bitch, he looked good in the two-tone raglan shirt, slate torso, long navy sleeves. It strained across his huge chest and biceps, barely containing him.

She still wasn't used to it. He had always been brawny, but he had put on so much more muscle mass while Kjartan had possessed his body. After disposing of his own 12-year-old *shell*, he'd trained with Kristján to test the limits of Kjan's strength. Eve wasn't sure they ever found them.

"What size is this? Extra small?" she joked. He was massive now, yet most of his wardrobe was still from before.

Kjan chuckled, his lips hovering over hers. "It's a large. Same it's always been."

"Speaking of large..." Eve drawled, dragging her unrestricted hand up his chest and giving his pec a firm squeeze.

The fabric stretched thin beneath her touch. She wondered if it were to give up its fight should she just nick it with her fingernail—or her canine, whichever.

She briefly considered putting the shirt out of its misery... and herself along with it.

"You like?"

"I like." Eve sucked in her bottom lip to keep from drooling.

Kjan laughed again, nearly squishing her with one arm around her ribcage. That low rumble emanating from his chest and rising up his throat never failed to send a ripple through her body. The jolt shot straight south to her lower belly, where it looped.

Willingly, Eve followed him on an excursion that, like him, knew no boundaries when it came to imagination. Apparently, tonight, she would learn how to fly.

They made it about half a mile through the forest when Eve tensed up. "I think that's far enough."

"I'm not sure," Kjan swung around to face her, flashing fully descended fangs. "They might still hear you scream."

He stepped into her, and her palms pressed to his chest when his arm snaked around her waist in a possessive hold, his right hand shifting to the back of her neck.

Eyes emitting a luminosity as if someone had switched on a light behind them, he gazed down at her. "I fucking love it when you scream." Then his fingers flexed at her nape, and his mouth crashed to hers, his kiss igniting in sparks like the pyrotechnics above.

Eve's breath hitched under his fierceness. She matched his passion, each kiss more primal than the last as he walked her backwards. His teeth bit into the tender flesh of her bottom lip, healing it with his saliva as fast as he scored it.

Her feet came to a stop once Kjan backed her against a tree.

Eve rolled her hips into him. Their tongues still entangled, she traced the contours of his chest up to his defined shoulders and gripped him tighter.

Ragged sounds of pleasure muddled between them. His right hand groped her breast, the pressure points of his fingertips releasing little jolts of electricity.

A heady shiver of desire ran through her when his hand went lower. His touch brushed over the exposed skin where her sweater had ridden up, stalling there briefly.

With more deliberate sweeps of his tongue against hers, she felt the release of the button, the gradual drag of the zipper, then the warmth and pressure of him diving in.

Eve swallowed his hoarse groan as he made contact with the dampness gathered there for him.

"Just like I want you. So wet and eager to be filled." His touch traced her seam reverently over the lacy texture of her panties before dipping underneath. "Brace yourself," he uttered in warning.

Mouth heavy on her, he silenced her cry as he slid three determined fingers home, pushing them knuckles-deep along her walls.

A gratified hum breached his kiss. "Your cunt is so fucking tight," he grated out against her lips.

Eve surrendered a whimper.

"Grind yourself against me. Ride my fingers," he said, retracting and diving back in. "Let me feel you stretch. I want you ready to take me."

Rocking her hips to meet his motion, Eve complied.

"That's it, Dove."

Wet, squelching sounds chased his thrusts while white lights popped behind her eyelids as though the fireworks show had moved into her head. It made her dizzy, but he felt so good.

Eve couldn't stop. Her hips jerked with his slick glide. Every time he retreated, a new zap of pleasure jolted over her clit to free a whimper.

The returning rumble from his throat was thick with need, coaxing her toward release. *Oh God…*

"Kjan!" Eve spasmed in his unrelenting hold, her nails digging into the thick muscles of his shoulder as she climaxed.

Pinning her to the jagged shape of the tree, he relinquished the assault on her lips, but his tenacity didn't let up.

A sinister heaviness hung in the air.

"Do you feel that?" Eve panted, finally drawing full breaths again.

The sharp points of his canines lingering at her jugular made her uneasy. Kjan didn't respond. His skin was humming again, just like it had inside the cave. He kept the electric current transmitting from his fingertips going while they pumped in and out of her, and as his arm ensnared her waist beneath her sweater, his touch raised goosebumps all over her body.

An alarming rush of cold mixed with the adrenaline in her veins. Kjartan, as the son of the God Hǫðr, had the power to draw electricity from objects through the air if a strong current presented itself around him; he had explained the ability like a black hole, and apparently his father could do much worse. He could also expel the charge from his body at will, which he had happily demonstrated by electrocuting Eve on the 4th of July. Kjan had that power too, though he insisted he couldn't control it as well.

She clung to him, the poignant sensation too intense to tolerate. Fireworks popped and whistled in her eardrums, adding to the onslaught.

"More, Dove," he rasped, his chest rising with strained breaths. "I want you drenched."

Bucking to meet his thrusts, she chased another spark of pleasure racing through her.

"Higher." His heart raced with her own while his palm forced her skyward relentlessly until she couldn't climb any further.

Arched against the tree, he nearly lifted her off the ground. "Fly for me, Dove. You're almost there. Let me hear your cry."

Tears stinging her eyes, Eve obliged, and wailing, she took the plunge.

She crashed to the bottom so hard she thought she might pass out, and maybe she did, because suddenly both of his hands were at her waist.

Kjan held her upright as vertigo hit her like a truck. Her knees buckled. She trembled all over.

"How–how did you do that?" she stammered. They were out in the middle of nowhere. There were no power lines or street lights out here. Nothing but the two of them, and yet he was charged to the tips.

His reply made her bristle. "It's you."

He unwound her arm from his neck and kissed along the inside toward her wrist, his lips prickling with the same subtle jolts. A dull haze coated his eyes. "I feel it flowing through me. You are breathtaking, Eve… exquisite… ravishing…"

His tone eerie, as if in a trance, he bit into the heel of her palm.

A drop of blood trickled down her forearm. He traced it with his tongue back to its source before wrenching her mouth to his, fingers twisted in her hair at the base of her skull.

"Kjan, wait." She broke free, blinking through the fog in her brain. She was still shaken by the experience and needed a minute to process. "Please," she begged, bringing her hands up between them.

With the tree harsh against her back, Eve found herself literally stuck between a rock and a hard place. It was too much. The taste of her own blood was suddenly freaking her out. Her hair stood on edge. Her instincts warned her of a threat.

Kjan let out an angry growl as she pushed at him but didn't back off. Her heartbeat doubled, then tripled, when the growl came back deeper… and louder.

Much louder.

"WOLF!" Eve thrashed violently, her eyes falling on the enormous, wild animal over Kjan's shoulder.

Her voice finally got through to him. He whipped around, shielding her with his body.

"It's huge," she mouthed, cowering behind him.

There was a long silence before Kjan responded. "It's not a wolf," he said hesitantly. "It's a shifter."

"As in *shapeshifter*?" Eve gripped the back of his shirt, her fists so tight her nails dug into her skin through the cotton fabric.

Kjan kept his eyes on the animal glowering down at them. It was as tall as a horse. "Do you remember the raven on the patio at the penthouse back in summer?"

"Yeah."

"I think it's the same one."

"WHAT!" *First vampires, then Norse Gods, and now there are shapeshifters?* "You mean you knew that it was a shifter then, and you didn't tell me?"

"I didn't want to worry you," he bit back, teeth clenched.

Eve threw her palms up, flashing jazz hands. "Well, I'm worried now."

The wolf—shifter—thing—*whatever*—gnashed his giant fangs as if it didn't value her snarky tone. Its eyes narrowed into slits, and if she didn't know any better, she would've guessed it was trying to communicate.

"Is it talking to you?"

"Not to me." Kjan glanced back over his shoulder, the bright green in his irises locking on to her. "To *him*."

Eve's mouth felt dry, and she tried to swallow, but the cotton ball in her throat went nowhere.

"What does it want?" Her voice came out hoarse as she choked on the question.

"I don't know. All I get is an emotional grid. No words." Kjan paused like he was reading the air. "He's… angry."

"Get in line," she scoffed, muttering under her breath. Who didn't have beef with the *HIM* Kjan was referring to? His Sire probably had a long list of enemies.

Kjan reached back to take her hand but trained his eyes on the beast. "I need you to do something for me, Dove. Whatever happens, don't let go."

Huh? Eve was confused. "Why would I—"

The clearing flashed in bright blue light, illuminating the branches of the trees upward into their crowns. His fingers closed tighter around her hand, crushing it in his grip as the corner of his mouth raised into a wide grin.

No, it can't be…

Kjan would never…

Eve's vision blurred. Something pulled at her. Her limbs tingled as if they had fallen asleep, making her body go numb and cold. She struggled to stay on her feet, fatigue suddenly overwhelming her.

The last thing she saw was the wolf stumbling backward, then everything went black and her body hit the ground.

CHAPTER

21

KJARTAN

'*WHAT DID YOU DO?*'

"Relax, she's unharmed… just taking a little nap," he assured his host. "I needed a boost, and she was the only available source. She will be fine. Now, hush."

Kjartan regarded the lupine creature as it snarled at him, exposing a row of razor-sharp fangs, each one longer than his fingers.

The wolf's paws rivaled the size of its head, and its nostrils flared when catching the change in his scent. Ears perked in his direction, nothing escaped its eyes. They burned with a deep orange glow, like fiery orbs of amber.

"Here I am." He spread his arms wide as he spoke. "What is it that you want from me?"

A faint green mist rose at the wolf's feet, twirling around its legs like miniature cyclones and twisting its form. The long fur whipped in the winds until the cloud engulfed the beast's entire shape.

Its head was the last thing to vanish within the veil, leaving nothing but the bright orange eyes behind, and when the mist cleared, a handsome young man stood in its place. The fact that he was fully clothed made one thing clear: he wasn't just a shapeshifter, he possessed magic.

The hem of his open wool coat flapped around his knees as he moved. He was dressed like an emo-punk, black from head to toe—black turtleneck sweater, black jeans, black motorcycle boots with buckles along the sides, and black leather driving gloves—revealing only his fingers and face. He appeared no older than eighteen.

The only color in his getup came from the bright copper-red streaks in his hair, which was otherwise as dark as the rest of him. Long black waves fell down his back like the tail feathers of a raven, but the sides of his head were braided, creating a sort of fauxhawk. He was taller than Kristján, though rather scrawny in comparison.

Kjartan raised his voice, annoyed at the stranger. "Why put on this charade?"

"I do not converse with humans. I consider them beneath me," he said in Old Norse.

He spoke with superior eloquence despite his juvenile look, and he clearly understood English, yet Kjartan chose to humor him, switching the language. "Then I assume you have not met many of them."

In the two hundred years since his escape from the mountain, Kjartan had enough experience with them; bad and good. He had seen the power of love and friendship that these mere mortals were capable of. No God had ever shown him the same courtesy. Not even his own blood. Despite their flaws, he had grown to respect and eventually care for the species.

"And I think you have been around them too much." His tone was crude and irreverent, spewing arrogance while he sauntered closer. "It has clouded your judgment. Look at you… possessing a human… and even falling in love with one. It rolls off you like a stench," he added, wrinkling his nose.

His boots stopped only three feet in front of him. He had to be 6'10". Kjartan felt the power emanating from the boy. It tingled on his skin. He had never seen magic beyond his own. And never laid eyes on anyone besides his mother who wasn't from this realm. The kid was clearly no ordinary shapeshifter. From what he had been taught, they usually had only one animal form they could change into. Was he a God too, like himself?

"Who are you?"

The stranger raised his chin like he wasn't already tall enough. "They call me Hrafni," he declared proudly.

Kjartan frowned. "The Raven?" *So obvious.*

"The very same. But you can call me Raf."

"Let me guess," Kjartan cut in, directing his focus away from the array of piercings along his ears. He noticed that the tips weren't pointed, so the kid wasn't Álfar. "Because of the color of your eyes?"

Raf was the Icelandic word for amber. It was still one of the closest related languages to the one that was spoken by the Old Gods of Ásgarðr.

The boy flashed a sly grin, the light in his irises alive with a raging flame. "I was born during the Great War," the shifter went on. "In Níflheimr."

"Born?" Kjartan felt dumbfounded. Níflheimr, he remembered, was the world of fog and ice. It belonged to the kingdom of Hel, daughter and last living offspring of Loki; *living*, of course, being a relative term. The Queen of the Dead presided over the fallen. The rest of her siblings had been slain during the aforementioned war.

Yes, Kjartan had caught up on history after his escape. The events of Ragnarǫk had come into full swing right around the time his curse had set in.

"Nobody is *born* in Níflheimr," he argued. "It is the realm of the dishonored dead, occupied only by the ones who died in their sleep, of illness, or as cowards."

"After my father's death, my mother fled Ásgarðr and hid herself away with the help of my sister. Well, half-sister." He shrugged offhandedly.

Kjartan felt a stab in his gut, timid to ask his next question. "Who was your father?"

"Can you not guess it?"

A ripple passed over him like the surface of water when touched, and the boy's appearance changed. The copper in his hair spread across his head, erasing any trace of black, and his face grew more defined with age.

Kjartan forced himself to blink. In front of him stood a man he had only heard of, and yet he knew who he was. The resemblance to the boy was uncanny: same height, same build, same eyes, but his hair was a fiery mane instead of black.

He was Loki.

"That… that is impossible." A tremble of fear snaked up his spine. Kjartan shrank back without taking his eyes off him as the illusion came toward him. "All of Loki's sons are dead." The 8-legged stallion he birthed himself, the serpent, the wolf, and even Narfi, the only mannish one, not born unto the giantess Angrboða but to Loki's official consort. An Æsir Goddess.

He shook out his hair with a swivel of his head, and the ripple passed over him a second time. Hrafni changed back to his own adolescent form, with the same perfectly straight nose and high cheekbones. "I am the last of them."

The Great War had lasted, give or take, 500 years. Kjartan had been born six months after his father's execution and the death of Baldr, which had signaled the beginning of Ragnarǫk. Loki had freed himself from his binds toward the final days, so Raf must have been born approximately nine months later, assuming the term of a divine pregnancy was equivalent to a mortal. His own mother had never specified.

The pieces fell together at last. "Then your mother is Sigyn, the Goddess of—"

"The Goddess of Victory," he finished for him. "Unlike my late brothers, I possess magic of my own and prefer to walk in the footsteps of my father." His hands gesticulated as he spoke. "Creating chaos wherever I go."

"Is that why you are here? To play games?" Kjartan spat in anger. The trickster had endangered Eve in Iceland and threatened her again right here. He wouldn't tolerate that.

"No. I am here to collect a debt," he replied through his teeth. "From *you*."

Kjartan recoiled. "A debt from me? I do not recall making a bargain with you."

"Did you ever wonder how you made it out of the cave? It was my mother. Sigyn lifted the spell that bound you. She used her abilities to ward off the magical incantation that confined you and let you escape."

"Then I guess I should be thanking her," he snorted. "Where is she?"

Hrafni's jaw clenched, as did his fists. "She is dead. The spell took too much out of her."

Kjartan's throat burned with remorse. All these years, he had never known her sacrifice for him—a stranger. "I am sorry for your loss—"

"She gave her life to free you." The fire in the boy's eyes flared. "YOU OWE ME!"

How could it be his fault? He shook his head in protest. "I did not ask her for that."

But he *had* prayed for help... to anyone who might have answered his plea. Did that make him in a way responsible?

"Be that as it may," Raf continued, regaining his composure. "I am appealing to your honor. I begged her to do it because I thought we might have something in common."

"And what is that?"

"Our hate for the Gods," he sneered. "I seek retribution. Vengeance for what they did to my brother. My father has made many mistakes and suffered the consequences, but my brother Narfi was innocent. As were you. And my mother agreed..."

He looked distraught as he hung his head. "The Gods made her watch as they turned the wretched Oðinsson, Váli, into a wolf to tear him apart. Then they used his intestines to tie our father to the boulders...

"No mother should have to suffer through that..." his voice trailed off again. "In spite of all her loss and despair, she never lost her gentleness. Or her pride. She claimed victory over every challenge that was thrown at her."

Lastly, he fell silent, but his words still resonated in Kjartan's chest. He felt the boy's pain; he empathized…

…just like Kjan had empathized with *him*. Did that mean they had the same goal? Did they want the same things? He had once retaliated to get the Gods' attention and failed. Because he had been alone. But now… now there were two of them. And they both had powers of their own.

"It was *your* magic I sensed in Iceland," Kjartan acknowledged. And not only on Christmas Eve, but last year too. Raf had been one of the two presences he had encountered in the church's square.

A flash of contempt twitched the boy's lips. "I have tried to reveal myself to you before, but my attempts were impeded."

Kjartan assumed by the other one. Had he been in the plains as well?

"How did you manage the distance in such a short time?" He had gone from Iceland back to the States within days. Kjartan couldn't picture the punk on public transportation. He would consider that beneath him too.

"There are portals all over your precious little realm if you know where to look and how to use them." Rubbing his finger and thumb together, he produced a green flame that flickered wildly, although there was no wind. "It makes traveling much easier."

So no flying on a plane? Convenient!

"But why wait until now? You could have come to me when I was freed. Why did you wait?" For 140 years, he had roamed to hunt down the ones he had sired to regain his strength.

"I needed time," the boy divulged. "Losing her… I-I did not anticipate that. It broke me. When I caught up with you, you had your own plan in motion, and I was curious to see how it played out." He shrugged. "Too bad it did not. I was rooting for you."

After silence stretched out between them, the kid expelled a forceful breath, as though he was done reveling in unhappy memories and ready to move on. "I need your help. Merge your powers with mine. I cannot draw magic out of thin air like you. I can only draw on myself. And I need time to recharge. I cannot do this alone."

Kjartan took a wild guess at where his request was headed. "Your plan is to wage war against the remaining Gods in Ásgarðr? The ones responsible for your brother's fate are long gone," he reminded him.

"I do not care. I want them dead." Raf's eyes burned into him. "Every last one of them."

"I cannot help you." He shook his head vehemently in response. He had too much to lose.

"I thought you of all people would understand." He cocked his head, reviewing Kjartan with curiosity. "All this time free, and yet you never learned of your mother's fate?"

Kjartan stiffened, invisible hands squeezing around his throat. "What do you know of her?"

"That she is dead," he said with indifference. "I guess we have that in common too."

The words sucked the air out of Kjartan's lungs. He should have anticipated it, but knowing the inevitable truth struck differently. He had clung to ignorance instead.

His mouth vocalized the question, but the sound didn't reach his ears. It was no louder than his breath. "How?"

"She took her own life. Threw herself off a cliff. Perhaps she could no longer deal with the guilt of condemning you," he replied heedlessly.

Kjartan felt the noose tighten around his neck. The Goddess of Eternal Youth, Guardian of Immortality, *dead?* It was unfathomable. Despite all the evidence, he had always hoped to see her again one day.

He wondered what else he lacked knowledge of. He hadn't been able to find much on the Gods post-Ragnarǫk; the survivors seemed to have retreated and then become forgotten. But if Hrafni was here now, that meant the branches of Yggdrasill were still active.

Óðinn, the Alfaðir, had been in charge of the Mighty Yew before the Great War. Who was in control now?

Could it possibly be his father? Everything he knew about his own lineage would suggest that Hǫðr had taken up the mantle. He was associated with Eihwaz, the representation of Yggdrasill after all.

Something tightened around his chest. *My own father, one of the most powerful Gods left in Ásgarðr …*

Kjartan wasn't sure how he felt about that. He hastily brushed the thought of his father aside. Ásgarðr was no more home to him than Portland.

Frustrated at his persisting indecisiveness, Raf narrowed his eyes. "I am not going to sit back and watch you get cozy with your new family. *I* am your kin. You have nothing in common with these pests, sucking blood to survive like fleas." He stabbed his finger into Kjartan's chest. "You are better than them. *We* are better than them."

His orange eyes reflected no warmth, and his tone was bitter cold, the words shooting out of his mouth like shards of ice. He was resentment personified. "You should take some time to think on it. I will be in touch."

Hrafni stepped back as the green mist enveloped him again. From the fog, a pair of wings spread out, and a large raven took flight, aiming straight for the skies. A single copper feather still shimmered at its tail before it disappeared from view.

Creating the mirage of Loki had seemed like child's play, but shifting into the shape of an animal required powerful magic. The boy was not to be underestimated. Who knew what other tricks he had up his sleeve?

Kjartan kept his gaze on the black sky for a little longer, enjoying his moment of freedom, then he turned back to Eve, still unconscious at the foot of the tree.

"Out here in the forest? How could you?" He kneeled down beside her, picking twigs and leaves from her hair.

He could feel Kjan raging beneath his skin. *'Don't you fucking touch her,'* he sneered.

"She is too precious. She deserves better."

The second his hand brushed over her cheek, he was forced back into his prison, but it had been worth it just to feel her— an invaluable experience he would never again take for granted.

CHAPTER

22

KJAN

"**E**ve!"

Her eyes flew open. But the second they landed on him, she scurried back against the trunk, kicking up dirt with her heels.

"It's me," he assured her.

When he reached out, she swatted at his hand. "I know! Your eyes are green again."

Her response hit like a slap in the face. *She doesn't want ME touching her?*

Kjan swallowed his hurt at her rejection. "Are you okay?" He couldn't see any physical injuries.

"No, I'm not *okay*." She jumped to her feet, straightening her clothes with a scowl.

Right. Her jeans were still unzipped.

"Why would you do that? Why did you let him take over?"

Kjan stood too. The warm spice of her anger burned in the back of his throat, sharp and bitter like ginger. He forced his reply past the distinct taste on his tongue. "We needed him."

She balled one fist and took a step toward him, raising a wagging finger to his face. "You left me alone with him."

"I had it under control," he stressed to settle her outrage. "Your safety is one thing we both strongly agree on."

"Are you serious? Do you really believe the genie is just going to hop back into his bottle now that you let him out? Have you forgotten that he tried to kill you and almost strangled me?" Eve glowered, pointing at herself. "Because I remember his hands around my neck the last time I saw him."

Kjan sighed in defeat. "I had no choice. I couldn't protect you."

"You didn't *try*!"

When she walked away, he grabbed her arm to swing her back around, but she immediately ripped herself free with an expression that screamed *'don't touch me again'*.

"What was I supposed to do?" he asked without raising his voice at her. "The Raven has magic, Eve. *Actual* magic, not cute tricks like me. We needed to know what he wants, and he wasn't going to talk to *me*. He was going to attack if I didn't yield."

She crossed her arms over her chest. "So, what does he want?"

"His name is Hrafni."

"Hrafni?" she repeated after him with the silent *H* and the *b*-sound in the middle, giving the pronunciation a try.

"It means raven in Icelandic," he elaborated.

Then Kjan took a deep breath and recited everything from the beginning, all the details about who the shifter was, how he had aided his Sire in escaping the cave, and what he demanded in return.

Eve listened until he was finished, then, without another word, swung around and stormed off toward the house.

Reluctantly, he trudged after her.

The lights in the living room began to flicker before Kjan made it inside. He slid the glass door shut, hard, then instantly regretted it. He didn't want to break the pane in his frustration.

Lucas' mouth opened when their eyes met, but Kjan shot him a not-fucking-now-look, and he quickly closed it again, retreating into the study.

Smart choice, kid. This was not the time. Sparks of electricity prickled at his fingertips. The party was officially over.

"We were wondering where you guys went," Erik said from the loveseat. "You have been gone a long time."

He sat sprawled with Claire in his lap, fingers twirling a lock of her hair. Assessing the vibe Kjan was giving, his expression abruptly shifted to alarm.

"Everybody out," he roared as they all stared from Eve back to him, catching the same drift of tension.

She had made it halfway up the stairs when the crash of breaking glass from the study swung the room's attention around to the archway.

Everybody watched Caleb stumble into the living room, coughing violently while choking on his own blood.

The sound of a scream reached Kjan's ears, probably Emma's, as the boy fell forward on all fours to hack up more of the bright red fluid. His girl was the first one to rush to him, then more bodies shuffled around them, watching helplessly in horror.

Kjan folded his arms over his chest and hung back. He was determined to make this a teaching moment. A year ago, Eve passed out after taking a shot of Patrón. She had managed to keep it down without it tearing up her insides. It appeared that Caleb wasn't as lucky. He had gotten into his whiskey stash.

"Can't handle your liquor?" Boots planted firmly on the hardwood, he glared down at the choking kid.

His body would heal on its own, but not before a great deal of suffering. Kjan had no intention of stepping in. It was a dick move, and he knew it.

Emma's mouth fell open. Kneeling by his side, she ripped at Caleb's shoulder. "Why would you do that to yourself? You damn well know the risk."

The boy couldn't reply, so Kjan took the liberty to do it for him. "He wouldn't. Not without a good reason." He scanned the crowd for a particular missing face.

He saw Eve's eyes cut to him in his periphery, as though she blamed him for leaving the liquor out so the baby could get into it. "Do something," she urged, frustrated with his lack of action.

Caleb's muscles seized and relaxed in rapid intervals, sending his body into convulsions while the poison of the alcohol worked its way through his system. Kjan's blood would give him the little push he needed to jump-start the cell regeneration and hurry things along.

Expelling an exasperated huff, he rolled his eyes and reached into his back pocket for his switchblade. The double-edge popped free at the flick of his thumb, and he went around the heaving kid.

Kjan gripped the top of his shaggy hair and flung him backward, splaying him out on the floor. His dull brown eyes rolled up into his head, showing only white. His body kept twitching.

Switching the knife into his non-dominant hand, Kjan straddled Caleb's hips to stabilize his flailing limbs. With indifference to the pain, he closed his right fist around the steel and ripped it across in a smooth motion. It slashed his skin without resistance; he had just sharpened it yesterday. The sensation left him utterly cold. It was a paper cut compared to what he had been through.

Kjan slammed his bleeding palm down on Caleb's mouth. Fingers clenched around his jaw, he pinned his head, leaving barely enough room below his nose to breathe.

Eve stared wide-eyed. Emma's hands were clasped over her mouth.

Seconds crawled by.

Eventually, the convulsions stopped, and Caleb's body stilled.

The golden bursts in his eyes focused on Kjan. He removed his palm, and the kid let out a hoarse groan. "Thank you, Jesus. I thought I was a goner."

Kjan wiped the blade on his jeans and flipped it shut. "Take him home," he told Emma, giving the girl a quick glance.

Then he pushed off and faced Eve. "Happy?" he snipped at her in the same cynical tone she had fed him outside. He wasn't going to hide the fact that he had only done it for her sake.

But, of course, she wasn't. She was still fuming. Her lips twitched, biting back a retort as she spun on her heel and stormed off again.

The door at the top of the stairs slammed shut, making the peanut gallery shift awkwardly around him. The spicy kick of her rage had turned acidic from despair, but he could still filter out her unique scent underneath. She was crying.

"Get gone!" he gnashed.

He ignored the confused looks of his mute audience and chased the trail of spring rain upstairs.

Eve sat on the bed with her legs crossed and didn't look up when he entered. He closed the door quietly, sagging to the floor in front of it.

"Why did I pass out?"

His head shot up at the sound of her little voice. She didn't meet his eyes, watching her hands in her lap instead. Her tears had dried up.

"He can draw power from any kind of life force, not just electricity. He feeds off energy instead of blood." Kjan swallowed uncomfortably. "*Your* energy."

"He used me as fuel?"

"Yes," he exhaled slowly.

Eve winced, her face darkening. "And you said Kjartan turned the Raven down?"

"He did. But I don't think it's going to be that easy. Hrafni seemed pretty adamant about the life debt he's owed."

"We should warn the others."

"I'll tell Kristján to lie low."

Everyone should avoid Mount Hood until they took care of this problem. The shifter's business wasn't with them, but they could become collateral damage, and she would probably blame him for that, too.

Eve nodded her head silently.

Sitting on opposite sides of their bedroom, neither of them spoke again.

'I panicked. I never meant to harm her. She needs to know that. You have to tell her.'

He was referring to strangling Eve at the temple after she had chosen suicide over becoming his plaything. Kjan gave him a cold laugh. "You would like that, wouldn't you? Fat chance."

'Your touch can give her comfort. Why do you withhold it?'

"You know why," he snarled back.

'You could make it go away… I would.'

"Shut up." He clutched his head between his hands, his body trembling to keep it together. "Stop. Talking."

CHAPTER

23

KJAN

He gave up on trying to overturn her standpoint on his judgment. Before suffocating in the enclosed space with her, he trotted into the study to inspect the casualty. He was momentarily confused by what he was looking at. All the glass was clustered by the far wall across the room, as if someone had flung it intentionally.

Son of a…

His eyes found the label of the bottle among the shards—*The Van Winkle.*

The kid had taste. But why couldn't he have picked the half empty? Kjan had paid almost ten grand for the set; $3500 for the 15-year and $6000 for the 23-year that was now soaking into the rug.

He got down on his haunches, crouching in front of the remains, when he sensed the presence stepping into the doorframe behind him.

"Of course…" Kjan muttered without getting up or even turning to address him. "He took it from you and drank it in your stead, didn't he?"

At Lucas' silence, he continued, "He wanted you to see exactly what would happen."

"He just started chugging it." The boy raised his voice in defense; it carried no air of guilt.

Kjan groaned inward. The word *chugging* in context with the Van Winkle pulled at his heart strings.

"I knocked it out of his hand to get him to stop," he went on, washing his hands clean of any responsibility. "I didn't think he would really *do* it."

Hence the bottle hitting the wall. Kjan had already gathered as much regarding the scene.

"That should have been you out there on the floor, drowning in your own blood." Lifting one of the shards, he closed his hand around it. "You put the people around you in harm's way, and they're stupid for trusting you with their lives."

Kjan wasn't sure if that last part was directed at the kid or himself, but Lucas took the bait. "You still blame me, don't you?" Deep contempt spewed from his mouth with the accusation.

"Of course I blame you." Kjan pushed off his knees and rose to full height to face him. It was fitting that the sociopathic bastard was wearing black jeans and a solid black hoodie to match his soul. "You're the one who held her down—"

"And you're the one who branded her!" he shouted to his face.

A dead silence fell over the room. Neither one of them moved as they glared at each other. Kjan clenched his fist, the glass cutting into his skin. He focused on the pain instead of punching the mouthy little shit in the teeth.

Yes, it had been his own hands doing the deed, and if self-mutilation made any difference, he would have chopped them off for hurting her. But unlike him, the rest of the coven had been fully aware and in command of their limbs. He would always hold them accountable for their actions.

Jaw tense in defiance, Lucas' throat bobbed as he swallowed. Then the hard lines in his features relaxed. Kjan thought he saw an inkling of shame flicker across his eyes before they cut away from him to break contact first.

The boy clutched the front of his sweatshirt to needlessly readjust its fit. He seemed nervous all of a sudden.

Perhaps he's capable of remorse after all.

His molars unlocked and his mouth opened. "I apologized, you know?" he said with the slightest quiver in his voice. "Even let her hit me."

WHAT!

Lucas couldn't see the mix of utter shock and rage streaking across Kjan's face as he rambled on, "She doesn't blame me."

"I'm sure she doesn't," Kjan bit back. "She's a bigger person than I am. I don't forgive so easily." A bit of an understatement. He could hold a grudge for 955 years, no sweat. "Now get out of my house."

Kjan turned toward the fully-stocked bar. He chucked the piece of glass into the sink and reached for the Four Roses Single Barrel.

"I have a daughter," Lucas mumbled under his breath.

Kjan's hand caught around the bottle's neck. His Sire had taken the vein of every single one of his acolytes. Their blood had revealed their strengths and their weaknesses to him—any memory he chose within his reach. Kjan considered it an invasion of privacy, but he had done the same to Charlotte, his former *acquaintance*, to gain leverage on her.

Kjan rubbed his tongue across the back of his teeth, weighing the unlikely probability while assessing him warily from the corner of his eye.

He twisted the cap of the bottle with hesitation, All his Sire's memories were accessible to him. They shared one mind. "How did I not know that?"

With a shrug, he stuffed his hands into his pockets. "There are no memories of her in my head; I had never seen her. Things didn't exactly go well with her mom," he babbled without a filter. It was completely unlike him.

"But I ran into them a couple of months ago. She's seven now. I-I saw her and… it just hit me. I will have to watch her grow old and die. That's not right," he choked on that last part. "I don't know how to deal with that."

"The fuck you're telling *me* for?" Kjan raised the Bourbon to his mouth and leaned back with his elbow on the bar top, crossing his right ankle over the other. He considered himself the last person the kid would want to open up to. Why not Caleb? Or Kristján?

"I have to tell someone. I have no one else to talk to about this." Lucas lowered his eyes and rubbed a hand across the back of his neck. His hood was down now, as though he wanted to appear more sociable.

Kjan observed him struggling to find the courage to talk. Sharing made you vulnerable. He knew the feeling.

On a deep sigh, the boy's gaze lifted back to him. "You've had people you cared about. Watched them die. How do you do it? How do you deal with it?"

Taking another sip, Kjan let the liquor run down the back of his throat slowly, the smooth burn plugging the little cracks beneath the surface to form a new layer of scar tissue. "I don't! I bury it."

"And how's that working out for ya?" Lucas asked sarcastically.

Touché.

Lips parted, Kjan cocked his chin at an angle and chuffed. "Not well."

Point taken. He tipped the bottle in a feigned toast before bringing it back up to his lips a third time.

Straight from the bottle, instead of a funnel-shaped glass, the aroma was subtle, even for him. His nose only caught on to vanilla and freshly picked flowers because it was exactly the nuance he was looking for.

The immediate blast of flavor came with the spicy heat of rye, chased by the sweetness of honey, brown sugar, and a mix of fruit. He let the deliciously sweet hues and flavors make love to his senses, but they served as a poor replacement for the real thing when he couldn't have Eve. Even with the Bourbon's long finish that kept going and going… just like his insatiable little dove.

"Tell me something," Kjan prompted. "That man you butchered… did he deserve it?"

He just needed to know. Other than himself, Lucas was the only one who had ever ended someone's life, but the murder he had committed as a teenager was also a blank area. At least the motive was. Had there been one? How could he trust him?

Lucas smiled boldly. "Every bit."

It was a pun on dismembering his victim before slicing his throat. He had removed his hands first, then moved on to the genitals. It appeared personal, but my Sire never found a reason in the boy's memory. He had buried it deep. No one would ever get it out of him.

Lucas' expression turned pensive, and more mumbling followed. "I did something stupid."

Stupid, as in coldblooded murder, or…

Kjan felt his throat constrict—and not from the burn of the fine whiskey. He squeezed his eyes shut, dreading the boy's confession.

For fuck's sake, please don't tell me you tried to turn your kid.

Attempting to sire another while still a fledgling could be fatal on both sides. Even if she was just a small child. None of them were strong enough yet. And then there was the fact that SHE WAS A FREAKING CHILD!

"I bit Bayley," Lucas said.

Kjan's muscles sagged, and a breath of relief exploded out of him.

"I don't know why I did it. I didn't need to feed. I just… had this urge to bite her."

The boy marked her! He hadn't seen the plot twist coming. "Did she bite you too?"

"No," he replied quietly, sounding disappointed. "I wanted her to, though. I've offered her my vein before. But she turned me down."

Rejection's a bitch. No wonder he had been so irritable lately.

"She said she doesn't want me to think that my blood is the reason she's with me."

Bayley had always clearly disassociated herself from the asshole Jordan, who had tried to use Eve for that exact reason. A lot of vampires had heard the rumors of the Ancient One's powerful blood.

"She's been taking care of herself for a long time. She doesn't want to depend on anyone," Lucas elaborated on her stance.

"If that's true, then she's a good woman." Kjan's arm raised of its own volition as if in another toast.

Is that four? Or five? The whiskey was over halfway gone and seriously starting to kick in. His vision was swimming.

If he was lucky, he could get ten minutes of a decent haze to sedate his senses. If he slowed down and stretched the bottle, perhaps twenty. And if he mixed it with the smoke of a good cigar, he could get downright catatonic for a few blissful minutes. The fusion with the tobacco deepened the individual nuances in both while doubling the narcotic effect on his hypersensitive receptors. Unfortunately, never for long.

From what he could make out in the blur of Lucas' face, the kid didn't seem too thrilled about the response he got.

"Look!" Kjan started. He needed to get him out of the house. He wanted to be alone. "I'm not the right person to give you advice. You should talk to someone else. Probably Bayley, for one." She was older. She knew more than the rest of the coven.

"Or maybe a shrink. What do *I* know?" He twisted his mouth into a shrewd grimace. He didn't feel like sharing personal details. Not tonight. Not ever.

"You know, you're a real dick when you're drunk." The dark shape of Lucas' body turned toward the door and shrank in his periphery.

"Joke's on you, kid," Kjan muttered into the mouth of the bottle in his hand. "I'm always a dick."

CHAPTER

24

KJARTAN

After his binge, Kjan had fallen asleep in the study. His body was stretched out on the leather sofa along the wall by the windows. Kjartan could see the daylight peeking through a slim crack between the heavy black curtains.

"I know what you are thinking," the disembodied voice addressed him from the darkness.

"How could you possibly know?"

He identified the voice even though he had never heard it before, nor met the man—God—it belonged to. His debut now felt underwhelming.

"It is true, then… everything he told me?" His mother really had taken her own life to escape her shame.

"I beg of you, do not consider the alliance with the Raven," his father pleaded. "You have sworn an oath not to interfere. If you reclaim the vessel without the host's approval, you will be punished. I cannot help you."

"You have never helped me." Commanding Kjan's body in the man's dormant state, he tucked one arm behind his head, staring up at the ceiling to spurn the intruder.

In his periphery, a shape took form among the shadows, casually leaning his shoulder against the bookshelf.

I shift my sight toward it. His father's hair was the same shade of black his own had originally been, but longer, curling outward below the ears. His face was that of a man in his mid-thirties, barely older than Kjan. It was pale and stoic, like carved from marble. It pained Kjartan to think that he might have looked just like him had it not been for his curse.

Most striking were his father's eyes. A light shade of seafoam green in color, they seemed to stare right into his soul. It was hard to believe the God was blind.

"I am sorry. Truly." Although sincere, his tone made no impact. "By the time Baldr and I returned from Hel, we were focused on rebuilding our city… starting fresh—"

"And I did not fit into your pretty picture?" Kjartan interrupted, shifting on the sofa to angle his upper body more toward the dark figure across the room.

His father hung his head. "Too much time had passed…"

"You mean, I was already too broken to be fixed. You gave up on me." He raised his voice in accusation. "You abandoned me too!"

The thought rang on in his head, 'one of the most powerful God's', yet his own son was left to fend for himself in this wretched existence. "Am I still worth nothing?"

His father didn't wince. Didn't bristle at the personal attack. The rise of his chest with his breath remained flat. "You are right. I have failed you."

Cloaked in the shadows of the study, Hǫðr showed no visible reaction. Nor did he answer that last question. But he didn't deny the allegation, and that was enough of an answer for Kjartan.

"You never felt responsible," he argued. "And while we are on the subject of my unjust punishment…" Uncrossing his ankles, he sat up straight, propping one elbow on his raised knee. "Where is *she*? I do believe I deserve an apology from her as well." That shouldn't be too much to ask. It had been *her* magic cursing him after all.

Kjartan narrowed his eyes while he waited for a reply and felt a tear roll down his cheek. He was so angry he wanted to scream. So why the tears? He wasn't sad.

"She is not coming," Hǫðr said, sounding regretful.

"I am not surprised." No need to waste any more breath appealing to their guilt. They didn't feel the same way about family. Blood meant nothing.

Tapping the tip of his index finger to his thumb, he stared off at the pool table to the side. He didn't want to look at his father, even if he couldn't tell the difference.

"She has a plan," the blind God insisted with an air of encouragement.

Kjartan's lips twitched with ire. "I am sure she does." He swung his gaze back to the shape by the bookshelf. "That is why you are here. Frigg sent you to make sure I do not side with Loki's son. Are you afraid he might succeed?"

"Of course not."

"Not afraid? Or not sent by her?" Kjartan sneered at his impassive stare.

This father exhaled a long breath. "Neither. I swear, she did not send me. But she is probably aware that I came. Mother knows everything."

Was that an eye roll? Kjartan thought he had caught a touch of resentment in the way he used the word *mother*.

He suddenly had the strong sense that even the mighty God of Darkness was still very much under the command of a higher authority. Could it be that he was not free to do as he pleased? Whom did he have to answer to?

Right on cue, his father's body straightened as if someone had called his name, and his gaze darted to the ceiling. His eyes, though useless, seemed fully alert. His jaw was tense.

"I have to go," he murmured more to himself than to Kjartan, and with a soundless poof, the contours of his shape dissolved to merge with the shadows.

CHAPTER 25

HRAFN

They called him a *vargr* in his mother tongue. The term for a thief. An outlaw. Someone evil.

They were not wrong.

Raf was all that, and more. With magic in his veins and skills beyond measure at his literal fingertips, he was a force to be reckoned with. They could no longer deny it. The Gods had powers too, but did they share his dedication? His deep-seeded thirst for vengeance?

Even they feared him. Why else would Frigg order her lapdog to track his moves?

"He will be the first to fall." Standing alone in the unlit backroom of the tattoo shop, Raf curled his fingers toward his palm to summon the precious weapon.

Bright green ribbons mixed with black. He watched as smoke whorled above his hand to form the long, dark shape of a blade—a 10-inch cyclone dagger. Bit by bit, it became corporeal as though he was pulling the shadows from the room together.

Of course, the weapon had always been in his possession, hidden by magic, but never far from reach. He merely had to focus his mind to manifest it.

The weight settled against his palm. Despite being formed out of thin air, he knew the edge was sharp.

But would it be enough?

His muscles steeled when a shiver rippled over his skin, and nonexistent claws tore through his flesh. Raf wrapped a fist around the dagger and clenched his teeth to brace the serrating pain that followed the shift of his tattoos.

The black markings that covered every inch of his upper body—front and back, from his neck to his wrists and down to his groin—had a mind of their own since he was a child, rearranging themselves on a whim whenever he took the shape of a man.

The one on his chest was the only one that never shifted from its location above his heart:

Skuldina—the debt.

Although not his to settle, the debt remained his destiny, his one constant, his only desire.

After an agonizing moment, the pain subsided, and the voices from the shop's front tuned back into his ears: the melodious drawl of a female and one other. A large male.

Raf had gained entry through the vents by momentarily shedding his bipedal form. The ferret was his favorite after the raven, perfect for making a quick escape and staying hidden. He could squeeze into the smallest spaces much like a mouse.

Or rat.

The chime above the door went off, followed by the arrival of a third mortal. Another male but not as burly.

"Hey, Torres. Is she here?"

Raf recognized the abrasive tone, although it was laced with desperation tonight. He had tracked the interesting boy to this shop once before. That was how he had found out about the establishment's peculiar owner.

"Maybe," he drawled in a deep timber.

"Please, I need to talk to her."

"It's alright, Angel. You can let him in," the female interjected.

"Your call." Scuffing sounds carried across the floor as the big man stepped back. "But one word, and I'll send his ass flying to the curb."

His heavy footfalls closed in on Raf when the woman addressed the boy out front. "You know how he gets," she said with a soft laugh. "He can be a little overprotective."

Raf had seen the large male—*Angel*—during his last scout. But even if he hadn't, as someone who consistently traveled the nine realms, he wasn't easily intimidated by the brute's size or his array of facial piercings. On the contrary. The black buzz cut and perfectly trimmed line of a beard were surprisingly ordinary. As was the darker shade of his skin.

He blends in well with these mortals.

"Are you the one they call *Weaponsmith*?" Raf asked to give himself away the second the male entered the room.

Angel's pale blue eyes narrowed on Raf lurking among the shadows. "Who wants to know?"

"Someone who has dealt with your kind before... *Dvergr*," he sneered.

Angel took one step. The point of a knife bit into the soft tissue beneath Raf's jaw in the next beat.

"Call me dwarf one more time," he dared in a low growl, fangs unsheathed.

He had been only *half*-dwarf prior to his transformation into one of the blood suckers.

With a slight tip of his head, Raf shifted his eyes to regard the claw-like blade protruding from the male's ring around his middle finger.

Jewelry that turns into a weapon at the flick of a wrist? How practical.

He returned his attention to the pale, narrow slits at his eye level. "I'm in need of your skills."

The muscles in Angel's jaw twitched. "I work by appointment only."

"I'm not here for *ink*," Raf grated out, his patience thinning. "I mean your *special* craftsmanship."

Angel drew a thoughtful breath, then sheathed the claw and straightened. "Go on," he prompted with a nod.

Raf raised his chin, weaving a coaxing tune into his voice. "Your kind is famous for forging magical weapons," he noted to entice the smith's interest. "If I were to provide you with the proper material, would you be able to create one that can kill a God?"

More than just anticipated curiosity, surprise flickered in the large male's features.

Raf took his cue. Lifting his hand into view, he revealed the shadow blade he had been hiding beneath his coat.

At last, the smith's eyes grew huge. His lips parted. In Raf's open palm, the slim tri-blade rippled. Shapes like black Damascus steel twisted around themselves as though it were alive, pulsing with power. The shadows that rendered its form remained in constant motion.

"It's one of the Dark One's weapons," Angel uttered in a fearful tone, taking a step backward. "How did you get that?"

"I would rather not say." He had plucked it from in-between his own ribs after their last close encounter. The wound left behind had taken weeks to heal.

"I can't work with that." Angel shook his head. "No one can. The structure of the material can only be altered by *him*, the one who created it. It's made of *his* shadow. His physical form."

Raf already anticipated as much, but a growl rippled in his throat nonetheless. "Then tell me," he pressed, closing his grip around the dagger. "Since you are of no other use to me. Can it kill a God?"

As long as Frigg's pet remained alive, his efforts were doomed.

Angel's expression darkened. "Perhaps," he replied gruffly, crossing his muscled arms over his chest. "But only if wielded by one. A *full*-blooded God. Not a half-ling like you."

A weight dropped in his stomach. Raf had been afraid of that. His father had been a *Jǫtunn*, a giant, and a God merely by title, not blood.

More than ever, it became clear that he *must* find a way to persuade Kjartan. He needed the Haðarson.

CHAPTER
26

EVE

The sense of dread had woken her before sunrise. She was bleeding again. She knew what it meant. Knew why this kept happening too. She had taken a life, and now the Gods were punishing her. The Goddess Frigg herself, patron of marriage and motherhood, did not deem her fit to be a mother. It would never come true.

Images of a young man flooded her mind, his hair dark, eyes green. He did not know that she had been with child again. Having lost four unborn in the same manner, she had feared the inevitable outcome to repeat itself. She had sneaked out of the house to wash in the river. She could not bear breaking his heart and losing that innocent, boyish grin he carried just for her. Kjartan was still hopeful, ever the optimist. He could never know.

She had always differed from the docile women in the village. And they avoided her for it. Hated her. So the two of them lived on the outskirts. Even as children, Kjartan had been the only one not looking to change her. He accepted her for who she was. The notion that she ordered him around was simply foolish. They did not understand the way he could wrap her around his finger without trying, and she could never turn him down. He always knew what she needed... knew her better than anyone.

Or *did,* before he had sailed to Ireland.

For the full cycle of a year, he had been gone, and ever since his return, she was forced to keep secrets from him. The truth would destroy him. He would never forgive himself for leaving.

The bitter consequences still haunted her dreams: the boy with the black hair, the babe she had been forced to give away. A piece of herself, but also a piece of the man she had murdered.

Out of the six times she had been with child, destiny had chosen *that* babe to live—*his* babe—while all her others had perished in her womb, never living long enough to take their first breath.

Yet *he* lived. It was Fate's cruel hand. Fate needed the boy to exist, and she believed that she had been determined to be the vessel to bring the babe into this world for a reason. This was *her* destiny.

As she stood still in the waist-deep water of the river, the disruption of the surface closed in on her. He came up from behind, moving silently like a predator.

His arms encircled her waist, and he pulled her against his bare chest protectively, his large shape swallowing her up. His skin was flushed, warming her body in his embrace and chasing the nightmare away.

"Elskan mín," she addressed him, melting in his comfort.

Eve had overheard Kristján address Kría with the same term once. Elskan meant *darling* or *love*.

He lowered his head, his cheek at her temple, speaking words in Old Norse Eve didn't know, and yet she understood the meaning behind them. He was worried, scolded her for leaving without waking him. When he asked for her reason, she wouldn't give it and refused to return home with him just yet.

He kissed along the column of her neck while her fingertips raked through his dense beard. With sweet words of endearment and a particularly devoted caress of her curves, he managed to persuade her in the end.

"*Kona,*" he whispered lovingly in her ear.

Eve recognized the word as clearly as the timbre of his voice. *Wife.*

Her sight went fuzzy, and the scene disintegrated in front of her as she was sucked through a vortex.

Gasping, Eve tore away from the vision. Her eyes instinctively skimmed her body, hands patting herself down. She wasn't wet, or bleeding, but she knew that what she'd seen was the truth. She'd been in the woman's head… shared her thoughts. She'd *been* Kjartan's wife—Kjan's wife—*Thórunn.*

Eve examined her shaking hands. They looked exactly like they'd always looked, but they also resembled the woman's.

She slid the ring off her thumb to see the little beauty mark right at the front. It had always been there; she'd seen it millions of times. It was unremarkable, really: two small, brown dots, one slightly bigger than the other. But their positioning had been identical on Thórunn's hand.

She rubbed her palms on her bare thighs. Her skin was crawling with ants. Every inch of it. It wasn't even noon, but she was wide awake now.

She sensed Kjan in the study and, without thinking, sprang for the door. In a rush, she flung herself down the stairs, stumbling over her feet, catching the top of the newel post at the bottom.

The commotion had him bursting out into the living room, poised for a fight. His eyes lingered on her naked legs for a second, then locked with hers in confusion. "Are you alright?"

"Fine. Well… no… not really," she stammered, short of breath.

He read her face, and his expression darkened, but his fists unclenched. "The nightmare again?"

"A different one." Arms wrapped around the wooden post, Eve swallowed, and he waited for her to elaborate. "Your wife! The dream was about her."

"Eve," he sighed her name, and his shoulders dropped in visible annoyance for bringing her up again.

"You were there too," she detailed further. "I saw you… by the river. Her name was Thórunn."

Eve let her words sink in. She needed him to believe her.

His brows creased into a mask of confusion. "I never told you her name."

"I know." There was no other way for Eve to know unless she'd really shared the woman's mind.

Kjan dismissed her. "You must have heard it somewhere. "*He* must have mentioned it, and I just forgot."

"No!" She let go of the banister, shaking her head as she walked up to him. "Kjartan only referred to her as your wife. He never told me her name, either." Eve held out her hand, drawing his attention to the marks on her thumb. "And what about this?"

His expression was clear. She knew what he was going to say. "Coincidence," he scoffed, unimpressed. "It means nothing. Lots of people have those. Let it go. It was just a dream."

"She had a miscarriage," Eve blurted. It was another detail he had never disclosed.

Her words had the desired effect. Kjan tensed briefly and then crossed his arms over his chest, meeting her with an incredulous stare. "Which time?" he countered, still demanding more proof for her argument about the memory of the river.

"Fifth."

A smirk tugged at the corner of his mouth. "She only had four." He was gloating, thinking he'd successfully discredited the authenticity of her vision.

"No. She had another. She kept it from you because she didn't want you to worry. You found her in the water after she'd sneaked out of the house before sunrise. *That's* how I know. I *saw* it." Eve dropped the whole load on him without drawing a breath.

Kjan uncrossed his arms and took her hands in his, meeting her with a stern look. "Eve, stop. She is not haunting you. Her soul is at peace."

He'd seen her, spoken to her in Fólkvangr when he himself had crossed over. If anyone knew if her ghost had any unfinished business, it was him. But there had to be an explanation. "Why do I look like her?"

"You don't. Your eyes are blue, same as Joe's. Your hair is a different shade of brown—"

"But not the same as my parents," she interrupted. And they both knew that was where the short list of differences between the two women ended. Kjartan had told her so, and Kjan hadn't denied it.

His lips curled up into a subtle but genuine smile, trying to curb her paranoia. "You're nitpicking. Why are you obsessing over this?"

"Doesn't it seem at all strange to you?" Besides the *Brooker-blues*, she had nothing in common with her family's looks.

"No. A lot of people resemble someone they have no connection to. Please, Dove… give it a rest." His thumbs stroked across the back of her hands in his gentle hold.

Studying Kjan's face, Eve recalled the images of the young man from her dream. He looked the same, yet totally different. There had been no pain in the deep shade of emerald. No Guilt. No regret. No signs of the trauma he would have to face alone.

With his face unchanged, his eyes revealed his true age. There was a depth to them that she couldn't put into words. They held patience, and concern, but they could also carry rage. Every decision, every consequence, all his careful calculations… they were there in his eyes, always two steps ahead to be prepared.

Eve gave up and pursed her lips. Pulling her right hand free, she absentmindedly rubbed her arm again. The crawling sensation from earlier persisted.

He caught on to the involuntary reaction immediately. "What's wrong with your arm?"

"I don't know. It's itchy."

With a tight grip on the bracelet around her left wrist, he pushed up the sleeve of the oversized sweater she'd slept in. She shuddered as the fabric scraped along the branding.

"Does it hurt?"

"It burns." Eve cringed, staring down at the bright blue mark.

After forcing the hot iron emblem into her skin, Kjartan had sealed the wound with a salt and cobalt pigment mixture to lock in the color. It was the same electric shade as his irises. There was nothing magical about the process, but it was a bindrune, after all. They were known to be a source of supernatural power.

Kjan studied her face. "How long has it been feeling this way?"

"I'm not sure. A few days, maybe? No," she corrected. "Since the cave."

"Why didn't you mention it?"

"I didn't see a connection until now. Do you think the cave affected me like it did you?"

Kjartan had chosen the Futhark as his symbol, a unification of life and death. Kjan had the same combination of *Berkano* and *Eihwaz* carved into his heart. It had given him life through death, and Kjartan himself had found new life in shedding his own body.

The ancient magic in the glacier had changed Kjan physically. Had it done something to her as well?

Brows pinched, he looked worried but didn't answer. She had no idea what he was thinking. There was only the steady rise and fall of his breathing. Did he know what it all meant? Did Kjartan?

"What's happening to me?" Eve whispered as he pulled her head toward his chest. "How could I possibly know any of this? *You* didn't even know. It felt so real."

"Dreams always do." He weaved his fingers through her hair. His voice was calm, a stark contrast to the rapid thumping of his heart in her ears.

"What if it's something else? What if…"

She let her thoughts drift off while she searched for the right words. "I feel this connection… like I *was* her. Before I was me."

"You're referring to reincarnation? Being reborn?" Eve nodded, looking up at him. "No." He shook his head again. "It only occurs within a bloodline—the soul of an ancestor passed down to a descendant. What you're proposing is simply impossible."

Eve slipped her hands out of his grasp and rubbed at her temples. A pounding headache crashed down on her, her mind whirling like a merry-go-round, unable to focus on what was real anymore.

Kjan covered her hands with his own and lowered his forehead to hers, his breath warming her lips, and his touch soothing her instantly. "Let it go. Please. I chose you. I don't want you to be anyone but yourself."

"I miss you," Eve murmured. "I miss *this*."

His knuckles traced the curve of her cheek, and he lifted her chin. Pain showed in his eyes. "You think I don't? I want you, Eve. I always want you… so much…"

His words broke off into a hoarse whisper as he bent down and brushed her lips, tenderly, thoughtfully, coaxing her into a kiss.

A trail of warmth chased his fingertips, where they stroked down her shoulders and back. He didn't urge her toward him. His caress—like his kiss—was so soft, so gentle, it hurt. It filled her with wanting.

Leaning into him, Eve deepened the kiss. His hard body flush with hers, she groped down his front, one hand hooked to the waist of his jeans, the other gliding lower.

Heat swelled between her legs when she felt the evidence of his arousal strain against her palm, throbbing like the beat of his heart. He let out a ragged breath so thick with desire it evoked a tremble in her core.

Yes, that was what she wanted.

"Come to bed with me," she purred, beckoning him upstairs.

Kjan didn't need further encouragement. He was right on her heel when she spun around. The bedroom door swung shut behind him with a ruthless push, then both of his hands were back on her.

Slipping under her sweater, he dragged it up and over her head, leaving her lips just long enough for her to suck in half a breath. Eve clasped the back of his neck, not letting go as he flicked her tongue with his, and their kiss grew more heated.

Kjan nudged her toward the edge of the bed, where he sat her down before leaving her mouth. He backed away, his gaze roaming her naked skin, his velvet touch caressing her thighs.

Eyes blazing with desire beneath his long, dark lashes, he dipped low, showering her legs with more kisses and letting the scruff of his beard brush along the sensitive insides. Every contact was a meticulously calculated move.

His fingers slid beneath her underwear and slowly stripped it too. Arching off the bed, Eve felt a delightful shiver run up her spine that made her weak in the knees.

Judging by his dark chuckle, Kjan knew exactly what kind of effect his teasing had on her.

He straightened and rose, looming over her, all 6'4" of him. He looked like a God. Reaching up over his head, he ripped his own shirt from his torso, unveiling his glorious chest with the Helm of Awe on his right pec and a raven framing the left. He sent the piece of fabric flying and, lastly, got busy with the front of his jeans.

Eve leaned back on her elbows to watch him undress through the gap between her knees, her eyes glued to his hands as they moved over his body. Flexing under his movements made shadows bounce off his corded muscles and melt with his tattoos in the dim light. The snake that coiled up his left arm took on a life of its own once he lowered himself down.

She took it all in: the view, his irresistible scent, the feel of his weight on her body. She welcomed the radiant warmth of his skin, eagerly drawing him close.

Her fingertips grazed the raven tattoos on the sides of his head. Nestled between her breasts, he bit through the front of her bra, and the two halves sprang open at will, making way for his tongue to venture freely.

The groan he let out resonated in her ribcage. His hands squeezed her curves, molding her shape into him while his lips moved up her sternum to the hollow between her collarbones.

When his mouth found the crook of her throat right below her jaw, Eve sucked in an unsteady breath. The impressions of his fangs were subtle, but every cell in her body went on high alert.

Adjusting her weight, she nudged him onto his side, and he complied, but she caught a change in his demeanor. Something shifted in his emotional grid just like it had in the clearing last night.

An air of frustration rose around him. Lacking its familiar affectionate touch, Kjan's hand strayed from the small of her back to her ass, kneading her flesh in a fierce grasp.

With the steep points of his fangs still near her exposed throat, Eve's pulse ran amok. Legs entwined, he rocked against her, a low, guttural sound surging from his throat as if he were holding a demon at bay. His fingers raked her body viciously, nails cutting into her skin and drawing blood.

No. This isn't right. This isn't him.

"Kjan…"

Rising panic weaved through her voice. Squirming underneath him, she dug the heels of her palms into his chest, but he didn't back off. He seized her wrists. With an angry grunt, he urged her onto her back, locking her arms above her head.

"Kjan, stop! You're hurting me," she cried. "What's gotten into you? This isn't like you."

Kjan didn't meet her eyes. Keeping her caged beneath him, he dropped his head on her shoulder. "It's the only way I can be with you. Alone. The only way I can shut *him* out."

HIM? His Sire? "What are you talking about?"

When Kjan raised his eyes, there was a faint hue of red at the center of his green irises. Beneath those dark lashes, he appeared to be in pain.

"He doesn't like it when I'm rough with you," he explained in an agitated tone. "I can't keep sharing you with him, Eve. He feels everything I feel. He's always there… with us." He tightened his grip around her wrists. "It's the only way I have you to myself."

Eve stared at him in disbelief, eyes wide. A shadow crossed his face, turning the muscles as hard as stone. Last night he had seemed possessed, and that was before Kjartan had *actually* possessed him. Kjan had that same look in his eyes now. The look that told her nothing was going to stop him.

"Let go." Fear forced its path up her throat, choking her plea.

"No."

That was it. One word. That was all it took to bring her entire world crashing down. His voice so callous... so foreign...

"What do you mean, *no*?"

Her eyes filled with tears. She had expected him to break under the pressure sooner or later, but never like this. Would take what he wanted... even if he had to take it by force?

She ripped her hand free in a last attempt to break away, but as she tried to scramble off the bed, he caught her around the waist and pulled her back under him, face down. "I need you, Eve. More than you know."

He had trained her to fight back, but she couldn't fight him. His betrayal of her trust sent a paralyzing shock through her muscles.

"Please, don't do this," she whimpered.

His right arm tightened around her ribcage. "You're mine, Dove. He can't have you." Then his left hand ripped her head back, and his fangs struck.

Eve's breath shot from her lungs in a single burst. She couldn't draw another. Everything stopped in that moment. Time. Space. Thought. It all ceased to exist.

There was no physical pain when he plunged his canines into her jugular. But despite the endogenous morphine secreted with his bite, she felt herself crumble. All the trust and unwavering loyalty between them were gone in an instant, washed away by the feeling of utter betrayal as he forced her into submission.

He didn't drink from her, though; his bite was an assertion of dominance.

Kjan retracted his fangs at last but made no motion to move off. His breath hot against her cheek, he claimed his place between her legs, holding her captive with his own unyielding body.

What was he waiting for? Her consent?

'I need you more than you know.'

Was this what he'd meant? That she was the only one who could give him what he needed? The only one who could ease his agony?

Eve closed her eyes, gritting her teeth. Her voice cracked from hurt. "Get it over with!"

CHAPTER
27

KJAN

The full impact of what he had done struck the instant the taste of her blood registered on his tongue. Kjan's body went rigid.

She was right. This wasn't him. What was he doing? When had he become this? A man who took what he wanted without mercy. Who took from his mate against her will.

"Get it over with!" Eve hissed.

Her words struck so deeply into his soul they shattered it. And he deserved the blow. Deserved even more. She didn't want this. Didn't want him.

Was I really about to—

No! No, he had bitten her, but he wouldn't have.

Running his tongue across his lips, Kjan released the fist in her hair. A bittersweet undertone chased the palate of her crowberry-wine-like blood. He had taken what had not been freely given.

He had acted as if on a primal instinct, compelled to mark her as his again, have her to himself, make her understand how much he needed her—needed their physical connection. He was her mate, dammit. There was no denying your mate what they needed. Nothing was off limits. How many times had she offered him her throat before?

Oh, who was he kidding? He knew this was different. His violation had corrupted this most revered act between them, and he couldn't take it back. Couldn't even get an apology out; he felt stunned.

"Get off me!"

The grating tone in her voice was laced with venom, and he complied, throwing himself back onto the pillows.

"Eve… please." He needed to explain.

"No!" she spat, sliding off the bed to gather her clothes that were scattered on the floor. "I heard what you said, but that doesn't make it right. I'm not going to let you use me to spite him."

Fuck! She was right again. This was more about his Sire than it was about her. The leech's voice in his head had driven him to reclaim Eve out of jealousy. She was the innocent, caught between battlefronts.

Expelling a sigh of surrender, Kjan dragged his palms up his face and lodged them in his hair.

He tracked her movements from the corner of his eye while staring at the ceiling fan. She slipped her underwear on first; next was her sweater, and she pulled it down over her naked breasts because he had trashed her bra; the cute mint-colored one that matched the cashmere top—

Wait! Is she leaving?

The thought made him bolt upright in alarm. "Where are you going?" With his sight now trained on her, she had his undivided attention.

"Home!" Eve rammed her feet through her pants and yanked them up.

Home? His mouth went dry. She was referring to the penthouse at Waterfront. The cabin no longer felt like home to her.

Kjan let his shoulders drop as he watched her leave. Had he really expected anything less? He owed her to be better.

The moment the door slammed shut, sharp pain exploded in his skull. It appeared his Sire had something to say as well.

Kjan's palms shot to his temples. Writhing in anguish, he locked his head in a vise and squeezed his eyes shut.

While waiting for the pain to stop, Eve's words echoed in his mind. *Get it over with?* At what point had sex become a chore?

He dragged the knife from his pocket along his forearm in a sense of penance.

Letting his blood drip onto the gravel by his boots where they were planted in the driveway, he offered it to the earth for what he took from Eve. Though he knew it wasn't nearly enough.

Curling his fingers into a fist, he brought forth more and prayed that the Gods would grant him forgiveness.

His head hummed along quietly. He wasn't sure what time he had lost consciousness. When his senses finally returned to him, it was late in the afternoon.

Kjan felt drained. He needed to feed. But that required him to be around people, and he could hardly tolerate them on a good day. Human emotions in large gatherings wreaked havoc on his receptors, and he was already irritated as fuck. He needed someplace peaceful to calm his edge.

One place came to mind.

Kjan let the twin-engine of the Harley loose. Gunning it down the mountain road, he hailed the wind like an old friend he had neglected too long.

He steered the bike to Cathedral Park at the north part of town, where he ditched it in the parking lot. Making his way on foot toward St. John's Bridge, he caught the last rays of the sun between the stunning buttresses.

He admired the architecture despite its oppressive Catholic charm. Not something *he* would choose, but it was a popular spot for wedding ceremonies during the summer months. On the first day of the new year, it was a lot less crowded, yet not deserted.

He sat on the steps below the bridge and stared up at the beautiful arches. Sending his empathic feelers out, Kjan was able to draw from the aura of a few joggers that passed by, paying him no mind. He kept his eyes on the sky as the sunset cast shades of pink and purple onto the snowy slopes of Mount Hood.

Eve and him had watched the sunsets from all angles around Portland. He had even talked her into the five-mile round trip hike to Angel's Rest. Rocky dormant volcanoes, wildflower meadows, river views… anything to get her mind off flying back to Iceland.

It hadn't been enough.

He had been careless for taking her to the glacier. The immortal's essence ran in her blood too, even though they didn't share a direct Sire-bond. The old magic in the cave had fused with the runes in her skin and triggered a link to the past. More accurately, *his* past. Kjan couldn't see the connection. It didn't make sense. What was he missing?

He didn't want to show his concern in front of her, but he was genuinely scared.

He wondered if she was looking up at the sky now. Nothing could fill the gaping void in his chest, his heart was always with her.

He mulled over Kristján's comments again. Did Eve really expect them to get married at some point? What difference would it make?

In the Christian sense, he was no longer bound to his wife after death, but what about the afterlife? Assuming, he ever managed to find his way there. Kjan still firmly believed in it. He had seen Thórunn with his own eyes. The Gods Baldr and Hǫðr had not been figments of his imagination.

Was it guilt from choosing Eve over her that kept him from making the commitment?

How could he reject the woman he had loved as a human with all his heart since they were children? He couldn't do that to Thórunn, even if he didn't love her the same way anymore. He had sworn an oath to honor her. Always.

His focus shifted. The lights that lined the trails began to flicker, and he retracted his greedy tentacles before they ran out of control and he accidentally shut down the power grid.

Unintentionally, his feelers hooked into a couple walking past the steps under the bridge. The man was cradling an infant in his arms, shielding it from the cold, while the woman pushed a stroller. Father, mother, child. They looked so happy. So complete.

Leaching off their affection for one another, Kjan's heart felt heavy again. *Why did it have to be a family?*

Feeding off others' emotions was easier when he was disconnected from them. Strangers didn't supply him with a lot, but it was just enough. Using Eve was on another level. Like comparing watered-down gasoline to jet fuel. Feelings of attachment made the whole ordeal too personal.

Releasing his hold on their auras, he concentrated his attention on the things he could actually control. How was he going to face Eve? There were no words that would right his wrong. Would she even hear him out?

Hands clasped in front, elbows resting on top of his knees, Kjan glanced down at the inside of his left forearm. The sleeves of his shirt were pushed up, and he hadn't bothered grabbing a jacket on his way out. Not even a scratch was visible in the ink where his skin had healed from the cut. The blade had been perfect, resulting in a laceration so smooth and fine the tissue had stitched itself without a seam.

The self-inflicted punishment had been far from satisfactory, though. He couldn't reach deep enough to cut the despicable darkness out of himself.

His eyes traced the lines of ink. He had gotten the tattoos on his left arm touched up after the motorcycle wipeout at the temple erased the entire midsection of the serpent and left his repaired skin a blank canvas. He had drawn the image out himself from memory for the artist.

He had gotten a few voids restored over the decades, but none as big as that last one. The components of the new ink weren't the same as the original ash and charcoal mixture, but the artists had blended them smoothly nonetheless.

The Futhark rune bands that snaked around his forearm in between the other images were unaltered. They spelled the names of the people he held most dear: the mother he never met, the father who left, and the wife he lost. A single *Sól* was added below Thórunn's name. The rune represented the sun, the great wheel of power, but for him, it simply meant *stelpa*—girl—for the daughter he hadn't been able to claim because she had been stillborn.

He had wrapped her in linen, then placed her in her mother's arms as he had buried them together, exactly the way Eve had seen it in her dream. It was nearly the identical scene that had repeated itself for Kjan back in Florence when he had buried Andromeda's victims with his own hands.

Why am I clinging to this heritage?

For a reason he couldn't understand, he continued to recover this exterior—this history of the human he had once been as if it were the last piece left of the man.

The tattoos were a reminder that he hadn't always been this monster. That he had a family once: parents and even a crazy Seiðr-witch for a grandmother. Although, she had been better known as the village's mad woman.

Kjan's head snapped around at the startling sense of someone breathing down his neck. His keen eyes searched the area and landed on a black pair of flapping wings as they settled in the crown of a tree.

He bared his fangs, and his hibernating passenger stirred, catching the scent of the shifter as well. The bird taunted him with his high-pitched caw, daring him to make the first move. He perched on the branch, squawking impatiently.

What's he up to?

'*He wants me to make up my mind already,*' his Sire answered. '*Choose a side.*'

The Raven ruffled his feathers in response and jerked his head as if giving directions. Then he took off south…

Toward Waterfront.

CHAPTER

28

EVE

She turned at the sound of footsteps behind her and shrank back in surprise. "Styrr!"

The boastful giant trudged up the stoop like he was the Jarl in charge, his long black braid resting over his mighty furred shoulder.

Unlike the noble warrior he wished to be, he was only known for his brute strength, not his smarts. The braggart was flaunting a fresh wound below his right eye that stretched down his cheekbone. A crooked smile, as though he were pleased with himself, peeked out between his braided mustache.

"Nice face." Thórunn stifled a gleeful grin, commenting on the still bloody mar. "Parting gift?" She knew exactly who the gracious benefactor was.

Gloating, despite the humiliating proof someone had bested him in a fight, he leaned his massive right shoulder into the cottage's siding right by the door, cutting off her escape route.

"Where is that rabid guard dog of yours when you need him?"

"He is not my dog," she sneered back, trying not to let her alarm show.

He shrugged, a malicious spark in his piercing blue eyes. "My mistake." Crossing his arms over his enormous chest, he pushed his entire weight into the wall. "I figured since he always cowers by your feet and the way you order him around. What kind of man tolerates that from his woman?"

His hand stroked his beard in a lazy motion while his gaze roved the curves of her body. She knew what he was considering behind his sharpened expression.

Her throat growing tight, Thórunn expected the worst. He wouldn't leave before getting exactly what he wanted. Out here, no one could hear her screams.

And no one would come to her aid if they did.

On a bluff, she jerked to the side as if to run past his left. The moment Styrr's shoulder separated from the house to block her path, she ducked through the gap on his right. She was small, and people always underestimated her physical responsiveness, but her limbs were as quick as her tongue.

As she lunged through the threshold, she tried to shut the door on him. Her breath caught in her throat when it slammed against his big boot already over the sill.

At the forceful thrust of his hand, the door burst open, and he took a full step inside, and then another, the thumping of his heavy footfalls louder than her heartbeat.

Thórunn stumbled backward. The huge shape of him blocked all sunlight from outside. He had her trapped.

"Someone should teach you your place." His mouth curled into a vindictive grin, twisting the gash at his cheek. "On your hands and knees."

The next moment, Styrr grabbed the hair at the back of her head and rammed her forehead into the wall, nearly knocking her unconscious.

Fear ignited in her chest. The room was spinning, and her legs buckled before he yanked her around to face him.

Fists clenching the linen at her front, he pulled her up close. "If your husband is not going to do it, allow me," he snarled, baring his stained teeth.

Bile rose in her throat. His breath was sickening. She drew back and spat in his face to demonstrate her revulsion further—

His hand shot out so fast. It was no more than a streak in her vision, and then a hot sting flared, numbing half her face. The momentum knocked her to the floor.

"You should have kept him on a tighter leash," he taunted with a pitiless laugh.

Dizzy from the hit, she struggled to get up, but he descended on her with his overpowering weight, driving her knees into the floor and crushing her beneath him.

With his fingers twisted in her hair and his other hand at her elbow, his grip on her was merciless. He yanked her head back, bringing her up close so she could see his face.

"This is how a woman like you should be treated," he rasped in a vile tone.

Flailing in his snare, she clawed at him in an attempt to drive her thumbs into his eye sockets. His cruel laugh curdled the blood in her veins.

He repositioned his grasp around her throat, both hands forcing her head to the ground, and choking her into submission. She had no chance of getting out from under him.

Her muscles went limp. Too close to blacking out, she felt her mind slipping and fought harder to stay awake.

His weight shifted off her hips to haul them off the ground and ready himself. She didn't scream when his free hand fumbled with her robes. Didn't even cry when he pushed himself into her. She refused to give him the satisfaction of drawing a single tear from her. He would *not* break her.

Thórunn closed her eyes and prayed for it to end…

And then she would kill him. She vowed by the Goddess Freyja and all those who witnessed the heinous violation that her assailant would not leave this house alive.

She focused her mind on the bleating goats out back, drowning out the sounds of him until, at last, Styrr's body stopped jerking on top of her.

With his final grunt, her eyes flew open. Stretching her arm above her head, Thórunn reached for the heavy iron kettle on the table.

She curled her fingers around the long handle. The weight strained her wrist and forearm so brutally she could barely lift it with one hand from her position. But unable to free herself from the man's massive weight, she had no other option.

Ignoring the sharp pain shooting through her arm, she tightened her grip and pulled with all her might.

The kettle swung in a perfect arch to find its mark at his temple. Eyes closed, Styrr never even saw it coming.

His body tumbled off her instantly. It dropped like a stone onto the floor, blood trickling from his skull where she cracked it. He didn't move, but his chest rose with jagged breaths.

The kettle slipped her grip, hitting the ground with a dull *thud*, and then the house went silent.

Thórunn felt nothing as she straddled his chest. Her small hands locked around his neck, thumbs pressing into the soft notch on the front of his throat, just like Kjartan had taught her.

Styrr never regained consciousness. Never opened his eyes again.

CHAPTER

29

EVE

id that really happen?

Eve hadn't even remembered crashing on the couch when she'd woken from the latest dream drenched in sweat and her body sore in all the wrong places.

The aches in her muscles seemed to confirm her question, but they were really the aftermath of her own nightmare.

He was so stubborn, always carrying the weight of the world alone, never admitting weakness or asking for help.

She had often wondered how it worked with two souls in one body. Eve had foolishly assumed that Kjartan's mind had been *powered down*, supposedly like his own last year in Iceland. Instead, his Sire had been fully aware this entire time. She was such an idiot.

Curled up in a blanket, and her hair no longer wet from the shower, Eve sat on the patio, still nursing her injured pride.

She had prepared herself for Kjan's bite, but when his canines had driven deep into her skin, it had shattered her.

The horrible memory from the temple with Kjartan had bubbled up; that night she had chosen death over compliance. He had tried to force her into submission too, but Kjan was the one who had succeeded.

She had given in and granted him permission to use her in any way he needed because she loved him, but he had broken her trust. By taking her vein, he had made her relive the worst moment of her life.

Twisting the bracelet around her wrist, she looked down at the bindrune that appeared in the gap of the platinum cuff. The ends of the bracelet curved in opposite directions: one in the shape of a wing reaching up her forearm, the other in the shape of an arrow pointing toward her hand. It had an emerald triangle at the head, just like the pendant of her necklace.

The two were a matching set now. Kjan had commissioned both pieces for her after his own designs, using her tattoo as inspiration. The ink on her right wrist was a feather-tipped arrow, overlaying an abstractly drawn angel wing. The pendulum of her necklace looped through a decorative wing at her throat and created the Y-style of the entire piece.

The flat arc of the cuff was about a quarter of an inch at its midpoint and inscribed with the words *'I Will Always Be With You'.*

It had started out as a Christmas present and then turned into his parting gift for her when he had expected to die during the merge with his Sire. Kjan always flipped the bracelet around to avoid looking at the mark—*His* mark.

Berkano—the rune of Baldr, symbolized light, life, and fertility. It looked like the letter *B*; only the rounded shapes were pointy like triangles.

Eihwaz—the rune of Hǫðr, symbolized death, rebirth, and the eternal cycle of all things. It was made up of one long vertical stave with two shorter lines branching off at each end. The top one was angled down and to the right like a flag on a pole; the bottom one was angled up and to the left like a checkmark.

Eve walked the tip of her index finger over each individual line burned into her skin. In Kjartan's crest, the symbols were attached at their vertical staves, with Baldr's rune nestled just below his brother's.

Is the mark causing the dreams?

She rubbed her bleary eyes. The sun had just crept below the horizon, the last hues of pink and purple fading behind the mountains when the deep roar of the Harley's engine announced its approach.

She still didn't know squat about motorcycles, except for the sound of this particular model: the FXDR 114. The bike was as flashy as the God who had picked it, and the turbo was one of the loudest she had ever heard.

Kjartan had an arrogant nature. He was impulsive, impatient, and immature—despite his considerable age of 1800 plus years. Eve figured for an Asgardian divinity that only equaled the human age of the early twenties. It fit his behavior. Kjan, on the other hand, really was 983 years old. They were so different from each other.

Regardless of his temper, the few times she'd been intimate with the immortal, he'd touched her reverently and with great care, as if afraid to hurt her by accident. She'd recognized her own need for acceptance in him. He'd wished for her to choose him freely, and her rejection had broken him. His fear of abandonment had pushed him into a very dark place.

Kjan was the polar opposite: calm and restrained—mostly. His footsteps made no sounds on the carpet, and his presence bathed the sterile high-rise apartment in a warm glow.

Hands in his pockets, he lurked silently by the patio door. She sensed a mix of remorse and worry in him.

"You talk in your sleep sometimes," Eve said, breaking the ice. "But you don't talk to yourself, do you? What does he say to you?"

Now that she knew Kjartan was always aware, it was like a veil had lifted. His lips had been moving in the forge because he'd been arguing with the voice in his head.

Her disclosure caught him by surprise. His posture stiffened, but he didn't look at her when he confessed. "He tells me that you were better off with him instead of me. He makes sure I don't forget."

Eve gave a soft laugh.

He lifted his eyes from his boots, and they must have landed on the purple bruise at her neck, reminding him of what he'd done, because a cold breeze drifted her way.

He cleared his throat. "I won't stay. Just let me feed you, please."

"I'll heal on my own," she said, shutting him down.

The hurt showed on his face, but Kjan didn't argue with her. He turned to leave.

Eve tossed the blanket and leaped off the lounger. She still had a few things to get off her chest. "I asked you... *begged* you to talk to me. All those days you couldn't sleep, hiding in the forge. Why did you keep it from me? Did you think I was going to reject you?"

He swung around aggressively, raising his palms. "You're rejecting me now," he pointed out.

"That's not the same. I'm not judging you for something *he* did. We could have figured this out together, but you didn't trust me."

"There is nothing to figure out, Eve." He raised his voice, clenching and unclenching his fist like he wanted to punch something. "I am stuck like this. Telling you wouldn't have made a difference. It would have just scared you."

"You're right. I *am* scared," she admitted. This wasn't him. Not the Kjan she knew. He would downplay issues, bottle things up, but these mood swings, these fits of rage were foreign to her.

Actually, they aren't.

The revelation struck her. *He's scared, too.*

Fear blew the hinges off the tightly sealed storm doors that kept his emotions in check. That was when his anger took over.

He spun away, and Eve watched him pace the dark living room—or rather, stomp back and forth; *thump, thump, thump,* his boots went with each stride, his breaths falling fast and short behind.

"I don't know what to do." Fingers running through his dark hair, he shook his head. "I hate that he's there whenever I touch you, breathing down my neck. I can feel him squirming… every second… of every day… itching to take over. And I know he can."

A heavy side of guilt followed her realization, watching him unravel. He had chosen to return to her despite the steep conditions to remain Kjartan's vessel. He hadn't just chosen *her* over Thórunn. He had chosen *this*, this torture, over freedom. How long until it broke him entirely?

His pacing didn't slow. "I'm so fucking paranoid, I can't breathe. I'm afraid to lose control… to him… to what's happening to me."

Did he mean what the fits of jealousy made him do when he was forced to share his mate with another?

Kjan's grip tensed in his hair, pulling at the roots, knuckles white. His voice grew more agitated. "They wanted to teach him a lesson, but *I'm* forced to share his punishment. *I'm* serving his sentence too. I'm stuck in this hell with no way out." He released the hold on his hair and stopped mid-stride to face her. "I'm right back where I started. Nothing has changed."

Nothing has changed?

Like she'd made no difference in his life? Their relationship: meaningless. Her existence: insignificant. Saving his life: a waste of time!

Eve couldn't hide the blow. The impact of his words dawned on him as she hid her face behind her hands.

Kjan rushed up to her. "I'm sorry. Eve, I'm sorry… I didn't mean that." He brushed her hands aside and wiped her cheeks. "I swear I didn't."

Cradling her face tenderly, he took a deep breath as if it were the first one he'd taken all night. "You are everything to me. What I did is unforgivable. How can you ever trust me again?"

He didn't expect her to answer. Lowering his forehead to hers, he let the soft touch of his fingers drift over her naked shoulders and down her arms until his hands found hers, his thumbs caressing the inside of her wrists—his left on her tattoo, his right on her branding.

The mark hummed.

'The truth would destroy him. He would never forgive himself for leaving,' the imported thought echoed in Eve's mind.

It wasn't her secret to tell. Thórunn had taken it to her grave. But if they really were related, could she be reaching out to her through the visions now?

"I felt her love for you," Eve whispered uneasily. "And yours for her. I've never felt anything so strong."

Kjan gave her hands a squeeze and nudged her forehead more earnestly. "Yes, you have… right here… between us," he said, drawing the words out. "This is real, Eve. Don't you dare take that from me. It's the only thing keeping me going."

"But it's not enough, is it?" Her bottom lip quivered, and she had to use her teeth to keep it steady.

Kjan straightened apprehensively. When her eyes flipped to his, he stared at her blankly.

"I had another dream."

"Dove…" he groaned, dropping her hands.

"Just please, hear me out before you shut me down again." Eve twisted the clunky ring on her thumb, her gaze steady on him. "I've been digging into my family tree, but I only managed to trace it back a few hundred years."

"Enough!" He threw up his hands in frustration. "I can't do this again."

Eve shuffled after him as he walked away. "But you can't deny that there is a possibility. We're talking about a thousand years. Who can really track their bloodline that far back?"

"Fine." He whipped around, the warmth in his eyes gone. "You want to do this now, then have at it."

He slumped onto the stool by the kitchen island, raising only one foot onto the rail, like he didn't intend to stay there for long. Propping his chin up on one elbow, he kept his eyes level, but his expression was far from welcoming.

Holy fuck! I'm about to shatter his world.

Eve inhaled a deep breath, watching his leg bounce up and down. "You said you don't want me to be anyone other than myself, but what if this *is* me? Or *was* me?"

"Eve, it just can't be," he said, rubbing his eyes with one hand. "You've seen it yourself. Thórunn didn't have any children. None that lived anyway."

"Not with you," she muttered.

His body went rigid as his eyes locked onto hers. "What did you say?" His brows furrowed, anger crossing his face.

Eve took a step back, the shock from those three words slipping out of her mouth robbing her of speech.

"Oh no,"—he pushed off the stool and stormed toward her—"you don't get to say that to me, and then back out. You're the one who started it."

Her legs balked, and he was on her in four long strides, hands clamped around her upper arms. His expression was seething with rage, ready to lash out at her.

"First you tell me that my wife had a miscarriage she kept from me, and then you say that she gave birth to another man's baby? How dare you?" He hovered over her like a lightning storm. Lips twisted in bitter contempt, his stare bore into her with stark, cold intensity.

Eve shrank back. The ire in his voice triggered the short hairs at her nape. Her focus shifted back and forth between his glowing red eyes. Her lips quivered, searching her mind for words, but there were none.

"Stop it, Eve." His fingers dug deeper into her arms as he shook her. "I don't want to hear any more of this."

He glared at her for another second to let his plea sink in, then released her, his eyes downcast. Shoulders sagging, he pivoted on his heel and bolted for the door.

A question burst from her lips so fast she had no time to consider the ramifications. "Who's Styrr?"

The muscles in his back tensed at the sound of the name, and Kjan stopped dead in his tracks, fists balled.

He turned his head over his shoulder first, and then slowly, his body followed, boots set apart in a defensive stance.

"Where did you hear that name?" he asked with a slight tilt of his head, his eyes just two narrow slits.

"He had black hair and a scar on his right cheek, which *you* gave him."

Eve watched the color leak from his face as his jaw dropped. She forced the dry lump down her throat to get through the next part. "He was the one who raped her after you left for Ireland. She begged you not to go, but you did anyway. You were gone for an entire year, and she was never the same when you came back. You thought she resented you for leaving, but she couldn't tell you the truth. She knew it would kill you."

Eve covered her mouth with both of her hands to stop more words from spilling out. She had opened a gate. She wasn't able to shut it.

Halfway between her and the door, Kjan stood rooted to the ground, wide-eyed, face pale, no longer flushed with anger. His muscles were rigid from head to toe.

He didn't blink.

His gaze dropped to the floor, staring at the space between them as he put the pieces together. He knew she was telling the truth.

She watched his breath pick up. It came in sharp, rapid bursts when he clutched his chest, and he swayed for a moment before reeling around to charge out the door.

Eve had no time to process. Shrill laughter erupted outside on the deck behind her, chasing shivers down her spine.

She swung around and was met with the strangest sight. A teenage boy with long dark hair, dressed in black from head to toe, stood smack in the center of her patio.

He shot her a devilish grin. "I could not have played that better myself," he said slightly accented. As he chuckled in glee, the wicked orange glow of his eyes added to his deranged impression.

With his long scarf flapping around his neck in the wind like a noose, the freaky goth reached for the metal rail that ran along the edge of the patio to hurl himself onto it. The shiny buckles and steel-toes of his boots gleamed in the light coming from the living room.

Balancing his feet on the bar as if it were a wooden plank, he straightened and took a gracious bow. "Thank you, dear. I really appreciate all your help."

Help? What help?

Then he stretched his arms out by his side and flung himself backward off the railing.

Eve charged toward the ledge, but when she leaned over, a huge bird shot past her face and soared to the sky.

It was *him*. The one Kjan had called *the Raven*.

How long had the son of Loki been standing there, watching them? What had he overheard?

Her heart was bounding out of her chest. Her mind was racing. Kjan had been distraught when he left, susceptible to his Sire overpowering him. Is that what the Raven meant by her helping? She'd made him vulnerable. She'd sold him out and opened the door for Kjartan.

CHAPTER
30

KJAN

He turned nuclear. White-hot pain ripped through his body, lighting up every nerve ending. Flames of blind rage licked along his veins, and he could feel his blood boiling, the blistering sensation beneath his skin fueling him.

He didn't recall the ride back. Hadn't noticed the change in scenery as it had shifted from city to highland in front of the headlight. He couldn't even tell if he was still breathing.

All at once, the FDX came to a stop at the head of the driveway, and his hand dropped from the throttle, killing the engine. Things were moving on their own; he was on autopilot, his vision red. There was no air in his lungs. Just. Fire.

Making his way to the forge around the house on foot, his eyes fell on the double-sided axe still wedged into the stump out front. He ripped it free with one hand in passing, not slowing toward his destination.

BAM! The bottom of his boot collided with the door.

The sound rebounded and amplified in his skull. Bursts of wood went flying inward as if from an explosion. It wasn't locked, but the gap between the barn doors couldn't fit all the rage he was generating.

Gripping the weapon with both hands, he started swinging, blowing the entrance wide open. Each crack of his axe split the wood anew, splinters spraying around him like the blood of the enemy he envisioned before him.

And Kjan didn't stop there. Clearing the threshold, he went to work on anything that caught his eye without focus: the shelves, the walls, the workbench… he left nothing in the wake of the savage blade. Tools went flying, bouncing on the floor, clashing into things, ricocheting…

He didn't duck or pause. Kjan kept swinging. Everywhere he looked, he saw the bastard's face. His smug grin. His hands on Thórunn.

He should have killed Styrr instead of giving him a warning. It had only provoked the brute, and he had gone to her for retaliation. When he hadn't been around after his return, he assumed Styrr had gotten the message. How could he have been so naïve? It was all his fault.

The voyage to Ireland had brought nothing but regrets. Why had he gone? What had he aspired to find there that he didn't already have at home? Why had he let his father talk him into it?

He should never have left. He could have lived one content lifetime instead of a hundred wretched ones. He would trade a thousand miserable years for just fifty happy ones with her.

As his vision blurred, the blade of the axe struck something solid. The metallic clank trembled up his arms, and the wooden handle slipped his grasp.

Splinters from where it was cracked had drawn blood. He didn't feel it. On the outside, his body was numb. But on the inside, he felt everything. The shame, the guilt, the pain his betrayal had caused her. It all crashed down on him.

Then he saw the blow torch rolling to a stop at the tip of his boot. The inferno blazing inside him wasn't hot enough to consume him. He needed more.

Approximately 3000 degrees more.

CHAPTER

31

EVE

Eve floored the pedal of her Grand Cherokee. She'd figured he would either head for the temple in the caverns or back to the woods behind the cabin where the shifter had revealed himself. But having struck out with her first choice, finding no sign of the Harley at the cave's entrance, she was now racing toward the cabin.

She was relieved that she didn't have to make the terrifying descent down the winding stairs into the heart of the temple. Eve never wanted to step foot in there again. But the pit in her stomach continued to churn. Kjan had been right. She did need to feed.

Her sight drew to the sky, and an icy cold crept up her spine. Smoke was rising from the direction of the house.

Nerves jolting beneath her skin, she pulled the Jeep into the driveway and then slammed on the brakes. She narrowly avoided crushing the Harley, which lay haphazardly on the ground like discarded trash.

Through the windshield, her focus shot up, and she gasped. The cabin wasn't on fire. It was the forge.

Eve jumped out of the SUV and raced toward the shed around the corner. Smoke stung her eyes. They watered, and she forced herself to blink through the irritation.

Then she glimpsed his dark silhouette, standing out against the background of the bright red flames just a few yards ahead. He had his back turned, hunching over the damage like a crazed animal. His hands still twitched by his side.

She crooked her arm over her face, blocking the smoke from getting into her lungs. Kjan glanced over his shoulder when she approached—

Eve stumbled backward. No, not *Kjan…*

KJARTAN!

His blue eyes glared at her, illuminating the short distance between them. The sight of him sent a hum of dread through her veins, and she felt the tingle across her scalp as the blood drained from her head.

Her legs trembled. Her mouth opened in shock. "WHAT DID YOU DO?"

"I didn't do this," he snapped back, defending himself. "I had to put your man in a timeout before he burned the whole place down… and himself along with it," he added after pausing for effect.

Kjan set it on fire? WHILE INSIDE? Eve stared at him blankly. "W-what happened?"

"I think the aftermath speaks for itself." He turned his gaze back on the rubble and scoffed. "And you thought *I* had a temper."

Her muscles sagged with relief. For some reason, she felt comforted by the thought of Kjartan getting him out in time. She hated to think of arriving here and not finding Kjan. Or his body.

Eve edged closer to his side, and they stood in silence, watching the flames devour the little shed.

Six months ago, when she'd seen him last, he'd told her that everyone's path was predetermined by the Norns, and despite free will, there was no escaping it. But since nobody knew their truc destiny, one should always strive for aspiration and never accept defeat. As a child, he'd been destined to spend all eternity trapped in a cave until he'd found his loophole. He had escaped his fate.

Eve, on the other hand, was a firm believer in shaping her own future with the choices she made every day. Yes, there was the fact that she was a descendant of Kjan's wife, but what were the odds of them ending up in the same house at the same time?

Joe had picked the place after her parents died.

Eve had chosen to run off after her breakup with Bobby.

Kjan had chosen to turn her in spite of his last experience going horribly wrong.

Kjartan hadn't been able to complete the possession, and she'd bumped into him in Iceland, of all places.

Had all that really been predetermined? Or just a string of bad luck?

"In case you're wondering if I'm reconsidering my stance on fate," she prompted, breaking the silence. Kjartan angled his head in her direction, but her eyes stayed focused on the fire. "I'm not."

Eve wasn't convinced. There were an awful lot of coincidental factors at play. All which could easily have been avoided by making a different choice. One little shift, and none of them would be here right now. Who would make this kind of effort? Why?

She decided to let it go and steer the topic back to the present. "I saw him. The shifter," she clarified. "He was at the penthouse."

"What did he say?"

She turned her head timidly, only enough to read the reaction on his face. "He thanked me for my help. Apparently, he believes I assisted him in some way."

Kjartan knit his eyebrows in deep thought. Eve could see the wheels behind them turning but couldn't tell if he was surprised or if he had known about the plan all along.

"What's going on in your head?"

His focus shifted back to her. "You need to feed," he said, staring at her with a disapproving scowl.

"I'm fine." She was getting really tired of people calling her out on it.

She felt her equilibrium tilt before she finished the thought, but Kjartan caught her around the waist to keep her from keeling over.

He tilted her chin up. "You were saying?"

Gazing into his brilliant, electric blue irises mere inches from her, she was sucked down the rabbit hole. Eve recalled every moment she'd spent with him, every second she'd tried to erase—not just the bad ones, but the good ones too. Like the first time he'd kissed her, hardly subtle, and yet he hadn't forced himself on her. And at the penthouse, when she'd willingly given herself up to him.

All the buried memories were still there. All the ways he was different from Kjan.

His thumb brushed across her lower lip. "He won't know. His conscience is dormant. Completely oblivious," Kjartan whispered, reading her guilty mind.

He had never used contractions in his vernacular before. He sounded just like Kjan. If it weren't for his eyes, Eve couldn't tell them apart.

Fully aware of his hands on her body, the fragrance of charred wood, pine, and freshly brewed coffee encircled her. She almost forgot where she was.

Bonfire?—No.

Fire?—Yes. The forge was burning.

Eve shook herself free from his spell. "We don't keep secrets from each other."

He raised a cynical eyebrow, but held his tongue. "I would never treat you the way he did."

"No, you only strangled me half to death." She glared up, reminding him of his own shortcomings.

"I'm sorry. I will never forgive myself for that. My approach was… misguided… and thoughtless. I believed that it was for the right reason. I was so desperate—" His voice cracked. "I'm truly sorry, Eve."

His honesty surprised her. His words sounded genuinely sincere.

He loosened his grasp, but kept her steady as she swayed. "It's your call. I will not force you," he said, rubbing salt into the still-fresh wound left by Kjan. "But you can't deny that you're hungry. Let me feed you."

Eve shook her head.

"You want answers, and I want you to take my vein. The way I see it, it's a win-win."

She wagged her finger in his face. "That's blackmail, but I shouldn't expect any less from you."

"You hurt my feelings. Just a drop then," he offered as a compromise. "It will be enough to heal that foul mark on your neck. It deeply offends me."

Eve thought long and hard about his offer and then gave in. "Alright. But just a drop," she insisted.

"Here is to cheating, stealing, fighting, and drinking."

"What?"

His eyes flared brighter as he grinned smugly, the tip of his fangs flashing, biting his lip. Then he crushed his mouth to hers.

The distinctive taste of his blood flooded her senses before her body went numb in his arms. Fingers twisting gently through the hair at her nape, he held her off the ground, his other arm hooked around the small of her back.

Powerless against the subduing effects of his blood, Eve lost herself in the moment. Her skin tingled as it mended within seconds.

"Dammit," she barked, shoving against his chest when he released her. "I should have seen *that* coming, too."

"You can't blame a desperate man for taking a chance, Love," he winked. "A deal is a deal. You get your answers."

Kjartan rambled on as they walked into the house. Eve chose the kitchen as the most neutral space; she wasn't going to get cozy with him on the couch in the living room or in the dim light of the study.

She tried her hardest to ignore his wandering gaze on her. She wished she'd picked a different wardrobe. With that gleam in his eyes, he was no doubt picturing her naked. He probably had an eidetic memory and recalled every freckle on her body. *Awkward much?*

"You really love to hear yourself talk, don't you?" she remarked.

"For once, someone other than him can actually hear me. And he usually just ignores me. Do you have any idea what that's like?"

Hands gesturing wildly, eyes darting, he jabbered on, "He is so dull. I honestly don't know what you see in him. I mean, he meditates more than a damn monk. What's up with that? And then he hides out in this stupid forge of his when he should be with you. It's so goddamn hot in there, I'm literally dying, and I know he is too, but it's all worth it as long as he can keep me away from you, because that is the whole plan—"

"Oh. My. God. Will you ever shut up?"

His shoulders dropped as his expression darkened, jaw clenched, eyes no longer bulging.

Reluctantly, he planted his butt on the stool across from her but continued glaring with discontent.

"Thank you." Eve took a closer look at him now. It was so hard to tell them apart. "You talk differently. You used to sound so… I don't know… *uptight.*"

He folded his arms over his chest with the cocky arrogance she was more used to. "He's rubbing off on me. I'm conforming to my new environment."

"I think he's been hanging around Caleb and Lucas too much. *Their* crude vernacular is rubbing off on *him*." Kjan had never been big on profanity before, but lately he was dropping f-bombs left and right.

Kjartan threw back his head and laughed. "Oh you poor sheltered girl. You clearly don't know much about Viking Age insults."

Eve couldn't tell what shocked her more: the fact that the boys weren't to blame for his vulgar slang or the fact that his laugh was identical to Kjan's. They were more alike than ever before. Except for their eye color.

'*Eerie as fuck*', she heard Caleb's voice in her head.

The muscles in his face got serious again. "My father came to see me. He inquired about my intentions in regards to joining the Raven."

Eve hesitated, chewing her lip. "What did you tell him?"

"I understand how Hrafni feels," Kjartan admitted. "He's the son of Sigyn, yet he's not accepted among the Gods. His brothers were slaughtered, he wants the Gods to take responsibility for what they did. I have suffered more than anyone under their rule; of course I relate to that. We are both outcasts. Unwanted. I don't belong here. I don't belong anywhere."

"Sounds like you hold a grudge," Eve noted. "Are you going to do it? Help him wage war against the Gods?"

Kjartan cocked his head. "What do you think? You believe I'm reckless enough to challenge them? What could I possibly gain from helping him?" His eyes stared straight at her, challenging her to read his mind.

Eve shifted the weight on her feet uncomfortably. Technically, he was holding Kjan hostage at the moment, and that was exactly what he had to gain from the situation. "Let him go. Please."

He folded his arms over his chest with the defiant arrogance that pretty much summed up his character. He looked more like a pouting child than a God. "Are you sure that's what you want?"

She glared at him, hands on her hips, and he threw up his palms. "Fine. But if you change your mind…" Brows arched, he let the words drift.

Eve scowled at his suggestion. Did he think she'd call on him to take back over? Clearly, he'd enjoyed his little taste of freedom.

She knew he'd sworn a blood oath not to hijack his vessel, and he'd only broken it to save Kjan from the fire, but would he break it again if she asked him to?

"Just offering."

Kjartan gave a shrug, and in the blink of an eye, his body slumped on the stool.

Eve caught him by the front of his shirt before he fell backward, but the momentum of his weight ended up pulling them both to the floor. She crushed into his chest with a *thud*.

"Ugh. Jackass."

Kjan jerked awake, eyes wide.

"Not you," she blurted. "Are you okay?"

His hand seized hers at his front, his other arm snapping around the small of her back in a panic. "What happened?"

Eve pushed off, extending her hand down to him. "What's the last thing you remember?"

"I was in the forge," he replied, taking what was offered and rising to his feet.

"Actually, I take that back. You *are* a jackass!" Anger flaring, she punched her fist into his shoulder. "What were you thinking?"

He caught her wrist and yanked her into him, a look of remorse on his face. "I wasn't. I'm sorry."

His hand reached up toward her face and swept a strand of her hair back behind her ear. His subtle smile dropped when he saw her neck unblemished.

Kjan did the math, and there was only one possible explanation for the rapid healing.

He didn't say a word but averted his eyes, and Eve noticed the jerk of his Adam's apple as he swallowed.

She felt so guilty.

KJAN

She had taken *HIS* vein.

Eve had refused him but accepted *his Sire's* blood! What else had he missed?

Kjan could smell him on her. He imagined the immortal's greedy hands, his prints like smudges under a blacklight only visible to him.

His stomach hardened, then a burn crept up the back of his throat. Her rejection was acid spreading through him, poisoning him little by little.

"I have to go," he said, pulling away. "To the temple."

"The temple?" Her hands gripped his biceps, and there was worry in her deep blue eyes. "Let me go with you."

He could tell she didn't want him to leave her again, but he couldn't be around her right now.

"No!" The word came out too harsh, his brain was a scrambled mess. "I-I wouldn't ask you to go back there. I'll go alone. I heard this voice—" He rolled his eyes. "Not the usual one, a different one, while I was *under*. I don't know what it means, but maybe I'll find answers there."

Kjan was about to turn toward the backdoor of the kitchen when he faltered. "Will you wait for me to return?" he asked hesitantly.

He couldn't say for sure if he wanted her to stick around or go back to the penthouse, but a sixth sense told him that he probably shouldn't be left alone. There was still a possibility of him doing something drastic. He was no longer calculated and organized. He had become an unpredictable, emotional wreck.

Eve nodded with a tight smile. "Of course."

CHAPTER
32

KJAN

Kjan reached the bottom of the narrow staircase, which led to the maw of the beast. To each side, tunnels branched off, reaching deeper into the heart of the mountain and forming a maze of catacombs.

For no reason at all, he glanced around the darkness as if to make sure he was alone. And, of course, he was.

The large double doors that opened into the ceremonial chamber were made from solid slabs of stone, four inches thick. A heavy chain was wrapped around the curved iron bars that sufficed as handles, and a big lock hung from it. Kjan had the only key.

He unwound the chain and pushed one side open just far enough for him to slip through.

The air was stale and damp, littered with particles of dust floating suspended in time. Unlike the glacier cave in Iceland, it was completely man-made, yet it gave him the same tomb-like feeling. Kjan had the urge to turn around and confirm that the door behind him was still ajar, propped open to keep it from slamming shut. He hated the idea of being trapped underground.

As he glanced across the span of the chamber in the dark toward the altar at the far wall, he could make out the markings on the ground. An Ægishjálmr, the same symbol he had tattooed on his chest, was etched into the rough stone floor.

The Helm Of Awe, or Terror, was formed by eight identical staves that represented *Elhaz*, the protection rune. When painted between the eyes, the trident-looking arms reaching outward were supposed to strike fear in enemies, while the circle in the center was believed to give the wearer spiritual and physical protection as well as victory in battle.

Ironically, the old magic had never done either for him, but he was hoping his luck was about to change. He had a more direct line to the Gods nowadays, and the capabilities behind Eve's bindrune were just too convenient to be a coincidence. He couldn't ignore what was staring him right in the face.

Kjan's gaze brushed over the chains anchored into the floor—the set that had held his arms in place during the transference ritual. There were a few throughout the chamber, but the two reinforced cuffs they had used on him were different from the others.

Lucas had known Angel Torres, the craftsman behind the work, for a while. The boy told the immortal that other than producing *'sick tatts'*, he also had an astonishing gift for metal crafts.

No one knew how he worked his so-called magic, but the strange vampire claimed his cuffs could even hold a God.

His Sire had no intention to find out for himself. He mistrusted the man on principle. There was something unsettling beneath his vampire hide. Something that was not human.

Kjan crossed the distance to the altar and lit the two blood-red candles on the iron stands flanking the stone top. He remembered the simple ritual the immortal had used to evoke the clairvoyance incantation, but his own blood was far less potent.

His grandmother had told him stories about the Völva, the practitioners of Norse magic known as *Seiðr*. She had even believed that his mother had been a descendant of a very long, very old line of Völva. Naturally, Kjan had not shared her conviction. If his mother had seen her fate of dying in childbirth, she could have prevented it.

Second sight or prophecy-telling had been the most notable among the many *Seiðr* rituals used to reveal the hidden secrets of the mind, and it had been through a similar ritual that his Sire was able to tap into the magic to hear his own prophecy from the Norns.

Only to fail regardless.

The problem with the knowledge was that the meaning wouldn't be clear until it came full circle. It hadn't done him any good.

Nevertheless, the magic *was* present here.

Kjan inhaled a deep breath and leaned back against the altar. The dust irritated his lungs, lacerating his throat on the way down. He tasted copper.

His eyes roamed the chamber and then dropped to the immortal's *throne* in the center. Seriously, the bastard had no taste. At least, the black leather wingback chair Eleanor gifted him had style—Baroque, but still. The giant piece of granite wasn't just uncomfortable, it was an eyesore. All Kjan could see was a highchair, lacking the restraints for the perpetual child with the bratty attitude of a toddler.

The chair's dimensions were only *slightly* excessive. The seat was nearly four feet wide, and the oversized back towered at six feet in height.

The single thing that saved the throne was the carving on the inside of the backrest: a Web Of Wyrd.

Skuld's Net, or the *Weave Of Fate,* was a symbol of the Norns, the Shapers Of Destiny. According to the lore, Yggdrasill, the Tree Of Life, which tied the Nine Worlds together, had three roots with three wells watering it.

At the first well, the Well Of Urðr, three wise women watered the root. Urðr was the oldest and represented the past. She passed along the thread of an individual's fate chosen at birth to her sister Verðandi, representing the present. She, in turn, gave the thread to the youngest sister, Skuld, who would then cut the *'Thread of Life and Death'* with her scissors. She represented the future and was also a Valkyrja in the service of the Goddess Freyja, Queen of the Valkyrjur. Her legion of warrior women was known as the *Choosers of the Slain*, as they chose the fate of the warriors on the battlefields.

The numbers three and nine were fundamentally sacred numbers. The *Matrix* of the symbol on the stone was made up of three sets of three lines, one set vertically and the other two diagonally in opposite directions, all intersecting.

The web signified the deep, interweaved fabric between the past, present, and future of all living things within the entire cosmos; subsequently, if you looked closely at the image, you could make out every individual Futhark rune.

In the Old Faith, runes carried within themselves the destiny of the whole universe. His grandmother used to lecture him that all stages of one's life were linked and impossible to separate. *'Our deeds in the past will affect our present, and our actions in the present will in return affect our future'*. The Web Of Wyrd was a simple masterpiece of completeness with one important message: DON'T FUCK IT UP.

A female chuckle erupted from the other side of the throne, which was blocked from his view by the high back. "A coarse choice of words, yet it gladdens me that you remember its importance."

Her tone carried a lyrical charm that was almost hypnotic. It was the same voice he had heard in his head. *She* was the one who had summoned him here.

Kjan's feet should have been rooted to the ground, but his boots started moving, circling the stone chair in a wide berth, eyes glued to the space where her head would appear.

With each step he took, more of her was revealed: first, robes of deep green silk pooling at her feet, then her elbow propped on the armrest, and lastly, her stunningly beautiful face, resting on long, delicate fingers—a ring on every single one.

Sharp, piercing blue eyes stared back at him, watching him curiously as he searched for identifying characteristics. Her skin was like porcelain, smooth and flawless. Her caramel-colored hair cascaded in large waves down her back. On her head, she wore a crown of gold that shone as bright as the sun in the faint candlelight. It was inlaid with shimmering emeralds of various sizes and matched her massive necklace. A heavy cloak made from falcon feathers covered her shoulders.

The warmth of her aura bathed the grand chamber in a soothing honey glow. It settled over him like a blanket, instantly calming his inner turmoil. The sensation spurred a memory of his grandmother pacifying him when he was a child. It was the same kind of comfort he had felt all those times she had tucked him in.

The Goddess in front of him radiated beauty and love. It was clear to see why she had such a pull on men, human and immortal alike. Slouching sideways on the throne, her knees crossed, facing him, she waited patiently for him to add up the details.

Frigg and Freyja were two sides of the same coin. Her knack for jewelry and her famous cloak, which would let her take the shape of a falcon, were naturally the biggest clues. The outfit was a bit dramatic, and Kjan wondered if she always dressed like this or if she had gone overboard just to impress him.

He almost felt flattered, but then he remembered why he was here. Frigg was associated with the Norns, spinning the golden threads of fate they weaved and cut. She was assumed to know everyone's destiny but kept the events that transpired in the nine realms secret. Frigg was also the mother of the Light God Baldr and his twin brother Hǫðr, aka the God who had fathered his infamous passenger.

Kjan was little amused by the family reunion. Since she was here, the circumstances must surely be dire.

"Lady Frigg," he inclined his head in a respectful nod, addressing her in English since she had done the same. "I am honored by your presence."

She straightened on the throne, her hands resting comfortably on either side of her atop the extensive armrests. "Kjartan, son of Mýrkjartan, Ásgarðr requires your service."

Kjan nearly choked. "And what service might that be?"

"Do not play coy with me. You know very well why I have called you here." She brushed her hand through her hair, and golden earrings gleamed between the strands as she moved. "Hrafni is a threat. He must be eliminated."

"He said he came to claim a debt he is owed."

"Yes, his prophecy will hold true: Hann skal heimta skuldina," she said in Old Norse—*He shall claim the debt.*

Kjan snickered sarcastically. "What could *I* possibly do? He is the son of Loki. Last I checked, I'm not a God."

What makes me so special?

"You are more important than you can imagine," she replied in an effort to boost his self-assurance. "You have a way with words. You must convince him to change his mind."

"You butchered his family, and you expect me to clean up your mess?" Kjan's tone took on a dangerously snarky edge.

Frigg scowled. "I was not involved in the crime against his brother. His father had it coming; we all knew the prophecy."

"And the only reason you refuse to intervene is because you know he's right."

Her chest shot forward, and her fingers grasped the edges of the stone. "Hold your tongue! You speak of things you cannot possibly understand with your feeble human mind." Her eyes flared brightly, casting the blue light off the walls all around them.

Kjan didn't cower. "He deserves everything he asks for, but you want to save face," he said, standing his ground.

"And what would you do in our stead, *strákur*?"

Boy? Kjan almost laughed out loud. No one had addressed him with that term since he was three feet tall.

He stuffed the smirk. "Make a deal," he suggested. "Offer him a place in Ásgarðr. He is the son of two deities; he deserves as much."

Frigg's face softened, and she cocked an eyebrow. "Are you still talking about the trickster-spawn, or are you referring to someone else?"

"The Raven," he grumbled, his eyes doing another annoyed roll around the chamber.

"It is too late for that. He is too far gone, blinded by his thirst for revenge," she gritted out through her teeth. "You must make sure that Hǫðr's boy does not join him. Keep him from collaborating with the outcast."

"If you want this so badly, why don't you just take care of it yourself?" Kjan's fingers twitched. He refrained from balling them into fists in front of her.

Frigg's expression stayed unshaken. "We cannot interfere."

Kjan snorted. "You Gods are so self-righteous."

"Careful, my patience is running thin." She tapped her long, thin finger on the stone armrest. "It is forbidden. I must abide by the rules just like everyone else."

"What higher power do *you* answer to?"

Her eyes narrowed into slits. "One that is bigger than Gods," she replied, annoyed. "Destiny! You see, the fabric of life and time, as well as our universe, is like weaving together numerous individual threads to create a whole tapestry. Every single thread is essential. One of them comes loose… it affects all. It is a very delicate affair. The boy is disruptive. Like his father. He has a power of persuasion that steers others from their predestined path. If not handled, he can cause irreparable damage to the matrix."

"So you read his fate and you didn't like what you saw?"

"I have seen his destiny," she said, her fingertips grazing over the large jeweled necklace. "Trust me, you will not like it any more than I. But it is not in my power to deter it."

"I don't want any part of this."

"Not an option. Sometimes fate requires a little nudge in the right direction. We need your help. You owe us a favor."

Kjan's fingers twitched again. He didn't like her allegation. "I owe you nothing."

"Do you not enjoy our gift?" Frigg pursed her lips suspiciously.

He felt a jolt in his bones. "Gift?"

With the smooth roll of her wrist, she turned her hand over, palm facing up, and above it, gray smoke began to swirl. At first nothing but a blur, slowly a face emerged from the coils. Kjan recognized her anywhere, smiling up at him, blue eyes sparkling.

"Eve? I don't understand."

"She was fashioned after *her* image." Frigg opened her left hand, and a second cloud of smoke appeared, taking the shape of the woman who still stirred a deep pain in his chest.

His breath caught in his throat. "I have suffered enough," he said, turning his gaze away. He couldn't look at her, even if the image was an illusion.

"Yes, you have suffered many hardships in your long life, Kjartan, warrior, aptly named. The Norns wept for you the day you were born." Genuine sorrow showed in her expression. "I am sorry it took so long. But you were not ready."

Weren't ready?

He had to be driven to the edge of death a second time? Lose a mother. A wife. A daughter. All for what? To have him standing here now?

"Did you know?" he blurted. "You're supposed to have foresight more powerful than the Alfaðir. Did you know everything that would happen?" He could hear the tremble in his accusation with his own ears.

Frigg cocked her head. "If you believe that, then you know I could never say."

Well, if that wasn't admission, he didn't know what was. So, there he had it.

"Why?" he asked on a long breath. His shoulders felt as though the ceiling of the cave was weighing down on him.

There was something familiar about the way she smiled, but he couldn't put his finger on it. "To guide you in the right direction. I have always been there for you in one way or another, even if you did not know it. Thórunn's bloodline descended from one of my very own Valkyrjur. I sent her to you like I sent your mother to your father."

"My mother?" Kjan couldn't believe what he was hearing. Tears gathered in his eyes. "You have been meddling this whole time?"

"The blood of a seer ran in her veins. As it does in yours. Unfortunately, the ability to harness the gift is only passed down to the female line."

"Then you must have been so disappointed when I was born a male and made a kink in your plan," he grated out.

"Not in the least. You are exceptional and everything I knew you would be."

"Even though your plan backfired?"

"Who says it has? Your mother… Thórunn… even your friend Eleanor—they were my chosen."

He recalled his friend's final words of a dream she had in Marseille about a woman in a falcon cloak. "You asked her to sacrifice herself for me?"

"I did not. She offered. She was deeply devoted to you. They all were; no one needed any sort of persuasion. It was their decision to walk the path I lit. You included."

Yes, he remembered. "It was *your* voice I heard in the harbor that made me turn toward Anne, and then again in the woods, alerting me to Eve. You were there when I killed her."

"Only to observe," Frigg admitted. "But I made sure you caught her scent."

Her scent! *The arrival of spring… The return of life…*

"You sent them straight to me. Why the effort? Why would you do all this to influence my life?"

"You have immense potential. But you needed Andromeda to make you grow up. And you needed Eleanor to show you that you could love again. I put them in your path."

"They were nothing but pawns to you? Tools to weave your stupid web?"

"Your mother was a daughter of Skuld. Do not insult her memory. She was very precious to me. Your grandfather was the tool," she added dismissively.

"And yet you let her DIE!"

His last word briefly rebounded off the walls. He expected her to scold him for raising his voice, but she stayed calm and waited for the silence to reclaim the cave.

"Your mother knew her destiny, and she embraced it without reservation. She had the heart of a true Valkyrja. As does your little dove." She chuckled. "Funny coincidence, that nickname you picked for her. I definitely would have chosen her as one of my warriors."

And the Goddess had chosen *him*, too. Groomed him for *this*. "You helped *me*, but locked up your own grandson for all eternity out of spite?"

"The cave was for his own protection," she explained. "When he left, I assisted in the only way I could: by staying away. But that does not mean I abandoned him. He remained in my care."

In her eyes, Kjan could see a lot of the fierceness Freyja was known for and very little of Frigg's gentle, motherly virtues.

"It is not hard to be both," she replied, reading his mind. "Show me a mother who cares about her children, and I show you a woman prepared to wage war to protect them."

He supposed there was truth in that.

"Do not resent me for my actions, Kjartan. I have barely done anything. I tweaked her looks here and there a bit… It was irrelevant. You know you would have fallen for her regardless. Your love for her is not through her appearance. You love her for who she is underneath. All the choices you made were your own."

And in his heart, he knew she was right. He had chosen Eve as his mate. She was his match.

"Like it or not, warrior, the three of you are bound by fate, your lives intertwined by the choices you have made. Go now." She waved him off. "Before you insult me further, and I decide to punish you for your insolence after all. Be with your little Valkyrja."

CHAPTER
33

KJAN

Had he replaced the chain?

Kjan's body was back on autopilot with no memory of the drive back. He was just glad he had taken Eve's Cherokee instead of the Harley. She had conveniently left the keys dangling in the ignition.

The bike was still in the driveway where he had kicked it onto its side. The guilt had struck like a bomb in his chest, grief bursting the dam wide open and flooding his body until there was nothing left of him. *He* was to blame. For all of it. His conscience couldn't handle the shame. He had wanted to burn in the flames.

That was when his Sire had taken over. Kjan's memory was blank. How much time had he lost?

The sun was peering through the dark clouds as he made his way inside. The storm would take care of the forge fire in case there was anything left to burn.

Eve had fallen asleep on the couch, curled up like a ball. Her features were tense. Even in her sleep, her face showed worry.

Made for me? He kept repeating the words in his head.

He had been waiting for something, though, hadn't he? Salvation? Redemption? A sign?

He didn't know for what, but he hadn't wanted to give up. He had clung to hope, as all humans did, and then she had come along.

Kjan scooped her into his arms and carried her up the steps to the bedroom.

Hazily, she opened her eyes when he laid her down, and before he could pull away, her hands grasped the front of his singed shirt. "Please don't leave." Her voice cracked as she began to sob. "I'm sorry. He tricked me. I didn't want to."

"I know." He clasped her fingers and drew them to his lips, kissing them softly.

"Don't let go. I can't take another night away from you."

Neither could he.

Kjan felt the wall between them crumble. She shoved against the bricks he had erected around himself, clawing, and ripping them free with her bare hands one at a time until her fingers bled.

He let her in. All armor dropped as she smashed through his emotional shielding once again.

Kjan kicked his boots off at the side of the bed and wrenched his shirt up, chucking it into the far corner. But he didn't remove his jeans. And he lay down on his chest, his hips angled away. Having her body pressed up against his was too much, too soon. He had to earn his way back.

Settled beside her, his gaze riveted to her lush, strawberry mouth with its irresistible draw only inches from him.

His breaths grew heavy.

The knuckles of his right hand brushed the soft curve of her cheek as she faced him, but his eyes refused to pull away from her lips when they parted slightly, the tip of her tongue darting out to wet them.

Kjan wanted nothing more than to force *him* out of her. He wanted his own blood to replace any remaining traces of his Sire in her veins.

Eve reached for his hand, sliding her fingers between his, and once her mouth opened again, her brilliant white fangs were fully descended.

Raw lust overrode his senses at the sight of her, nerve endings firing vigorously in his brain. To make matters worse, she closed her eyes and dragged the steep point of a canine across his wrist to torture him.

Then she drove the little daggers home. The muscles in his back spasmed as sweet pain shot up his forearm.

Kjan chased the pleasure, squeezing his eyes shut. Sparks popped like fireworks behind his lids, and his gums throbbed from his own fangs itching to break free.

But instead of sinking them into her, he turned his head and punched them down on the bicep of his left arm, hard, while muffling a strangled moan. His hips ground into the mattress underneath him on impulse. This woman could bring him to his knees with just her bite.

Willing his eyes to open, Kjan watched her swallow him down. With every draw that she took in, filling herself, she chose him over the immortal.

When she was done, she ran her slick, warm tongue over his skin to seal the wounds. Unnecessary, but so gratifying. He steered her plump lips toward his, savoring the last taste of his blood in the kiss.

"I shouldn't have run out of the apartment," he said softly, nuzzling her cheek. "I was too afraid to hear the truth."

She shot him a critical look. "Why did you go to Ireland in the first place?"

Her question didn't surprise him. Why would a man choose to leave his wife for a year?

His eyes caught on the shiny ring on her right thumb as her hand rested on her chest. Kjan stared at the round, one-carat diamond in the center. Four white gold bands melted together created the wavy free form: her mother's engagement ring, anniversary band, and both her parents' wedding bands. He wondered how perfect their marriage must have been. In ten years, Thórunn and he had not been granted the blessing of a child.

"Do you remember the old cathedral in Dublin I told you about?" He didn't expect her to. He had only mentioned it fleetingly once when they had talked about architecture. And she had been half asleep in his arms at the time.

"The Viking one," Eve confirmed with a bob of her head.

"Iceland had just officially converted to Christianity. A Viking King founding a Catholic church was a big deal, especially for those who held onto the *Old Ways*. My father and I sailed with a small group." It had taken them five days out on the open ocean to reach the islands on the west coast of Ireland.

"You were gone for a long time." Her fingers grazed lazily over the short-cut sides of his hair, tracing the lines of the tattoos around his temple while he talked.

"I couldn't convince him to come back with me. He said the island was cursed."

Kjan paused, thinking of the last time he had laid eyes on the old man. He had been in his early fifties, Kjan twenty-six. "I had never seen my father happy. Not truly happy. There had always been a sadness to his smile. Iceland represented death and grief for him. In Ireland, he seemed at peace. The idea of starting fresh gave him hope. When I sailed home, he stayed behind. We said our goodbyes, and I never saw him again."

"Never?" Eve echoed, wrapping her mind around it.

Kjan shook his head.

"What about your grandmother?"

"She had wandered off into the mountains before we left."

"What do you mean *wandered off*?"

"It's not as strange as it sounds," he snickered. "It wasn't unusual. She used to say that she felt closer to the Gods among the volcanoes and glaciers. One day, she didn't return. She knew her time was coming to an end."

Eve grimaced, and he couldn't help but chuckle again. "Times were different."

"Apparently," she remarked. "What happened at the temple?"

Kjan draped one arm over her and nestled closer against her back, kissing her shoulder. "It can wait," he said wearily. He didn't want to open that can of worms right now.

KJARTAN

'Don't do this. She wouldn't want this for you,' Kjartan pleaded with the madman.

"Stop. Talking. You didn't know her, she wasn't yours to protect… she was *mine*. She was my entire world, and my foolish ambition killed her."

Kjartan felt like he had no choice. He watched Kjan's rant until he took it too far. The heat from the flames was bad enough, he had no desire to find out what it was like to be burned alive. Though they healed quickly, the pain was very real. He vividly recalled the image of his own body being consumed by fire after the transference of his mind into Kjan's vessel. He wasn't going to let the maniac burn. Eve would blame herself, and that was simply unacceptable. If his actions were for her sake, he wasn't technically breaking his oath. Her mental state was as much a concern as her physical safety. They both agreed on that.

Kjartan seized his opportunity when Kjan's defenses were down. The man's spirit was weakened by his self-loathing and guilt, making it too easy to reach in and overpower him. His consciousness unfolded like the sail of a ship in the wind, and once it spread to his fingers, he was in full control.

And so was the fire.

He found himself trapped amidst the blaze, flames licking at him from all sides, catching bits of his shirt on fire. The shed's walls moved as if they were alive. Black smoke blocked his sight of the ceiling, the wood creaking above him as it bowed.

The roof wouldn't hold much longer, the forge was beyond saving. *Time to pull out.*

Kjartan was about to lunge for the doors when a beam crashed down in his path, only narrowly missing his head. Sparks exploded out of it as it slammed into the ground, more smoke and ash stinging his eyes.

He shielded his face while dodging a second one landing in front of him. He could feel the embers burning his skin, and panic gripped him as his vision cleared. The path to the door was now blocked.

The realization struck him like a full blow to the gut. He wasn't going to make it.

Before Kjartan could brace himself for the worst, the barn doors burst open, ripped straight off the hinges.

"Need a hand?" the cocky voice bellowed.

The beams by his feet began to jitter and then followed the same trajectory the doors had taken.

As the dust slowly cleared, Hrafni's silhouette appeared in the opening, leaning smugly into the frame. He jerked his head over his shoulder, beckoning him out, but Kjartan hesitated, pretending to be underwhelmed by the little magic trick.

With a feral groan, the ceiling of the shed broke free. Raf's hands shot upward to prevent the roof from collapsing, his long coat swaying from his quick response.

Green light protruded from his fingertips as he held the weight in place. "Any time now," he gestured with a little more urgency, his eyes glowing a deep amber color in reference to his nickname. "I cannot hold this forever."

This time, Kjartan took the cue and dove through the opening. He landed with a heavy grunt, clearing the threshold just before Raf dropped the load.

The ground shook, the weight turning the rest of the forge into rubble.

Kjartan coughed the smoke out of his lungs and rolled onto his back, glowering at the flames as they continued in their frenzy.

His Samaritan stepped into view, looking down on him, sprawled on the concrete. "Miss me?" he asked, grinning wide. "I told you we make a good team. You are lucky I was in the neighborhood."

"Convenient," Kjartan bit out, sitting up.

"Hey, I had nothing to do with the fire." The Raven raised his hands in defense. They were burned. The black leather of his fingerless gloves was melted to the skin on his palms. He didn't seem to care.

"You are the son of Hǫðr, and a descendant of an Æsir Goddess. You have magic in your blood, but you are not using your full potential. You could do so much more than merely snuff out energy. I can teach you."

He held out his hand to Kjartan, who refused the help and got to his feet without the assist. He wouldn't give him the upper hand by expressing his gratitude.

"I want no association with *her*," he said, putting emphasis on the word. "*She* is the one who imprisoned me."

Even as he stood tall, the son of Loki was still taller than him. "The more reason to take what is rightfully yours," Raf pressed.

Kjartan shook his head. "I have no desire for revenge."

He made an attempt to walk past him, but the half-giant blocked his way, splaying a singed palm on his chest. "Where are you going? You and I have unfinished business."

"Watch it," he snarled back, baring his fangs.

The shifter's eyes flared in a darker shade of orange. "Or what?" he taunted.

Kjartan growled low, grinding his molars. "You might as well start digging your own grave. Vengeance will not bring you peace. It will not make you feel any better."

"No. You are right." Raf dropped his hand. "It will not make me feel any better. It will not make me feel anything. But as long as it makes them feel just a little bit worse, it will be worth it. All Frigg cares about is her precious *Web* and how it *aligns our universe*." His hands gestured mockingly. "I seek to plunge it into chaos. Is that not supposed to be my legacy? The Gods reaffirm me every chance they have. They never let me forget who my father was."

Raf cracked his knuckles as his tone grew in animosity. "You fought your fate once, against all odds, but that did not stop you. Deep down, you knew this girl was not destined for you, and yet you did everything in your power to change that. You failed, because you were alone. I am your only way. We are linked. We can try again… together. I will help you break free from the shackles of destiny. 'Old sin creates new debt', she told me. 'The debt is mine to claim'. That is my prophecy. My fate, Haðarson."

Kjartan's insides steeled at the sound of the name, the only one he had ever been given… through default, not devotion.

"Frigg gave you a prophecy that would lead you to me?" Kjartan mused. "Why would she reveal a way to disrupt the matrix? It makes no sense."

"She underestimates the bond between us… does not believe I could get you on my side, but we both want the same thing, brother." He spread his arms out to his sides, gloating. "A chance to prove we can be more than what destiny tells us to be. We are more than mistakes she can lock away and ignore. I am the closest thing you have to family. Me! Not these mortals you consort with."

Kjartan knew he used the term 'brother' to emphasize their affinity. To sink his claws deeper into the wounds which yearned to heal.

And it worked.

Guilt settled heavily in his stomach. He longed for the connection.

When he didn't get a response, Raf's impatience escalated. The half-giant stepped right up to him and glared down, his smile now small and cruel, drilling his finger into Kjartan's chest. A chill ran down his back that could have made a Frost Giant shiver.

"Your father is the God of the Accused. God of Atonement and of Redemption. Who are you to turn me away?" he asked with breath as cold as ice.

"I am over it." Kjartan shrugged to feign disinterest, but deep down, the Raven's temptation festered.

"Are you sure about that? I can sweeten the deal for you," Raf offered, his brows raised expectantly. "Just name your price."

Kjartan swallowed, his eyes shifting uneasily between the Raven's. He could see his point. Understood his reasoning all too well. He had tortured and killed to get where he was. Then everything changed. Did his affection for Eve make him weaker or stronger? The latter definitely applied to Kjan, but what about him?

The reject and the outcast working together?

The sound of Eve's SUV coming up the road made both of their heads snap to attention.

"Maybe it is time you figure out where your loyalties really lie," Raf hissed. "We will finish this later. I will be waiting." Then he vanished in a puff of green smoke.

Kjartan stared at the empty space where the boy had stood, then recoiled. A serpent slithered out of sight beneath the underbrush, the telltale copper streak on its back standing out against the black-scaled body.

CHAPTER
34

EVE

She looked up from her laptop. Kjan came around the house on the footpath from the forge, his expression sullen. "Anything salvageable?"

He'd been rifling through the debris for hours, avoiding her. After making up last night, she'd hoped they could move past the lingering issue together, but when she'd found him by the shed earlier, the wounded expression on his face was still there.

She'd retreated to the patio, giving him space to work out his frustration on his own. He would find her when it was done. He always did.

"I dried the blades and put them in the garage." Rubbing his hands on his jeans, he squeezed into the pod with her. The heavy rain had turned what was left of the forge into a black pile of metal and ash.

He pulled her legs across his lap and tucked her bare feet under the blanket. "Would it kill you to wear some damn shoes?"

"What, like a rusty nail from the forge, is going to be the death of me?" she mocked, snubbing his criticizing tone. "I had my tetanus shot before you killed me, you know?"

Eve waited for him to laugh, or at least give her a weary grin for the joke. His face remained stoic, like he hadn't even been listening.

She lifted her hands to smooth the deep crease between his eyebrows with her thumbs. "You still haven't told me what happened last night." Cradling his head, she wiped a dark smudge off his forehead. "Spill."

"I was recruited to stop the Raven… prevent the two from joining forces against the Gods."

"Recruited? By whom?"

He didn't look up, faking a sudden fascination with the pattern of the fleece comforter. "Frigg," he murmured.

"*Frigg* was the one whose voice you heard?" Eve's eyes nearly popped out of her head. "Of course she would suggest *you* for the job instead of getting her own hands dirty. Hypocrite. Why does she assume Kjartan would even consider it?"

His frown deepened. "She knows that he does. She knows everyone's fate. It's not exactly a far reach; they have a common goal. Revenge!"

"Kjartan doesn't want revenge. He told me himself that he doesn't hate them." He'd made the statement nearly a year ago, but last night he'd given her no indication to assume his opinion had flipped.

"Things have changed, Eve. He has an ally now."

"*You* are his ally. You have a truce." He had sworn a blood oath to Kjan not to reclaim his body unless Eve was in danger. The oath was the only thing that kept the powerplay between the two in balance. Not to mention, Kjartan owed him for accepting the deal to return.

It made her wonder what would've happened to him had Kjan chosen to stay with Thórunn. Was there another place for him to go? Or would he have simply ceased to exist?

"Loki's son has a silver tongue. He's persuasive."

"Then *he's* the enemy we need to focus on!" Eve exclaimed. "Hrafni came to the penthouse after you left. He just showed up on the patio."

Kjan's expression was one of utter shock. His conscience really had been completely unaware during her talk with his Sire. "He tried to hurt you?"

"No!" Interesting, how their reactions differed. Kjan's first concern was for her safety.

"Then what did he want?"

"Nothing. I mean, he didn't say much. Only thanked me. And then dove off the rail."

"Thanked you? For what?"

"I'm not sure," Eve replied. "I was worried that he was going after you, but when I got here, you were alone... um, I mean, *Kjartan* was alone."

Kjan exhaled frustratedly and pinched the bridge of his nose. "What did he tell you? Did he talk to the Raven again?"

"N-no. At least... I don't think so," she stammered. "He didn't say that he saw him." She tried to recall his exact words.

"You mean, you didn't ask."

A thrum of tension rippled over her from the sharp edge in his tone.

"I…" She opened her mouth, but the words failed her.

"Then we have to assume that they talked."

"He told me he didn't agree to anything. He wouldn't lie to me."

"Yes, he would," Kjan snapped. "You can't trust him, Eve. He's been meeting with the shifter behind my back. I'm sure of it."

He leaped out of the pod and headed toward the patio doors. "I had the chance to get rid of him. I should have taken it," he muttered to himself, raking a hand through his hair.

"What are you talking about?" she called after him.

"At the cave." He swung around. "When we went back. I could have left him there. I could have ended it. None of this would be our problem right now."

"But you didn't. Because that's not who you are." Kjan was kind and compassionate. Not malicious.

"What if, subconsciously, the only reason I went back was to trap him?"

"You really believe that?" She furrowed her brows. Why did he see himself in such a negative light?

"I don't know. I keep asking myself if I made the wrong call. What if the roles had been reversed?" Kjan shook his head as if he were clearing it. "We can't trust his words."

Eve didn't want to believe it. He'd seemed sincere. Kjartan had never openly lied to her. He would bend the truth to his advantage, but he wouldn't knowingly put them all in danger.

"He can't go against you. He has sworn an oath to uphold the truce, right?"

Kjan's dark green eyes stared at her like she was missing the point. "He doesn't have to break the oath himself, Eve. The Raven will do it for him. They have a loophole."

What loophole? As long as Kjan didn't concede, his Sire couldn't overpower him. And there was no chance in hell he would give up.

"I don't know…" Eve tucked her hair back behind her ears. His speculation felt like an overreaction to her. It had to be the paranoia talking.

"Why are you defending him? Why are you taking his side?"

"It doesn't feel right. It doesn't sound like him."

"DOESN'T SOUND LIKE HIM?" He raised his voice, jealousy pouring out of him. "You base that on WHAT? A week you spent with him. You don't know him the way I do. You can't trust him."

Eve lowered her eyes. Kjan was being unreasonable. He was accusing Kjartan of betraying them without giving him the slightest benefit of the doubt. "Let me talk to him. Give him a chance to explain—"

"You don't believe me? You're choosing *his* word over mine—"

His voice faltered, and he took a step backward, his face turning to stone as the deep red color replaced the last emerald shimmer in his eyes.

Kjan stormed off, suffocating the flames of the firepit in his icy wake and slamming the glass door behind him. Eve ducked back into the pod as it exploded into pieces, shattering the entire row of panes along the side of the cabin.

Her body trembled from the blow. She stared at the little crystal shards glittering all around her in the faint light of the stars above.

CHAPTER
35

CALEB

"C'mon… pick up," he muttered into the speaker. He recognized that look in Lucas' eyes. He was about to snap.

Caleb had seen his best friend go off before, and everyone in his proximity was likely to catch a fist once he got going.

Why'd the asshole have to make that comment about Bayley's rack?

No way was Lucas going to ignore that. He would make the guy eat his words… along with his front teeth.

"Let it go, Luke. Ah've been dealing with the likes of him for a long tahm. He ain't worth the trouble you'll get in." Scrunching her perky little nose, Bayley shot the loudmouth a narrow glance before returning her focus to the ticking bomb beside her. "Please."

Her dark brown eyes were rolled way up to look at Lucas, but he wasn't listening to her. His chest heaved against her palm as he glared straight ahead at the other guy.

He and his friend were laughing now. The one who'd let the comment slide had his elbow braced on the bar's countertop, a beer in his meaty fist. He nudged his buddy in the side. "Look how the little woman sticks up for him."

Their shit talk didn't end there; more insults kept coming over the bar's general volume. Every word was perfectly audible. Caleb's teeth started itching.

Both guys were tall and sturdy, bigger than Lucas, but they had no idea what they were facing. And the *'little woman'* was just as vicious as the man—vampire—beside her. She just had better self-control. If they both let loose…

Caleb hung up, then redialed, his thumb slipping across the screen. Kristján was taking too long. Maybe he could get—

Glass shattered beside him. The crash jolted right up the roots of his hair, and he saw Lucas clutching the neck of the Dos Equis the motherfucker had been holding a second ago. He must've ripped it right out of his hand and slammed it into the edge of the counter. The bottom half of the bottle was gone, its remnants scattered by Lucas' feet.

"Your cock's not going anywhere near my girl." He raised the jagged ends of the green glass between them as he leaned into the guy whose face had gone pale. His mouth hung slack, and he looked like he might piss himself.

Lucas' fangs were definitely showing now. He went on in a low, grating voice no less sharp than his weapon, "The only place it's going to go is down your throat when I feed it to you."

Caleb's hand started shaking. The unnerving sound of the dial tone kept drilling through his eardrum.

"Shit-shit-shit." Someone was going to get hurt.

Or killed.

KJAN

She's choosing him? HIM?

Kjan was falling, spiraling, his body moving forward, down a dark abyss with no floor to catch him. Eve had been the only other person who hated the immortal as much as he did. The only one whose loyalty he had never questioned. Her unexpected change of heart was like a knife in his back—or more like a broad sword by the weight and pain of it.

He hadn't told her about his proof because he wanted her to trust him regardless. It shouldn't have been necessary to sway her judgment. Where had he gone wrong when the woman who was supposedly made for him chose someone else over him?

Kjan anticipated his Sire's self-satisfied laughter, but it never came. There was nothing. No taunt, no sneer, no malice. Just more silence.

And he did have proof that the leech had made contact with the Raven again: the mud on his boots.

When he kicked them off by the bed, there had been only dry dirt on the soles from his trip to the cave, but when he picked them up later at night, they had been wet. He had been out in the woods after the rain, and Kjan had no recollection of the meeting with the shifter.

Last year, his Sire had chained his mind to keep him restrained but aware of his surroundings. Every action, touch, or word spoken… he had been there. Right up until he put his final plan into motion, and decided to shut Kjan out.

Like last night.

As if trapped underwater, his sensations had been cut off from the outside world. The bastard was deliberately blocking him out to keep him in the dark, and Eve was falling for his act.

It was no longer the two of them versus the immortal and the shifter. It was three against one. She was helping them. Unwittingly. Kjan knew that if he lost her, he was done. It wasn't Hrafni who would put the final nail in his coffin. It was Eve.

His Sire's words repeated in his head about Andromeda having been unable to kill him directly because she had still seen him as her mate. How could he not think of Eve at the temple on the night of the blood moon?

She had turned the stake on herself rather than on him.

But was that really the work of the mate-bond preventing them from killing each other, or was it something different?

Kjan's mind started reeling. Could it be some sort of failsafe, preventing you from killing the one who made you? He hadn't been able to kill *his* Sire. And unlike Eve and Andromeda, he had tried.

What if it really was impossible to physically turn against the one who sired you? What other option did he have?

He picked the Harley off the concrete and set it upright to inspect the damage. The paint job had suffered the most, but everything else looked decent. Definitely drivable. He scanned the driveway.

Where the fuck's the damn helmet? Whatever. He didn't need it.

His phone buzzed, and he rejected the call without so much as giving the screen a glimpse. He shoved it in his back pocket and got on the bike. He was itching for a good fight. If he was careful, he could pick one with a human, and if he was lucky, he might even find a vampire to take his rage out on. Downtown was always littered with creatures of the night, but they usually gave him a wide berth. They knew what was good for them. They could tell he was different. Stronger. Faster.

Kjan really hoped to get lucky tonight.

He pulled up to the shifty dive bar and killed the ignition. The rampant ambiance of the bar was exactly what he craved. Maybe he could talk himself down by feeding on the scum that dwelled here.

His cell continued to vibrate in his pocket, and he ignored it. He slithered through the doors, drawing little attention, except from a woman in a scrap of black that couldn't legally be called a dress. Barbie's brunette twin looked him up and down with lustful eyes, chewing her blood-red lip. She forgot all about the guy drooling over her fake tits.

Kjan pressed on, nudging past the rest of the clientele toward the booths on the other end where he parked it. Slouching low under the dim lights, he closed his eyes and sifted through the different emotions in the cramped space.

An uneventful hour crawled by in a mostly orderly fashion, with a few insults flying here and there when the mellow tide suddenly turned. An altercation broke out at the bar, instantly turning into a skirmish as two drunk idiots started shoving each other.

Years at his club in Vegas had drilled him to break up any kind of argument that threatened to become violent and dangerous to innocent bystanders. Collateral damage was unacceptable.

He kept his head down. *Let it go. It's none of your business.* Only his eyes didn't obey the command sent from his brain. He glanced in the direction of the bar.

Fuck. The shorter one of the two was *his* idiot.

Lucas' white-hot aura stood out of the crowd like a flare. Fists twitching by his side, his body was braced to attack.

Bayley was there, too. Her long blonde waves whipped around her head. She looked terrified while tugging on his arm. Her elongated vowels and the muted *r*s—the exact opposite of the Icelanders and Nessa—carried over the noise all the way to him, but Lucas ignored her pleas.

The tiny girl was just as bossy as Emma, yet small enough to fit in his pocket. If it weren't for her boobs. At barely over five feet, she was rather top-heavy and liked to show them off as much as Dynja did. Originally from Georgia, she had worked her way around the west coast as a night nurse over the past eleven years. She got her blood supply from a local hospital, where she currently pushed shifts. *Must be her night off.*

Kjan pulled out his phone to check the missed calls. All three were from Caleb. And what do you know? The kid emerged next to Lucas with Kristján flanking him on the other side. The situation was under control, no need for him to step in.

His resolute commitment fell through the second his mate's presence registered. Her head bobbed through the crowd, shoving at guys twice her size.

Eve reached the bar where Kristján was holding Lucas back. She was livid. She went off on the boy, grabbing the front of his shirt to pull him down to her eye level, her lips moving fast.

Kjan's skin caught fire. Every fiber in his body told him to step in and protect his mate from the threat. Lucas was unpredictable. He could crush her.

The unimaginable happened next. She got through to him. Whatever words were leaving her lips actually made an impact, and Lucas' shoulders dropped. His fists unclenched. Even Caleb and Kristján cringed uncomfortably and took a step back.

Kjan remembered the boy calling her scary. He was right.

Eve let go of his shirt and stabbed her finger at his chest to make one more point. Then her posture changed. Her head whipped around in Kjan's direction, her eyes locking with his in a glare that sliced him open from gut to breastbone.

He had been made.

CHAPTER 36

EVE

Eve couldn't believe her senses; she thought her mind was playing tricks on her. Kjan was *here?* Sitting back in the dark booth and enjoying the show?

She sucked in a breath. "What the fuck was that?" she went off, planting her palms flat on the table in front of him. "You were just going to sit there and watch?"

He held her gaze, unoffended. Tension prickled over her skin.

Eve slid into the seat across. His scent was dark and cloudy; no more hints of sweet cherry. Something had changed in him.

"Go home! You shouldn't be here." His eyes narrowed to show his disapproval of the place.

He was right. It wasn't her kind of hangout, but she wasn't going to let him tell her where she could or could not go.

She folded her arms over her chest and leaned back. "Caleb called me because he couldn't reach you. You didn't answer your phone."

"Why am I always the one expected to clean up their mess?" he sneered, thick with disdain.

Eve was reminded of the night he had hesitated to help Caleb. "They come to you for help."

"Great," he huffed. "I'm the fucking babysitter."

"Caleb looks up to you. They call on you because they trust you. We're a family."

"Ha!" A sharp laugh burst out of him at that. "Dysfunctional like one, true." He rolled his eyes.

"Wow! Tell me how you really feel, why don't you? Where is this hostility coming from?" It was clear now that the problem wasn't that he thought they didn't want him around. *He* was the one rejecting their coven.

"I don't trust them," Kjan replied brusquely. "They turned on you once. They will do it again. *He* sired them. They are bound to *him*."

Eve's jaw dropped. "Then by default, so are you," she countered his absurd reasoning. "He turned them into mindless drones. You know that. You were there at the temple," she pointed out. "They didn't like being controlled any more than you did. Kjartan didn't—"

Boom!

Eve jumped when Kjan's fist slammed down on the table, the impact shaking the top like an earthquake and knocking over the menu stand.

"Stop using that name!" he growled at her over the noise of the bar.

Red flames licked through the emerald in his eyes. "That name is dead to me. Just like the man it belonged to. The bastard stole everything else from me. I will not have him take that," he gritted out through his teeth, nostrils flaring as he forced heavy breaths.

Eve exhaled harshly to pull her thoughts together. It was like talking to a stranger. "He… he didn't give them a choice," she continued calmly. "Do you really believe they would have gone along with that of their free will?"

"We will never know," he underlined in a cynical tone, letting his words dangle in the air for a moment.

Then his glance darted to the bar and back to her, his mouth tight, and he leaned in closer across the table, lowering his voice. "Eve, you're kidding yourself. You have nothing in common with them. You still have actual family, remember?"

She raised her eyebrows, giving him a pointed look. "Which you made me give up," she retorted.

"Bullshit! I never told you to cut Joe out of your life. That was your choice. Don't you dare put that on me. I would give anything to—"

Kjan froze without adding the rest, his eyes wide in surprise at his admission. All anger washed away.

"*To revoke your choice?* Go ahead. Finish that sentence," Eve dared him.

She held her breath as she watched him grind his teeth through sealed lips. The bitterness in him ran so undiluted it bled through his skin into the air. The tang mixed with the smoldering anger she was trying to hold back herself.

The muscles in her jaw and shoulders flexed. What shot out next wasn't something she would've said to him a mere week ago. "I'm sorry you blew your only chance at reuniting with your *real* family. Maybe you shouldn't have made such a rash decision."

Eve pushed out of the booth and lunged for the exit without looking back, tears muddling her vision. She didn't want him to see her cry.

KJAN

A shard of ice lanced through him. She thought she had taken the words out of his mouth, but she couldn't be further from the truth. What had made him choke up was the fact that he had used the exact wording his Sire had thrown at him after the incident with Lucas. *'I would give anything to trade places with you'*, he had said.

…give anything…

Still, Eve got it wrong. *'…give anything to have a family of our own'*, had been at the tip of his tongue.

He could never give her that. And he had ripped that future away from her too.

The hollow sensation in his gut came back, and his stomach tightened. Replaying her interaction with the guys in his head, something struck him that he hadn't fully realized until now. She *had* friends. She *had* a family. Eve had managed to become an integrated member of the group where he had not. The failure on *his* part had made him the sole outsider.

Kjan felt the darkness pulling him away from the light and couldn't fight it.

CHAPTER

37

EVE

She clenched her teeth to keep them from chattering.

Arms wrapped around herself to brace the cold, Eve stood on the patio, wondering how long it would take for her to turn into an ice sculpture; she could practically feel the little crystals form inside her blood.

She focused her mind on the physical sensation to prevent a total meltdown. The blast of his rage shattering the window panes had sent a chill so deep down her bones she still felt the shiver.

There was no moon tonight. The sky stretched out like a gray canvas with only a few stars visible in the brightly illuminated view of South Waterfront.

Eve reminisced about the night they'd hiked to the glacier. She'd never seen so many stars. Not even the view from the cabin compared to the wasteland of black ash and snow-covered mountains. She hadn't properly appreciated the tranquility of it all at the time. Now, she'd happily volunteer to crawl back into that hole and hide.

Peering straight down over the edge at the long drop, she felt neither angry nor relieved when the throaty rumble she knew wasn't the sound of thunder rolled in.

After leaving Kjan at the bar, she didn't want to go back to Mount Hood, so the penthouse became her refuge once again; whether from the world or from him, she hadn't decided. Though she should've known he'd find her anyway.

He always did.

Eve sensed Kjan's presence in her skin like the warm golden glow of a sunrise. He appeared in the patio's doorway, and she gave a quick glance over her shoulder.

He looked uneasy with his hands shoved deep into his pockets, trying to figure out the right words to approach her. He probably expected her to kick him out. She had good reason.

"I hate this. I hate the fighting."

"All we do is fight. Make up. Then fight again," she grumbled. "Why did you come?"

"To tell you that you're wrong. I don't regret staying. It's the only thing I *never* regretted," he emphasized.

"You've been keeping everyone at arm's length, and now you're pushing me away too. I used to feel you in my head, but you closed yourself off and pulled so far away... I can't reach you." She hugged herself tighter. "This jealousy is eating you up. I don't know who you are anymore."

Testing the water, he dragged his boots on the ground. "I don't want to push you away, Eve," he said softly as he stopped beside her.

Turning his back to the skyline, he leaned against the metal rail. His deep bottle-green eyes fixed on her, he uncrossed her arms and slid his hands into hers.

His touch was timid, with a tremble so subtle she might have imagined it as he entwined their fingers. "You are the last person I want to push away."

She raised her gaze to his. The little part of his soul within her strained to reconnect with itself. It wasn't the same. The glow of his aura remained shallow somehow, only skin-deep without reaching her heart.

He lowered his forehead to hers. "The truth is," he said, "the anger, the rage… it's because I'm scared. Terrified. If I lost you… it would be the end of me."

Eve scowled. "I love you too, you know? You think it's any different for me?"

The corner of his mouth drew into a small grin just before he swooped down and kissed her, but the second they touched, his insistence fled.

He released her hands, his fingertips skating idly up her arms to her shoulders, and Eve felt herself melt into his kiss, the warmth spreading over her skin like a blanket.

The brush of his lips was ginger and light. He wouldn't take what he so desperately wanted. He waited for her to come to him, coaxing her tongue into seeking out his.

When his fingers wound through the hair at the base of her neck, it was too easy to get lost in the moment and forget about the world around them. She wished they could hide in this bubble forever.

He broke away, drawing a jagged breath. "You make it so damn hard to keep my priorities straight, woman," he rasped.

"You are the ideal of temptation. This is not what I came here for, but when I touch you, it's all I can think about."

His fingers twitched nervously, cradling her head, and then his gaze flitted to the sky above. "The new moon is a symbol of a clean slate. A new beginning," he said, focusing back on her. "I hurt you, and I'm not taking that lightly. I swear I will earn back your trust if you give me a chance to prove it."

"You have to promise me that you won't let him come between us anymore," Eve demanded, meeting his eyes as they stared into her soul.

She reached for his hands, and his focus flittered briefly to the runes on her wrist.

"No one will come between us," he vowed, kissing first the blue brand, and then sealing his promise against her lips.

When he pulled away, his gaze dropped down the low-cut front of her T-shirt, regarding the goosebumps among other perks on her chest attentively. "And you're not freezing on my watch," he added, dragging her inside.

Curled up under the warm comforter on the bed, time stood still again. Here, nothing could harm them. No Hrafni. No Kjartan. With Kjan by her side, she felt safe. Everything was perfect. Together, she knew they could conquer anything.

He took her hand and kissed the knuckles of her fingers as Eve nestled into the crook of his shoulder, which was somewhere along the lines of snuggling with a red-hot lava rock. The fog in his eyes had lifted, giving them a significantly brighter shimmer of green.

"Did it ever cross your mind to just drop everything and leave?" he asked out of the blue. "Let this whole mess be someone else's problem?"

Eve grimaced at the coincidence of him bringing this up now. It was all she'd been thinking about for the last few hours. "You mean, run from responsibilities? That doesn't sound like you."

"If we could run away from all this… start over somewhere new. Would you do it? Would you leave with me?" he asked, his eyes suddenly sparkling with enthusiasm.

"You're asking me to run away with you?"

"Hypothetically."

"Where would we go?"

"Doesn't matter. Anywhere."

"Yes," she replied decisively, cupping his cheek, her thumb grazing his stubble. "I would. I love you, and I would follow you to the end of the world. To a place where it's just you and I. No Gods. No magic."

Eve's tone lost its cheerfulness. "But there's nowhere we could hide from them."

"You're right," he said with disappointment, as if she had taken the wind out of his sails, crushing his perfect fantasy. "Forget I mentioned it."

He pressed his lips to her temple and then fell back into deep thought. "Maybe we should just go for a drive. Take the bike out."

"Me on the Harley?" Eve blurted surprised. "That would be a first. You've never taken me on it?"

"Then it's about time, Love. Tomorrow night."

Renate Rowland

CHAPTER 38

HRAFNI

Raf discarded the charred piece of wood and wiped his hand on the dark denim as he sat cross-legged. The friction against his palm made him cringe. The pads of his fingertips had been the fastest to heal with the use of very little magic, yet the rest of the flesh remained tender and the muscles stiff.

The low temperature inside the house did not aid his recovery. His current lodgings were meager and at the same time represented a luxury. In animal form, he did not require much space or a roof over my head.

As a man, however, he was cold.

Raf was reminded of Níflheimr. The world of his birth was colder than cold. A murky mist hung heavily, hiding the sky and cloaking the landscape in gray. The ground was equally shrouded by chilly fog, and he had always hated it there.

But the tremble in his bones was more than climate-related. He felt the pulling sensation across his skin despite the layers of clothing. His entire body ached, not just his palms.

He gave his injuries another critical look, then flipped his hands over. Traces of charcoal stained his nails.

Blocking out the pain, he worked his fingers to force mobility back. The wounds impeded his dexterity, and thus his magic. He could not afford to lose the advantage it gave him.

While flexing the little joints, his eyes sprang to the wall before him, which was no longer blank. The knife in his heart twisted deeper until he had to avert his gaze.

Another shiver ran across his body. *Cold... always so cold ...*

And hungry, his empty stomach reminded him with a growl. Because, unfortunately, he also needed food to keep his magic up.

But large prey was scarce in these temperatures. And although meals were the easiest to come by as a bird, he could not consider digging caterpillars out of the ground particularly satisfying for long. Other than snatching a rabbit as the wolf two days ago, he had relied on fish from the nearby lakes.

Raf pushed off the floor and left the little house through the window of the second story.

Of all his forms, the raven came most naturally to him. While the wind beneath his wings gifted him the feel of freedom, he could cover great distances within minutes.

The city, of course, offered an abundance of food sources, but he refused to pick at the trash left behind by humans or choke on their diseased rodents. With a quick slide of his hand, he stole apples right from under the vendor's nose. He stole anything he wanted.

He liked roaming the city. The streets were crowded during the day, masses of strangers passing by, paying no attention to him. He was anonymous. An ordinary face amongst many—though he was significantly taller than most when he chose to walk in his true form.

He did on occasion.

He had his ways of seizing opportunities to play little tricks here and there, keeping himself entertained. And if he was lucky, he had the chance to mess with the angry one some more. The one they called Lucas. Raf would whisper into his mind, and he always took the bait. He was so full of doubt and self-loathing that it was too easy.

Manipulating *any* human was easy. They were weak.

He sat down on the roof of an apartment building. The hands on the church's clock tower told him it was 8:30 in the morning. The sun had risen a little while ago, but it was hard to tell through the black clouds. Rain was imminent.

He gave his wings another flap, then sailed down into the dark alley, where he shifted. When he emerged onto the sidewalk, he stepped right into the human traffic to merge with the flow.

He kept his eyes on alert for any potential victims—people who were distracted with their attention on the little devices in their hands. There were so many, it took no effort at all.

Shoulders squared, his right side bumped into a man coming toward him. He quickly apologized, giving his most unassuming smile before moving along. The gentleman never noticed Raf's hand slipping into his coat pocket.

He repeated the spiel two more times, lifting the paper currency from the billfolds, then discarding them in the cans lining the street.

Somewhat familiar with Portland now, he recognized the individual buildings that had originally felt like a maze to him. He was more accustomed to open fields and plains, or the occasional old-growth forest.

He sought out the same café he had visited on his last trip here. Choosing a seat in the back, he gave the table next to him a glance—sausage, eggs, and bacon.

Not for him. He kept his order simple. And he had a craving for something sweet this morning. A celebratory treat. Last night's unexpected events had worked out in his favor.

The man across from him shifted uneasily, but not because he was uncomfortable in his seat. His stare kept landing on Hrafni, though he tried his best to avoid getting caught. It drifted over every visible body part of his, and he felt his skin flush under his clothes.

Raf reached into the man's mind. *Look again!* he said in a low, entrancing timbre.

The man complied on command, his Adam's apple jerking from the surprise of finding Raf staring right back.

Amusement tugged at the corner of his mouth, and he cocked his head in satisfaction. He liked the positive attention. Reveled in it. It was something utterly new to him.

And maybe to the man across as well. Flustered, he wet his lips, then swallowed again as he dropped his eyes.

A moment later, he pushed to his feet and almost tripped over himself to escape.

His interaction with the waitress was similar. She, too, blushed and hid a shy smile when she brought his order.

"Much obliged," he said, keeping his eyes on her instead of the plate-sized waffle she dropped in front of him.

He noticed the nervous flutter of her lashes, but she held his gaze until she turned away.

Too easy.

Sucking the last bit of powdered sugar off his fingers, he watched the downpour through the window while contemplating his return flight. For all he knew, he could be delayed here for hours.

Drawing up a random portal in an alley was beyond his skill—there was only one God powerful enough to do so—and the natural gates he had to rely on only occurred around waterfalls, since they received their magical powers straight from the well in Níflheimr.

The roaring spring called Hvergelmir in the center of the realm of fog and ice was known to be the origin of many rivers all over the nine realms, thus creating a network for him to travel. Through a waterfall, he was able to produce a doorway to get him anywhere he wished, in this world or any other.

Yggdrasill had gates on Miðgarðr, of course, but they were heavily warded. Opening any to the other eight realms would trigger a magical resonance alerting the tree's infamous guardian. Raf knew because he had tried. To keep magical interference to a minimum in the realm of mortals, Ásgarðr had decreed it off limits. Like a habitat sanctuary for their little pets. Access was only granted to the elite. Raf naturally did not fall under the term.

But he had a plan for that. He knew a way around… if you were willing to take the risk.

And Raf was.

Alas, a running stream was not to be reached on foot in these conditions. He had to wait. Although not for long. The rainfall soon began to slacken.

Raf paid and left a generous tip that was double the check before rising from his seat. He found human money strange. When had they given up on hard metals for payment? Gold and silver made much more sense. Why paper? It was worthless.

Swiping an apple from the buffet on his way out, he stepped into the freezing drizzle. His muscles tensed. He hated this. Why could fate not have sent him someplace warm?

The street was less crowded now. Few people still rushed between vehicles and buildings to find shelter. He rounded the corner to the nearest alley for a little bit of privacy. Feet firm, he closed his eyes to calm himself. Once the noise of the city completely disappeared, he was able to shift.

He landed back in the same woods behind what was left of the forge. The ground was wet, but it was no longer raining.

He ruffled his feathers to shake off the remaining drops, then returned to his innate shape. His hair stuck to his face, and he was soaked to the bones, freezing.

Channeling the spark of his essence, he felt his chest warm as his magic flowed from his center of gravity outward toward his hands.

He reached up, brushing his fingers through the plastered black strands on his head that he had neglected to braid this morning. The ripple of magic following the motion dried him instantly, top to bottom.

Much better.

He gave his neck another roll, chasing away the last chills, then he sensed it. A familiar presence lurked among the shadows between the trees. The same one that had been stalking him for months.

"I know you are there," he called out in a singsong voice that carried a goading lilt. "Third time's the charm."

First at the warehouse in Portland after Kjartan's deal with the Russians, then again in Reykjavík, and now here. He kept interfering, blocking Raf's magic, so the Godling couldn't sense anything.

A sudden gust of wind rose from the ground by his boots, twirling and twirling around him until it engulfed him entirely.

The cyclone became a swirling wall of black in front of him, a shadow, so dense no sound or sight could penetrate it. There was nothing to see, save for his loose hair whipping across his face with the motion. In the eye of the storm, he was cloaked in darkness, cut off from the forest, although he had never physically moved.

Angry sparks tickled at his fingertips as they ignited like flint, emitting a soft crackling that persisted in his coffin. "Show yourself, coward," he called into the vortex.

A cold laugh answered over the thrashing of the wind. Then the twirling gusts faded to a light breeze and, lastly, died away, releasing him back into daylight.

A dark figure manifested among the shadows and took a casual step forward. He was tall, broad, and looked every bit the warrior his name declared him to be. His expression was hard, no longer amused.

A black void emanated from his shape, like the opposite of a halo. A sort of armor, perhaps? It appeared to suck away anything in existence around him.

Raf fought against the urge to shrink back. He knew he should have been cowering. So naturally, he did the opposite. "Look whom she sent… the cripple."

"Watch your tongue, boy."

"Or what?" he taunted with the intrepidity of a madman. "Will you smite me where I stand? You are her executioner, are you not?"

Hǫðr took another reserved step toward him. It was fascinating to watch him move. There was no uneasiness in his stride. "I am not here to fight you, Lokason. I have come to mediate."

"Ha!" he chirped. "One outcast to another?"

Hǫðr's pale green eyes focused on the source of the insults, his blind gaze only slightly tipped downward as they stood at equal height. His shoulders were relaxed and his arms hung loosely by his side, but Raf knew he did not necessarily require his hands to work magic. He could do things with the sheer will of his mind. He was considered one of the powerful three—perhaps even more powerful than his twin.

"Return the blade."

"What blade?"

"*My* blade!"

Could the blind God sense it on him? Raf wondered whether he was able to track him through the weapon. If it was indeed made of his shadows, there had to be some kind of physical connection.

But apparently Hǫðr could not take it from him by force. Not unless Raf lifted the cloaking spell of his own magic.

"Ohhh! You mean the one you left in my ribs?" he mocked with a dramatic eyeroll. Then his features turned hard again. "No."

The insolence did not appear to ruffle the God before him. "What is it that you want?" he prompted calmly. "State your retribution so we can be done with these theatrics."

"I want Váli's head on a stick. Skaði's too." More lively sparks crackled around Raf's nails. The tension pricked along his forearms under the sleeves of his wool coat.

His answer spurred a derisive huff. "You expect me to offer up my own brother?"

"It would only be fair… since he tore mine to bits."

He had been told of Narfi's bravery for not uttering a single cry when being ripped open, his guts spilling out. Raf could be brave too. "A brother for a brother," he suggested. "You cannot be overly fond of him yourself, considering he was conceived for the sole purpose of killing *you*." As retribution for him slaying his twin and to restore balance.

"Which he carried out swiftly. I do not resent him for doing his duty."

There was no rancor in his tone as he spoke. Was the God of Darkness and Winter really as cold as he appeared to be? Was there nothing he cared about?

"I know you were there last night too… watching from the shadows. Yet you did nothing to save your own flesh and blood." Raf had sustained injuries saving *his* son. Was his Sire not the least bit grateful?

"Listen to reason, Hrafni," he said with the patience of a father. "There is so much anger in you that you cannot grasp the consequences of what you are attempting. Stop your madness." His brows pinched, and Raf thought he recognized the hint of regret in his stark features, the first real emotion he had shown until now.

But Hǫðr was not a father. He had no right to the title. Or the authority.

Rage exploded in Raf's veins. He would not be undermined by the likes of *him* who thought themselves above all others.

Feet set apart, he leaned his chest forward in an aggressive stance. "Fate is on my side. I am not afraid."

"You cannot succeed."

"Not on my own," he sneered. No, indeed, he could not overpower Frigg's executioner on his own. "But I am no longer alone in my cause. *Syndin skapar skuldina*—The sin creates the debt—*Your* sin became *his* debt, and I shall stake my claim NOW! The debt is MINE!"

The tattoo on his chest flared, and the burn stretched across every inch of his body as the ink shifted anew.

Raf swallowed his agony. He would not reveal his pain.

At last, Hǫðr's tone grew pressing. "You claim to seek the destruction of destiny, yet you cling to your prophecy."

Yes, he believed in his prophecy. Believed he was destined to aid the Haðarson in breaking the matrix—though he had refrained from mentioning to Kjartan that he would have to take on his own Sire.

His son's magic was the only kind that could rival the dark God's own, and by merging theirs, they would take them all down. One by one. Hǫðr would only be the beginning.

A fiery sphere formed itself in his palm before he could stop it. It burned bright with the flames of his hatred.

Could the blind God feel it? He stood no more than half a body's length in front of him, his demeanor unchanged.

Raf drew a silent step back, keeping his weight on the ball of his right foot and his sights on his target. The muscles in his shoulder flexed, invisible under his clothes even to a man with the ability to see. The chaotic force behind the projectile buzzed against his bare skin.

Now!

He jerked his elbow back, then his palm shot forward, fingers splayed on the release. Green flames surged past the extended tips, making his nails glow... he could see the imminent clash just beyond his hand...

The fireball imploded against Hǫðr's chest, delivering no impact.

As if swallowed up by a black hole, the darkness surrounding him had suffocated the green flames. He never even flinched.

But then he blinked. Once. And when his eyes flung open, the strange pale color was gone. Along with his black pupils. Two solid orbs of arctic white stared back at him.

A shock wave ripped through the air. The violent compression of the disturbance nudged him back, and the clearing plunged into darkness as though he had suddenly become blind himself. All he saw was the white sheen of the God's eyes. The pearly surface had a ripple effect that was utterly mesmerizing.

A hand collared around his throat, then Hǫðr's low voice spoke so close, he felt his icy breath across his cheek. "Do you feel that?"

Something else wound around his ribcage, pinning his arms down by his sides while squeezing the air from his lungs.

"That is me, slowly teasing the life out of you until there is nothing left."

Raf gulped through the constricted pipe in the God's grasp. "You... wouldn't... dare," he clipped out. Hǫðr was under orders to '*mediate*', after all, was he not?

The shadow snake around his chest squeezed tighter, and he felt his ribs give under the pressure. "Test me," Hǫðr hissed in challenge.

Branches cracked close by, but the God's blind stare remained level on him as though he were looking right through him.

Then he was freed.

All restraints dropped away, and Hǫðr vanished into thin air before Raf drew his first breath. A burn lingered in his ribs and throat that was more from the humiliation than the stranglehold.

His left hand curled around the apple in his pocket, his right rose to the single word stitched across his chest. His fingers traced the five runes he knew by heart.

There was no doubt in his mind that Kjartan could overpower his father. He had the means. All he was lacking was the proper motivation.

Raf would not give up. He knew well what was at stake. If he failed to persuade his ally, they would send him back. And he could not endure the cold again. Never again. He would rather die than be forced to go back to the world of primordial ice. He did not belong there.

Lifting his gaze to the sky, he removed the fruit from his coat and launched it toward the tip of the pine. Then he charged after it, unfurling his wings mid-leap to catch it in his beak.

CHAPTER
39

KJARTAN

He waited until Eve dozed off and her pulse slowed to a soft rhythm, her chest rising slightly with each shallow breath. The door clicked shut quietly behind him as he slipped out.

He hated seeing Eve hurt. Especially knowing he was the cause of her pain. That look in her eyes when she left the bar was the last straw. He had to save what was left.

The words had come easy for him because she made things simple. There was nothing else in the world he cared more about, and he would have told her anything she needed to hear, but every sentence out of his mouth had been true. Because the biggest lie had been staring her right in the face.

He had gone back to meet with Hrafni after the rain had finally let up:

The shifter was sitting in the crown of a large Douglas fir in his human form, leaning back against the trunk behind him.

Kjartan couldn't help picturing the boy making the climb, though it was more likely he had flown up as a raven.

"It's too bad she does not love you back," he called down from the tree, one leg dangling underneath the branch, the other one bent to prop his arm on his knee.

There was an apple in his hand that he was playing catch with, lazily tossing it a few feet into the air, then capturing it in his palm like it was a baseball. He was no longer wearing the ruined gloves, and Kjartan noticed the tattoos on the backs of both hands. They stretched halfway up his fingers.

"She will never feel the same way for you. Never see you as an equal." He caught the bright green fruit on its last drop and sat up straight, redirecting his attention slightly down toward Kjartan on the ground. "Not as long as that human soul occupies your vessel."

With an air of mischief, he slowly spun the apple between his slim, long fingers, his eyes drifting over Kjan's body in disapproval. "So, what is it that you truly desire, son of Hǫðr? Anything you want. I can make it happen."

He took a large bite and leaned back against the tree, gazing at the passing clouds in the sky as he chewed.

Kjartan's heartbeat hiccupped, but his lips stayed sealed. He couldn't bring himself to say the words out loud.

Leaves rustled as Raf scrambled in the branches, then leaped to the ground, landing with a *THUD!* worthy of a giant's spawn. The impact of his heavy-soled boots sent a shockwave through the earth.

The complacent smirk on his face gave the impression that he still hid an ace up his sleeve.

"I can get rid of him for you," he said, meticulously setting one foot in front of the other. His black scarf trailed behind him in his slow stride, blending with his long hair.

As he strolled forward, he passed the apple back and forth between his ungloved hands, tempting him with the forbidden fruit. There was a strange hue to the ink on his hands.

"You do not have that kind of power," Kjartan stammered, watching him play with the orb that had a chunk missing on one side.

The skin on his palms was still raw but had receded to the color of a severe sunburn. Despite his magic and his divine blood on his mother's side, Loki's son didn't appear to be healing as quickly as he did himself.

Raf danced the black, almond-shaped tips of his fingernails over the polished green and came to a stop right in front of him. "I do not. But Hel does. My sister will make sure that he crosses over safely this time. You have my word on that." He spoke the last part against the fruit before taking another crunchy bite out of it.

Kjartan felt his pulse in his throat now. "I... I cannot do that to her. Eve would never forgive me."

Hrafni pitched the apple over his shoulder and pursed his lips maliciously while keeping his stare fixed on him. "She does not have to know. Anything you want," he repeated the words directly into his mind like a spell, pointing his finger at Kjartan's blue eyes.

A single luminous green cord of light spooled around it, unwinding itself at the tip of his nail and becoming individual wires of a cable. The filaments extended like the tendrils of a jellyfish.

Rooted to the ground, Kjartan watched the threads of light stretch toward him. It triggered a tingling sensation in his eyes and was so bright that it blinded him momentarily.

"A little gift to help you with your decision. It's a simple illusion, not nearly as sophisticated as shapeshifting," he bragged, throwing his hair back over his shoulder, "but it will hold up. The glamour will disguise the true color of your eyes. Do with it whatever you want," he added with a suggestive wink, then pulled the same disappearing trick as the night before. In seconds, the only thing left of him was the discarded apple in the underbrush at the bottom of the tree.

A glamour? Kjartan had heard of the trick before, but he had never tried to perform it himself. That was what Hrafni had used to appear in the form of Loki. He had not, in fact, shifted into the shape of his father. A glamour was an enchantment that worked by creating an illusion and displaying the desired image like a screen. Could he really pull it off?

He stared at the hardly-eaten apple for another minute, wondering if Raf had picked the taunting fruit purposefully because he knew what it represented for him. It was a painful reminder of his mother, Guardian of Immortality, and an Æsir Goddess like Hrafni's.

Yes, they were indeed kin. Two rotten apples from the same divine tree. All their glorious potential wasted.

Kjartan left the penthouse to return to Mount Hood.

"Did you enjoy my gift?" Legs casually stretched out in front of him, Hrafni looked up from his spot under the tree in the woods behind the cabin. "Did you wrap her around your finger?" he insinuated with a juvenile grin.

Kjartan scoffed in response.

"I shall take that as a *yes*." Lifting his hand from his lap, he jabbed the tip of his index finger toward Kjartan in approval. "You really are a great liar."

"I did not lie," he sneered.

Raf scrunched his face in a skeptical grimace. "Whatever you need to tell yourself." He leaned back against the tree trunk, clasping his hands behind his head. "Looks like you have no more trouble overpowering your host."

"His resistance is fading. He is losing the desire to fight back." It had been so easy to take charge of the vessel at the bar. A smooth transition. No one had noticed.

Glancing up, he tilted his chin at an inquisitive angle. "Do you think he suspects anything?"

Kjartan shrugged. "It makes no difference. He never trusted me in the first place, and look where that got him." Consciously aware or oblivious, Kjan was too weak to regain control now. It didn't matter whether he listened in.

"So what is your plan?" he asked. "How do you intend to reach Ásgarðr without alerting anyone?"

"Through Hvergelmir."

That name robbed Kjartan momentarily of breath. The churning maelstrom in the underworld was the primordial spring of several poisonous rivers, which earned their bounds the moniker *Shore of Corpses*. The waters cut through the gray and frozen landscape of mist, killing everything it touched. Including Gods. One had to be mad to go through there.

"Yggdrasill is guarded by magic, but its gate in Níflheimr is compromised," Raf went on explaining.

Before the events of Ragnarǫk, a dragon used to live at the bottom of the well. Supposedly, it had gnawed on the root, leaving it dead.

"I can produce a portal to Hvergelmir in the waters of Thor's Well outside of Portland; the place where the big oaf punched a crater into the earth with his mighty hammer. And once we step onto Yggdrasill, it's merely a stone's throw to Ásgarðr."

There was a lightness to Raf's tone that made it sound like child's play, but Kjartan wasn't fooled. It couldn't be that easy. There had to be more to it. He was talking about *Ásgarðr*. The mighty realm of the Gods.

"And assuming we survive the jump, what will we be facing once we get there? An Army?" *My father?*

Kjartan wasn't ready for that.

"You promised to teach me more," he reminded Raf. "Teach me how to tap into my soul's power."

He seemed to believe Kjartan had the abilities to strike down anyone who dared to stand in their way. How much was he really capable off? He needed to know.

Raf's lips stretched into that characteristic sinister grin of his. "I thought you would never ask."

Removing one hand from behind his head, he rolled his wrist in a showy motion before holding it out palm up. "I will teach you," he said, his fingers curling as if weaving invisible threads. "And then we will find out what you are capable of... with this."

Shadows gathered in his splayed palm, rendering the shape of a dagger. The cyclone form rippled with life and Kjartan knew immediately what it was. He felt its power. Recognized its familiarity. At its core, it contained the same force that had gripped him once before, prepared to tear him from his vessel.

"Where did you get this?"

Hrafni shrugged. "Finders keepers."

"And you would simply hand it over to me?"

"Call it a gift of my devotion. It's yours… *if* you join my cause," he emphasized, then retracted his hand, making the weapon disappear again.

At last, a blade that connected Kjartan to his heritage—something the Russians were never able to procure for him.

How had Hrafni gotten his hands on it?

"So?" Raf's brows winged up. "Are you in?"

Lips slightly parted, Kjartan traced the top edge of his teeth with his tongue, contemplating his answer. "Tell me something." He paced a few steps by Raf's crossed ankles. "Why did Sigyn stay with Loki? Despite everything he put her through… his transgressions, the public humiliation."

"He truly loved her. She knew that. And Angrboða was different. She was more like his first wife. Sigyn accepted the giantess' claim to him, but there was no deep affection between the two. My father's heart belonged only to my mother."

"Wish I could say the same." Kjartan slid his hands into his pockets and hung his head. "My mother rarely spoke of my father. The few times she mentioned him… it did not sound like love. Respect, for a son of Óðinn, but not love. At least not the kind I have seen firsthand." *The kind that makes you sacrifice yourself without a moment's hesitation to protect the other*, he thought to himself. "Maybe Gods are just different. Choosing only one mate seems absurd if you are eternal."

"The entire notion of having a mate is absurd." Raf uncrossed his legs and pushed off the damp ground, wagging his skinny finger in Kjartan's face. "Loyalty! That's the only thing that matters. Not love." He let himself fall back against the tree trunk to prove his point.

"Any other questions?" he barked annoyed, folding his arms over his chest.

"The runes on Eve's wrist. Is that your magical handiwork?"

"Partly. The magic of the glacier triggered the brand, opening a window into her bloodline. She can glimpse moments of her ancestors' lives, but I control which memory she sees. I chose the perfect ones."

Kjartan gasped. "Why?"

Raf's eyes glowed with hubris. "Because I am my father's son. I revel in mischief... create chaos wherever I go." He snickered. "Just ask your friends. I had a blast chasing them around Reykjavík last year. I watched them run scared like roaches before they called you, crying for your help."

His amber irises twinkled with amusement. "I also used a glamour to make that old man Cooper think he saw you at the abandoned warehouse when he shot that boy. And let's not forget about the one I poisoned. I took a page out of your little friend's playbook for that one. What was her name again? Andromeda?"

"That was you?"

Raf cackled like a witch, doubling over. "Oh, you are so easy," he quipped, slapping his thigh. "And predictable."

Kjartan felt his temperature climbing, bringing his blood to a boil. "This is all just a game to you?"

"No, it is far more than that. You were nesting. Becoming complacent," Raf berated him. "You needed motivation, and I gave it to you." A pale green shimmer rippled over him as he threw up another glamour. Only this time, it wasn't the image of Loki staring back.

The half-giant's towering height washed down to below Kjartan's, his hair faded to a warm shade of chestnut, and his irises ignited in a burst of blue. A perfect vision of Eve appeared in his place.

Kjartan's eyes went wide. "Stop this!" he growled at the illusion as he ambled toward him, a sensual sway in his hips. The dark green silk moved against his body like a second skin.

"I'm a shapeshifter. I can turn into anyone the situation requires," he said in Eve's voice with a perceptive chuckle that made his eyes sparkle just a little brighter. "In case you need a little more motivation." He clasped his arms around Kjartan's neck and pressed his body up against his, teeth tugging at his full bottom lip.

Kjartan squeezed his eyes shut, but he couldn't escape the illusion. It even smelled like her. The scent of spring flowers and sweet apples encircled him, drawing him back to the first time he tasted her lips, only a few hundred yards from where they stood now.

Her kiss had been soft, her touch timid, and he had been craving her ever since. But this wasn't real, he told himself. This wasn't Eve.

Kjartan forced his eyes open for reassurance. His breath caught in his throat as his gaze fixed on Raf.

"Come on, I know what you really want. Don't fight it," he whispered, his hand caressing Kjartan's cheek. "Or is this more like it?"

His eye color started to change into a pale green with golden flecks in the center of his irises. His hair darkened a few shades and extended into long braids that had little white flowers weaved into them.

Before Kjartan stood the woman whose face still haunted him. The woman from Kjan's memory. "Thórunn," he sighed.

In shock at the reveal of his heart's desire, his hand darted out, grabbing Raf by the throat and pinning him against the tree behind him. "I said STOP!" Kjartan bellowed.

Twigs behind him snapped, and in an instant, everything else seized to exist.

Gods no!

Her voice was so soft it barely carried. "What is this?"

CHAPTER
40

KJARTAN

A crippling panic locked his muscles in place. She had picked the worst moment to show up.

"Eve!" His eyes shot to the real version of her and then back to the shifter, who was still caught in his grip. He had changed back into the emo punk, but she had seen everything, and he knew exactly how bad this looked from her perspective.

Kjartan removed his hand from Raf's neck to let him go as Eve stomped toward him, brandishing her fists. "Kjan was right," she shouted out of anger at herself. "I trusted you. I defended you… and you… you betrayed us!"

She shoved at him, battered his chest with her little hands, and threw all her built-up emotions at him.

Kjartan snared her wrists. "No, you didn't. Not the way you trust *him*."

"So you're going to sell him out? After everything?" Eve ripped her hands free and leaped backward.

But in her attempt to get away, her feet caught on the roots in the rough underbrush. She tripped, and when her rear hit the ground, she landed badly on her wrist.

Agony wrenched through him as she winced and clutched her forearm to her chest. Kjartan lunged for her. "I'm sorry," he muttered frantically, dropping to his knees at her side. "I didn't want this, Eve. I swear I never wanted any of this. All I wanted was you."

Her pulse was rampant, the pounding of her heartbeat so loud in his head he couldn't hear his own. Everything was going wrong. She wasn't supposed to be here.

"I know why Frigg locked me away," he continued through the tears stinging in his eyes. "She knew what I would do… what I would become. She was right to do it. I am a monster. I keep hurting you."

Eve let go of her wrist and put her hands on his shoulders. "You made a promise. Please, Kjartan, if you cross that bridge, you can never come back."

"I know," he exhaled woefully. "That's just it. You will never reciprocate what I feel for you and—"

"You don't love me," Eve jumped in. "It's not real. You are projecting what you feel onto me because you can't have *her*. I saw her—I mean *him*!" She pointed at Hrafni. "He took her shape right there."

Kjartan grabbed both her arms to get her to focus on what he was trying to tell her. "I don't fit in here," he said with a resolute edge. "Kjan is accepted… loved. I'm merely tolerated. I want to be chosen, Eve. Chosen for who I am, not because there is no other option."

Her voice was calm and soothing when she spoke. "I know exactly how you feel," she told him. "I've felt that way my entire life too, but you have people who care about you here. You are not alone. What about Askja? Don't let him pull you into his madness. You are not like him." Over his shoulder, she nailed Raf with a glare.

The shifter laughed in his high pitch. "You think *I* am the villain here? I'm the hero in this story. I'm the only one who will tell you the whole truth."

"What's he talking about?" Eve's brows furrowed as she looked at Kjartan.

Raf didn't wait for him to reply. "Even your precious lover Kjan left out a minor detail. Why do you think you look exactly like his wife?"

Eve's shocked gaze darted back and forth between them.

"Because Frigg created you this way," Raf said in his next breath, answering his own question. "How would you feel if you found out that you were nothing but a pawn in someone else's destiny?" he asked, baiting her. "Like an accessory. That your entire existence is based on compensation. Would you still believe in fate and trust those who shape it?"

Kjartan could see the wheels in Eve's head turning. He felt her pain in his own chest. She wasn't just questioning *his* feelings for her; she was questioning Kjan's.

Hrafni's magic wasn't the only threat. He had the power to convince people that their worst fears were true. The power to make them doubt their own existence. The trickster was more dangerous than he had expected.

Eve's lips parted, but it took her a few more seconds before she managed to speak. Her breaths were feeble and shaky. "What else did she say?"

Kjartan turned over his shoulder. "Please, give us a minute."

Raf grumbled with discontent, but when his form imploded in the puff of a green smoke grenade, he felt relieved.

He stared off at the ground. Eve's mood would not improve after hearing the specifics. He was playing right into Hrafni's hand.

"You are Frigg's gift to Kjan," he said at last. "A payoff for bringing about Thórunn's and his mother's deaths. Fate put you on this path, so he can fulfill his destiny."

He searched her blank stare for any signs of credence. Would she believe the sincerity in his? They were his own again. He had dropped the glamour spell.

"But that's not what you are to me, Eve." He clasped her trembling hand, and she didn't flinch away. "We were never meant to be together. That's why this is real… you and I."

He needed her to listen, just for another minute, to make her understand his reasons for this ultimate decision.

It *was* final. There was no going back.

He tenderly uncurled her fingers and traced the lines of her palm as if he were reading her fortune. "Two souls can't exist in one vessel. One of us has to go; there is no other way. I'm going to set things right. I have overcome every obstacle in my way to be with you, and I would do it all over again just for this opportunity… no one can take this from me."

The pressure in his nose became unbearable, and his lips trembled so badly he almost couldn't get through this last part. "Remember that your fate can be whatever you want. You're the one choosing your path. I just wanted a chance to—"

Her hand ripped out of his grasp with a jolt as her outcry pierced through the woods. The flutter of wings followed the shrill sound as flocks of startled birds took flight from their shelters.

Kjartan jumped back in alarm, his palms up, no longer touching her. Cold sweat prickled at his back.

Eve's body went limp, and she collapsed onto the forest floor, eyes rolled back into her head, showing only white.

No-no-no… what happened? He wasn't done talking.

His hands fumbled around her body, searching for an explanation. He swatted at the twigs by her legs. His fingers felt numb.

Then he spotted it. The black snake coiled between her ankles, the bright copper stripe on its back glimmering like the spark of a brush fire.

"NO!" Kjartan yelled. "What did you do?"

The shifter slithered free and turned back into human form. "Eliminated your distraction," Raf gnashed as if he wanted to chew the redundant response up and spit it back at him. "I need your undivided attention. You will help me finish what I started, or she will stay in this comatose state," he hissed. "You will cast Frigg's *proclaimed Paladin* out. I want him gone. Whatever he means to her… I will put an end to it. And once we get rid of him, her web will wither."

CHAPTER

41

KJAN

He thrashed aimlessly to catch his breath, but his lungs filled with more icy water, and his strength was fading.

Kjan was drowning.

The pool he found himself in was as dark and frigid as the glacier cave. His fatigued muscles screamed in agony from the cold. Needles drove into his skin.

He had fought his restraints. Had struggled against the chokehold. Over and over, he had tried to reach the surface. Every time he broke through, he was dragged back down into the deep, hands grabbing him from all sides, pushing and pulling until he couldn't tell which side was up.

As the water burned in his lungs, his body became numb. Kjan closed his eyes and prayed for death. He longed for peace.

'He shall come for her,' the female voices chanted. *'He will plunge his sword into her flesh to whet its edge on her bones until the blade runs red with her blood.'*

A prophecy? He had no strength left to fight… couldn't save her…

He drifted, semi-consciously, in the darkness, listening to the incoherent mumbling of voices around him, when suddenly his senses came rushing back. A hand clasped his forearm and yanked him upward toward the surface.

Kjan landed hard on his side, his body slamming into solid rock like the hole in the ground had coughed him up and spat him out.

Despite the pain, he willed himself to move. He pushed onto all fours, heaving violently to force the water out and the air back down into his lungs.

He didn't have a chance to take a proper look around the grotto. From the corner of his eye, he saw the figure in the shadows, and before his aching muscles had time to protest, he lunged at the shape.

Kjan crushed the intruder's spine against the cave wall with a full body blow, expelling the air from the man's lungs. At first glance, he thought he was facing off with an evil version of himself, but when he focused his eyes, he wasn't looking at his reflection.

Nor was he looking at the 12-year-old boy he remembered. He saw a man in his early twenties with pitch-black hair and irises as cold and blue as ice.

If the volcanic glaciers of Iceland were a person, this was what they would look like. He was a spitting image of the blind God Hǫðr.

Clutching the front of his shirt, Kjan let out a roar and threw a right punch, flinging his Sire's head to the side.

The most exhilarating sensation of triumph rushed him at the impact, but when he drew his fist back again, ready to dish out another one, his opponent dodged it. Kjan's fist drove into the rock wall, sending debris scattering.

A burning sensation licked across his bleeding knuckles, and he missed blocking the knee that buried itself into his side. Catching only a flash before pain crashed through his jaw, a fist knocked his field of vision to the left.

The taste of blood hit his tongue.

Kjan swallowed the bitter trace away. It was the first time since the transfer that he was physically face-to-face with his Sire. And even though this was all still happening inside his head, he was able to touch him. Hurt him. Here, they were equals.

The man opened his mouth, but Kjan had no interest in his speech. "No more tricks," he roared, his suppressed rage bubbling to the surface. "I'll kill you with my bare hands."

Still fisting his Sire's shirt at the neck, Kjan grabbed a hold of his other shoulder and threw himself backward, pulling the bastard along with him. Shoving his boot into his gut on the way down, he vaulted him over his head.

He heard his body drop somewhere a few feet behind him and pushed off the ground, flexing his fingers to work the throbbing ache lingering in his hand.

Poised in a fighter stance, his enemy rose as well. "You know you can never beat me," he taunted. "Not out there and not in here. But if that's how you want to do it, let's see what you got."

With a savage battle cry, Kjan charged again, and fists started flying. His Sire dodged two hits, then his left return collided with Kjan's cheek. His head snapped over, blood spraying out to the side and his brain bouncing loose in his skull.

His vision rippled, but instinctively, he ducked and was able to avoid the follow-up from the other side.

Keeping his weight light on the balls of his feet to move quickly, he dodged another fist. His Sire was left-hand dominant; Kjan was right but efficient with either, and the knuckles of his left hand landed square beneath his opponent's chin, kicking his head back. He stumbled two steps before recovering.

Kjan darted forward and swung his elbow at the man's cheekbone, making contact with his nose along the way. Another painful sting shot up the bones of his forearm thanks to his wall-punch earlier. But it hurt less than the impact on his knuckles. Here neither of them had the ability to heal from the wounds inflicted.

His Sire's right arm drew back for a counterpunch, and Kjan was ready to catch his wrist in mid-air.

"Welcome to *my* world, bitch!" Holding firm, he yanked him close and rammed the front of his skull into the bridge of his nose. The crack of the break was crisp and clear.

Head lolling, blood trickling down his nose, his balance was off, and Kjan took advantage, aiming a vicious right hook at his jaw. He didn't care about the pain anymore. This was *his* subconscious. *His* dominion.

He heard the sharp snap and caught the deep crimson reflection of his eyes in the icy blues of his Sire before he went down. The back of his skull cracked hard against the uneven stone, but he remained lucid, his hands clawing at Kjan's chest to shake him off.

"You should have left me down there," he said in a menacing growl, squeezing his grip tighter around his rival's neck. He jerked him up and then slammed him down a second time, leaving a small, dark red stain on the ground.

Kjan's focus slipped for a fraction of a second, and his Sire landed a firm hit on his temple. The impact was enough to blur his vision and momentarily gain the upper hand in the struggle.

As they wrestled on the ground, throwing punches, each one causing bones to crack and splinter, the fight took on the proportion of a UFC match—minus the gloves. The immortal's palm clasped around the front of his throat, but before he could crush his windpipe, Kjan rammed a knee into the side of his ribcage, then unloaded a forceful punch to his Adam's apple.

Choking on his own blood, his Sire cursed under his breath, then backed off. "Stop… fighting," he croaked, coughing up the red liquid. "Stalemate." Then he fell back onto the ground next to Kjan, their heaving breaths billowing in combined rhythm through the cavern.

They lay side by side, sprawled out and exhausted. There could be no winner; the fight was a deadlock—their strengths a perfect match—with neither one of them able to overpower the other.

Kjan's eye socket throbbed, and his nose felt like it was broken. He had to remind himself that none of this was actually real. The fight had been a physical manifestation of their separate minds clashing. And it had ended in a grueling draw.

"Why did you pull me out?" Kjan rasped, his voice hoarse, his throat sore.

His Sire wheezed as he gave him a weak laugh. "*Now* you want to hear what I have to say?" His head bobbed wearily in Kjan's direction. "I didn't come to fight you. I came to concede. All I ask for is a chance to say goodbye first."

CHAPTER
42

KJARTAN

He charged at Hrafni with the speed of a cheetah. Fury exploded in his veins, igniting his muscles. Then he pounced, lips curled into a snarl, fangs gnashing.

"I'll shred you to pieces for this!" he roared, seizing the lapels of Raf's coat. "I will never join you."

Kjartan's fists cut through the air like axes flying at a target. Each one hit with deadly precision, again and again, so sharp and crisp his hands began to emit a faint blue glow.

By keeping him engaged in close combat, Kjartan didn't grant him an opening to use his magic. A punch to the throat collapsed Raf's airway. His eyes blazed as rage flared across his face. He didn't heal as fast as Kjartan or the vampires. The gashes on his eyebrow and cheekbone were deep.

The half-giant wasn't a fighter—wasn't built like Kjan—but his muscles were surprisingly solid for his lean frame. And though he had been relying on his magic skills to win his battles, he moved with lithe agility.

The brawling was fierce, unrelenting, from either side. It pushed them closer to the edge of the drop-off where he knew the soil was soft. Kjartan felt the slight shift beneath his tread, then both of them lost their footing.

He couldn't tell who went over the hillside first. The earth beneath their feet dislodged and gave away, one dragging the other with him.

Tumbling head over heels down the ridge, they became a tangled mess of flailing arms and kicking legs. The merciless terrain scraped and cut Kjartan's skin, mixing his blood with the dirt. Raf's coat snagged on rocks. It ripped as they made their steep descent, skidding and rolling like conjoined twins.

The landing came with an abrupt stop between a pair of boulders that left Kjartan on top yet with his shoulder dislocated. Raf recovered too quickly from the fall and managed to shift back into the shape of the raven before Kjartan could land another blow.

As the green smoke swirled around them like they were in the eye of a tornado from *The Wizard of Oz*, he lost his hold around the bird's neck.

Claws the size of a man's hand snatched at him, and his long sharp talons dug into Kjartan's forearm when he blocked an attack from his beak.

Flapping hysterically, the shifter swatted at him, and one of the large black wings collided with his head.

Kjartan fell back, and Hrafni took the chance to escape, but his wing was badly injured, which made his flight choppy. He narrowly missed a large branch as he coasted through the trees before vanishing from sight, squawking furiously—no doubt, a raven's version of heated curses.

Looking back up the steep slope they had toppled down, Kjartan wished he could grow a pair of wings right about now too. He blew out a heavy breath and snapped his shoulder joint back into its socket with a nasty *crack*. Then he tackled the ascent.

The dreaded picture that awaited him at the top was even worse than his imagination. Eve's skin had turned ashen and cold. The veins on her arms created a roadmap underneath the translucent gray.

Raf would pay for this. He would find a way to kill the shifter, and there would be no more sympathy... no compassion... no forgiveness.

The evil spawn would die.

He kneeled beside her nearly-lifeless body. Her pulse was so weak.

What if I can't save her? What if my blood isn't strong enough to counter Hrafni's venom?

Kjartan's thoughts were racing as he freed his arm and bit into his wrist. His divine blood spilled from the deep gash in a stream along his forearm, soaking the bulk of his sleeve.

"Please, Eve," he begged, pressing the wound to her lips. "Don't give up now. I need you to fight."

The toxins of the yew in his blood only lulled her under further. The properties of his were so vastly different from Kjan's despite sharing the same body.

"Please wake up. I only wanted a chance to say goodbye."

The deal was done. He had already given his oath to Kjan after leaving her bed, but he needed her to know what he was giving up. Needed her to know his sacrifice… see the good in him… hear the words from *him*.

"No… no, not like this," he mumbled to himself. "Please…"

Hrafni had magic, but he did too. And if the shifter could tap into his own essence to fuel his magic, then so could he. A sacrifice would amplify his capabilities even though he lacked the skills. There was no power greater than that of a sacrifice.

And Kjartan was willing to offer one. For *them*. Their love was the realest thing he had ever seen. He would burn up his soul and destroy himself to give Eve and Kjan a chance.

The blush did not return to her cheeks, her body remained motionless in his arms, her heartbeat faint. The solution was so obvious. It wasn't *his* blood she needed. She was beyond his reach—no link, no spark to pull her through.

Kjartan dropped his wrist and pulled her into his chest, cradling her head gently under his chin. As he entwined his fingers with hers, he wished he had more time. More time to breathe in her scent. More time to touch her velvety skin.

Eternity wouldn't be enough to absorb it all. Bathing in her light was like trying to soak up the sun. He wanted to draw out their final minutes and make every second count.

"You and I, we could have been real, Eve. We never had the chance to find out… I was too late… you chose him."

Kjartan squeezed his eyes shut against the building pressure behind them. "Maybe in another life, you would have picked me."

He couldn't hold back the tears any longer. He rocked her tenderly and let them run. Laid himself bare for her, though she couldn't see it.

"Kjan loves you. Don't doubt his feelings for you. He chose you the way you chose him. *I'm* the one who doesn't belong. He should have cast me out to save himself—"

A sob hitched in his throat. The tight knot burned as he swallowed. "I need you to remember that it was real… at least for me."

Brushing her hair from her face, he leaned down and kissed her forehead, whispering his last words to her. "Goodbye, Love."

CHAPTER 43

EVE

For a split second, she wasn't sure she'd caught it right; the word was only off by one letter. *'Love'*, he'd called her. Kjan never used that term. There was only one person who did.

It took Kjartan's slip-up for Eve to realize the man in her bed was not who he pretended to be. Imaginary hands crept around her throat as the ruse came to light. She couldn't fathom how effortlessly he'd deceived her.

But two could play that game. Forcing her heart rate steady, she played along, and when he left in broad daylight, she followed the imposter back to the cabin.

The scene in the clearing was a nightmare on a whole other level. From her hiding spot, Eve watched a freakishly accurate version of herself put the moves on Kjartan. Was that how Hrafni had persuaded him? By offering to help him regain permanent control over Kjan's body?

She'd seen enough. Eve was about to step out and confront them when the shifter changed his shape again. She froze in her move. Their similarities were uncanny—besides the fact that the woman looked like she'd jumped off the page of a Viking history book.

Before Kjartan appeared a female with long braided hair and a fierce look in her eyes. She wore a medieval navy blue apron dress that split open at the sides and a simple white tunic underneath. A belt was tied into a knot around her waist. Her feet were bare.

Enraged by the trickster's games, Kjartan pinned the woman against the tree by her throat. The sight virtually knocked the wind out of Eve, she couldn't keep quiet any longer. Hrafni was the son of Loki, God of Lies and Deceit, untrustworthy by nature of his blood. So why was Kjartan working with him?

She knew he was cunning, every move a strategically laid-out plan, but the truth came down on her like a house of cards. The shifter kindly put the bigger picture into perspective for her: Eve was a diluted copy of the woman Kjan had lost. The woman he was meant to be with.

Kjartan tried to convince her that her fate could still be whatever she wanted it to be, but the revelation left a bitter taste in her mouth. Eve felt cheated. She didn't know what was real anymore. Where was her free will in all this?

The last thing her brain processed was the acute stab at her ankle and the agonizing pain shooting up her leg. She felt her mind separating from her body, her consciousness tearing away from her physical form.

"Wake up, *dúlla*," a woman's voice ordered her in heavily accented English. It sort of sounded like Kría's or Dynja's, only still thicker than the Icelandic brogue she'd become so familiar with.

What had she called her? *Dúlla?* The girls addressed each other with the same term sometimes.

Eve's eyelids were heavy as she lifted them, and a friendly face came gradually into focus: eyes that were a mix of gold and peridot green, pale freckles scattered across her sun-kissed cheeks and nose. The sun gleamed around her like a halo.

Blinking away the haze, she recognized the warm smile of the woman hovering over her. Four small braids embedded with little white flowers crowned the top of her head. They were weaved in an intricate pattern to combine into a single strand down the back.

The rest of Thórunn's hair spilled over her shoulders like a waterfall. It was so long that the ends pooled on the grass around her. Her hands rested in her lap.

Eve sat up to look around. She was no longer on Mount Hood. They were in a meadow that was covered by a blanket of the same white flowers Thórunn had in her braids. Over her shoulder, Eve saw the little farmhouse from her dream. The wooden porch wrapped around the cottage, and she heard sheep bleating in the back.

Her gut felt heavy. It was *their* home—Thórunn and Kjan's.

"I know he still loves you," Eve said to her without meeting her intense stare. That was why the Gods had used her looks. Thórunn was the original; Eve merely the copy who took her place.

The woman shook her head. "He does not. He loves *you*, and that is all well. Do not feel guilty," she assured her when Eve lifted her gaze back up to her. "I release him from his oath," she declared, her voice warm and without a trace of resentment for feeling cheated or forced to relinquish her claim.

Eve's breath hitched with relief.

"What's happening to me? Why can I see you?" she asked, a sudden alarm ringing in her ears. Thórunn was in Fólkvangr, the field of Freyja's chosen in Ásgarðr. Did that mean she was dead too?

"You are descended from my blood, and the Raven is using you," Thórunn replied with a compassionate smile. "Everything you saw is true. Do not let him drive a wedge between the three of you. You all need each other. You are stronger together, and the trickster knows it."

She clasped Eve's hands, and then her face turned grave. "I choose him. You must tell him that. *I choose him*," she repeated.

"Him?" Eve's mind felt foggy. *Does she mean—*

"Aye, *dúlla*," she said with a wink. "I know you are a smart one. You are the balance. You need to fix it."

The vision of the scene rippled like water disrupted by a skipping stone. The outline of Thórunn's body faded into the blinding brightness behind her.

"Wait!" Eve called after her. "Don't go." She needed more answers.

"I'm not the one leaving." She grinned. "I'm counting on you, Eve. Do not let me down."

The light of his aura penetrated her chest, and a humming glow spread through her. It enveloped her heart, holding it in a ginger embrace that warmed her from the inside out.

Kjan was calling her home.

CHAPTER

44

EVE

Her senses perked, and she *listened*… to the thrum of his voice, the beat of his heart, the rhythm of his breath, the rushing of blood in his veins…

The sound of him was a song composed only for her ears, and it guided her out of the darkness.

Her eyelids twitched as awareness crept through her, gradually chasing away the numbness from her face, down her chest, and over her heavy limbs.

Eve found herself in bed, swaddled like a newborn and, yep, definitely naked as she freed her arms from the constraints.

Kjan's heavy left arm draped over her like an I-beam. He had a towel wrapped around his waist, and his hair was still damp. She vaguely remembered being in the shower, the cool, black marble pressed against her back, and him holding her upright while she went in and out of consciousness.

How had they gotten home? The whole thing was a blur.

Her blood-drenched clothes lay on the floor at the foot of the bed. What had he done? Rip his arm off to open a vein? He was so dramatic.

And thorough.

Guilt burned like acid in her throat. How could she have been so blind? Their mind-body-soul connection was always disrupted with Kjartan. Empathic link to his mind: check; comfort from his touch: check; but when it came to his essence, the part that was truly him and not physically Kjan, there was no bond. That was why his blood changed depending on who was in control.

She inched closer, a whisper on her lips. "I messed up."

Kjan hugged her into his chest without opening his eyes. He smelled so good. Eve wished she could bottle his scent and wear it like perfume, then she could inhale the rich dark chocolate fragrance all day.

"He lied," she continued, tracing the scar in the center of his chest below Muninn's wing with her fingertip. "You were right from the beginning. He betrayed us."

"No, he didn't. He opened his mind to me and showed me the truth," Kjan elaborated. "He had no intention of joining Hrafni. He was stalling. Turns out, I could have saved myself the fight." He chuckled softly. "But it felt so good."

"What fight?"

"Never mind." He exhaled, pressing a kiss to her temple. He sounded tired, but Eve didn't sense any of the resentment in him that had turned him so bitter at the bar.

She interrupted the silence. "Why didn't you tell me what Frigg said?"

"Because it's insignificant. I know what you're thinking, and you're wrong. I'm not projecting."

"Did you turn me because I looked like her?"

"No. I brought you back because you didn't deserve to die for my mistakes. It's the honest truth."

He clasped her chin gently between his index and thumb. "Eve, listen to me. You are not what the trickster says. She might have created you in Thórunn's image, but you are still your parents' daughter. They raised you. Joe raised you. They all made you the person you are. With your own hopes, your own dreams, your own choices."

"But… Hrafni said I was made for you." A compensation, he'd called her.

"No, Dove," Kjan said, the green in his eyes so deep and calm. "*I* was made for *you*. Everything the Gods put me through was to forge me into the man you deserve. A man you could love. I'm nothing without you."

Eve snorted. "You lived for a long time before I came around."

"Existing in a vegetative state is not living. You changed everything."

"You put too much value into my presence. Your existence doesn't depend on me."

"Oh, I beg to differ." Kjan snickered, head-butting her affectionately.

"I felt lost before you changed me. I never thought I would have anything in common with a godly being, but I know what it's like to not fit in. You still feel that way now." Eve linked her fingers behind his neck. "You know, if you didn't hate him so much and actually took the time to look, you'd realize the two of you are a lot alike."

"I dare you to say that again," he taunted, kissing the soft flesh under her jaw. "No, I take that back. I should punish you for even suggesting it."

He clasped her right wrist lightly, stroking her forearm with his thumb. "But first, I'll make love to you," he said with a soft murmur, sealing his mouth to hers.

His hand brushed along her arm and shoulder, down the side of her body, gliding meticulously over the thin sheet covering her. The smooth silk slid voluntarily across her skin, offering no resistance as he cruised her curves.

Eve's breath became strained. His touch was warm through the subtle fabric, turning her limbs to putty.

She tugged on his towel, but he slapped her hand away. "I'm not that easy, woman," he chastised her. "I'm going to hold on to my grudge just a bit longer. You don't get to touch. There must be some form of consequence for your gullibility."

So maybe keeping her warm wasn't the only reason for trapping her in the sheet.

Eve groaned in disapproval, but when Kjan lifted off the pillow and rolled her onto her back, she didn't put up a fight. He ripped the terry cloth aside and spread her legs under the sheet that still covered her.

Cradling her hips with a firm grasp, he yanked her flush with him. The silk bunched in his lap and slick warmth welled as he molded his body into her shape. The friction of the sheet increased the coveted sensation, liberating a reserved whimper from her lips.

While his tongue licked its way further into her, he drove her higher, chasing her release. A feathering sensation, like a myriad of kisses all at once, rose across her skin. She felt him everywhere—the bond of her mate, reaching out, caressing her mind with a velvet touch, and even the swelling in her chest from his own arousal.

She felt what he felt.

Their souls were forever connected as one by the vow they had taken to never forsake each other. No matter what. Two threads, winding together to form a stronger line. A double helix.

Eve's arms tensed around his neck, her fingers teasing through his hair. Her quivers became more urgent, her moan more desperate…

The orgasm shattered through her, the surge tingling every nerve in her body, and before she could catch her breath, his hand shot beneath the silk to rub at her clit.

She twitched and squirmed in his hold, nearly breaking her back as she arched.

It was torture. Sweet, sweet torture.

Kjan hummed with satisfaction. His thumb made a slick pass down her seam, then back to her sensitive nub, giving it another skillful flick.

He tipped his head back, and his lips parted in a raspy moan. "All that honey just for me… every last drop… mine."

Lastly, he ripped the sheet out of the way. He kicked her leg over his shoulder and sank into her in one sharp thrust.

Eve cried out as the poignant pleasure seized her belly. Bringing his full weight down, he buried the length of him deeper inside her. And she welcomed him. Welcomed all of him to make their bond whole.

"Look at me, Dove," he ordered her. "I want you to know that it's me. No one can ever take my place, do you hear me? No one."

He took a clipped breath and straightened. "You're mine!" Keeping a possessive hold on her, his fingers caressed along the outside of her raised leg while his lips trailed the sensitive inside of her calf.

Kjan was gorgeous to watch as he worked her, stroking her with each deliberately prolonged drive. His muscles flexed under his skin. The tattooed wolf that snaked up his right shoulder seemed to grin wickedly, as if enjoying her attention, and the ridges of his abs deepened.

His hooded eyes riveting to her, he drew his hips back, then filled her again to the brim… so slowly.

Eve whimpered.

"Can you feel me in your head?"

"Mm-hmm." Her body was preconditioned for his touch. A tingling sensation hummed beneath her skin, matching the frequency he was giving off.

Eve ran her hands over his chest, rolling her hips to meet the magical slip-and-slide of his deep drive. She felt his heart pound against her palms. Her gaze lingered on the pulsing artery at his jugular that pumped his blood with each thundering beat.

Kjan's body tensed. His throat jerked as he clenched his teeth, and then a savage growl erupted from his lungs. Eve bit her nails into his skin when his fangs flashed between his lips.

Fuck. That's so hot.

Watching him come pushed her over the edge again. Sparks ignited like flint where they were joined, and she bridged off the bed, her hands flying up to the headboard.

The flat wooden surface gave her nothing to grab onto. Contorting in bliss, Eve settled for the corners of her pillow, clawing at it while she wept through her release.

Kjan let her leg slip off his shoulder and eagerly answered the call of her nipples. He claimed one with his mouth, circling it with his warm, slippery tongue. Sucking and lolling along the crest, he pinched the other between his fingers.

As the shockingly raw high subsided and her pulse settled, Eve let go of the pillow to walk her fingers through Kjan's hair. "Did you know that male sharks sometimes bite females to get them to mate?"

She no longer held his actions against him. They were vampires. A degree of violence was in their nature. Why else would they have fangs?

Face buried between her breasts, Kjan gave a muffled grunt of disapproval. She chuckled and tightened her limbs around his huge body, which was already smothering her under his weight.

"Swear it will always be me, Dove. Swear you will always remember this." He looked up at her, his eyes dark and serious. They held too many emotions for her to count.

"I swear it." She cupped his face and drew his mouth to hers.

Forehead pressed to her temple, his lips parted with a heavy sigh. "I don't want this day to end."

Eve's eyes flicked to the window. The setting sun was already low in the sky. She trailed the edge of his jaw with her thumb. "I'll come with you. Wherever you go, I'll go."

He covered her hand with his own. "I know," he said with a weary smile.

His eyes shot to the window with a distant look, then he kissed the center of her palm. "It's time."

CHAPTER
45
EVE

She hopped into the Cherokee's passenger seat. "Where are we going?"

"The temple," Kjan replied. "Hrafni wants me dead. He'll show. Or I'll track him down." He shrugged his powerful shoulders. "He's injured. I don't know how long it will take him to heal and regain full power. We can't waste this opportunity. This ends tonight."

And she would be right by his side. Eve knew on his own, Kjan would fail, but she was the key to uniting him with Kjartan. *'You are stronger together'*, Thórunn had said. Three against one—enemies to allies—that was the only way to beat Hrafni. Not alone. Not divided. Only as one strong unit would they prevail.

And the dream of Thórunn had revealed something else. Kjan didn't love her anymore, but someone else still did. And she was choosing Kjartan. He had a place where he belonged after all. He just didn't know it yet.

If his father is a God, does that automatically grant him entry to Valhǫll or Fólkvangr to be with her? How could Eve possibly fix *that*?

She wasn't exactly sure how it would work, but once this was over, once Hrafni's threat was eliminated, she would tell him, and they would figure it out together. Together, they could face anything.

Kjan turned onto the obscured dirt path. It was littered with bushes and overgrowth, and the number of divots made the headlights bounce in front.

As he rounded a final turn, her Jeep pinpointed their destination, dousing the exterior of the entrance in an unkind illumination that sent shivers down her spine.

Kjan shut off the engine and swung his door open to get out.

There was no real footpath through the tangled mess of thorns and weeds, and even his footprints from the other night had washed away.

Eve looked up at the sky as she slipped out. She could see the waxing silver crescent of the moon disappearing behind a thick, dark cloud. "There's another storm coming in."

"Afraid of a little rain?"

He pulled the old, rusty steel gate at the front open with a painful screech. It wasn't locked, and she followed him through, giving his ruggedly handsome get-up a critical once-over. He was wearing a pair of waterproof dark brown Harley Davidson's. The 6-inch ones with the steel toe.

"You got boots on. I'm wearing sneakers. Wet shoes are the worst... I'd rather be barefoot."

Her skin crawled. The passage was dark. Kjan took the rustic torch off the wall and pulled a lighter from his pocket. A rag was wrapped around the top of the hefty stick. The odor of lantern oil tingled in her nose.

He held his lighter up to the rag, and a flame quickly sprang to life, the fire reflecting in his eyes.

"Watch your step," he said, holding out his hand to her.

Eve took it gratefully, and he led the way down the narrow staircase.

When they reached the bottom, he nestled the torch into the empty cradle by the door and dug a key from his jeans. He unhinged the padlock attached to the chain and removed the links from one of the handles, leaving it to dangle on the other one.

He took a sideways glance at her, the flames of the torch dancing playfully around his crooked grin. "You look even more irresistible in the light of the fire."

"Likewise," she said, returning the compliment.

Eve felt her cheeks burn hotter, but it was doubtful he could tell since they were already flushed from the radiant heat the torch threw off. For a split second, she forgot the threat they were facing.

Kjan pulled the solid stone doors open, making it look easy. The stale air from the chamber caught in her throat, little dust particles choking her on the way down to her lungs.

Her heart plunged into the pit of her stomach. She couldn't stop the dreadful pictures springing to life in front of her eyes: the coven in their blood-red robes, surrounding her during the ritual… Kjartan holding her down as he drained her… Kjan pointing the stake at his own heart, begging her to kill him…

the deadly silence after he collapsed on the ground and she clung to his lifeless body…

Eve took a shuddery breath, shaking the images off. Stepping over the threshold, Kjan lit the two candles by the door with his lighter first, then went along the wall to light all the others so she could see better. Her night vision wasn't as good as his. She felt his gaze on her, watching her every move.

There were twelve candles in total, six on each side. Eve preferred the temple dark. The iron chains that had once held Kjan were still anchored to the ground with large hooks. She recoiled as she looked at the dark stain where his blood had spilled.

A chill raced up her nape. Kjan sensed her dismay and took her clammy hand. He was eerily calm.

"What now?"

"We wait," he shot back, nudging her toward the floor.

He took a seat on the ground next to the throne, leaning back against it. Gods forbid, he actually sat on it. He probably thought he'd get struck by lightning for blasphemy or something.

Eve dropped by his side, the cold sensation of the stone shooting right through her jeans.

Kjan looked down and clasped his free hand over their entwined fingers in his lap. "Have I ever told you how proud I am of you? How fortunate I feel for watching you become this strong, independent woman… who's not afraid of anything?"

He gave a soft chuckle, bumping her with his shoulder. "I dismissed my responsibilities, and you stepped up. You handled Lucas when I dropped the ball. It's not me they look up to. It's you."

"We make a good team," she added boastfully.

Kjan shook his head ever so slightly, rubbing her hand. "It should have been you from the start. You made the plea for them. You took them in. I was just along for the ride."

He turned toward her, his eyes even more cryptic than before. "You don't need me as a brace anymore. It's time for you to spread your wings and fly on your own, little dove."

Sudden panic hit her like a gunshot. "You're scaring me. Why are you saying it like that?"

He hooked his arm under her legs and draped them across his lap, scooting her closer. "You can live without me. I know you will survive. You are stronger than me, Eve."

There was a series of rapid metallic clicks, like the sound of a ratchet, and then something snapped shut around her ankle.

In disbelief, Eve looked at the shackle he had fastened. Despite the torture-dungeon vibe of the temple, her shackle was a modern cuff with a rotating arm. An iron chain connected to it, similar to the other ones in the chamber.

NO! No-no-no. What's he doing?

"I'm going after him, and this time you will not follow me."

"But I want to help you," Eve uttered as she scrambled off him and fumbled with the heavy links.

Her mouth went dry when her eyes traced the length back to a massive hook anchored into the ground behind the throne. She pulled hopelessly on the chain. The anchor didn't relent.

Eve whipped around in a fury. "Why are you doing this?"

"I'll finish this alone. I cannot endanger anyone else. This is *my* fight," he reasoned. "Don't you see? This path of destruction follows me wherever I go. I kill everything I touch. Everyone I try to protect ends up dead because I can't protect them from *me.*"

"What happened to Thórunn wasn't your fault. You didn't know—"

"But I *did* know!" Kjan cut her off. "I knew that if I left, she would be vulnerable. *I* brought this on her. *I* did this. To Andromeda… and to you. I shouldn't be close to you. I should never have been born. Every woman who has ever been close to me has died. My mother, my wife, my daughter, Eleanor, Charlotte, Anne," he blatantly rattled off the list. "They're all dead. You're the last one left, Eve. I can't take it."

Eve grabbed his shoulders and shoved him back against the hard throne. He remained stoic.

"Stop blaming yourself for their deaths. You didn't kill them."

"I killed you!" he parried. "And I killed Eleanor."

Eve hesitated, her words catching in her throat. She couldn't argue with that one. "It was her choice to give her life for yours."

"And what do I have to show for? What have I done to honor her sacrifice? Perhaps this is it. The reason I was born. The reason I was spared so many times."

His voice was strained but resigned. In his eyes, she could see that he was already gone, an empty shell in front of her.

She didn't hold back her tears, letting them race openly down her cheeks. Her lips quivered. Her breathing shook. She didn't know what to do. "Why does it have to be you?"

"Because there is no one else." Kjan cradled her face in both of his hands and wiped her tears gently with his thumbs. "I love you, Eve… with all my heart… until its last beat. But you won't change my mind. I'm going after him."

"And if he kills you?"

"Then so be it."

Averting her eyes, he coldly plucked her hands from his shirt and rose to his feet. "You have to break the mark. I held on to the link with Anne because I deserved the pain. I don't want you to suffer the way I have. You have to reject the bond between us."

He can't mean that! He can't really mean that!

Eve wanted to scream. Tears gathered under her chin, and still, he just stood there.

Kjan took one last look at her down on her knees and then turned his back.

There's only one who can stop him now.

"KJARTAN, HELP ME!" she screamed from the top of her lungs. "Don't let him walk out. DON'T LET HIM LEAVE ME!"

Her sobs cut off her words, but she would beg his Sire to overpower him if it kept him from leaving.

Eve watched his body go rigid. Then he turned back, slowly, his eyes dark.

"I should have known you would try to use him against me," he said with a weary smirk. "But I'm afraid we both agree on this."

There was only tenderness in his tone. No anger. "There's something I need you to do."

Eve glared at him with no inclination toward humoring him with a favor.

"Go and see Joe," Kjan elaborated. "There's an envelope in the top drawer of my desk. I left him the farmhouse. Tell him whatever you want, but don't give up on the relationship you can have with your uncle. Not while you still have the chance. Trust me, you will regret it one day," he finished, facing the doors.

Eve braced her free foot against the throne's base to pull harder on the chain. The cuff cut into her ankle with the shift in position, and the links burned in her grip. She knew they were tearing her skin, but she refused to give up. She pulled and pulled.

The iron slipped through her bloody fingers, and she fell backward.

"I will hate you for this!" She shouted the empty threat as he locked her in.

"Good. I'm counting on that."

KJAN

He sealed the doors shut. Palms pressed against the stone, he lowered his forehead in between.

He felt Eve's heart break. Despite the massive slabs in his way. The agony, the rage… all directed at him. He felt it. Her pain was his pain.

No more.

Kjan's fangs descended. Focusing on the cold, hard barrier in front of him, he fought the line connecting them. He forced it away, pushing against her pull.

His body ached. It didn't want to let go.

The bond beneath his skin began to jitter as it threatened to tear. The tremble was so powerful his hands shook.

He pushed harder, dug deep into his soul to claw at the roots that were entwined with his heart.

A silent scream forced its way up his throat. His fingers curled with more determination… his nails scraped against the stone…

And then it was gone, the link to his mate ripped from its socket, a gaping void left where it had disconnected.

His chest felt hollow. His knees weak. A dead numbness crept over him.

Kjan's hands dropped to his side, and he stared at the doors for another second, picturing Eve on the other side.

Will she hate me enough?

He had done his part. Now she needed to do hers. She needed to sever her half of the bond before his lungs took their last breath so he wouldn't drag her with him.

'That was unusually cruel of you.'

"But necessary," Kjan responded to the disembodied voice. "You and I both know this is not working. We're trapped together; neither one of us is free. There's only one way out of this hell. And I'm ready."

His Sire hadn't been able to overpower the Raven on his own. Two sacrifices were better than one.

He looped the chain around the door handles and left the key in the padlock after pushing it closed. There was no cell service down here. He would leave a note at the cabin. Sooner or later, one of the others would come looking for them at the house, and that way, at least they knew where to find Eve.

He could still hear her screaming after him, but he was not sorry. She would sit this one out. *Yes*, it was cruel. But also safe.

Taking the steps two at a time, Kjan left the catacombs and took the Jeep back to the house.

There was still no sign of Hrafni.

Thanks to their little tumble down the slope together, he had a pretty good read on the boy's scent now. The fall had cut more than just his coat, and the distinct trace of his blood had burned itself into Kjan's brain.

He also had a hunch about where the trickster might be hiding out.

Going around the back of the cabin, Kjan entered the living room through the non-existing glass wall. Besides the vacant frames, there was no hint of the devastation. Eve had diligently picked up every last piece.

For a moment, he just stood there, picturing her crossing the broken shards on her bare feet. His petty jealousy had caused her so much needless pain.

He had no regrets for ditching her, and yet her final words about hating him stung. Kjan clenched his fists, then went down to the garage.

His minor attempts at any kind of energy manipulation were considerably inferior to Hrafni's magic, but he wasn't going to face his enemy empty-handed. There was only one weapon in his collection suited to fight a God.

He dug through the metal he had salvaged from the forge and found what he was looking for. From a pile of throwing knives, various daggers, and an unfinished sword, he pulled his father's axe—well, technically his mother's.

It was fitting. If he was going to die with a weapon in his hand, he wanted it to be this one.

Even in the Viking Age, the privilege of owning weapons of such quality belonged exclusively to the noble elite. They came at a high cost and were therefore a symbol of wealth and status. Kjan had always wondered how his mother's ancestors had come by it. With Frigg's confirmation of her Valkyrja heritage, it made sense now. *Chosen by the Gods themselves.* His bloodline *was* noble; only not in a material sense.

And it seemed fate had delivered the magnificent weapon to him a second time. For exactly this purpose.

It felt the same in his hand. The new leather wrap was smooth, and the blade was sharp, but he wished he had had more time to polish it.

He brushed his thumb along the sharp edge. She had never tasted blood by his own hand before. Tonight, he would make her sing.

"He wants me dead. So I'm going to give him what he wants. But not before I make him pay for hurting her."

'Hrafni will never stop. He must die.'

Kjan had no expectation of walking away from this fight alive, but he would be damned if he didn't take the Raven down with him.

"Then let's finish this together."

CHAPTER
46

KJAN

Unlike the last time he had walked to his death at the temple to meet his Sire, he was calm now—his breaths: long and deep; his pulse: low and steady; his steps: strong and sure.

He *was* ready. He would face his end with clear eyes and resolute faith. Eve was out of harm's way, and there was no doubt or worry about her moving on and making it through the difficult stretch that lay ahead of her.

Kjan dropped the Harley at the edge of the train tracks, where he had first heard the Raven's laughter. He focused on the particular scent that stood out among the pines: mint and something fruity.

Orange? Or grapefruit perhaps?

A cinnamon undertone added a kick of heat that burned in the back of his throat, and a clear picture of his prey formed in his mind. The shifter was close.

Gripping the axe handle tighter, Kjan paused. "Grant me courage and steady my hand as I face my enemy," he said in his mother tongue, sending a prayer to Týr, the bravest of the Gods.

Then he followed the unique trail further into the woods to a small abandoned shack, where he found Hrafni perched on the porch rail.

He wasn't sitting on top, his feet resting on the second level. No, he was balancing on the balls of his feet, elbows propped on his knees, hands clasped in front.

His black coat hung motionless behind him, just like his sleek, long hair. Only his face and fingers were showing. The fresh cut above his left eyebrow had already scabbed over.

He watched Kjan approach and cocked his head expectantly. His eyes were two shiny obsidian orbs, as if he were observing his surroundings through the view of a bird. Then he blinked, and they turned back to their predominant amber color.

"Well, well, well," Raf exclaimed. "Look who decided to make an appearance. Did the traitor tuck his tail between his legs?"

The fingers on Kjan's left hand twitched involuntarily in response to the insult. His Sire didn't like the accusation.

He felt a sudden throbbing pain in his left eye. His vision blurred briefly and then came back into focus.

"You can take it up with the both of us," Kjan replied, glowering.

"So I see." Hrafni shifted his gaze between the different colored irises—one green, the other blue, Kjan assumed. "Does that mean you two are sharing now? Did you manage to wake her?"

Kjan's grip tensed on the axe's handle at the mention of Eve. "Enough with the pleasantries," he barked, baring his fangs.

He whirled the axe once like a windmill at his side. "You're going to pay for what you did."

Raising the blade above his head, he pointed it toward the powerlines. A bolt of blue lighting jolted from the wire, and crackling thunder shook the earth as it collided with his axe.

Kjan felt the humming of the weapon shooting up his arm, the wooden shaft splintering in his grasp. He didn't flinch. He absorbed the power as it flooded through him.

Tendrils of light coiled wickedly around the handle of the axe. They slithered and twisted around his biceps all the way to his shoulder, sparking like live wires. Hungry tendrils bit into his skin to fuse with his body.

Hrafni rose to full height on the rail. "Impressive," he sneered, looking a little surprised. "But do you really think you can keep up? I have been practicing magic since I was born."

He took a step forward and dropped straight down, landing softly on the mossy ground. "It's in my blood."

Kjan lifted his chin, unintimidated. The electrical charge in the air around him crackled. It was palpable.

Staring at the cut above Hrafni's left eye, he began to wonder. The shifter wasn't healing as quickly as a vampire. He would eventually, because he was a God, and he would recover from his wounds faster than a human, but maybe not fast enough.

Suddenly, Kjan saw a glimmer of hope. This was his chance of making it out alive... if he could just get close. "Bring it, *Witch*."

One corner of his mouth drawn up into a smug grin, Raf turned his hand outward in a smooth motion. Green fire ignited in his open palm, shaping itself into a sphere above his curling fingers.

Kjan stared at it, temporarily transfixed by the glow. In the next moment, Raf flicked his wrist, and his hand shot forward, releasing the flaming orb.

Kjan only had a fraction of a second to react. He lunged to the right, and the projectile blazed past him.

"Your aim sucks," he taunted.

His relief at the miss was short-lived, however. Hrafni immediately summoned another ball in his right hand, tossing it a few inches in the air and catching it back in his hand the same way he had done with the apple. "I'm just getting warmed up."

"You like playing with fire?" Kjan continued to poke at him. Maybe if he agitated him, his temper would affect his targeting skills. He had no chance against the trickster's magic. He had to find a way to get closer.

"I should have let you burn," Hrafni snarled, throwing his second pitch—sidearm again.

Kjan ducked low, sprawling out in the dirt. He could feel the heat of the flame darting right over his head.

His eyes followed the trail of the fiery little comet. The tree behind him wasn't so lucky. The green fireball had split the trunk in two. The halves splintered like they had been struck by lightning.

He was already back on his feet when Hrafni prepared for another throw. As the projectile hurtled toward him, he swung his axe and deflected the attack. The baseball from hell reversed its trajectory with a returned-to-sender label.

Hrafni cursed, dodging it, and stumbled.

"You shouldn't have come here," Kjan shouted. "You should have stayed where you belong."

"What makes you think I belong anywhere? I was a pariah from the moment I was conceived. I am the epitome of an outcast."

There was a twinge of empathy in Kjan's chest. He had heard that exact story before. He understood why Raf had sought them out. Kinship was a big motivator.

"So instead of deviating from your father's path, you followed in his footsteps, bitching and moaning about how your life's tough?"

"I never wanted to be like him!" Hrafni yelled back. "I tried to make amends for Loki's flaws, but no one gave me a chance. I was pushed into this role by fate. Now I will burn it to the ground."

Kjan scoffed sarcastically. "Way to go and prove everyone right."

The fury showed in Hrafni's expression. This time, he conjured two flaming orbs, one in each hand by his sides. The green glow placed his face in a menacing light from below. The otherworldly illumination flooded the clearing around the small cabin.

He flung them at Kjan with such velocity, they were no longer spheres but blurry streaks charging at him. He swung his axe blindly at the targets.

The weapon vibrated in his hand as contact was made, and sharp pain raced up his arm, but the blade reflected the blasts. One shot straight over Hrafni's head. The other skated along the ground, digging a trench through the earth and stopping short at his feet.

"You are stronger than I expected," the boy noted, commending Kjan's vehement efforts to stay alive. "It seems I chose the wrong man for the job. I should have approached *you* as an ally instead. I could have offered you a deal too."

Kjan's ears were still ringing from the clash like he had been in a car accident and gotten personal with the front airbag. Hrafni's words snapped him to attention.

"I know what you want," he droned on. "I can read your heart just like I read the coward's inside you. You wish for the woman to have a future. A normal life. Everything you cannot give her. I can take the curse from her. I can either cure her of the affliction or I can cast the traitor out of you. The choice is—"

"Can you take her memories?" Kjan interjected. "Can you erase me from her past and make her forget she ever met me?"

The Raven's sly grin grew wider. "Yes, I can."

Kjan's thoughts were suddenly swimming. Was there a way to take it all back? To right his wrong… to save her from all the heartache he had caused her?

He recalled the images of Eve and Claire sitting on the wall, joking around with Caleb. How comfortable she was with all of them. Even the night at the bar when she had gotten through to Lucas. He had no right to take that away from her. She had been unhappy as a human. Now she truly flourished. She was home.

The choice had to be hers, not his. "No deal," he called out to Hrafni.

"Fine. Your funeral," the trickster snapped, grimacing.

He swung his arms forward in a wide arch around his body, slamming his palms together in front with the crack of lightning.

On reflex, Kjan raised his axe like a shield and took a step back, digging the soles of his boots into the ground to brace himself for the impact.

The blade absorbed the energy of the shifter's magic. The force of the blast pushed his feet backward, making him skid in the dirt, but his body was unscathed.

Flames converted into electricity, and the amplified current surged over his skin. The muscles in his back flexed as he gathered the charge, then reflected all of Hrafni's magic back at him in a single swing of his axe.

The boy hunkered down, arms crossed in front of his face, but the thrust of the shockwave knocked him over regardless. Hrafni went down on his knee, bracing his fall with one hand on the ground behind him.

Not giving him a chance to recover from the blow, Kjan charged at him, weapon raised, but as he aimed for the neck, the solid structure of the boy's body dismantled like a school of fish.

The blade cut through air, the momentum of the axe knocking his weight off balance. There was no obstacle. No body. The image before him had been an illusion.

Kjan had fallen for the deception. He whipped around to find the trickster standing tall, smiling.

"Fooled you," he said with a wink. "I cannot be harmed by my own magic."

Enraged, Kjan swung his axe sideways at his throat again. Raf's eyes glinted fiercely. His forearm shot up to block the fatal hit, his raven hair flowing out behind him. Green sparks erupted.

The kickback from the collision rattled through his bones. Kjan held on tight, but the blade fractured under the impact of Raf's magic, losing its electric charge.

Shock replaced his rage, giving Hrafni the opening he was looking for. Flames burst from his palm as he struck Kjan dead center in the chest.

It took no time for reality to sink in. It was over. Pain detonated inside his ribcage, vibrating through every cell of his body in an instant.

Eve's face flashed in front of him—her bright blue eyes that stared right into his soul. He remembered the first time she had smiled at him, shy at first, then growing in confidence as the weeks went on, waking something deep inside him that had been lost.

He remembered the pull he had felt toward her since the night he had turned her… the instant affection…

The impression of her at the gala in Eveline's gown was as vivid in his memory as ever—the way she had lit up the room with her presence, the moment he had known he was hopelessly in love with her.

The pictures kept changing, flipping through a photomontage of his short life with her: her carefree laughter echoing in his chest, her adorable scowl… the creases in her forehead when she was deep in thought. All the stolen glances at her profile whenever she hadn't been looking…

And the heartbreaking disappointment in her eyes when he had forsaken her in the catacombs.

The final image of her hurt the most.

The pounding of his heart slowed its assault on his temples, and the air in his lungs stalled as he took his final breaths. He felt the axe slip from his grasp before his body hit the ground.

Panic flooded Kjan's senses as the blade landed out of his reach. He would die without a weapon in his hand, forever denied access to Valhǫll.

His last shred of hope disintegrated with the shifter's flames. The reunion with loved ones had been his saving grace. Knowing he would get to see his mother… perhaps his daughter.

Raf stood over him, looking down. His splayed left hand hovered above Kjan's body, immobilizing him. "I'm afraid the Álfaðr's Hall will not be your destination," he said, retrieving Kjan's weapon. "But I keep my word. My sister will take care of you. I respect your efforts, mortal."

He raised the axe in his right hand. "It was never personal."

"It was personal for *me*," Kjan rasped, the noose tightening around his neck.

As his gaze wandered the constellations in the sky, his ears perceived a rustling among the trees in the distance.

Wings?

Hrafni didn't seem to hear it.

Something flew through the air. Perhaps a Valkyrja would come for him after all.

Kjan imagined his mother, a woman he had never met, a descendant of a Valkyrja, according to Frigg. He wanted it to be her.

The blade gleamed in the moonlight as it struck his chest.

CHAPTER
47

EVE

The entire blade had penetrated Hrafni's chest. The curved handle of her karambit was the only thing visible.

"You know those aren't meant for throwing, right?" Lucas frowned at her from behind the tree he was using for cover.

Eve ignored his criticism while peering over her shoulder around her own tree to see the clearing. "How else was I going to get it to him? Now Kjan can just pull it out."

"Using the witch as a knife block? Nice!"

She tapped her index finger to her temple. "It's not just a pretty hat rack. I do actually think things through."

"Perfect aim, too."

Eve pursed her lips bashfully. "Yeah, let's pretend I was aiming for his chest and not his crotch."

Lucas muttered something in response, but she didn't quite catch it. She was already sprinting down to Kristján's position.

They'd strategically split up into pairs surrounding the shack. Caleb and Emma were to the left, Dynja and Parker to her right, past Kristján and Kría. Askja and Nessa were positioned behind the small wooden structure, and Claire was somewhere among the trees with Erik.

Bayley was on standby for medical emergencies. She'd once stitched up Lucas from a gunshot wound, and she was a vital asset on this plan, even if they healed quickly from any injury.

It had taken Eve a hot minute, but Thórunn's words eventually clicked. *'Stronger together'*. It wasn't just about the three of them. She'd referred to *all* of them—their coven, their family.

And they were all here, of their own free will, to protect one of their own. Whether he liked it or not.

The epiphany had come to her in the temple, of all places. That was where Kjartan had taken control over the others and merged his mind with them to increase his power.

Kjan would have never agreed, but the choice wasn't his to make. He didn't know that after her ex, Jordan, had handcuffed her in the warehouse two years ago, Eve had googled her way through different options of escape. When she'd slipped the cuff, she'd called for help, and none of them had turned her down.

The blue and green light show had lit up the sky for miles, making it easy to spot the battlefield from the top of Mount Hood. It seemed they'd arrived just in the nick of time too. Kjan was on the ground, motionless, but alive. She could feel him, his heartbeat weak… so weak.

He was adrift somewhere out there, and if he wasn't reaching for her lifeline, then she would have to do the angling.

Lucas stayed right beside her, not letting her out of his sight and being overly protective. He clearly wanted to prove himself.

"We need to lure him away," she told Kristján as soon as they caught up with the couple.

"Shouldn't be a problem," the giant replied. "He knows we are here now. He is going to turn his attention on us."

Eve nodded. "Keep him distracted."

"What about *Sleeping Beauty*?" Kría asked, glancing at Kjan.

"He'll recover once we get some distance between them. I hope," Eve added nervously. "Just get me to him."

Taking a deep breath, she shoved the throwing knives into Lucas' hand and ducked out of sight. She was relying on Kjan to draw on her energy field once she got close.

Hrafni's eyes scanned the edge of the woods, nostrils flaring as he sniffed the air. He couldn't see them yet, but Kristján was right. He definitely knew he had company. The knife sticking out of his chest was the biggest clue.

He dropped Kjan's axe and conjured up a pale green glow, which spread quickly over his entire body.

In her peripheral vision, Eve could see the group stepping out of hiding, and Hrafni's head snapped around to Caleb first, who appeared to his left.

As he pivoted his weight to charge the boy, she took her shot, approaching from the blind spot on his right.

Head down, Eve dashed out recklessly from behind her cover—

And froze.

The goth kid towered in front of her, standing way over 6 feet, murder in his eyes. How the hell had he moved that fast? He'd come out of nowhere. A second ago, he was yards away, lunging himself at Caleb, and now he was standing in front of her, blocking her path.

He was taller than Kristján but slender in build. Nonetheless, he was frightening. His orange irises glared down at her, paralyzing her with fear. Her instincts told her to run. The hairs on the back of her neck prickled. He was Loki in the flesh. Well, almost.

Eve felt the air passing by her head, and he flinched as a slim knife struck near his collarbone.

Speaking of great aim, she was glad that Lucas had some practice with blades himself.

Hrafni's silhouette flickered, and that was when she noticed it. There was no karambit sticking out of his chest, and his body had lost its glowing luster. Through his fading shape, she saw him still standing over Kjan, solid and luminous.

Eve swallowed the knot in her throat. The one that had charged at Caleb was also an illusion, and there were four more in the clearing engaged in hand-to-hand combat with the others.

Lucas must have figured it out at the same moment, because he flung the next knife at the real version of the trickster. It sliced through his coat and struck his back just below his left shoulder blade.

Hrafni roared with anger. He dropped the act, and his clones exploded in green starbursts.

As he whipped around to face his attacker, a third dagger came toward him, but he readily blocked it with a wave of his hand. Lucas had earned his full attention.

With the Raven's back turned, no longer incapacitating him, Eve could feel Kjan's pulse accelerating rapidly. He was moving.

His left hand reached for the piece of steel in Hrafni's back before his feet were even steady on the ground. The 5-inch blade was buried so deep in his muscle that Kjan pulled his body backward onto his knees without dislodging it. Then his right hand reached around and gripped the curved hilt protruding out of the shifter's chest. He yanked it free, spattering blood in a high arch.

Eve felt a spark of pride in taking credit for the flesh wound.

She saw Kjan's lips moving, but whatever he said to Hrafni didn't carry. He kept his voice intentionally low. Everyone was watching. The entire coven's eyes were on them. She knew Kjan didn't like the attention.

Planting his boot in the center of Hrafni's back, he kicked him forward to retrieve the throwing knife from his shoulder.

The witch landed with his hands stretched out in the grass, then spun around. A green mist rose around him, swirling like a funnel. As he scrambled backward on his haunches, his long legs disappeared into the cloud, and Loki's spawn emerged as a raven.

She heard Emma gasp as the girl cowered behind Caleb. The others stood equally amazed with their mouths open.

Eve determined the bird wasn't as terrifying as the wolf, and nowhere nearly as freaky as watching a scantily-clad clone of herself put the moves on Kjan—or Kjartan. Whichever. She was getting really fed up with this doppelganger-charade.

Though Hrafni initially took flight, he was unable to rise fully to the sky. With his large black wings flapping wildly, he crashed into the second-story window of the shack.

More smashing and breaking sounds followed his landing, then the thrashing stopped and a bright green light flashed through the cracks of the building.

Eve kept her eyes on Kjan, waiting for a sign that the coast was clear for now. A blade in each hand, his shoulders rose and fell with long breaths. He was still in full attack mode, body poised in a fighter stance.

Lips peeled back over his fangs, eyes frantic, he looked gruesome. Specks of the shifter's blood stained his face like freckles.

Eve almost didn't recognize the man she was looking at until his shoulders dropped and his posture relaxed. She took her cue and ran for him. Fear could no longer hold her back.

KJAN

Eve lunged at him, sparks in her eyes that did *not* come from the joy of finding him alive. She pegged him with a punch to the jaw that made his teeth rattle. The anger behind her fist was genuine. He actually saw stars.

Kristján seized her arms and pulled her off him to give him a chance to recover before she tried to swing again. Still clutching the blades, Kjan didn't have his hands free to defend himself from the wrath of his woman.

The giant hoisted her into the air as she continued to kick and squirm in his hold.

"Let go of me!" she barked at Kristján. "Put me down right now!"

"Hurts, don't it?" Lucas mocked, shooting him a sideways look as he rubbed his chin.

"Like diving head-first into a brick wall," he snorted. "And before you ask, *yes*, I have done that."

Dynja stopped short by his side, her mouth gaping in awe. "Woah! Your eyes. They are two different colors."

"I know." Kjan brushed off her marveling. He didn't want to discuss the fact that there were currently two helmsmen steering his ship. He nodded at Kristján to release Eve.

"You sure?" the tall blond asked, raising a questioning eyebrow.

"I'll take my chances."

Kristján dropped Eve onto her feet. Her face burned red, still seething with anger. She fixed her disheveled clothes, tugging roughly on the sweater that had ridden up her belly underneath the open parka during her scuffling, then her eyes flashed to Kjan.

"Eve," he started defensively.

She took two steps toward him, shoving her finger in his face. "Save it! I'm not here for an apology."

"Why *are* you here?"

"*We* are here because you can't do this alone. Kjartan increased his power by taking over their minds, and he drained me to fight Hrafni off the first time. If he can, then so can you."

Possessing the coven was his Sire's domain. Kjan refused any further association with the immortal's vile acts. "I-I can't," he stammered.

"You can! You know how."

Kjan shook his head vehemently. He would not become a hypocrite. "Eve, no. I don't want to. It's wrong to take control like that—"

"You wouldn't be forcing your will onto us," she reasoned. "We concede."

Eve paused her argument and waited for him to consider it.

She was right, but the stakes were too high. If he lost control and fucked this up—or worse, Hrafni beat him a second time—they would all die. Their lives tethered to his was too great a responsibility. He couldn't be trusted with that.

He searched her eyes for any mental reservations. Her expression was that of perseverance.

"You used me to recharge. Just imagine how much stronger you can be if you draw energy from all of us," she continued.

Kjan looked at the group and tensed. All eyes were on him. Kristján had one arm around Kría, Caleb was squeezing Emma's hand for reassurance, Erik stood with Claire next to her twin brother Parker and Dynja, and even Askja was staring at him intently with her warm, honey-colored eyes as she leaned into Nessa, her head on her partner's shoulder.

He scanned the emotional grid of the group and found no sign of objection or hesitation among a single one of them. Not even Lucas.

He handed the boy the dagger blade he had so skillfully thrown and switched the karambit into his left grip. Scooping his boot underneath his axe, he kicked it off the ground and caught it mid-air with his dominant side.

OATH BOUND

Damn this woman!
Damn them all!

CHAPTER 48

KJAN

A power surged inside him he didn't know existed—the strength of his ancestors, flowing through his veins.

Kjan could feel it driving him. He reached deep, summoning every ounce of his being, his essence, within his core. It came to him effortlessly as he called it forth, drawing it out of Eve and, with the link to his Sire, out of the others as well.

They stood behind him like a wall, unwavering. Without touch, through the kinetically charged air alone, their energies merged. Willingly given, it was more powerful than he could have ever imagined, and it restored the spark inside himself.

With his mother's axe in his right hand and Eve's karambit in his left, Kjan was bound for the ramshackle.

Dark storm clouds started to form overhead. Lightning bolts flashed and illuminated the scene as if Þórr himself had joined their ranks for support. The crackling thunder was deafening. It rattled the abandoned shack.

He sensed Hrafni's godly presence on the upper level as he kicked in the flimsy door. No creaks or sounds of movement came from the wooden floorboards above him, but the half-giant was still there. Hiding.

Kjan crossed the space toward the stairs. His eye caught on the handrail. It was covered in a black, soot-like dust. There were more of the same streaks on the walls as well.

He dragged his forefinger through the filth and rubbed it between his thumb… *yep, charcoal.* Just like he had suspected. *What the fuck?*

He wiped the questionable stuff on his leg. Flipping the handle of the knife in his grip so that the curved blade went backward, point down, he crept upstairs.

Despite the old wood, the fall of his boots was imperceptible and light. He blended into the shadows, moving as one every time a flash of lightning shot through the house.

When rounding the corner of the landing to the other half of the stairs, he could see the top. Wooden slats fenced both sides of the opening. The stairs emerged smack in the center of the second story, giving Hrafni the upper hand and leaving himself vulnerable to being attacked.

Kjan raised his guard on the ascent. Just as expected, he was met with one large single room. The steel handle of the karambit dampened with sweat in his palm, and his nerves twitched, but he pressed on.

Conquering the final step, he wrinkled his nose. Not because there was a particularly pungent odor that irritated his senses, but because of the sadness of this place.

His view no longer obstructed by the rails, he took it all in. Broken furniture was spread without order, discarded, and scattered across the floor. The rusted-out bedframe had wiry springs poking through the moldy mattress, and a sofa, badly stained with torn upholstery, was pushed against the far wall, which had dark smudges like all the others.

The black substance was all over the shack. Here and there, chairs lay thrown around haphazardly, and a table was knocked over, missing one of its legs. Only one of the three windows still held a pane. Not exactly homey.

There was nowhere for a man to hide, yet there was no sign of Hrafni. Kjan stayed on high alert, trusting his senses more than his sight. His scent of cinnamon and mint permeated the air. *Has he been staying here?*

He wasn't sure what had caught his attention, but before he could muster up an inkling of pity, an innate nerve response told him to duck right as a streak of green flashed over his head. It collided with the top half of the split window and shattered the glass.

Kjan whipped around to confront…

…no one. Nothing but empty space stared back at him.

The room was dead quiet. Besides his own presence and the chaotic furnishings, the loft appeared vacant.

His fingers twitched with anticipation around his weapons, his eyes raking the interior. "Nice place you got here," he taunted through his teeth. "No wonder you're so bitter. You shouldn't have fired the maid."

No reply came, but he noted a subtle shift in the temperature. Cool air brushed his face like a sheer curtain. "Show yourself, coward," he bellowed.

The trickster's shape materialized out of thin air next to the sofa, then by the bed, disappearing and reappearing in different places in the blink of an eye. He was moving too fast for Kjan to get a lock on him.

Hrafni knew he wasn't an adept fighter at hand-to-hand combat. His strategy was to keep Kjan at a safe distance by projecting green flames from his palms. "What is it about you, mortal?" he yelled, launching flare after flare. "Why are you so important to *her*?"

"I'm not here for Frigg."

"That's what you think. But she is playing us all."

Kjan deflected the fire, his index finger hooked securely into the ring of his knife, and he swung his axe, which still held its own despite the fracture in the metal.

The large weapon had a longer reach, but the curved blade of the karambit was short and required him to get a lot closer. *Unless…*

His skin rippled with power. Kjan spun around and nailed Hrafni in the chest with a perfectly executed kick that knocked him into the off-kilter tabletop across the room. The remaining legs collapsed under the weight, crushing beneath him.

A roar blasted through the open space in a mix of agony and rage. Scrambling to his feet, he picked up a chair with a wave of his hand and flung it toward Kjan, who evaded the object, more annoyed by the game than feeling threatened.

It would take more than hurling furniture to defeat him a second time. He knew failure was not an option. There was more to lose now than just his own life. They trusted him. He couldn't fail them.

When Hrafni tried to repeat the trick, Kjan hurled his axe at the chair, stopping it in its flight. "ENOUGH!"

The bass in his tone shook the floorboards beneath his feet.

'Let's make this a fair fight,' the familiar voice in his head chimed in.

His Sire's shape manifested right in front of him in the same form he had appeared in the imagined cave, with the same short black hair. He stood almost like a shield between them, his tall, lean physique mirroring the Raven's, but his body wasn't solid. It was merely an astral projection composed of his signature bright blue energy.

Beyond it, the witch's eyes went wide in shock.

The conjuring trick served as the perfect distraction. Kjan lunged through the flickering silhouette. His uppercut struck Hrafni's chin from below and sent him stumbling back five feet.

As he wobbled on his legs, Kjan charged him again, head first, arms caging his torso, and they both went out of the shattered window together.

Shards of glass that were still stuck in the frame stabbed into his sides. Tangled, they landed briefly in a sprawled heap on the porch's overhang before skidding over the edge of the slick roof and plunging to the bottom. Kjan's boots hit the grass, Hrafni's head smacked the last step of the porch.

In spite of the concussion he must have received on the drop, he was very conscious, and Kjan's muscles seized in a momentary panic when his feet were kicked out from under him. His spine smashed into the solid ground, and Hrafni advanced to leap on top of him.

Before his weight came down, Kjan raised his boot and rammed it square into his jaw, knocking his head back. Blood spewed, and Raf's skull cracked against the wooden steps a second time.

Kjan kicked his legs up and jumped to his feet. The kid stayed down, his chest heaving from the strain of drawing breaths. He must have cracked a rib.

Another lightning bolt shot from the sky and struck the power line above them. Clouds broke open in a downpour, wind whipping, pelting them relentlessly.

Stowing the knife that had stayed in his grasp during the scuffle, Kjan went for the boy's throat, clasping it with both hands as he straddled his chest. "I always finish on top," he hissed triumphantly.

Hrafni looked unhinged, his lips curled, eyes flaring deep red. His fingernails stretched into long, sharp points, like the claws of the wolf, but that was as far as he got. He couldn't shift his form. He was too weak to keep up the magic, and the deep gash from Eve's karambit was still oozing.

It was over. Kjan had the high ground. He would drain what little life Hrafni had left.

'Do it!'

He couldn't see him anymore, but his Sire's disembodied voice urged him on. He wasn't sure where it was coming from now. Behind him? His head? The second-story window?

"What are you waiting for?" Raf spat. "End it. Or I will make you regret it."

Only now did Kjan notice Raf's pale skin. His dull, bloodshot eyes. Tears gathered in the corners and ran down his temples. Like an addict who had used too much, his body was failing.

Kjan's breath faltered. His grip loosened.

'What are you doing?' his Sire objected. *'He is done. Kill him!'*

"No," Kjan muttered.

'He hurt Eve. He must die!'

"NO!" he repeated, raising his voice.

Eve was right. Kjan had a lot in common with his Sire. And he could see himself in Hrafni, too. All the anger and resentment, the hidden self-loathing…

He recognized the signs. They were a cry for help. Hrafni was just a kid, a one-thousand-year-old Asgardian, the equivalent of a human teenager. His half-cocked plans of declaring war on Ásgarðr and the Gods were the rage of an overconfident adolescent. He hadn't considered the consequences; and not just the ones for failure. Because what if he *had* succeeded? It would have plunged the nine realms into chaos.

Was that really what he wanted? For all the worlds to burn?

No. He was a victim of abuse and neglect, lashing out, becoming the next abuser in line. The cycle had to end.

"I have felt what you feel. I've been there," he yelled over the storm showering them and his Sire's angry ranting. "You have to let go of the hate. Take it from someone who's held on to it for way too long. Revenge won't bring back what you lost. Your brothers… your mother… they're gone. They wouldn't want this for you."

The boy's features twisted. "How do you know what they would have wanted?" He glowered, his nails digging into the material of Kjan's shirt at his biceps. They were black. Not just the tips of the almond shape. Part of the cuticles too. But it didn't appear to be polish.

"No parent would want a life of hate and anger for their child."

"That's all I have left. I begged her. She is dead because of *me!*"

"It was her choice," Kjan argued. "Your mother didn't want you to be alone. She wanted you to be happy, so you would let go of revenge." It was a mere assumption, but he could relate to Sigyn's reasons. He would have done the same for his daughter. For his family.

"I thought I could never have a family—or even deserve one—but here they are." Kjan's gaze drifted over the clearing. The wind was starting to die down, and the rain was slowing to a drizzle.

A hundred yards away, they all lay unconscious on the ground, but he could feel their heartbeats. Steady. Strong. Each and every one of them. They had come for him. His family.

How had he not seen it? Eve had made the connection. She had accepted them. Why hadn't he?

"Life comes at you fast sometimes," Kjan reminded himself. "In the blink of an eye, your whole world gets turned upside-down, but that doesn't mean you stop going. You adapt. This doesn't have to be your end, Raf. Your mother's death wasn't your fault, and you shouldn't have to pay for your father's sins. Don't force my hand." He gripped the kid's collar tightly, their faces inches apart. "Yield!"

"I-I can't... I can't go back there," Raf stammered fearfully, clipping his speech. "I will not die in that forsaken place." He fought against the hold on him, his legs thrashing.

Kjan pinned his shoulders with full force against the ground. "Yield to me, and I will make sure you won't have to go back to Níflheimr."

The boy hesitated. "You can't promise that," he refuted.

"I will speak on your behalf. I swear on my honor, I will implore Frigg to pardon you, as the Old Gods are my witnesses."

"Why should I trust you?"

"I'm the only chance you got. Now say the words."

Hrafni's eyes narrowed as he weighed his options, revealing obvious apprehension toward a dreadful outcome. He detected no deceit in Kjan's vow, because there was none.

"I yield," the Raven uttered grudgingly.

Kjan released him. Bracing his hand on his knee, he pushed off but stayed right on top of Hrafni. The storm had passed at some point, and it was no longer raining.

He pulled the karambit from his pocket and dragged the curved steel across his own palm, then handed the knife down to the boy. "Swear it," he demanded.

Raf accepted the blade with reluctance and sat up. Repeating Kjan's action, he spoke in Old Norse, "By spilling my blood, I hereby surrender and swear to renounce all desire for vengeance."

Kjan opened his hand to him, and Hrafni reached up, clasping his forearm in the traditional custom of pledging mutual respect and agreement. There would be no mixing of their blood.

He returned the knife with a sulky expression. "Happy?"

"Good enough." Kjan slid the karambit back into his pocket, the sharp tip going right through the denim in the process as he stepped away.

He had barely moved from his position when the ground started quaking and he stumbled.

With terror in his amber eyes, Hrafni scurried backward, helplessly. Kjan could hear his heart pounding.

"No! No! You promised... I trusted you," he cried.

The earth split beneath him, opening into a crevice to swallow him up. He clawed at the soft ground as it gave way, nothing but darkness to meet him.

In shock, Kjan shuffled away from the hellish chasm, the chill from the boy's screams still cutting through the earth as it re-sealed on top of him.

"Do not feel guilty," an enchanting voice drifting across the clearing said. "It is not as bad as it looks."

Frigg sat on the porch railing, her feet dangling out from underneath her wispy sky-blue gown. Her hair was done up, revealing long diamond earrings that grazed her shoulders.

Hands clasped in her lap, she leaned her back against one of the vertical posts that supported the overhang. "And I will honor your plea," she continued with a benevolent smile while Kjan stared at her dumbstruck. "You made a great sacrifice. You fought with the power of your soul as well as the power of your heart. And you won."

Was this it? Had she come to claim the barter he had made? Would she take him home now?

He felt no different. His boots were still planted on the ground. He wasn't dead. "Then why am I still alive?"

"Death was inessential. You offered up your soul freely. The mere bargain was enough. You have a noble heart, Kjartan, son of Mýrkjartan. You have proven your compassion. You are indeed forgiving and merciful."

He let her words sink in. "The glacier was a test, wasn't it?"

"It was. One that I knew you would pass with flying colors, as the humans say. We all played our part—some more willingly than others. Mercy was yours: seeing yourself in the shoes of another, finding good in evil where others are blind, forgiving an enemy even when you have the upper hand," she recounted. "You had forgotten your greatest strength, Mýrkjartansson. No one but you could have gotten through to the boy."

"Where did you take him?" Kjan wondered, replaying the horrific scene in his head.

Frigg dismissed him with a wave of her hand. "He is no longer your concern. I will handle the terms of his punishment personally, but I promise you that he will be judged fairly."

Her body straightened on the rail, and in the next moment, she materialized in front of him, her form iridescent, shimmering with the colors of a rainbow. Standing tall now, she was Kjan's height.

"I never doubted you, sweetheart," she said, raising her hand to his cheek. "I knew you would do the right thing."

Her touch was solid, gentle, and warm. The display of affection made him feel like a boy again. Cherished. Loved.

"And I was never the one teaching the lesson," she remarked referring to the comment Kjan let slide about his Sire. "*You* were. You *and* your mate. Your actions will influence the destiny of many. We are on the cusp of great change. All because of you and your little Valkyrja," she finished with a somber smile.

A few loose strands of her hair billowed in a nonexistent breeze, then her presence vanished like a feather caught in the wind. The only thing left behind was her lavish scent as it lingered in the air.

Kjan glanced back over his shoulder, his heart suddenly racing. His feet lifted off the ground, weightless, as he sprinted toward her. None of them had come around yet after he had physically depleted them.

He skidded to his knees and scooped Eve into his arms, sweeping the matted strands of her wet hair from her face.

His throat choked up. He didn't feel their bond. He had ripped out his half; had she done the same? Had she freed herself from him at last?

He held her tighter, his fingers clawing at her parka. His body trembled. His breath hitched. "Don't let it be gone… please."

Her eyes flew open, instantly turning back to rage when they focused on him.

"You fucking bastard," she huffed. "You locked me up—"

Kjan's hand grasped the back of her neck, crushing her lips to his to shut her up… just for a second… just to feel her… to feel *something* from her, even if it was anger.

He broke away on a gasp. "And I'll do it again. No matter how much it hurt."

Eve shoved at him, her fists battering his chest, her tone furious. "I'm still mad at you."

"I'll do whatever you want." The words spilled from him without a filter. He needed her to listen, if only for a moment. "If you want me to leave, I'll disappear, and you never have to see me again. But you have to say the words… I-I have to hear them coming from you."

Kjan hung his head. He couldn't look at her. There was no connection, no link, no oxygen in his lungs. He wanted to tell her how much he loved her, but the words were too simple. They didn't feel enough.

He held his breath, waiting for her answer. A tear rolled down his cheek as he squeezed his eyes shut and endured the silence that seemed to last forever.

Please don't make me go…

CHAPTER
49

EVE

She could sense the fear in his voice. That was how much he trusted her. He laid it all bare, the side of him that only she was allowed to see. Eve was the one he permitted himself to be vulnerable with. Completely unguarded. It was everything that had been missing when he left her at the temple. She recognized how much courage it had taken him to tear out his own heart and lock it away to keep it safe.

Eve captured his face between her hands and pulled his mouth back to her. With great relief, he wrapped his arms around her waist, kissing her deeper, neither one of them getting enough.

"I love you," he uttered through choked breaths. Pressing his forehead against hers, he hugged her tightly into his chest.

Eve felt her ribs protest briefly before he eased up. "How did you get out of the cuff?"

"Shoelace," she replied with a half-shrug. "After Jordan kidnapped me, I watched a tutorial on YouTube. Wouldn't have helped me with my hands tied behind my back but worked just fine on my ankle."

Kjan looked baffled. "What about the chain on the door?"

"You left just enough slack in it for me to squeeze my hand through and reach the key," she added to the details. "The damn thing fell shut once, nearly taking my hand off. I had to prop it open with one of the iron candle holders."

Eve paused and scowled. "Why was there a shackle behind the throne anyway? If you wanted to tie me up, all you had to do is ask." Tugging on the front of his shirt, she batted her lashes, hoping he'd take the hint.

Kjan covered her hand with his own, stroking the back with his thumb. His voice was husky when he spoke, eyes glued to her. "I'll keep that in mind."

A flush rose in her cheeks, and he reveled in it with a dark smirk on his lips. Eyes glued to her, he read her response like an open book.

Kjan let her dangle for another moment, drawing her hand up and softly kissing her fingers, then he released her from his hook.

Curbing her wandering thoughts, Eve glanced around. She'd been the first one to wake, but they all began to move now. She didn't even remember passing out. "What happened?" she asked, rubbing her temples vigorously.

"I didn't kill Hrafni. I couldn't. Because of you. I saw something in him that reminded me of myself... something you said. I don't know how, but I got through to him. He agreed to a plea bargain, and she took him."

"Who?"

"Frigg. She came. She took him with her. I don't know where."

Askja's head popped up behind him. "She was here? Does that mean it's over?"

Kjan nodded slowly. "It is. He's gone," he said, focusing back on Eve.

"You said that already."

"No, Eve." He took her hands and placed them on either side of his head. "*He* is gone," Kjan repeated more clearly.

Her lips parted with a sharp inhale. This time she understood his meaning.

KJARTAN

He sat in the grass with his right leg bent, the left knee raised to prop his cheek on a fist. He was dressed in the same outfit his mind had conjured up inside Kjan's head—standard black jeans and a gray button-down shirt—because none of it was real.

His gaze dropped to the hand by his ankle. It wasn't corporal, but it was *his* hand. Not Kjan's. Not the hand of a child either. The hand of a grown man. *This* was what he had pictured when imagining his adult self. He knew what his father looked like now and knew his mother's looks too. He was something in between.

It hadn't been difficult to manage, and he realized that he had never needed someone to teach him how to use his powers. Like an intuitive awareness, he simply knew how. He always had, even back when he created his very first neophytes.

He watched the coven—*his* coven, technically—rise lethargically off the ground, clearing the cobwebs from their minds. Split into pairs with their mates by their sides, they all gathered around Kjan and Eve. Except for Lucas. He stood by himself, but even he wasn't alone. He had Bayley. His feelings for her were reciprocated.

Kjartan had not felt this lonely since he escaped his icy prison. "This has always been my destiny, hasn't it? Being alone?"

He didn't look up to acknowledge her arrival. Frigg sat down beside him, unbothered by his disrespect for her. She hugged her knees into her chest, clasping her wrists over her ankles. "Destiny means following your heart," she replied.

Plucking at random blades of grass, he sighed in frustration. "What if my heart's greatest desire is not fated to be mine?"

"You do not know your future, elskan. *'If you want something, never give up'*. Your words, not mine, but fairly accurate nonetheless," she added, meeting his puzzled scowl with a warm smile as she tilted her head in his direction.

He remembered saying those exact words to Eve. They didn't make him feel any better now, and he wondered if it had been the same for her then.

"Kjan was the better man. Again. I would not have shown him mercy. I would have killed Raf in cold blood."

"Come now. Do not be so hard on yourself. Your blood runs anything but cold," she teased. "You are a—what do they call it? Hothead? You need someone to cool your temperament."

Another lesson for me to learn?

He had overheard what she said to Kjan. And it was true. Beyond this final lesson in mercy, these mortals taught him to become a better version of himself. Taught him patience, compassion, humility, and the true meaning of love; all qualities that seemed to run scarce among Gods.

Kjartan shifted impatiently. Raising his other knee, he crossed his arms on top and dropped his chin. "What now?" he asked with resignation.

"It is time for you to come home."

His breath hitched in a panic. There could be but one reason. "Will I be punished as well?" he muttered uneasily. He had witnessed Hrafni's unpleasant departure. Would he have to face a similar doom?

She gave a soft laugh. "No, elskan. You will be rewarded."

"Rewarded?" He raised his head, and his eyes shot to her. "For what? I have done nothing to deserve the honor."

"But you have." She nodded encouragingly. "You had the chance at personal gain for the price of betrayal, and yet you chose loyalty. You have proven your allegiance to Kjan, Eve, and us. You have earned it. It is time to take your place. Your father is waiting for you… and he is not the only one."

Kjartan couldn't fully read her expression, but his blood raced with a new purpose. Would things finally change for him?

"I need to ask a favor." There was one last thing he needed to do before moving on.

Frigg pursed her lips as if she already knew.

CHAPTER 50

KJAN

He closed his eyes and inhaled her exquisite scent, their limbs entangled in the large bed. He had efficiently screwed her lights out; though she had used a more vulgar term to describe it.

He never did. Not with her, and she deliberately poked fun at him for it.

The crude vernacular simply didn't do it justice. Eve was so much more than a gratifying fuck to scratch his itch. She alone held the power to reign over all his senses. He was hers to command.

And they both had the bite marks to prove it.

Eve hadn't held back her anger at his actions. She had met him with every ounce of her fire, ripping his shirt, pushing and pulling, challenging his dominant nature until he reclaimed what was his…

What had always been his.

She had never broke her half of the bond… never let go. But she had made him earn his redemption. The aftermath showed with streaks of blood and clusters of down feathers redecorating the bedroom.

She had bled him but wouldn't let him bite her in return.

Eve had pleasured him with her mouth, leaving him aching to sink his fangs into her as he climaxed, but she denied him that. And when she rode his cock to another release, she withheld herself again.

It wasn't until he came a third time, taking her from behind, her body caged beneath his, that she bared her throat to grant him his claim.

And Kjan drank.

He gorged myself on the irresistible wine that was her blood as he filled her.

Worn out, she had drifted off to sleep blissfully while Kjan couldn't let go. He couldn't peel himself away from her. With her skin warm and her breaths deep, he forced himself to stay awake.

It was still dark outside when he sensed a presence in the house. His eyes sprang open, darting aimlessly as he pinpointed the sensation. The presence was downstairs—back porch. He had told the others to make themselves scarce for at least a month. *'Don't call or even think about showing up unannounced,'* had been his exact words. He had gone as far as threatening mutilation, so he knew it wasn't any of them. But the presence was familiar.

Too familiar.

Kjan slid out of Eve's arms and grabbed his jeans from the foot of the bed; smudges of red marked his chest like war paint. He followed the pull as if answering a call, staying vigilant, though there was no notion of danger or malice in the air.

A stiff breeze hit him through the shattered-out panes to the patio, and once he reached the bottom step of the front room, he saw the flames.

His Sire stood in front of the firepit, a self-sufficient grin on his face. "Sorry to interrupt. I wasn't going to enter without permission, but I had to get your attention somehow." He motioned with his thumb over his shoulder at the fire.

Kjan still wasn't used to seeing him as an adult version of the 12-year-old boy. Like he was an actual person now. "Why are you here?"

The immortal pointed at the wicker lounger closest to Kjan. "To return this," he replied. "Wouldn't want you to lose it again after you traveled so far to get it back."

Kjan frowned, taking a step around the chair to see past the backrest. His brows lifted in surprise. His axe. "You didn't have to."

"I wanted to," his Sire shot back. "And to be honest, I wanted a chance to say goodbye."

Good riddance. "Where are you going?" Kjan didn't really care as long as he wasn't sticking around.

He responded with a single word. "Home."

His eyes lifted to the dimly lit sky as wood crackled in the flames. The sun was gradually stretching across the vast distance, forcing away the darkness, but the luminous orb was still visible.

"It's the first one of the year," he said. "The Natives call it Wolf Moon. It represents letting go of the past and embracing a new beginning. Can you feel its power?"

"No. I'm not a witch," Kjan replied sharply. "I don't practice magic."

His Sire chuckled softly, splaying his hand on his chest at the reference to him using the moon's power. "Touché." Then he held out his arm expectantly. "Here is to new beginnings."

Kjan suppressed a laugh. *A peace offering?* As if a handshake could make up for everything and settle the rancor stirring in him. But if it meant being free of the parasite's lingering presence…

Pressing the tip of his tongue against the back of his teeth, Kjan hesitated briefly before accepting what was offered to him.

"To new beginnings," he concurred with a nod.

He grasped the immortal's forearm in a firm shake, the same way he had done with Hrafni. His touch was hot, burning Kjan's skin, but he didn't shrink back.

The gesture only lasted seconds, then the impression of his shape vanished, snuffed out like the flames in the fire pit.

Can he travel through the shadows like his father now?

Kjan rolled his eyes. He hoped he would never cross paths with another member of their family again.

He dragged himself upstairs, flexing his fingers, clenching, and unclenching his fist. The stinging pain in his arm persisted. The nerves tingled madly, with spasms shooting up and down.

Kjan chose to ignore it, and by the time he returned to the bedroom, he had forgotten all about the discomfort. The lovely bouquet of spring flowers in full bloom filled the space from wall to wall. Her irresistible fragrance was enough to make him hard again, but then Eve stirred, flashing him her naked backside.

Damn! He couldn't keep his hands off her.

She roused when he joined her. Arranging his body against hers, he nuzzled the stretch from her shoulder to her ear. "Wake for me, Dove," he purred.

Her left arm lifted sluggishly. "I'm awake," she mumbled, her eyelids fluttering lightly but refusing to lift.

She reached back, her fingers raking through his short hair. "Prove it," he taunted encouragingly.

He turned his head, and his lips grazed over the blue mark burned into the skin on her left wrist. He could see a clear image of the runes glowing brightly in his mind's eye. *Eihwaz*: regeneration, immortality, sense of purpose. *Bjarkan*: personal growth, liberation, family… and new beginnings.

Eve rolled onto her back, raising her legs at his sides. Kissing the front of her throat, he reached for her hand, tracing the length of her arm with a light touch.

As he weaved his fingers through hers, his forearm brushed across her brand. Sparks virtually ignited between them, welding their bodies together.

He had the urge to dive head-first into her divine honeypot, but she wasn't ready. Wasn't wet enough for him just yet. So he took his time, sliding gradually deeper, succumbing to the blazing heat of her core.

The need to bury himself inside of her consumed him when the plea reached his lips. "More, Dove. Take all of me."

He could give her the most vulnerable parts of himself, knowing she would keep them safe. She was his shelter. His armor.

Her walls stretched to welcome him, squeezing his aching length so sweetly before adjusting again and again.

Kjan relented a groan. He felt his cock swell against the pressure. Her body wrapped around him and swallowed him up. On every hungry drive of his hips, her body came alive for him.

"*Now* you're awake," he emphasized, nipping at her lips. Her sweet nectar poured between them as he sank in to the hilt, coating every inch of his shaft.

He captured her moans of pleasure and relief, dragging them down into his throat to draw her into him.

He let her warmth, her essence, become part of himself, merging their bodies as well as their souls. They were one being, one force, two halves of a whole.

CHAPTER
51

EVE

She sat in the middle of the bed, her hair draped over one shoulder. It was still dripping wet from the invigorating shower they'd just enjoyed together.

Her eyes skipped over the pages in her hand she'd pulled from the desk. "Why didn't you tell me about this? These are dated months ago."

She was holding the papers of the deed for the farmhouse her uncle Joe and she had shared with Kjan for ten years, never knowing the hermit in the upstairs studio owned it. "And signed by *Morgan Lewis?*"

One of his aliases, she presumed. What happened to his alter egos once they had outlived their purpose? Did he kill them off or simply let them vanish?

Kjan came out of the walk-in closet wearing a clean pair of dark blue jeans and a different shirt. Eve had taken the liberty of putting the one he'd originally chosen on herself.

"A 70-year-old man from Colorado enjoying a nice and quiet retirement," he elaborated with indifference.

"You've lived in Colorado?"

"I have lived in a lot of places. But I have always liked mountains." He sank onto the bed and crossed her legs over his lap.

"How do you pick these random names?"

"By their meaning. My father's name, Mýrkjartan, means *Sea Warrior*. All my aliases are some form of *ancient fighter from the sea*."

"Huh. Kinda predictable, don't you think?"

"*You* didn't figure it out." He tapped his index finger affectionately to her nose, a jaunty note in his tone. "You called them random."

"So why didn't you send them?" Eve wondered, setting the stack of papers aside.

He drew up one shoulder. "I don't know. I guess… I was kind of hoping we could deliver them in person… together."

Her brows lifted. "Together? As in *you-and-I-together* together?"

Her mouth felt suddenly dry. Too many questions began racing through her mind. She'd left home to protect Joe as much as herself. Her ex Bobby had already put two and two together. Eve had ditched her uncle without even saying goodbye and hadn't spoken to him in almost two years.

How would he react? What exactly would they tell him? Kjan had never talked about going public before. What had changed? Why was it important to him now?

Kjan sensed her reluctance. "I know you're worried, but family trumps everything. Joe is your blood. He will understand."

He closed his arms around her waist and pressed his nose to her cheek. "I don't want to hide. You mean too much to me, Dove. I want the whole world to know that you belong to me."

Eve scoffed. "*Belong* to you?" she echoed, repulsed.

She felt him smile against her skin, the stubble of his beard scruffy at her jawline.

His hand left her waist and drifted to her ankle, walking slowly higher up her leg. "Mine," he said as his fingertips brushed the outside of her calf, "mine," skimming along her thigh, "mine," rounding her hip and dipping under her shirt—his shirt—to her perked nipple that was surely hard enough to cut glass by now, and lastly, "mine," as he claimed her mouth with his own.

Eve took his motion to assert dominance as a challenge. *Two can play that game.*

Her hand grazed up his nape and then twisted roughly through his hair. She pulled his head back, exposing his jugular and subjecting him to her own claim. "Mine," she growled, right before her canines penetrated his skin.

His blood poured down her throat, lush and smooth. It pulsed in her arteries, merging their heartbeats into one.

Warmth spread in her belly, filling her to the brim, and yet she craved more. When had she last taken his vein? In the shower? Last night? It seemed like forever ago.

Kjan's arms closed around her torso, the softest moan on his lips. "Still hungry?"

"Starving," Eve rasped as if waking from a trance. She dropped her head on his shoulder. "Can we just stay in bed all night?"

"Are you assuming I had anything else on my mind?" He gave a condescending chuckle, raking his fingernails across his forearm absentmindedly.

He'd been scratching at it all night since waking up. There were visible marks over his tattoos, because his skin couldn't keep up with the healing. She'd first noticed them in the shower, and they still looked fresh now. "What's wrong with your arm? You keep scratching it."

"Am I?"

Eve scooted back, and Kjan sat up straight to study it closer. He had a strange look on his face, like he was feverishly trying to remember what he had for dinner last.

That was stupid, of course. It was the same thing he had the night before: *her!*

His hand rubbed across his forearm again, then his eyes darted rapidly back and forth. He was somewhere in his head, light-years away. Eve knew his tells. She couldn't reach him.

"Kjan?" she whispered, slowly inching for his hand as it started to shake.

He snatched it up before she touched him, seizing her wrist with a callous grip. His frigid stare went right through her, and a shudder rippled over her skin.

"What is it? What's going on?"

There was a nervous edge to her tone that Eve had no control over. The last time she'd seen that expression on him, he had nearly blown up the house.

KJAN

He had woken up with his arm resuming the throbbing program. It was an annoyance, more than anything else. He had ignored it, but now he saw it. *Óðal*, the O-rune in the band of his mother's name, was raised like a fresh burn.

Kjan's mind instinctively skipped through the list of meanings: The Óðinn rune, Allfather, inheritance, legacy, tradition, richness in the sense of home and family, symbol for male fertility—

He stopped dead, his heart hitching like the needle on a broken record.

Then he started again with *Bjarkan*: birth, female fertility, the unrealized energy of a mother's womb waiting for a spark to initiate growth—

His spark?

No! It couldn't be… it just couldn't.

The room started spinning. *Air!* He needed air. He couldn't breathe.

Kjan fought the nausea and dizziness. Eve's scent had changed, the hormonal shift giving it a distinctively sweeter and stronger nuance. She was already pregnant.

Eve's lips were moving, but he couldn't hear her over the rushing of blood in his head.

He let go of her wrist and stormed out the door, stumbling, nearly tripping over his feet, because he couldn't get away from her fast enough.

Distance as his goal, Kjan ran without a particular direction, past the hallway, down the stairs, across the patio, through the trees…

He broke down somewhere in the woods, miles away from the cabin, his body trembling as it went into shock.

Hunching over, he clutched his shirt in a vise grip as if that would somehow lessen the sharp pain in his chest. His heart pounded up his throat, making it harder to force air past the throbbing and into his lungs. Every breath he inhaled threatened to surge back up.

"Kjan?"

He snapped around at the call of his name, his eyes unfocused, but he recognized her voice. Askja appeared out of nowhere.

Or had she already been here?

He didn't know. He couldn't think. His mind was lit up like a Christmas tree from the sensory overload of his body.

She took a few steps, extending her hand toward him.

"Don't… don't touch me," he stammered, his tone more abrasive than he intended.

She didn't seem to take it personally. Her expression was one of worry, not fear before Kjan squeezed his eyes shut to stop the trees from swiveling.

The chirping of birds eventually brought him back. Askja was still with him, sitting patiently on a tree stump a couple of feet from him.

"I'm sorry," he apologized. "I didn't mean to sound so harsh. You were only trying to help."

It was the first time the two of them had said more than three words to each other. He didn't want to ruin the chance at fixing things between them.

"It's okay," she said, raising one corner of her mouth. A small dimple showed in her cheek, and the honey glow of her eyes was as warm and honest as ever. "Are the panic attacks always this bad?"

"No. It was the worst one yet. I thought," he paused and corrected. "I *hoped* they would stop now."

He used to get them regularly in connection with Andromeda. His link to her while she had been buried in the ocean had caused nightmares and inevitable bursts of anxiety. The same thing happened when Eve was agitated. Her emotions would flow into him and occasionally amplify. And all that had happened *before* becoming 'Mr. Split-personality'.

But that was over now. Things were supposed to be better. Not worse.

"Eve's pregnant."

The words spilled from him thoughtlessly. He didn't mean to say them. He had no desire to hear them out loud.

"Isn't that what you always wanted?" Askja sounded confused. He expected his statement to have a more shocking impact, but there was no trace of surprise in her tone.

Kjan's temper bubbled to the surface. "Did you hear what I said? Eve is pregnant!" he repeated, raising his voice.

"Then why aren't you happy?"

"Because it's not *mine!* How could it be, Askja? We can't procreate. He used me."

Kjan's fangs bit into his bottom lip to keep it from quivering. Blood welled under his tongue. He focused his attention on the physical pain he inflicted on himself. If everything else fell apart, it was the one thing he could control.

"*We* can't. But you're not like us. You were Kjartan's vessel. Your body has changed since he took it for a joyride.

All it needed was a little bit of rune magic." Her lips stretched thin into a nervous smile. "He gave you a gift."

"*His* magic. *His* spark," Kjan muttered under his breath. He had nothing to do with the *gift*. He was merely the courier. No more than an errand boy.

"It was conceived with your body. Biologically, it's yours. And the transformation you have been through at the glacier—" Askja's words cut off abruptly, as if she had said too much.

"Eve told you about that?"

She chewed her lips for a second. "She didn't have to. I felt it. I can sense the change in you."

She saw the confusion in Kjan's eyes. "I'm sorry," she went on, tearing up. "There is so much I wanted to tell you, I swear."

His vision narrowed on her. "What do you mean you *felt* it?"

"I'm a *seer*. I see and I hear things… sometimes."

Kjan felt like a veil started to lift in front of his eyes. "Why were you out here tonight?"

Her glance drifted to the ground, his valid question making her uncomfortable. What wasn't she telling him? What was she hiding?

"You have known this whole time?" His accusation came out angry, but it seemed justified now.

"No. Not until we all woke up in the temple together. It's like it unlocked something in my head." She made a wavey gesture with her hand. "That's when I heard her voice."

"Whose voice."

"Frigg's—Freyja's—whatever. She said she had kept Kjartan concealed from the Raven and then sent me, a descendant of herself, to watch over him once he was freed. See, when my son died, I lost all direction in my life," she rambled on without stopping at the vital piece of information. "My mother passed away two years earlier, and I—"

"Whoa! Back the fuck up. You're *what*?"

Askja stiffened and took a deep breath. "I'm a descendent of Frigg and an oracle, and as such, I am sworn to secrecy. Naturally."

"BULLSHIT!"

"I swear, I wanted to tell you every day. It was so hard to be around you and watch you suffer."

Kjan clenched his teeth. He was still bitter. "Why are you coming clean now?"

"I'm off the hook, so to speak. We are not allowed to talk about the future, only the past, and the knowledge will not affect your path from here on out."

"Why didn't I know any of that?"

"Because Kjartan didn't know. He only knew what I knew, and I had no clue until that night at the temple."

Same conundrum he had faced with Lucas' reveal of having a daughter he didn't know about.

"I lived a perfectly normal human life for 35 years. Well, more or less," she went on. "My son and my mother were gone. I barely knew my father. I was alone. I think that's when I heard her voice for the first time. Frigg sent me to find him. God, he was so fucking small, he reminded me of him."

She blinked away more tears, reminiscing about her son. "I watched over him… I took care of him. Frigg is not just some far-off ancestor of mine. She is my grandmother… on my father's side."

"Oh, gimme a fucking break," Kjan bellowed, throwing up his hands. "You're one of *them*. You really have one hell of a family there."

In his book, she was guilty by association just for being related to his Sire. *Freaking Cousins!* Who would have seen *that* coming?

Askja's face turned grave. "I'm not done."

"Fuuuck! What else is there?"

"You better buckle up, buttercup, because you're really not going to like this next part."

Kjan groaned. That didn't sound good. He figured it was appropriate that he was already sitting down.

Crossing his arms over his chest, he braced himself for the worst. "Bring it on."

"Like I said," Askja cleared her throat. "I don't know my father much. I was 16 when I saw him last, but I have always known where he is."

Kjan rolled his eyes. He was getting seriously impatient with her ramblings. "Cut to the chase, Askja. No offense, but why the fuck would I care about some schmuck the witch spawned."

"Because he's *your* father too."

His jaw dropped to the floor. "What did you say?"

"Our father is still alive," she repeated, her eyes dead serious. "Congratulations! You're part of the family now."

Kjan blinked, perplexed, and momentarily struck stupid. His lips refused the command to move. *The old man… alive?*

"Where… where is he?" He remembered his father as a kind but bitter man. Broken by loss. A family curse, it seemed.

"Back in Iceland. He's been there for a very long time. Long before he crossed paths with my mom. They were never married. It wasn't that serious, according to her." Askja paused for a sullen breath. "Frigg said he never forgave her for taking your mother."

A shell of a man.

Kjan remained stunned. *My father… a direct descendant of a Goddess?*

Askja… my sister?

And Frigg…

His mind circled around her words at the temple. Specifically around something she said about the potential of his blood. If his father was her son, carrying her gift of foresight, and his mother the daughter of Skuld, the Norn of the future, what did that mean for his own female offspring?

After no more response came from him, Askja slapped her palms on top of her thighs and rose from the tree stump, concluding her lecture.

"Do you want me to fill Eve in?" she asked over her shoulder before taking off. "It's okay if you need some time to digest. It really is a lot to take in."

Kjan vaguely felt his head bob.

"Oh, one last thing before I forget." She got down on her haunches to be at eye-level with him, her expression gleaming. "Just so we're clear, your child will be a God. Or Goddess," she added with a wink.

CHAPTER

52

EVE

3 months later—

Eve pulled the blanket back over her head, her muscles still weak and stiff from earlier. Kjan had turned on all the lights in the room, trying to get her to move, but she was having none of it. She didn't want to leave the warm bed.

"Are we actually going to dance with ribbons around a tree?"

"Pole," Kjan corrected her from the closet. "And no. I think we're just having a bonfire."

Askja had insisted on the public celebration of love and fertility since May Eve was associated with the God Frey and the Goddess Freyja. "How is that different than any other night we have the whole gang here?"

"Because we're doing it in the clearing instead of the back porch."

"So, using our football field makes it special?"

"It's bigger," he called back. "Why so skeptical? Just go with it."

Go with it? That seemed to be the new motto around here.

Eve had accepted the news surprisingly well. It was hard to judge what was more of a shocker: Kjan and her having a supernatural baby, or the fact that after almost one thousand years, he now had a half-sister. Oh, and not to forget the minor detail about being related to ancient Gods.

Who would've thought that his Sire had been his cousin all along? Talk about a fucked up family tree. No wonder Kjan's father had taken off.

Eve rolled her eyes—not that he could see her face under the blanket. "Fine. Whatever makes her happy. When are they getting here?"

"They're probably on their way already. She has a lot to set up." His voice was closer now, and before she could get a better hold of the sheet, he ripped it back.

Cold air bit into her skin, but the view was totally worth it.

Kjan hunkered down by the side of the bed, grinning from ear to ear. His hair had grown out enough to tuck back. His beard was the standard half-inch. "You're still not dressed," he observed. "What else can I do to motivate you?"

Eve crooked her finger, beckoning him closer.

The mattress dipped as he slid one arm underneath her and lowered himself down.

She triumphantly locked her limbs around him. "You're soooo warm," she groaned, skimming her nose along his neck. "And you smell perfectly delectable. I changed my mind. Maybe I do want to dance around a pole."

"I told you, woman, there won't be a pole."

"Oh, there will be." She baited him with the innuendo, pressing her hips up to him.

She let her tongue follow the trail her nose had taken up to his ear, then added in a whisper, "And I will be sliding down on it."

Kjan laughed wholeheartedly, his eyes sparkling. "That's your hormones talking."

"And that's somehow a problem?" True, she had been insatiable these past weeks, but she didn't remember him complaining. Ever.

Kjan shook his head, amused by her argument, and then relented. His free hand slipped under the T-shirt of his that she had slept in, and his mouth fused with hers.

Voices erupted downstairs, people moving about and doors slamming as their family let themselves in.

"Oh, hell no!" Eve shouted, crossing her ankles tightly at the small of his back. "I'm not getting cockblocked again."

Kjan gasped dramatically. "You kiss me with that filthy mouth of yours?"

"I show you filthy," she replied, nipping at his jaw. "Let them wait. We have time for a quick fu—"

He silenced her with a fierce kiss before she could finish the word.

"Hold on to that thought," he said, pulling away.

When he sat up straight, he dragged her with him. "I *have* to go," he apologized, unwinding her clingy arms from his neck. "And you better get dressed."

"Did you know a lioness in heat will bite her mate's balls if he can't keep up?"

That got his attention. "Okay, that's it!" He nailed her with a glare while scooting off the bed. "You're officially cut off from watching animal documentaries."

He spun back, his forefinger extended. "I can keep up."

Yeah, he could, but from his unsettled expression, he was probably considering sleeping with one eye open from now on.

Eve cursed after him as he left and then kicked the blanket to the floor defiantly. *Might as well*, she thought, stomping to the closet.

She rifled through various tops. *What to wear, what to wear?* Jeans? They were a good option to sit around a bonfire all night, but not very festive for the occasion.

She kept most of her dresses at the penthouse. Denim was the practical solution in the mountains. She had no idea what was appropriate for a traditional May Eve celebration.

Damn, she cursed again. She should just make the switch and get it over with. It wasn't like she'd ever move back to the city. Why had she been pushing it off?

Kjan had transferred all his stuff back here, except for Eleanor's furniture. Even his suits hung neatly organized, and when was the last time he'd worn one? He hated them. Yet here they were, in their *home*.

It *was* their joint house, wasn't it? She hadn't just moved into one of his properties. He was very clear that the cabin belonged to her as much as him, and he discussed any potential modifications with her.

He'd asked about her thoughts on how to fix the glass wall in the living room and rebuild his forge. Though Kristján and Erik had helped with the completion, her opinion mattered to him.

She rubbed her hand over her still pretty flat belly. What exactly was bothering her? They were having a baby. They couldn't be more thrilled. Everything was finally perfect.

Eve sighed, leaning back against the door. Something caught her eye on the floor under his suits.

She crouched on the soft carpet of the closet and picked up the white cloth, unfolding it in her hand. It was a monogrammed handkerchief, with the cursive initials *K.M.* embroidered on it.

Kjan currently went by the surname Murphy, but he *had* used others. She brushed her thumb across the elegant letters. They were a lot like his own handwriting.

She spied two more colored handkerchiefs on the ground by his dress shoes. The first one was deep red with the initials *D.M.* in bold black letters stitched in the corner—the infamous *Donovan Morgan*.

Eve shrugged with indifference. She accepted the fact that he'd lived many lives, and if the name held no more significance to him, then it didn't matter to her either.

The second one Eve had grabbed was a lovely shade of purple and had a delicate lace trim around the edge. This one didn't smell like Kjan.

She raised the little square closer to her nose. A very distinct trace of lavender clung to it. It was Eleanor's.

Eve's heart felt heavy as she unfolded it carefully. The embroidered monogram hit her like a blow to the gut.

E.M.

She vaguely remembered that Kjan had been using the name Kasey Murdoch at the time the two had met in Chicago back in the sixties. His former companion's last name had been Dale. Either her maiden name started with an *M* or the two had been posing as a married couple.

Eve tried not to focus on the image that popped up in her mind. He probably had it made for her in Paris.

She looked at the two handkerchiefs side by side: *K.M. & E.M.*

Her throat began to constrict slowly the longer she stared at it. Pushing to her feet, she put them away.

Eve settled for a pair of navy blue leggings and a red tunic-style shirt, then went downstairs, where she was met with the usual joyous chatter and laughter coming from the living room. But when her eyes fell on the girls, her grip tensed around the banister.

She was massively underdressed.

All six of them were dressed in pastel-colored gowns that drifted across the hardwood floor as light as air. Askja's and Kría's were lavender, Dynja's and Nessa's a sage green color, Emma's and Bayley's powder blue. Claire was the only one in a dusty-rose-colored dress.

Fresh spring flowers were weaved through everyone's preciously styled hair.

"Your color doesn't go with my hair. Go stand somewhere else," Nessa told Claire with a cheeky grin as she nudged her side.

"Wow! You guys look gorgeous. I didn't expect anything this fancy." Eve fidgeted nervously with the hem of her bright red shirt. She wanted nothing more than to crawl back under her warm comforter and skip the entire ordeal.

"Don't worry, sugar, I got your dress," Bayley said, hooking her arm around Eve's. "Let's get you changed."

The short girl spun her around on her heels and dragged her back the way she had just come down.

Eve stammered, confused. "W-what? Where are the guys?"

"They're setting up on the field," Kría answered. She was the last one to enter as they all crammed into the bedroom.

"Let me do your hair first." Claire shoved her toward the bed and motioned for her to sit.

Eve refrained from complaining and submitted herself to the complete makeover. It surely couldn't get any worse than her current unbecoming appearance.

Under Askja's watchful eye, Claire got started looping several ponytails on top of her head through one another. Eve had counted six in total.

Teasing the individual strands apart, she coiffed them into shape with little direction from her critical supervisor. She braided the sides next, then added white flowers, and a few tucks here and there later, she was done.

"I love it. I think it's your best one so far, Claire," Bayley said, handing Eve a small mirror so she could see for herself.

"Wow!" Eve exclaimed when she saw it.

There were simply no other words to describe it. Two slim Dutch braids adorned the side of her head on either side, tight enough to give her a facelift. On her crown, her hair was over four inches in height, and that was without the use of any products to give it hold.

The rest of her locks fell in natural waves loosely down her back, beautifully embellished with not just flowers but beads as well. Eve had to fight the tears and blamed it on the damn hormones.

In the corner of her eye, she saw Nessa unzipping the huge garment bag she'd been carrying. Eve's breath stalled the second the emerald chiffon bubbled out of it.

She leaped off the bed. "That's Eleanor's dress," she muttered. "How did you get this?" The crystals and beads crinkled in her firm hold when she hugged the embroidered bodice against her chest.

"Kjan gave me the key to your apartment." Askja replied. "I hope you don't mind. I had a hard time talking Emma and Bayley out of raiding your closet." She nodded her head in the direction of the accused girls, and they averted their eyes, looking very guilty.

"But there's no way I'll still fit in this."

"Don't be silly, las," Nessa laughed. "You're not even showing yet. Go put it on."

Eve disappeared with the gown into the closet. The embroidered lace bodice that came down to a deep plunge in the front zipped up without protest. She couldn't believe it. In a few weeks, she would've blown the seams at the waistline.

She turned around to look at the back in the floor-length mirror that hung over the closet door. The intricate lace on the backside was sheer, unlike the front, and dropped like a pair of wings from her shoulders.

The whole get-up made her think of Eleanor's last gala back in Seattle, where she'd danced with Kjan for the first time. She recalled the flutter of her heart, feeling his hands on her skin that night. He'd put on a suit—and tie—just to impress her.

Eve got briefly lost in the memory when the sound of an old truck rattled up the driveway.

She flew out of the closet and darted for the window, the girls gasping behind her. Ripping it open, she leaned her upper body out as far as she could on her toes and craned her neck.

Her eyes landed on her uncle's orange and white Chevy.

Eve stormed out of the room to race down the stairs, the girls rushing after her like chicks after their mother hen.

The concrete under her bare feet didn't slow her down. She reached the truck before Joe managed to even shut the door behind the woman hopping out of the passenger seat. She had blonde hair that was cut into a short bob, and her dress was a beautiful plum color. In her flats, she was the same height as Joe.

Eve released her uncle from a big hug that had almost knocked him over. He hadn't changed. Behind the blur of her tears, his dark blond hair was the same clean cut it had been for as long as she could remember.

His glasses were new but had a very similar style. The only thing different was his smile. And the fact that he was wearing slacks and a dress shirt; Joe preferred jeans and T-shirts like Kjan. Only wore suits to work at the hotel, where he'd been the night manager for years.

The night shift had made it easier to take care of Eve when he'd taken her in after her parents' deaths, but she'd always felt as though she was holding him back from living his life. Looking at him tonight, a huge weight lifted off her shoulders. Eve had never seen him happier.

Kjan and she had hand-delivered the deed for the farmhouse to Joe three months ago, claiming that Morgan Lewis was actually his father. Eve had been so nervous on the drive and then broken down crying in the kitchen for almost an hour.

She'd wanted to tell him everything, from her interrupting Kjan's suicide attempt to finding out he was the grandson of a Goddess. But he never would've believed her. The story was outrageous.

In the end, she'd decided to keep it simple: she'd run into Kjan a few times in Seattle, he'd offered to show her around the city, and things had gotten more complicated after that. He'd been worried about their age difference, and they'd split ways but stayed in contact when she'd moved to Portland alone. He'd eventually shown up to reconcile, and Eve had been radio silent because she didn't know how to tell Joe the truth.

It *was* the truth. Minus the crazy, supernatural details. And when it came to them not aging… well, they'd cross that bridge once they got there. Kjan had agreed to go along with whichever story she came up with.

"I hope it's okay that I brought a friend," Joe said with a shy grin. "This is Kate."

The woman flashed a nervous smile at the group crowding the driveway. Her eyes were a warm hazel tone, only slightly lighter than the freckles that stretched across her slender nose.

"Of course it is!" Kría shouted eagerly, clapping her palms together.

"Jeez, bug, look at you in that dress." Joe took her hand and gave her a spin. Her skirt fanned out like a big circus tent. "You look incredible."

"Doesn't she?" Dynja chimed in.

Eve felt herself blush. "Thanks, Joe," she said awkwardly. She was still very confused about what the whole fuss was about.

Joe hooked one arm around Kate and offered Eve the other one. "Ready?"

Another instant flashback sparked in the back of her head: Kjan leading her up the museum's steps. He'd granted her a glimpse into his life and thereby changed her own forever.

Eve shrugged and looped her arm around Joe's. "Lead the way," he said to Askja.

With the rest of the girls falling in line behind them, they followed the driveway's turn to the backyard and kept on going until they reached the football field.

Askja stopped suddenly and stepped aside, clearing the view for Eve, who'd been keeping her eyes on the ground. She had a hard time not stepping on the hem of her dress without heels adding a little extra height.

"Dayum!" Dynja blurted the combination of damn and yum from over her shoulder.

Eve looked up, and her body went numb, head to toe. She didn't feel Joe next to her anymore. Didn't see anyone but *him*. The whole world disappeared around them.

CHAPTER

53

EVE

She shook her head in utter disbelief as Kjan stood at the bottom of the hill. He'd changed out of his T-shirt and distressed jeans from earlier and was now wearing a two-piece suit: gun metal gray pants paired with a vest and completed with a tie. No jacket.

He had rolled up the sleeves of his button-down shirt, which was the same shade of lavender as his sister's dress. The tie was a deep green, matching Eve.

The sight of him sent unpredictable palpitations to her heart.

Towering next to him was Kristján, and past him she could see Lucas, Caleb, Parker, and Erik, all looking equally fashionable.

The pieces were finally falling together. Her chest swelled. It was all too much for her to take in; she was speechless. How had he done this without giving anything away?

Eve fought really hard not to tear up as Joe walked her down the makeshift aisle, lined by fist-size rocks and twinkling blue lights.

Her *betrothed* waited for her at the end, centered between two torches marking the entrance to a circle of flowers, leaves, and small branches. She identified myrtle and willow, but there were other scents in the air as well.

"You don't look like yourself," she said as she stopped in front of Kjan.

"Funny, I have never felt more like myself." He clasped her hands tenderly and kissed the top of her fingers, his green eyes beaming. She felt his heartbeat skipping in harmony with her own. "You freed me."

"You did that yourself."

"But you opened my eyes," he shot back, dropping to his knees in front of her. "It was always you, Dove. You came for me when I was dying, and you raised me from the battlefield. You truly are my Valkyrie."

Eve plopped down to join him, her gown doing a quick *poof* as she settled.

"Okay." Askja shrugged, bobbing her head in agreement. "I guess you can do this part on the ground."

She walked around the wood for the bonfire that was piled in the center. To the north side of the circle stood a table covered with red cloth, like an altar. Candles in different colors were placed on top, as well as a bottle, two drinking horns, an incense burner, and a... *long stick*?

"Divine Gods of Ásgarðr," she called out, "noble ancestors and those who have assembled here today, we welcome you to our sacred circle. We ask that you bear witness to this holy union of matrimony and that this marriage be a lasting bond of commitment and perfect love."

She picked up a lighter, preparing to light the two white candles positioned to the right and left forefront.

"We are all children of light," she continued. "Thus do I bring to flame these candles, one to represent the sun and our Spiritual Father, and one to represent the moon and our Spiritual Mother. May the light bring this union of Kjan and Eve to grow in health and joy."

After lighting the candles, she lifted one horn from its stand with her left hand and picked up a vile Eve hadn't noticed earlier with her right. She held them both high and poured the white, crystalline content of the vial into the horn, saying, "Thus are the salt and water blessed, purified, and mingled, that these lovers shall enter a circle made clean and pure, able to join themselves together in this rite, cleansed of all impurities."

Askja went around the circle, sprinkling the water, and then returned to the altar, lighting the incense next. "Myrtle to keep your love alive," she said. "Rowan to bring you luck. Oak to resonate fertility. And willow from the tree of moon magic to protect you on this plane of life. Thus is the incense made holy and its sacred scent carried around the circle, so the lovers shall enter this temple of Óðinn filled with blessings. May their lives be happy and filled with the riches of love."

Again, Askja walked around the circle, this time with the burner.

Returning to the altar, she picked up the staff that was taller than her head. Norse runes were carved along its sides in Younger Futhark.

Staff in hand, she approached Kjan and Eve at the circle's south gate. "An oath to love forever consecrated before the Old Gods, Goddesses, and our ancestors fastens a bond extending far beyond this life. Swear no words which you are unwilling or unable to uphold, for no lawful betrothal shall be broken with impunity."

Askja rapped the ground soundly three times with the rune staff. "I call upon the betrothed Eve," she said in a voice more authoritative than usual. "If you desire a sacred and binding union and vows made before us all, come now through the portal of this sacred wedding circle."

Kjan helped her up, and Joe guided her to the right side of the altar before turning to stand at the head of the circle beside Kate.

Eve's apparent bridesmaids joined in next, forming a crescent with Nessa in the lead and Claire at the end.

Askja rapped the ground with the rune staff again. "I call upon Kjan. If you desire a sacred and binding union and vows made before us all, come now through the portal of this sacred wedding circle."

Kjan stepped forward and walked to the east position in front of the altar opposite Eve. His groomsmen, led by Kristján, copied the ladies, framing the other half of the circle.

Erik closed the temple's gate with Claire in the south.

Askja returned to the altar and picked up the salt water she'd mixed. "I give you the blessings of Frigg," she announced and dipped a spring of evergreen into the horn.

After anointing first her, then Kjan, she held out a chalice of what appeared to be clear water to Kristján, and he dropped something small from his pocket into it. It was heavy and made a metallic clunking sound when it sank to the bottom of the cup.

He held on to the chalice while Askja used a red cord to bind Kjan's left wrist to Eve's right. "This cord is a symbol of your passion, a bond of love and commitment to each other. May this tie, unbroken, always serve as a reminder of the vows you make today."

Next, she filled the second ceremonial drinking horn with, what do you know, traditional mead. Picking up the horn, she guided Kjan and Eve to Parker, who marked the east point of the temple, holding a blue candle.

She spilled the drink on the spot and lit the wick. "You begin your journey of life shared," she recited, "bound together by the vows of this rite. Many are the years you will share, and countless moons may you watch together. If you keep your vows, your sacred trust, happy will be the number of your days. May the keepers of the sacred winds whisper joy into your life. May you delight in each other's love for all your years unto death. Share the great mysteries of life and let your spirit be as free as the falcon's flight."

Askja led them to Claire at the south point of the circle. She poured mead on the ground again and lit a red candle in the bridesmaid's hand. "You begin your journey of life shared, bound together by the vows of this rite. Many are the paths you will share, and countless summers may you pass together. If you keep your vows, your sacred trust, happy will be many of your days. The past is in flames; you are forever changed from this day on. May the fires of love kindle your passions for each other throughout all your years. May your love rise anew, an eternal flame, to light each day."

Lastly, Askja guided the bound couple to the west point of the circle, where Kría waited with a green candle. She poured the horn's contents and lit the flame. "You begin your journey of life shared, bound together by the vows of this rite. Many are the dreams you will share and countless tides of life to ride. If you keep your vows, your sacred trust, happy will be many of your days. Share the waters of life and share the reflection of love in one another's soul. Together, explore the laughter of rain and the mysteries of love, and in love, share the tears of life."

Askja completed the ritual by leading Kjan and Eve back to the altar at the north point. She poured mead one last time and lit the final yellow candle. "You begin your journey of life shared, bound together by the vows of this rite. Many are the roads you will take and endless the nights of your love. If you keep your vows, your sacred trust, happy will be many of your days."

She gave Kjan a subtle nod, and he clasped both of Eve's hands.

"My sweet Dove," he said full of reverence while gazing into her eyes. "I praise the Gods every day for your patience with me. For standing by me as you have, with strength and grace in equal measure. And I beseech them to grant me the wisdom to always see you for who you are inside, so that I may love you as you deserve. You are my best friend. My light in the darkness. My soulmate—"

His voice cut off, choked with emotion, and Eve gave his hands a light squeeze of reassurance.

"You are the keeper of my heart," he went on after closing his eyes for a second to swallow. "I love you, and I will cherish you forever, in this life and beyond. I vow to always take joy in your presence and feel fortunate for the gift of your love. Walk this path with me, as I will do with you, sharing with each other the moments of our greatest happiness as well as deepest sorrows."

His words were so beautiful, Eve's heart threatened to burst. Tears streamed down her cheeks as she heard more sniffing behind her.

Askja accepted the chalice from Kristján and held it out between Kjan and Eve. "As a ring is a circle unbroken, so too may your vows stand unbroken against the tests of time. Take these rings, warmed with the blessings of all those assembled here and made sacred in the holy fire of your love."

Kjan reached into the cup to fish the ring from it first, then slid it onto her trembling finger. With her free hand, Eve did the same, retrieving the second ring and placing it on his.

"Ringed and bound, are you now ready to avow?"

"I am." The declaration shot from Kjan's lips as though he'd been waiting a lifetime to say it out loud.

"I am," Eve repeated after him.

"Brother, do you take your chosen and beloved mate, Eve, to be your lawfully wedded completion, to have and to hold, from this day forward, for better or worse, for richer or poorer, in sickness and in health, until death do you part?"

"I do."

"Will you keep your love and trust," Askja went on, "caring for and cherishing your beloved? Will you keep the promise of this rite?"

"I will," he affirmed.

Askja turned to Eve. "Sister, do you take your chosen and beloved mate, Kjan, to be your lawfully wedded completion, to have and to hold, from this day forward, for better or worse, for richer or poorer, in sickness and in health, until death do you part?"

"I do," Eve replied.

"Will you keep your love and trust, caring for and cherishing your beloved? Will you keep the promise of this rite?"

"I will."

Turning toward the gathered group, Askja proclaimed, "You have declared your consent before your Gods and Goddesses within this holy circle. May the Goddess Frigg strengthen your consent and fill you both with her blessings. By the witness of our Gods, Goddesses, and ancestors—and by the legal power of the state of Oregon," she muttered under her breath, "are these sacred vows made manifest. May this mead bless this union and sanctify it for our Gods and Goddesses. Enjoy," Askja added with a jealous edge, handing the horn of mead to Kjan.

He took it with the hand that wasn't tied to Eve and tipped it back, then returned it with an arrogant smirk.

"I hereby pronounce you husband and wife. You may now kiss your bride."

Kjan didn't wait for Askja's clearance. He tugged on the cord and pulled Eve to him.

His honey-coated tongue from the mead was so much sweeter than the harsh burn of Bourbon. Her head started spinning, but he kept her steady in his embrace, never wavering, never relenting.

"You said you wanted me to tie you up," he whispered against her lips, giving her wrist another tug.

Over his shoulder, Kristján cleared his throat aggressively to remind them of everyone's company. Kjan ignored him. He pressed another tender kiss to her lips, letting his fingertips graze down the side of her face before easing back.

Claire and Erik came up from the south end and handed them the lit torches. With their hands still bound by the ceremonial cord, Kjan and Eve ignited the bonfire together.

After the untraditional ceremony, Joe and Kate came over before taking their leave.

"Well, that was certainly something different," he began. "Definitely the most beautiful wedding I've ever attended. I didn't take you for a heathen."

"My sister has been planning this for weeks." Kjan gave Eve a sideways glance, his arm squishing her side. "Thank you for coming all the way out here. It means a lot to us both."

"I don't know what happened between you two," Joe addressed Eve now, "but I can tell one thing: that man is crazy about you. I'm happy you found each other. And it looks like you finally found your place." He gestured toward her new-found family and gave an approving smile. "You have this light inside of you that makes people want to bring out the best in themselves. Your dad had that too. I'm so happy for you, bug. I wish you two all the best."

"Thanks, Joe."

Eve recalled his plea to her. He had wanted her to make something out of herself, and well, she had. She was the freaking leader of a vampire coven. Too bad she couldn't tell him that.

"Love you, bug." He gave her one of his big bear hugs that lasted anywhere from three seconds to five minutes.

"Love you too."

"Don't be a stranger now, okay?"

"I won't," Eve replied. "I promise."

"Kjan, take good care of her," Joe said, shaking his hand.

Kjan repressed a laugh. "She's the one taking care of me."

Joe nodded and then disappeared with Kate over the hill. The rest of the gang sat down in the grass, huddling around the fire. They had added more torches in a wider circle around the makeshift temple.

Pulling Eve down in front of him, Kjan slipped the cord from their wrists and stuffed it in his pocket.

"You have no idea what effect this dress has on me," he said hotly against her neck. "I wanted to rip it off the first time I saw you in it."

Eve thought she could paint a pretty accurate picture in her mind of the impression it had on him. She was also very aware of his body pressing up against her curves every time he shifted only a fraction of an inch.

"So, what did you think?" Askja asked, bringing the sexual tension boiling between them to an abrupt stop.

Eve blushed like she'd been caught with her pants down. Kjan, of course, looked unruffled.

She cleared her throat, dragging her thoughts out of the gutter. "To be honest, I was expecting a virgin sacrifice in my honor," she joked. "But I guess we can do without one."

"The night's young. I can go find you one," Caleb offered from across the fire. "It won't take long. I can sniff 'em out from a mile away."

Emma scowled at him while everyone else laughed. "What? The bride gets what she wants, and we both know it ain't gonna be you."

Her face turned promptly red, and it had nothing to do with the heat of the flames.

Caleb leaned down and whispered something in her ear that brought her smile back. Then he kissed her cheek and gave her a tight squeeze.

"Virgins are probably hard to find at weddings these days," Eve said, stroking her belly. "Hell, I didn't make it past 17, and I never even contemplated going the distance with any of them."

"*Them?*" Kjan asked with a slight cringe in his tone. "Many?"

Eve glared at him, reluctant to give a number; no matter how small and insignificant it was.

"Fine. Keep your secrets, woman. I'm not judging."

She exhaled an exasperated breath. "Okay, it's not a surprise that Bobby wasn't my first, but at least my number is not in the millions."

Kjan laughed. "You actually think I kept count?"

"Whatever." Eve rolled her eyes. "I'm not jealous. But I am curious how many virginities have fallen victim to your irresistible charm."

"I'm guilty of Anne, yes, but that's where my line of virgin sacrifices ends."

She raised her eyebrows in a questioning arch. "What about your first time? On your wedding night, maybe?"

He scoffed, amused. Hadn't he taken his wife's virginity? "What's so funny?" Eve asked. "If *you* weren't, at least *she* must have been a virgin."

"She was," he confirmed. "But you didn't know her. I didn't take anything. It was always *her* way." He brought his lips up close to Eve's ear. "*She* was the one who did the taking."

A vivid picture of a more docile Kjan on his back and Thórunn on top of him burned itself into her memory. *Huh, who would've thought?* Granted, he'd mentioned her dominant traits before.

Well, good for her.

Eve had told him about the brief moment the two women had shared in the meadow and about his late wife's choice. "Does it bother you that she's with him now?"

"No," came his brisk reply. "I think she's good for him. She'll keep him in check. He needs a firm hand of guidance," he added in a light tone, and Eve caught a smirk just before his lips drew into a tight line.

He set his chin down on her shoulder. "Can I ask you something?"

"Anything?"

"Why did you choose Lucas as your second?"

Kristján had been Kjartan's, and he was the oldest and most responsible one, but it never felt right to Eve. "Are you jealous?" she teased. "You know he's only second after you, right?"

"That's not why I'm asking," he said with a soft chuckle. "I don't have to worry. The kid wouldn't know what to do with you. He couldn't handle your appetite. It's just an unexpected choice. He always seemed shady to me… hiding things."

"And that's why I picked him. He reminded me of you."

"Me?" The touch of his chin lifted off her shoulder in surprise.

Eve cocked her head to the side with a scowl. "Misunderstood. Lost. Moody," she pointed out. "Sound familiar? He needed a purpose. I wanted to give him a chance to prove himself. You know, you could always practice your dad skills by mentoring him." She lifted her eyebrows in hopeful expectation.

"I'll think about it," he grumbled, snuggling back into the crook of her neck.

Eve fought a grin. Then her hand rubbed over her belly again, and he covered it with his own, entwining their fingers.

"You're worried," he observed, rocking her gently side to side.

She stared down at their hand-forged wedding bands. He'd used a different design to create the matching set. Where his and Thórunn's had been three heavy iron strands weaved into a simple braid, Kjan had chosen the style of a Celtic love knot for her. The symbol represented their intertwined lives and their eternal, unbroken love for each other.

"Aren't you? You've been through this before."

Kjan drew little circles on her belly with his thumb as he held her hand. "This time, I know everything is going to be fine. It helps to have a seer in the family."

"Askja is not allowed to talk about future events."

"She told me just enough." Kjan pressed a kiss on her neck, then withdrew his hand. "Come on. I know what will cheer you up," he said, hauling Eve to her feet.

Bunching the front of her dress with both hands to keep from tripping, she followed him, and they made the short hike up the hill back to the house.

When they reached the patio, he carried her across the threshold before towing her through the living room into the very dark study.

"Where are we going?" Eve picked up her skirt with one hand now. He didn't slow his stride. He appeared in a hurry.

"To officially break in the pool table."

"That's how you plan to cheer me up? You want to play pool?" And hadn't they broken in the table months ago?

He stopped on the short side and spun her around to face him. Her butt hit the edge.

His response was blunt. "I want to fuck my wife." Then he dove into the crook of her neck, nudging her backwards.

An exhilarating thrill raked through her while greedy hands worked their way down her body. "Without witnesses," he declared, his tongue flicking at her, lips hovering over the sensitive skin at her jugular. "I'll happily omit that tradition."

"Look who's got the filthy mouth now, you savage Viking."

Kjan's hands shot under her dress, and his fingers bit into her ass, confirming her suggestion with hard proof.

"Æ, kona."

EPILOGUE

KJARTAN

He stepped out of the portal his father had so graciously called forth for him and found himself standing in a meadow that was part of Fólkvangr, Freyja's domain. His eyes were immediately drawn to her radiant presence. That was how magnificent she was. A splendid beauty with a brilliant soul more luminous than any star he had ever seen.

And he had seen a lot. Even the sun didn't compare. It only enhanced her natural light.

She sat in the clearing. The rays bounced off her head, bathing her in a dazzling glow, her hair shimmering like gold. It was a few shades lighter than Eve's and cascaded in luscious waves down her back, so long it merged with the grass.

A lamb nestled by her side, and she was rocking a small bundle in her arms.

Kjartan left the shade of the tree that concealed him. He felt his hands sweating. He was nervous. It was strange that something so simple as perspiration could make him feel so alive.

Thórunn lifted her head as he advanced, and his breath caught in the back of his throat. Her eyes… they were exactly the way he remembered them: pale peridot green with a burst of golden flecks in the center.

Frigg had told him that she was waiting for him. He couldn't believe it. Had to see it with his own eyes.

Now he was here, and he still didn't believe it. *Why would she choose me? A reject!*

Thórunn tilted her head with an affectionate smile, and the words escaped his mind. She took his breath away. He didn't know what to say. Didn't know how to address her.

Silently, he dropped down on the grass beside her. She didn't appear to mind. The babe cooed blissfully content in her mother's arms, and something stirred in him he hadn't felt since his own mother had abandoned him.

Gazing into the baby girl's eyes, he felt safe. She felt like home.

"She is beautiful," Kjartan said after finally regaining his speech. "What is her name?"

"She does not have one," Thórunn replied. "Her father never had the chance to claim her."

According to the old tradition, when a child was born, it was placed in the father's arms, and if he accepted it as his own flesh and blood, he would choose the name. This precious little soul had passed on before Kjan, her biological father, ever had the opportunity.

Thórunn placed the babe in his arms. "She is yours if you claim her."

Kjartan shook his head. "I cannot… I-I could not…"

"He will not mind," she reassured him, then withdrew her grasp.

Despite his mind protesting, his trembling hands accepted the treasure she offered him.

He stared at her in awe, holding her lovingly against his chest. She was so small. So fragile. And in that moment, he knew he would give his own life to protect her.

"What is her name, elskan?"

"Eva," he said, the first one that sprang into his mind. "Her name is Eva."

"A good name," Thórunn agreed. "'Tis fitting."

To breathe. To live. To give life.

If it hadn't been for Eve running away from home at that fateful moment, none of them would be here now. She had been the key. She was the mother of all life, and through her death, she had brought change beyond her own world. Her bloodline was the future.

Kjartan lifted his sight from the infant back to Thórunn—*his* beacon, *his* savior. His feelings for Eve had always been filtered through Kjan; the mortal's body had been his conduit. Now that they were no longer sharing one vessel, Kjartan felt his own heart racing for the first time, and as he looked into Thórunn's eyes, he understood the oath.

"My body… my mind… my soul," he pledged.

THE END

Afterword

Although Kjan and Eve's story comes to a close, my story is far from over. The Web Of Wyrd series will continue with Book Four, the first of the sequels centered around characters you have already met in this trilogy, and I can't wait for you to officially meet my next MMC.

Subscribe to my newsletter or follow me on Social Media for updates.

As you have noticed, I chose to highlight Caleb and Lucas by giving them their own POVs. I have something planned for them in the future and want my readers to know a little bit about their deep friendship in advance.

And of course, Hrafni will be back.

Acknowledgements

I want to thank my amazing beta team:
Kelsey Stone, Hilary Preston, and Toni Middleton.

My Street Team without whose support I could never have done this:
Manda Baumgardner, Jennifer Clarke, Tiana Cole, Conny Dochantschi, Casey Hayes, Caitlin Horst, Robin Mannon, Hope Mosley, Chelsea Smith, Cyndall Tolley, and Kendra Demello.

As well as all of ARC readers.

Thank you all so very much for your continued support.

References

Old Icelandic Calendar:

Winter months
- Gormánuður (the end of October marks the beginning of the winter nights and a new year)
- Ýlir (late November; beginning of Yule)
- Mörsugur (begins with the winter solstice: the first full moon following the first new moon in late December)
- Þorri (Miðvetr – Midwinter; late January; end of Yule)
- Góa
- Einmánuður

Summer months (the beginning of spring is celebrated as the 'first day of summer' in late April)
- Harpa
- Skerpla
- Sólmánuður (Miðsumar – Midsummer; summer solstice: the first full moon following the first new moon in late June)
- Heyannir
- Tvímánuður
- Haustmánuður

Hallgrimskirkja – [hatl-*krims*-kirk-ya]; doors and plaque text

Irish drinking toast:
Here's to cheating, fighting, stealing, and drinking.
If you cheat, may you cheat death;
If you steal, may you steal a woman's heart;
If you fight, may you fight for a brother;
And if you drink, may you drink with me.

<u>Ásatrú hand fasting rite:</u>

Vows and prayers were adapted from Ásatrú ceremonies. Ásatrú, which stands for Æsir Belief, is the religion of modern Heathenism, a contemporary Germanic Paganism, based on Norse Gods.

Thank you for reading

Please consider leaving a review however long. A review is always appreciated.

Bonus Material

Find my other works and the official SPOTIFY PLAYLIST to this book on

www.runikpress.com/renaterowlandbooks

While you're there, don't forget to sign up for my newsletter, so you won't miss anything.

Author Bio

Renate Rowland is an author of suspenseful Paranormal and Contemporary Romance. Born and raised in Germany, she grew up with the sagas and mythology surrounding the Norse Gods, but it was her passion for vampires and Viking lore that inspired this trilogy. After being fortunate to have called three different continents her home, she has settled with her family in the US. She is an artist at heart, and although she expresses that in various ways, she held on to her stories until she felt it was time to give them air and let them breathe on their own. Finding much inspiration in music lyrics, she is driven by the desire to create something as powerful and moving as the artists she admires.

www.ingramcontent.com/pod-product-compliance
Lightning Source LLC
Chambersburg PA
CBHW070301310726
48976CB00005B/1526